"Timely, germaine, and relevant. A medical thriller attuned to the direction medicine is heading."

Dr. Dean Edell, Nationally Syndicated Physician, KGO-TV, San Francisco.

"A great story full of delightful characters, amazing twists, and fascinating information. As compelling as a Kellerman novel, while also offering a helpful crash course in clinical information systems and new technology. This book should be required reading for every healthcare professional."

Mary Jo Monahan, Deputy Director, Family Service Centers of Pinellas County, Past President, Florida Chapter, NASW

"Riveting, exciting, and alarming - pushes us face-first into a kind of heathcare management that only George Orwell could have foreseen."

Dick Finnegan, The Executive Speaker.

"A lively, engaging, and fascinating story that shines a scrutinizing light into the dark corners of healthcare. Richly drawn characters in all too common struggles."

A. Nicholas Groth, Ph.D. Psychologist,
President, Forensic Mental Health Associates

"A gripping and compelling story that brings to light the challenge of modern medicine in the age of industrialized managed healthcare. A good and powerful read, and I learned a lot. His thoughtful prose and insightful humor gently walked me through the most complex computer systems."

Dan Kearney, CEO, Psychiatric Hospital-Orlando

"TERMINAL CONSENT is an exciting and terrifying account of medicine gone awry. The novel is both illuminating and shocking in its depiction of managed care practices that are fast becoming commonplace. Clever, lively, and easily understood.."

J. Ted Giuffrida, M.D., Florida Radiology Associates.

"TERMINAL CONSENT was absolutely wonderful. The situations that I read about are a part of my world and I was scared down to my shoes! Thank you for this tremendous story.

Gail Farmer, RN, Director of Utilization Review

8 →

TERMINAL CONSENT

Michael Freeny

PRESS

William Austin Press, Inc.

𝕾𝔱. 𝔓𝔢𝔱𝔢𝔯𝔰𝔟𝔲𝔯𝔤
𝔍𝔲𝔫𝔦𝔬𝔯 ℭ𝔬𝔩𝔩𝔢𝔤𝔢

Published by
William Austin Press, Inc.
Orlando

TERMINAL CONSENT

Copyright ©1998 Michael Freeny
All Rights Reserved.

Library of Congress Catalog Number: 98-71196

ISBN 0-9663686-6-5

Cover Design–Greg Sammons

Printed in the United States
April 1998

Acknowledgments

So many gracious and knowledgeable people contributed to this project. I'd like to give thanks to them all. To my wife, Gloria Gluskin for her honest editing. To Annette Habin for her hawk-eye proofing and to Ron Habin, Ph.D., for his consult on issues of health and the elderly. To Hal Stokes of AAA-Information Systems for his expertise with mainframe computer protocols, and his wife, Bobbie, who generously advised on medical procedures. Dennis Wilcox of the IBM Corporation provided excellent advice on computer hardware and large information systems.

Thanks to a dear friend, Tracy Heath, for her insight in developing suspense and plot consistency. A special thanks to Richard Simon, publisher of the Family Therapy Networker, who gave me the first opportunity to air these issues in a national forum. Malcolm Harriman, who, as CEO of Health Expert Systems, always encouraged and supported vigorous dialogue about the important issues of technology, healthcare, and privacy. To all the manuscript readers whose advice flowed freely. And finally, to that wonderful resource called the Internet.

For my loving wife, Gloria, who believed from the beginning and to my children, Erin and Sean, who made it a true family project.

A note to the reader.

Although this is a work of fiction it is based entirely upon real technology. No machine, process, or protocol was invented for this story. Only the characters and companies are fiction. The technology is used everyday.

Chapter 1

The crisis case was passed to Jenny Barrett before she was completely seated at her workstation. She spun in her chair and tapped the computer keyboard to awaken her dozing monitor, which soon displayed a cautionary message, "Suicide Risk–Immediate Action Required!" It was a code three case, an adolescent girl in Atlanta, Georgia, recently discharged from a five-day psychiatric hospital admission.

Jenny was 2,100 miles away, encased in a corporate glass cubicle in Woodland Hills, California. The emergency required quick action and medical expertise. Jenny, a clinical psychologist, felt fully prepared as she tapped the keys of the 15 million dollar computer system that would assist her in any intervention. The continent that separated her from the client was a minor inconvenience, for distance has little meaning in cyberspace.

The original caseworker who received the call had assessed a potentially lethal situation, despite the client's denial of suicidal intent. The company's diagnostic computer agreed with the data it had reviewed, and commanded, "Route to crisis team!" Unfortunately, the "team" for the day was Jenny. She had recently been appointed the new Director of Member Services for Progressive Psychiatric Management, the managed healthcare company located in a Los Angeles suburb. Her staff was busy training new employees in the art of "tele-medicine" and phone counseling. Jenny was also flanked by two interns, who watched as their mentor psychologist donned a telephone headset and logged onto the computer.

"This is Jenny Barrett, may I help you?" she asked.

"Jenny, this is Clair Lendt in Member Services. I'm speaking with

April Louise Scott from Atlanta. April, are you there?"

"Yes," replied a soft voice, with the muffled nasal sound of someone who'd just been crying.

"Jenny, April just got out of the hospital four days ago. She's being followed by a Dr. Winslow for aftercare. She stayed home from school today and says she doesn't think she can go on. Her boyfriend doesn't want to see her anymore. I told her you were a specialist in these matters."

"April," asked Jenny, "is that what's going on?"

"Yeah," replied the teen, with a curious laugh. A message scrolled across the bottom of Jenny's screen while she listened to April. It was from Clair, who was still listening, stating that there was a good chance April had taken an overdose of medication about twenty minutes ago, though the teen had denied it. The parents were at work and the patient was alone at home. The chart showed a history of two prior suicide attempts, one nearly successful. This was far beyond Clair's level of expertise, and Jenny was the most senior clinician available.

This was a demanding case to confront at 8:30 in the morning, even for a seasoned clinician. Jenny glanced at the interns seated behind her, their lips drawn thin with tension. She knew they were thanking their lucky stars it wasn't their call. Jenny hoped to use this case to illustrate modern crisis intervention techniques.

"Thanks, Clair. Do you feel comfortable speaking with me, April?"

"Yeah, I just want to get some help. I didn't want to leave the hospital. Now everyone thinks I'm crazy. I don't want to see anyone. Can you get me back to the hospital?" Within her desperate personal hell, April had already left Clair, embracing the new voice of Jenny to wring out some hope for redemption.

Another message scrolled up on the monitor. Clair asked Jenny to note the increased slurring in April's speech, which had been initially clear and articulate.

"April, I want to help you, but you have to help me first, okay?"

"Sure," said the teen, interrupted by a gulping sound.

"Are you drinking something, April?"

Jenny heard the clunking sound of a glass bottle hitting a tabletop or the floor.

"I have to get my nerves under control. I'm shaking all the time. Dr. Winslow says I need to be back in the hospital. Please say it's okay," she pleaded, on the verge of tears, her speech eroded into a continuous slur.

"April, did you take all your pills?" asked Jenny, as her fingers flew over the keyboard. The situation was deteriorating quickly. Before the teen could answer, Jenny had pulled up April's entire medical history on screen and was paging through it. The patient had prescriptions for a tranquilizer, an antidepressant, and a sleeper. A quick check of the pharmacy records found that a mail-order firm had filled the order, which meant all the refills for all the medicines may have been mailed in one package.

Jenny had the computer calculate a lethal dosage based upon the patient's recorded weight and known drug interactions. The machine assessed that the child had enough to kill herself twice, three times if she combined the pills with alcohol. The earlier sound of the bottle falling echoed through Jenny's head. It was time to act.

"April, do you expect anyone home soon?"

"What? Home. No, I'm alone. Always alone. No one will be with me. Alex told me to go to hell. He used me," she wailed. "He fucked me, then he fucked me again." She seemed to like the sound of that and started giggling a little, then she began to sing the phrase. Maybe April was pregnant, thought Jenny. On that hunch, she checked the hospital chart for the date of April's last menstrual period, but it was only two weeks ago.

Jenny muted the microphone, then addressed the interns. "This kid's in trouble. I think she took a serious overdose. As a healthcare company, we have rights to certain information." Another window popped up on her screen, which appeared to be a grocery list.

"I checked on the shopping habits of the family through their debit and credit card transactions," Jenny continued, "which show recent purchases of hard liquor. This makes the situation critical. I'm going to call the paramedics in Atlanta and get them on the way. I'm also going to break confidentiality and see if I can find a neighbor to help her out. She could aspirate and choke to death in an instant."

"April," said Jenny as she un-muted the microphone, "I want you to stay on the phone. Can you tell me if there's a neighbor who can help you?" Jenny didn't wait for an answer, but pulled up the patient's address and had the computer list all neighbors for ten houses in each direction. April hadn't responded to the last question, so Jenny said more loudly, "April, you must stay with me."

"I'm here," the girl replied, but not into the phone handset. "I'm here," she said again, as if taunting a playmate. Jenny believed the girl was being overwhelmed with the drugs she had taken and would soon lose consciousness. She instructed the computer to dial four of April's neighbors. Phone machines answered three times, but one was answered by an older man's voice.

"Hello," began Jenny. "Is this Mr. Dekens?"

"Yes it is. Who's this?"

"My name is Jenny Barrett. I'm a psychologist at a healthcare company in California. I need some help with an emergency next door to you. Do you know the Scotts?"

"Yes."

"I'm afraid their daughter, April, has taken an overdose of medication. I've sent for the paramedics, and we're placing calls to her parents right now. However, I'm worried that she may get really sick before they arrive. Would you feel comfortable going over there and checking on her until the paramedics arrive?"

"Sure. I know Glenn and Vicky have had a hell of a time with that girl. You say you're in California?"

"Yes, I have April on the phone, but she's fading out. I'd appreciate it if you could just help until the paramedics arrive. It should be just a matter of minutes."

"I'm on my way," Dekens assured her, then hung up.

April was no longer responding to Jenny's voice. She heard only grunts and whispered phrases, as if the teen was falling asleep. Jenny called Brimley Hospital to authorize readmission, and then made a final call to inform Dr. Winslow of the developments. A minute later Dekens and the paramedics entered April's doorway and Jenny breathed a sigh of relief. Dekens picked up the phone and spoke briefly, then handed the receiver to an EMT while Jenny instructed where to take the girl. He assured her that the girl was okay, but Jenny informed him of the quantities of medication that she could have taken and faxed the information to the emergency room. April was on her way to help.

"Good, a happy ending," Jenny thought as she turned to the gaping interns.

It was a picturesque Southern California spring day outside. Jenny and the interns sat in a cubicle, nestled deep in the hermetically sealed office building in northwest Los Angeles County. With a telephone headset clamped onto her light brown hair and a 17-inch monitor casting her face in a pale blue light, she hardly looked like a clinical psychologist. Yet she was one of the best in the company.

"I'm sorry," said Jenny in sympathy for the interns. "That was not a typical call. You'll be dealing with the usual garden-variety type of personal problems from the 2.3 million subscribers of Progressive."

"How . . . how did you learn so much about the girl? It was as if you lived next door," asked one of the interns.

"Tele-medicine. Cybercare. It's called all sorts of things. I know it looks intimidating, but it's hardly more sophisticated than using a telephone was in 1940. Here, let me take another call and show you how our usual clients access their mental healthcare."

A pleasant chirping sound emanated from the computer, which announced another call from the client telephone lines. Jenny's long fingers again moved quickly over the keyboard, obtaining client information even before she answered the phone. The caller had already passed through at least four levels of voice menus before being deposited into Jenny's lap. That usually meant the need for some real help, but it was far short of a crisis.

"Hello, thank you for calling the Warmline. My name is Jenny, may I help you?"

"I'm calling to get some help," said a female voice. "I don't know what to do. I think my marriage is falling apart. He just doesn't care about me anymore," she choked. "I can't go through another divorce."

Jenny smiled at the familiar words. She had worked the phones for three years and little could jolt her. This was more of what she wanted for demonstration purposes. With the confidence of a seasoned counselor Jenny said, "Hold on a minute, let me catch up. We can help you, but we have to take it slowly. All right?"

"I'm sorry, I just feel so lost and alone. If he's left for good, I might as well be dead," said the caller.

The call had entered through the "WarmLine" feature of Progressive Psychiatric Management, where they offered brief counseling and referrals to members of the health plan. Despite her promotion, Jenny and all senior management were assisting with the training of new staff due to a recent and sizable expansion of Progressive. The phones had been ringing incessantly since the company won the Tuckerman's Fried Chicken national mental health contract. She was drafted as part of a stepped-up training program to bring in more help on line. The two interns in training flanked Jenny, eagerly watching her navigate through computers, callers, and telephones.

The computer was clearly Jenny's link to all the resources she would need. Progressive prided itself on this state-of-the-art computer system, the envy of a highly competitive industry.

Jenny muted the phone to address the interns. "First, we check on who's calling. The computer uses caller ID to log the phone call and flash the name on the screen. It then automatically looks up their health plan so we can help the client." In a window on the monitor the computer displays a ten-digit phone number with a Colorado area code, followed by "Ramirez, Daniel B." as the registered owner of the telephone. Using the mouse arrow, Jenny highlighted the window. A separate window on the screen listed the members of the Ramirez family as shown on their healthcare application. Esther Ramirez was the wife.

"May I have your social security number?" asked Jenny, who again muted the phone to tell the interns, "I don't really need it, but sometimes the clients get upset if we know who they are before they tell us."

The caller hesitantly recited her social security number, then began to weep. "I don't know if I can go on if he's left for good."

At this second reference to suicide Jenny took some backup action. As with the previous call, she highlighted the address on the screen and instructed the computer to list all of Esther's neighbors. She turned to the watching interns and said, "I don't think this will get serious, but we're ready if it does." The preparation took only four seconds.

Jenny came back on line. "Esther, I think we can help you with this, but first I have to ask you some questions. OK?"

"Yes."

"How long have you and Daniel been married?" asked Jenny.

The shock of hearing his name hit Esther like a slap. "How do you know about Daniel? I didn't mention his name."

Adopting her most soothing voice, Jenny said, "Esther, I didn't mean to upset you. We list your husband on your health insurance plan and the computer brought it up when I checked on your benefits." Jenny eyed the interns to confirm her earlier comment about surprising clients with information.

"Of course, I'm sorry. I've just never done this before. He'd be angry if he knew I was talking to someone about our problems, but I just can't get through to him. Well, to answer your question, we've been married six years. Things started to get bad about two months ago. Now he hardly talks to me. Doesn't even touch me."

Jenny had heard it all before, a thousand times in her career at Progressive. "Let me check on your benefits," she told Esther. Then she instructed the interns, "In the corner of the monitor you'll see her benefits listed. I just wanted to buy some time to sniff around about hubby. I'm pulling his medical records right now to see if there's a reason for him avoiding her." Jenny let the mystery hang with the eager interns while she scrolled through Daniel's records. Within thirty seconds she spotted a clue.

"See there, about three weeks ago he saw his doctor for a UTI, a urinary tract infection. Most likely he had gonorrhea and his doctor fudged the record to protect him. The marriage has probably been in trouble for some time. He likely started diddling on the side and picked up a bug. We can't tell where he got it, but it's pretty clear why he wouldn't touch his wife. Hopefully, he learned his lesson. If he keeps this up, he might bring something terrible home, like AIDS. We'll refer her to counseling because Progressive doesn't need another AIDS case, and it's not excluded on this policy."

Jenny queried the computer using Esther's zip code and came up with the names of some counselors on the Progressive PPO provider panel. She gave the names to Esther and made her promise to call, noting the contact in Esther's electronic record.

"Welcome to psychotherapy in cyberspace," she told the gaping interns. "At times I still can't believe how easy it is to get all this information. Do you two have much experience on computers?"

The two interns hesitantly nodded. "We typed our papers on a computer," offered Natalie, "and did a little research at the library, but nothing like this."

"Do we have to learn how to run all this stuff before we can work with clients?" asked Melissa.

"Fortunately, the system is designed to be fairly user friendly. Progressive will train you well before you sit in the cockpit. You'll do just fine," Jenny said in support, remembering how intimidating these machines seemed. "Besides, MOM is very helpful."

"MOM?" asked Natalie.

"The MultiAxil Outcome Management system. We just call her MOM. It's the main computer program that runs everything, and she looks after us pretty well."

Another chirp signaled a caller. Jenny decided to squeak in another call before they broke for lunch.

"Warmline, this is Dr. Barrett, may I help you?"

"I think I need some marriage counseling," said a husky voice. "My wife and I, we're fighting all the time. We can't get along, always blowing up."

"Let's see if we can help you. I need your name and social security number," Jenny asked. Before the caller could respond, MOM had provided the caller's identification and confirmed eligibility. "Yes, Mr. Schultz of Houston. You are fully registered with Progressive Psychiatric Management. Tell me, how long have you been having this problem?"

"She's always been spirited and passionate, but it has gotten out of hand lately," he explained.

"Any recent changes in your life?" Jenny asked, searching the medical record for any clues.

"Well, to be perfectly honest, about two weeks ago she found out about an affair I had some time ago. It was brief and it didn't mean anything, it just happened. Now my wife's gone ballistic. Screaming all the time, crying, shouting how she hates me. I don't know what to do."

Jenny muted the phone and turned to the interns, "That's two affairs back to back. It's gonna be a long day." Back on-line Jenny said, "Mr. Schultz, I see from your medical record that you recently received stitches in your hand at an emergency room. Is that when you told your wife, Lucille?"

"Why yes," said Mr. Schultz, somewhat startled. "She got so angry she picked up a skillet and whacked me. The edge hit me in the hand, which caused me to bleed pretty badly. I had to get 13 stitches."

"Your medical record says it was a gardening accident," Jenny stated.

"Well she felt so terrible about it and I didn't see the point in bringing it up to the doctor. As I said, she's very spirited."

Jenny was typing in case notes as Mr. Shultz spoke. Check boxes on the side of the screen listed risk behaviors: suicide, homicide, drug abuse, domestic violence, etc. When she dutifully checked off the domestic violence box, MOM instantly displayed a new screen, highlighted in red. In the center of the screen flashed a message . . .

> "Warning. You have indicated that an act of domestic violence has occurred. This is a reportable event under California Penal Code 17654-V. The information is now being collected and packaged for transmission to the appropriate authorities. You must either transmit this material now by pressing the 'REPORT' button at the bottom of the screen or provide an explanation as to why it should not be transmitted."

The three of them stared at the flashing screen for a second. Jenny began pressing some keys to bring up another screen, but there was no response. The system required her to report the incident before taking any other action. She could think of no reasonable rationale to provide to avoid reporting, and she certainly wasn't going to risk her license. She moved the mouse pointer over the REPORT button key and clicked. Within three seconds MOM compiled and transmitted the report, then returned the screen to the case notes.

Jenny turned to the interns, "As you can see, MOM is very thorough in monitoring our legal reporting compliance. Child abuse, homicidal threats, domestic violence, they all get special attention."

"Mr. Schultz," Jenny began, "this office is located in California. As a licensed therapist I am bound by the laws of this state. The State of California requires therapists to notify the authorities of any incidents of domestic violence. You have indicated this is an unreported violent act. I'll have to report this to the local authorities in Houston." Jenny hated this part of her professional duties.

"But I don't want that. I don't want the police. We just need to get back on track. Some counseling sessions. Please don't report it," Mr. Schultz pleaded.

"It has already been transmitted, Mr. Schultz, but I can help you anyway. Let's see if we can find a good counselor for you," said Jenny.

"What do you mean it's already transmitted? I thought this was a confidential conversation. That's what the brochure says. How can you just run and tell the police?"

"Mr. Schultz, our talk really is confidential. But there are some limitations that were outlined in your original benefit agreement. I've pulled it up on my screen and I'm looking at your initials next to a list of exceptions to confidentiality. It's on the Global Release Form you signed with your benefits package. Surely you must have read it."

"What will happen now?" he asked in a disheartened voice.

"That depends upon the jurisdiction. Social Services or the police may want to talk with you and Lucille. They may require you to attend some domestic violence counseling."

"I suppose you can give me a referral for that."

"I sure can, but court-ordered therapy is not covered in your benefits package. It's almost universally excluded as a mental health benefit," explained Jenny.

"Wait just a minute here," said Mr. Schultz in an incredulous voice. "I called to get marriage counseling. You find out my wife hit me and immediately tell the police. Then you tell me because she hit me, the counseling I want is not a covered benefit. It's almost to your advantage to get my wife and me in trouble so you don't have to pay for anything. So why have I been paying you this money in premiums?"

"I understand how confusing this is, these systems are so big. However, Progressive wants to see you get the best care possible. Let's see what we can do. As you know, there is a reduced benefit for marital counseling. You have ten sessions with a fifty percent co-pay up to forty dollars per session. Let's see if I can get you an appointment with our local contract therapist."

"You mean I went through all this conversation, I have the police coming to my door and you only pay twenty bucks toward my counseling? I went with this policy because I thought it would be cheap, but now it may cost me a bundle." He hung up abruptly.

Jenny turned to the interns, who looked a bit anguished over this example of cybercare. "Yeah, I don't like this part either. Seems like there are more and more laws telling us how to treat clients. This new domestic violence reporting law is causing havoc on the lines. People are afraid to call. It's a part of the job I just hate."

"Still, it's amazing how quickly you put everything together for the client," said Natalie. "I worked at a Veterans Administration hospital and they were in the stone age. It would take me weeks to get the information you just punched up in a second. I had no idea."

"That was a tough call. You don't get many like it. Mostly it's matching clients to counselors in their area, maybe helping them get a clearer picture of the issues. Psychiatrists run Progressive, so they stay in tune with patient care. MOM just makes it much easier."

Chapter 2

Jenny logged off the computer as the interns babbled behind her in animated excitement at what they had just witnessed. The lesson was over for now. She smiled, listening to them rave about the power of the computer system and how easily information is obtained. Although these students come from the UCLA psychology program, Jenny knew these machines were not part of their education. The universities remain about ten years behind the times in teaching about client care technology.

The interns said goodbye and wandered off to another orientation meeting. Their presence spurred Jenny to remember her first days at Progressive, nearly four years ago. She was all of twenty-eight years old, full of idealism and grand plans. After what seemed like an eternity in school, she had finally completed the academic work for her doctorate in clinical psychology and was ready to join the ranks of the underemployed. She was ABD, all-but-dissertation.

Jenny had hoped to get a position at her last internship, a respected community mental health center in Hollywood. She could wear Levis and sweatshirts, and be freed of the tyranny of pantyhose. However, her idea of spending long hours sifting through the troubles of working-class clients was cut short when a funding grant was cut.

So she joined the throngs of recent grads looking for that first real job. Despite all of her networking through professors and referral sources, she found the Progressive job in the classified section of the Chronicle. She remembered feeling almost ashamed for talking with a "managed care company," the sworn enemy of all things good and wholesome. At least that was the popular view among her classmates. "How little we knew," she reflected.

By the time Jenny had secured an interview with Progressive, she was determined to pull out all the stops to get any job in the field. She vowed not to be one of those sad statistics; forty percent of her graduating class couldn't find work in the psychology field. Jenny had two great advantages over her classmates in approaching the rapidly growing firm — she was exceedingly competent on computers, and she was, in a word, gorgeous, a label she had spent much of her life trying to minimize. She had a slender, athletic body, inquisitive hazel eyes with flecks of gold, flowing brown hair, and sinewy arms ending with almost porcelain hands that had modeled in a few commercials. "Not bad for a ranch girl from Oregon," she often said.

Jenny hated trading on looks, but she hated unemployment even more. As her colleagues scrambled among public agencies, the Oregon country girl zipped on her corporate persona, including her pantyhose and a laser-printed resumé.

She fit the job like an glove. Progressive took a business approach to healthcare, so Jenny's down-to-earth pragmatism was welcome. Yet it was her knowledge of information systems, learned from her brother and years of office work, that proved to be her greatest advantage. Computers were everywhere in the new healthcare world, and it had become survival of the cybernetically fit. Jenny's unique blend of savvy, techno-smarts, and humanity helped launch her career at Progressive. She completed her dissertation in February and had yet to grow comfortable with the title "doctor." Most of the people at Progressive Psychiatric Management still called her Jenny and had to think for a second who "Dr. Barrett" was.

As Jenny zoomed through promotions and responsibilities, her goals began to change, or more accurately, expand. She felt privileged to be on the cutting edge of healthcare reform. Sure, it was nice to step into the shoes of a client occasionally and help them find the escape route out of their self-imposed prison, but Jenny saw herself more as an architect of care delivery systems.

She had also learned, while on the front lines of clinical practice, that too many people were trying to scam the system, and too many well-meaning therapists were helping the bad guys. At Progressive she felt she could pursue the bigger picture, the greatest good for the greatest number. "Whew," she thought, "I do have some high falutin' goals."

MOM's gentle chirp broke Jenny's reverie, announcing another call. Her screen flashed "Mark Lipton," a name that gave her a warm smile. He was a college buddy who now worked as a reporter for the Chronicle. Mark was brilliant, creative, and at times almost radical in his thinking about the forces that shape the news, and he always had an entertaining spin on things. They had been an item a long time ago, but now maintained a good friendship.

"So, what's the Chronicle's star reporter and greatest bun warmer doing," she asked as she answered the phone.

"God, I hate it when you do that," was Mark's reply. "I just can't get used to this caller ID stuff. I can't even surprise you anymore. By the way, my manager told me the reporter phones are caller ID blocked. How did you know it was me?"

" Hey, anonymity is for wimps. Besides, you don't have MOM on your side. Our computer isn't troubled by the little deceptions of a devious reporter. We're a healthcare company. We get special privileges. So how are you doing? I read your piece on Medicare fraud. Nice job."

"Thanks, it was a great piece, from a very humble guy. It even got picked up for syndication."

"And I thought you were headed for the fashion section," teased Jenny.

"Well you may be headed for the big time yourself. What are you going to do when Great Health Benefit takes over?"

"Say what?"

"Yeah, I just heard it from the business editor. Great Health Benefit is offering to merge Progressive into its rather humongous corporate bosom."

"Larry wouldn't let that happen," said Jenny, speaking of the CEO who had nurtured the growth of the company.

"He may not have a choice," offered Mark. "If GHB wants Progressive, I gotta believe they're going to get it. You mean, there isn't any scuttlebutt around the office?"

"Not a peep. There are always rumors about some large company nosing around, but nothing's ever come of it. Are you looking to do a story, Mark?"

"Well, I wouldn't turn down a few inside reactions. I know how much you like your job there. Why don't you ask around and see what gives?"

"Okay, I'll make some discreet inquiries."

"In fact, why don't we get together for dinner tonight?"

"Mark, I'm swamped. I can't get anything on the story by this evening."

"I know, I just haven't seen that toothy smile since Christmas. You got a better alternative?" Mark at times had the finesse of a pit bull, which made him a good reporter, but impossible to live with.

"Well, a quick check of my calendar shows a slim window of opportunity tonight, that ends at 10 P.M., I might add."

"Got it. I'll swing by around seven. Maybe pick up some hints for next Christmas."

"Say, doesn't Elaina Ruiz work for Great Health?" Jenny asked.

"Elaina, your rat-runner friend from college?" using a term they applied to any research psychologist.

"Yeah, you remember her. We were buddies in college. She was a whiz on computers and statistical analysis. Really helped me out on my graduate thesis. She graduated a year ahead of me and I think took a job with Great Health Benefit doing some big claims management project. God, I haven't talked with her since the conference last year. She'd certainly remember you. Why don't you give her a call?"

"Will do, and thanks. See you later. I'll bring Ouzo."

"You'll drink it alone."

"Okay, Cabernet."

"See you, Mark," Jenny said without thinking. She was on automatic pilot as she hung up, her mind swimming with the startling news. She wasn't ready for big changes in her life right now. "Why would Larry not tell the staff about this?" she thought, "he's usually so open." She logged off her computer to take a break.

Jenny put a call into her VP's office, Laura Paine, but ended up in voice mail. She felt pretty close to Laura and could talk openly. "Laura, this is Jenny. A little bird told me someone is moving to buy Progressive. Any words that you can share?"

Jenny got up and wove her way through the cubicles, looking out the expansive window at the blooms of late spring. From her third-floor office she could clearly see the gardens and individual flowers in the landscaping around the building. She wandered down to Armand's, the lunch bar on the first floor of the building. This was primarily a commercial area, so most of the patrons were in suits and business attire. She scanned the booths looking for a familiar face. Eventually, she spied a distinctive set of ears sticking out of a closely shaved head, the unmistakable signature of Al Friedman, senior clinical systems supervisor, a brilliant guy who gets so cosmic this planet can barely contain him. Jenny saw some space at the booth.

"Al, can I join you guys?"

"Sure, Jenny, slide on in. This is Bruce Wyle from MIS and Jackie Washington from Claims. This is Dr. Jenny from Member Services, that is, *Director* of Member Services if the company newsletter is accurate."

"Sure is," Jenny said with a grin, "which means I get to run the phones *and* get hollered at by VPs."

"They still have you on the phones? Must be that Tuckerman's Fried Chicken account, pushing everyone into overtime," said Al.

"Why? Is TFC driving their employees crazy?" asked Bruce.

"No," says Al, "pretty much like any other company, about three to five percent of employees. The problem's at our end. We weren't ready for that many new people in the system. However, Jenny, you'll be happy to hear we're working on another level of voice mail that may answer a lot of the client's questions. Give you some relief."

"You're gonna voice mail me out of a job someday, Al."

"That's the plan," he said with a sly grin, as he handed her a menu, "so you enjoy the good life now."

Jenny decided to bring up the Great Health Benefit rumor. "You hear anything new about companies moving in on Progressive, like a merger?"

"All the time," said Jackie. "But Larry isn't going to sell. This is his baby."

"A source, who will remain nameless, says there's talk of Great Health Benefit taking over."

"Please," said Al, "I'm eating. Don't start talking about cannibals."

"That bad, huh?"

"They're the worst. Eat their young if it was profitable. I've heard they have more member complaints than any other company in healthcare. They'll fight tooth and nail over itemized bills, even disallowing cotton balls. Still, the big employers love them because they keep health insurance costs so low. Heck, they probably haven't paid a claim in four years."

"Well, this source has heard serious talk on the street. You guys haven't heard anything?"

"You know," Jackie said, "we've had to pump up tons of claim reports, much more than the usual monthly stuff. Maybe they're looking at our numbers?"

"Please!" said Al, in mock exaggeration, while a string of beef and cheese hung from his mouth, "Stop it with the horror stories. Let's talk about something else. What are you planning for vacation, Jen?"

"Up to my parents' ranch in Oregon again. Blew out the budget on my Park City ski trip last February. Just gonna kick back on the ranch for a week. What about you?"

The group swapped vacation plans between bites of lunch. Jenny respected Al's opinion, and his gruff exterior couldn't mask the real concern he felt about the suggested merger. She felt bad for having alarmed everyone when she really didn't have much to go on. Even if it was true, they might not find out for months. She had no idea how wrong she was, or that in six weeks she would wonder if she could even survive.

***

Lawrence Harrington, M.D., the 59-year-old CEO of Progressive Psychiatric Management, stared out at the same spring day that Jenny had admired earlier. However, his view was more acute, more precise, desperately hungry to see the intimate details of life's seasonal renewal. "Cancer, what the hell," was his foremost thought. His wife, Carol, had received the diagnosis of pancreatic cancer two months earlier. Although her grandmother and two aunts had histories of cancer, none had been stricken at the early age of 52. He had been there when Dr. Watanabe sat them in his office and discussed the findings of Carol's work-up. Their heads were swimming with questions, doubts, and fears. The illusion of invincibility had been cracked. He wanted to protect her, fix it all, make it right. Above all he wanted to throw all the damn money he had made in this crazy decade of healthcare reform to one purpose: to save the woman he loved.

Carol had married him 31 years earlier, probably against her better judgement. Back then he was young, brash, overly confident, probably at great risk for early bankruptcy. Somehow in thirty-one years they had managed to make it work. They raised two healthy kids (well she did, mostly) who were now just finishing college. Much of their lives had been spent struggling to keep their kids in private schools or move into better neighborhoods. Like so many couples, their intimate companionship was catch as catch can. They had vowed to take romantic vacations, but somehow the family always came along. The phenomenal success of Progressive in the last eight years had consumed all of Larry's attention. Carol took greater command of the home front and they had even less time together. They were looking to his retirement in a few years as their time together. The diagnosis shattered those plans.

The discussions with the doctor and Larry's own on-line research through MOM confirmed only two things; she would be aggressively treated with chemotherapy and surgery, and there was 50 percent chance she would be gone within five years. Life without Carol had never been an option. He realized, with some embarrassment, that he had always assumed he would go first, probably on the way to some appointment in his frenetic life. Boom. No regrets, no goodbyes, no chance for grief or anticipation. Now he had to face a frightening possibility: life without his best friend and lover, and guilt over all the postponed chances to be together.

Two months earlier Great Health Benefit made a query to Progressive about a buyout. Progressive was such a hot property they received three or four queries per quarter, which they always turned down. GHB was persistent and began positioning itself for a hostile takeover. They apparently intimidated other suitors, for all queries from other companies were suddenly withdrawn. Few companies had the muscle or stomach to tangle with GHB. Larry could probably stall for a while, maybe a couple of years. He was still the very capable head of the independent organization, and the board of directors had complete confidence in him.

Carol's diagnosis had drastically changed Larry's take on his corporate life. Staring at the flowers below his window, he realized the decision had already been made deep in his heart. He must leave and be with his wife. Although Progressive had always been like a third child to Larry, he suddenly recognized he was no longer the mainspring, merely another cog in the wheels of a well-run organization. It was time to leave and be with Carol, for all the time they had left. The offer from Great Health Benefit was substantial, and coupled with his stock options, would give him more money than he could possibly use. It would allow him to purchase the best care available for her. He could nurse her back to health, as she had done for him countless times. It was time to be done with Progressive.

Larry's intellect quickly provided the corporate rationale for his departure to satisfy the matters of his heart. He had already told the board of directors that Progressive could not continue to develop in its present, independent form. They must affiliate with a larger national insurance company if they were to survive. At this point in the evolution of healthcare reform, Progressive could either be absorbed by another company, dismantled, or allowed to slip in market share. The days of independent operations were over. He had little doubt the board would approve the merger in their vote that night.

Larry hated that GHB was the winner in the negotiations. He foresaw the complete destruction of all that Progressive stood for. Great Health Benefit would replace his medically trained staff with bean-counters and burger flippers. The trade papers were filled with so many horrific GHB stories of patient neglect, denials of care, legal threats to providers, and gross violations of confidentiality. He felt a little like he was abandoning his staff to cruel foster parents.

The executives of GHB were aware Larry was disappointed by the merger, but weren't mindful of his hatred of the behemoth company. They had even asked Larry for a recommendation for one of his staff to move into a key position in their organization. Who could he suggest that would try to bring some humanity to this predatory beast? "Marge," he said to his secretary, "make sure I speak with Jenny Barrett at the meeting today and introduce her to Carter Newton."

Jennifer Helene Barrett was one way he could fight back. He had an opportunity to place her in a critical position, one that might make a difference. Carter Newton, a VP from GHB who was active in the negotiations, was searching for a key employee to help implement their new computer system. The person would be privy to the core workings of their decisions on patient care. If anyone would stand up for patient rights, it was Jenny. He had watched her mature in the last few years and believed she had much to contribute to the healthcare revolution. Besides, this merger short-circuited her promotion. GHB would obviously do some downsizing of the Progressive staff. Placing Jenny in the belly of the beast would at least give her a fighting chance.

As he turned in his chair Larry's hand brushed against the plastic mouse on his desk, waking up his computer screen from its slumber. Again he scanned the compiled data on Carol's cancer and her estimated chances. He had seen thousands of lives reduced to such numbers in his years of healthcare service. Somehow with Carol they looked obscene. With a click of his mouse the data evaporated. He began to draft his plans for the board of directors. If he was lucky, he could be out in two weeks.

Chapter 3

At six feet three inches, Crandall Bream stood out conspicuously among the protesters. He towered above the mostly female crowd outside an abortion clinic in Seattle. It was an unusually warm day for May, with a high temperature expected in the eighties. Handcuffs gouged his wrist, and the salty sweat added to the irritation.

Crandall had handcuffed his wrist to the wrought iron fence next to the clinic entrance. Other protesters had attached themselves to cars, parking meters, mail boxes, trees. One old man had padlocked his wrist to the clinic door knob. They meant to stop any abortions today, and were, so far, successful. No one, not even the clinic doctor, felt like running this gauntlet. Of course, this was not just an abortion clinic. It was a medical clinic, where many procedures were performed. None of the other procedures would be done today either.

The clinic administrator spent most of the morning trying to get the police to clear the streets so they could get back to work. The media seemed only mildly interested in the event. A news photographer barely stopped his car to click two or three pictures, almost a drive-by photo shoot. Two local TV stations swept their cameras over the crowd, but had to stay close to make it look like a sizeable group. Hardly forty people stood outside the clinic, despite the arrival of Mr. Bream. He felt betrayed by the local Christian leaders for not calling out the troops to make this a major media event. Nevertheless, Mr. Bream was slowly spiraling down in his notoriety and popularity.

Crandall Bream's career in spirituality began shortly after the death of his pregnant wife to a drunken truck driver. At 31 years old he had been married to Sandra for just two years. He had come and gone from the church throughout his life, taking little comfort or meaning in the rituals or traditions.

His greatest fault was an expansive ego, and he wanted a woman who could feed it well. Crandall was not particularly handsome and he hated rejection. Sandra was the first woman who seemed to love, or adore, him in a fashion consistent with his own self-image. He did truly love her in his own way, and was devastated when a slob with five prior DUI convictions slammed into her as she returned from shopping. She was four months pregnant. The autopsy report said it was a boy. Crandall hated God for six months.

A family friend met him at a social gathering around Thanksgiving and recommended he come to church on Sunday. Something in Crandall yearned for spiritual salve, and he accepted the invitation. The sermon, about abortion, stirred something deep in the man, and once again he embraced God. Crandall felt awakened by a new meaning and purpose. How could women voluntarily kill their children when his child had been so wanted? He became active in the anti-abortion movement, rose to a position of leadership, and ultimately launched a new career.

At one point Crandall Bream produced his own syndicated cable TV show, preaching the evils of Satan, smut, and abortion two nights a week. He was welcomed as a crusader into hundreds of churches, to stir the faithful and fight the tide of "child murderers." Crandall enjoyed the glow of fame and soon learned the price of continuing it.

He began to pull outrageous stunts to impress his following and keep himself in the spotlight. Although his antics never led to bombing or shooting people, he fiercely dogged anyone he thought was sympathetic to abortionists. His followers would stake out the homes of physicians who were suspected of performing abortions. He crusaded to have medical personnel who had assisted in an abortion be excommunicated from the church.

His most dramatic stunt, which also marked a sudden decline in his popularity, occurred when he infiltrated a major hospital while impersonating a physician. Crandall obtained and copied the medical files of about thirty women, including ten who had received abortions over a six-month period. The information was used to publicly harass the women and any of the medical personnel whose names appeared in the chart, which included doctors, nurses, and lab assistants. He called them co-conspirators. His goal was to remove the veil of secrecy surrounding abortion, but the plan backfired. The police charged him with impersonating a physician and fraudulent use of medical records. These charges were later dropped when it was determined he had only worn a white coat and a stethoscope, never once stating he was a physician. Still, even as he dodged the charges, the public grew suspicious of his motives.

At first he had seemed a man of true passion and commitment, yet his antics became increasingly hurtful and cruel. A local TV station manager got fed up with his theatrics and produced a "<u>Hard-Copy</u>" type exposé of Crandall Bream, focusing on the pain he had caused in his "noble quest." The final scene in the three-part series ended with a five-year-old girl, the daughter of a nurse, standing outside a hospital shouting in terror to Crandall, "Stop hurting my mommy!" Crandall went to embrace the child, but she stepped back and the camera only caught him swinging at the girl. She screamed again, fearful of an attack.

At the end of the broadcast, the image was frozen on the screen as the sounds of the cheering crowd faded away. The close-up shot of the fearful yet determined little girl became an anti-Crandall posture. His followers turned away. The church bookings ceased. He lost his cable show when the sponsors fled. Attendance at his meetings dropped to a dozen or so devout followers. At 42 years-old he feared he was near the end of his run. It would take something big to reestablish himself. Although Crandall still believed in the "cause", he also needed cash to continue the crusade.

Jerry Stack, Crandall's only remaining part-time assistant, pulled up in a large blue van about a block away from the clinic. With his freckled skin, blond hair, and lithe body, Jerry moved in a graceful, almost effeminate fashion. He had been monitoring the police broadcasts to see how seriously the situation would be taken. Crandall had been arrested many times, but his popularity kept him out of jail and serious trouble. The money had also purchased high priced legal talent. Jerry was worried that those benefits were fading fast. If Crandall didn't watch out, he could easily lose a case and end up doing some serious jail time. Jerry overheard the police coordinating a big presence at the clinic demonstration and decided Crandall was needed elsewhere.

Weaving through the crowd, Jerry slapped supporters on the back and sported a placard reading, "This war is for the children." Crandall spotted him approaching and guessed the reason. Jerry motioned slightly with his right thumb in a subtle but distinct gesture, like hitchhiking. It was the signal to leave. Jerry said out loud for the crowd, "Mr. Bream, you're desperately needed in a conference with the legislative committee of the Christian Coalition. There is a new opportunity for an anti-abortion bill and they require your input."

"Jerry, my place is here, on the front line with these good people.

We're stopping murder today." The crowded cheered in support.

"Yes, this is truly the Lord's work. Yet you can't miss this opportunity to serve an even greater good. Changing the law of the land. The cause needs you now to serve in an even mightier capacity."

Crandall turned with a look of ambivalence to the people around him.

"Crandall, go tell them the truth," someone shouted.

"Yeah, tell the legislature of the horrors in our clinics. Get those godless fools to pass some real laws," said another.

Crandall reluctantly withdrew a key from his pants pocket and unlocked the handcuffs from the iron fence. He kept the other end attached and dangling from his wrist as a symbol of commitment and rebellion. "I hear your pleas and I will heed the call. I will take our message to the leaders and see to it that this murder is stopped." Crandall and Jerry walked through the crowd, now delirious with pride and hope. In a half-hour the police would arrive to begin carting off the protestors. Crandall would be safe. And he would not be meeting with any committees or legislators.

As Jerry drove them away in the van, Crandall removed the dangling handcuffs. He slumped in the passenger seat. "Thanks again."

"No problem," said Jerry. "You in the mood to talk? I've got something hot to tell you."

"Let's get some lunch and go to your place. I'm getting too old for the gymnastics of protest."

They stopped at a Subway and bought some sandwiches with a coupon. Ten minutes later they were devouring them in Jerry's kitchen.

"So what's up?" asked Crandall.

"Well, as you know, our financial situation is grim. It's as if someone turned off the cash-flow spigot. We've gotta do something. We seem to have lost the support of the churches around here. So we need another angle."

"And that would be . . . ?"

"It's a little complicated. But I think it will work. You remember Elliot Mears, the computer hacker who turned to God about a year ago?"

"Vaguely. Didn't his wife decide to leave him when she was pregnant and then aborted without telling him?"

"Right. Really made him see the light. Well, I was talking with him last week at a barbeque. We had some beers, got a little loose, and he began talking about getting to all the women who have had abortions. Remember that Guttmacher Institute report that said almost half of all women in America have had at least one abortion?"

"Mother of God, do I ever."

"So does Mears. He wants these women to be held accountable. To be confronted with their sins and pay the price."

"What price are you talking about?"

Jerry paused for effect, "We ask them for donations to the cause!"

Crandall's mouth dropped open in perplexity. "Am I missing something? We ask women who have had an abortion to contribute to an anti-abortion cause?"

"Yeah."

"Well, there are two obvious problems with this approach. One, how do we find a list of women who have had abortions, and two, why would they contribute to our cause?"

"Mears says he can identify close to a million women who have had abortions, using data from healthcare and insurance computers. I'll explain that later. But assuming for a minute he can give us a list, how many women would be willing to pay to get their name off a publicly circulated list?"

"A publicly circulated list?" Crandall's eyes became wide with excitement. "My God, if we could break through the secrecy of abortions, it would stop the industry in its tracks. If people knew they would be exposed, they'd never go through with it."

"It would definitely give them second thoughts," agreed Jerry. "But we would need a dramatic revelation to the public that these murderous secrets are no longer secure. And we can get a lot of people to pay for their sins, or at least to have their sins removed from the list."

"What's your thinking?"

"If we can get the list, we'll produce a mailing to these women. The letter will contain enough facts to convince them we know of their past. We'll have to set up a few shell companies or agents to keep you clean. We can keep the donation reasonable, say thirty or forty dollars. If we even got 10 percent response rate on half a million women, we'd be in the big bucks. It would dramatically advance the cause, and put you back on the map."

A dark expression crossed Crandall's face. "This does sound a little like blackmail. If it were handled poorly, it could be a public relations nightmare."

"We can make it work," assured Jerry. "Crandall, this is a fabulous opportunity to put a dent in the devil's work. Only the liberal press would see it as anything but justice. And they ain't our friends. In one shot we could cut the abortion rate maybe 80 percent. No one could ever be secure in their secrecy. Even if you weren't associated with the fund-raiser, we'd be in a great financial position to push the envelope even further. Maybe get you back on the air. If people aren't getting abortions, they'll need help, guidance, support. They'll need spiritual leadership."

"Okay, I like it. Let's pursue this further. What's the next step?" asked Crandall.

"We meet with Elliot Mears. He's a major computer genius, but he can get a bit obsessive on the details. I believe he can do it. It's an amazing plan that could be executed quickly. It may take some front money, maybe fifty to eighty thousand."

"Those are some big numbers."

"Yeah, but the return could easily be millions of dollars, as well as thousands of lives. At least we should meet and kick it around."

Crandall weighed what he had heard in the last half hour. Jerry was loyal, dedicated, and much more practical than himself. He was one of the few people Crandall really trusted.

"Okay, set it up."

***

The lunch group broke up and Jenny headed back to her cubicle. The vacation talk had fired her up. Only a month until she got to kick back at her parents' ranch. It wasn't elegant, but it was needed at this point in her life. The winter ski trip wasn't able to salvage her one-year relationship with her former boyfriend, Todd, so they decided to end it amicably rather than risk slowly poisoning it. She half wished he would come up to the ranch just as a friend, but unlike Mark, Todd couldn't make the conversion to platonic friend.

The interns had returned to their seats by Jenny's desk. She'd have about an hour more with them, teaching them the ropes of modern mental healthcare. She could sense the mixture of awe and intimidation for the system. It was curious how each year her information support systems got more sophisticated and the interns' education stayed about the same. The universities were being left behind with their outdated ways. During lunch breaks the interns would describe lectures on Freudian theory and techniques. Jenny would smile at the notion of Freud's turn-of-the-century ideas being fit into today's lightning-fast systems. "Yes, Mrs. Smith," Jenny would role play in a heavy Austrian accent, "lie back on zee couch and place zee phone by your head. I vant you to say zee first thing that comes to your mind." It used to be a funny story, but in the last couple of years it seemed to be getting scary.

The students were farther and farther out of the loop.

"So, any questions about that last case," Jenny asked as she logged back onto the computer. Her only e-mail announced a management staff meeting on Friday. No word from Laura Paine on any scuttlebutt.

"I didn't realize you had to turn the guy's wife in just for hitting him with a pan," said Natalie. "When did that start?"

"A couple of years ago. They keep knocking down the walls of confidentiality. First we had to report anyone who was seriously suicidal or homicidal. Then it was any suspicion of child abuse. Now, any physical conflict between spouses, lovers, or domestic partners. It's not the greatest part of the job, but we have to do it."

"But it's as if Progressive benefits from it because they don't have to pay for treatment."

Jenny admired Natalie's bravery in stalking a tough issue. "Some companies may try to turn it to advantage, but fortunately Progressive usually doesn't. Larry Harrington, our CEO, even testified against the bill on the grounds that it would prevent people from seeking appropriate care. Say, didn't you learn about this stuff in school?"

Two blank stares was the response.

"Be sure you bring it up in class. Okay, let me give you a little orientation about counseling in the late 1990s. You may have visions of sitting in a private room with a depressed or anxious client and your job is to explore the person's history, their upbringing, the meaning of the symptoms, and finally reach an integrated understanding of who this person is. That about what you hope to do?"

Some hesitant head nodding was the more hopeful response.

"In your dreams. The pitch today is on short-term care. It used to be that therapists could see clients for decades of weekly sessions, kind of wandering down an aimless path to the soul. Unfortunately it cost a tremendous amount of money and no one was sure it really helped. Therapists felt that everyone had a right to therapy, and that anyone could benefit from it. Just about everyone had health insurance with some kind of mental health benefit. Almost like people were walking around with a golden ticket. The job of the therapist was to get the client to come into the office so he could punch the ticket to make a living."

"Everyone felt the benefit was just about infinite. Everyone except the employers, who were footing the bill. They got tired of paying for infinite therapy with no clear benefits. They finally said, 'Hey, let's ask these guys to show us what we're paying for. Let's find out what's the most cost effective therapy. Let's only pay for stuff that works.' So they began pulling back benefits, managing care, and success rates stayed about the same. So they pulled them back more, saving even more money. Still looked good on paper. So today our job is to help businesses save money while we get cheaper healthcare. It's called managed care."

Natalie and Melissa sat quietly, a little stunned. Jenny saw traces of fear around their rigid smiles. She hated stealing people's dreams.

"Look, I'm not saying you can't do the kind of counseling you want. I'm just saying the field is much more complicated now. It isn't just a private conversation between therapist and patient any longer. I wish they would clue you in at school instead of pushing horse-and-buggy ideas."

Jenny redirected their attention to the hardware on her desk. She offered a brief overview of MOM and how the system was tied into other major systems around the country. She explained how the client's record is automatically updated with every call, and how information is sorted, sifted, and transmitted to all the players. It was as if a dozen people were sitting in the counseling session, all taking notes for the bean counters who paid for treatment.

"The other major advantage of this system is what it does for the therapist," Jenny added. "We have instant access to most of the client's health claims history. We can compare their concerns with thousands of others and recommend the right treatment. As of six months ago the system will even check on treatment for us, alerting us when something isn't right. If we find a bad provider, we can alert the licensing boards immediately. It makes the mental health field much safer."

"But it does seem a bit impersonal," noted Natalie. "You hardly get to know the person over the telephone."

"I admit it's different," said Jenny, "but sometimes that's an advantage. Look how many people bare their souls on radio shrink shows. Heck, the Psychic Network makes ten million dollars a month. We're much more personal than that."

Jenny had logged on, ready to accept calls. MOM was soon chirping for attention.

"Follow along on this case and you'll see how personal it can get." Then she announced, "Warmline, this is Dr. Barrett, may I help you?"

"I'm not sure I should be calling," said a weak voice. "I don't want to get anyone in trouble."

"We're here to help you. You won't get anyone in trouble," assured Jenny. "Who am I speaking with?"

"Michelle, just Michelle. I called a while back to get some help. I know the doctor is trying to help, but I don't seem to be getting any better."

MOM had drawn a blank from the caller ID since the call came from the business phone for a large employer. "Are you calling from work?" asked Jenny.

"Yes, I'm on break at my desk," was the reply.

Up popped the employer's telephone extension directory and the current active extension number. Number 1244 belonged to Michelle Daniels, a 23-year-old clerical worker, referred five weeks ago for anxiety symptoms to a counselor, Dr. Marsha Wassermann. Jenny noted Michelle originally spoke on the EAP Warmline with Diane, who was off today. "What seems to be the problem?"

"Well, I'm just feeling worse and worse. I'm not sure what to believe anymore. I can't believe the things I'm being told," she blurted as tears started to flow. "Things are all messed up," she cried.

"Michelle, I'm with you and we can make this better," said Jenny, somewhat perplexed at the reaction. Diane's intake notes seemed straightforward. A 23-year-old college junior from Ohio, visits Universal Studios on summer internship. Decided she wants to stay and play for a while, postponed senior year and graduation. The father lowers the boom, says to do it next year after graduation and threatens to cut off her funding. Michelle was torn between independence, fun, and responsibility. The conflict produces anxiety attacks, she starts to miss work. Fearful of losing her job, she gets more anxious, has more attacks. The recommended treatment: outpatient sessions twice a week, medication evaluation, progressive relaxation and desensitization to manage anxiety. Resolve issues with the father, help her make a decision. They handled thirty runaway-to-the-theme-park-job stories every summer, which usually resolve in four weeks. "Is Dr. Wassermann helping?"

"That's just it, I don't know. She says I've been hurt very deeply. She says I could've been sexually abused by my father, and this is why I can't face him."

"Michelle, I realize these are scary things, but I want to be sure where they are coming from," said Jenny. On her screen popped up the recent statistics on Dr. Wassermann's client outcomes. There was also a screen that provided questions about treatment protocols. She read from the list. "Did you tell Dr. Wassermann you thought you were abused?"

"No," protested Michele, "I never imagined anything like that. My father has always been stern with me, but he's very fair. I know he wants me to do well. He just doesn't know how tired I am of studying."

"So where did the suggestions of sexual abuse come from?" asked Jenny.

"From Dr. Wassermann. She says that would be the easiest explanation as to why I'm having such a strong reaction to my father's demands to return to school. She says such power over a child is not usual and may suggest some other influence. Like I'm afraid of being abused again."

"Do you remember being abused as a child? Did your father hurt you? Did he touch you in ways that were uncomfortable?" asked Jenny.

"No. I mean, I don't know. I don't remember anything like that, but Dr. Wassermann keeps asking. We spend our time going over my childhood, looking for bad feelings or memories. I feel so bad after the sessions, I usually miss another day of work. I've never been in therapy before. I don't know what to do. She's the doctor. Isn't she trained to know these things?"

"She is certainly trained to help," acknowledged Jenny. "Did she teach you any relaxation techniques or thinking styles to help reduce your anxiety?"

"We talked about it briefly in the first session, but after that we just talked about my childhood," said Michelle with a little more composure.

"Did she refer you for a medication consult? Or talk about whether you wanted to go back to college or stay at Universal?"

"No, not really."

Jenny was annoyed by this. She felt the therapist had betrayed the client and the company. Over the last five weeks Dr. Wassermann had used about $1,800 of the client's $3,000 benefit chasing something that didn't appear to be there. She had not provided the client with common procedures that reduce anxiety in 90 percent of cases. There had been no medication evaluation. Dr. Wassermann had severely violated the treatment agreement she had made with Diane. What to do?

Jenny had MOM search the professional literature again with Michelle's symptom profile to validate the original treatment plan. She also had MOM find a procedure to reframe the treatment goals. "Just a minute, Michelle, I'm checking your benefits," she offered. The screen soon displayed the protocol notes.

Using her most soothing voice, Jenny said, "Sometimes therapists try to help clients by following a particular therapeutic path. They hope it leads to a solution to the problem. Sometimes it doesn't and you have to find a different path. Michelle, I'm going to go ahead and refer you to a psychiatrist, Dr. Jefferson, as we had originally agreed. I also want to speak with Dr. Wassermann before your next appointment, so I'll have to cancel the remaining authorized sessions until I speak with you again. Do you understand?"

"You mean I shouldn't go to Dr. Wassermann anymore, but you want me to see Dr. Jefferson?"

"Yes."

"I hope I didn't get her in trouble. She seemed nice," said Michelle, almost wanting to take it all back.

"We're with you Michelle. I'm sure we can get you back in control real soon, and this will be behind you. OK?"

"Thanks, I feel a little better. It's been so confusing. I'll wait for your call."

MOM flagged Jenny that a treatment extension request had been received yesterday on Michelle's case, from Dr. Wassermann. Although utilization review personnel hadn't reviewed it yet, Jenny called it up. After a brief scan Jenny's blood began to boil. Dr. Wassermann reported using relaxation techniques throughout the five sessions with no progress. She reported the patient refused a medication referral. Jenny believed Michelle's story, which meant Dr. Wassermann appeared to be lying in the clinical record. This was a serious violation of basic practice standards.

Jenny displayed the details of the other clients Dr. Wassermann had treated for Progressive. The global outcome stats looked suspicious; all eleven cases required over thirty-six sessions, three times the average for the company. She cross checked the cases by diagnosis, looking at the original diagnosis assigned by the EAP and the final diagnosis given by Dr. Wassermann. A pattern quickly emerged; no matter what the initial symptoms, Dr. Wassermann diagnosed 90 percent of her clients with post-traumatic stress disorder and childhood sexual abuse. These stats were way out of line with all other therapists on the network. A chill shot through her.

Jenny decided to investigate outside Progressive. Logging onto the central insurance outcomes database at the Health Information Databank, a massive collection of medical/psychiatric claims provided by most insurers in the US, a more advanced version of the Medical Information Bureau. Jenny told MOM to do the same comparison study on every claim filed under Dr. Wassermann's tax identification number. Within a few minutes Jenny had hundreds of client names scrolling across her screen, each carrying the final diagnosis PTSD. She captured the data, linked it to Dr. Wassermann's file, and prepared to act.

Jenny called Dr. Wassermann, but got only a voice mail system.

She left a message about the termination of further sessions with Michelle. The interns watched intently as Jenny auto-filled the complaint forms to be transmitted to the licensing boards, malpractice carriers, and related agencies. She hesitated in pressing the "send key," reflecting that her anger may be running ahead of her professionalism. Although the company would be immune from any legal action regarding the reporting of Dr. Wassermann, a ripple of doubt about taking immediate action coursed through her.

She turned to the interns. "At this point I've assembled most of what we need to investigate Dr. Wassermann," Jenny instructed. "But we like to give the provider every chance to explain their actions, so I'm going to send it to the director of provider relations for review."

Jenny placed an e-mail message for a consult on the case. The case would get an administrative and legal review before Jenny was advised on how to proceed. "I wonder if the pressures and isolation of private practice make people take such liberties," Jenny reflected out loud for the interns. She felt snug in her glass corporate tower.

The interns left for the day and Jenny began to close up shop. She had received an e-mail memo from Laura. It only said, "Rumors are flying as usual. May be a big announcement at Friday manager's meeting. See you there Ms. Director :-)", signing off with punctuation representing a sideways smiley face.

"Goodnight MOM" was Jenny's quitting time log off. She was leaving at 4:10 P.M., but she'd been there since 6:00 A.M. Her company was pretty good at flex time. She liked the company just the way it was and hoped any mergers wouldn't change things too drastically. Unfortunately healthcare had become one of the most unstable enterprises in America. Managed care companies started, merged, and failed with frightening regularity. It would be folly to think Progressive wouldn't succumb to some giant corporation soon.

Chapter 4

Mark Lipton spent the afternoon collecting interviews for a news piece on shady abortion clinics. A recent state study had found that roughly 20 percent of abortions were performed on women who weren't pregnant. Mostly poor women and frightened teens. The clinics or agencies would use questionable labs that always reported a positive pregnancy test. Mark even got a sympathetic physician to submit five samples of male urine to the labs, all of which came back positive. (He had mischievously left a message for his parents that he was about to make them grandparents.) The scam involved the simple financial reality of healthcare funding; no abortion, no money. Mark had been reporting the excesses of healthcare for two years, trying to make a name for himself in what he saw as the decade of healthcare reform.

Around 4:00 P.M. he tracked down the number for the Great Health Benefit claims division and called to see if Elaina was still working there. He remembered her clearly even though they were never close friends. She had hung out with Jenny's academic buddies and he had talked with Elaina maybe twenty times. She was attractive, extremely bright in the sciences, but very subdued and reserved, almost shy. He could imagine her doing well in a corporate environment talking *about* clients rather than *to* them.

"You have reached the claims division of Great Health Benefit. You may make a choice from the following menu . . ." stated the computer voice.

Mark instinctively pressed the "O" in the hopes of raising a human immediately, and soon the distinctive, non-perfect voice of a real female said, "Claims, how may I help you?" The voice was sunny, yet professional.

"I'd like to speak with Elaina Ruiz."

The human voice faltered, almost choked. There was too long a hesitation. "I'm sorry sir, Ms. Ruiz is no longer with the company." Clouds had suddenly blocked the sun in this voice. "Do you have a claim number so I can route you to the appropriate representative?"

"This is a personal call, from a colleague," he added quickly. "She volunteered to be on a professional committee. Do you know how I could get in touch with her?"

Again, a lengthy pause. Then the voice, now devoid of any sun, said, "Just a moment, I'll see if someone can help you." Mark began to feel alarmed.

"This is Peggy Koss, may I help you?" said a new, more sterile voice.

Mark repeated his request.

"I'm sorry, Ms. Ruiz left the company about three months ago. Of course, for security reasons I'm not at liberty to disclose any information."

"Could you get a message to her, my name and number?"

"I'm sorry, we have no current location on Ms. Ruiz."

"Maybe human resources has a forwarding address," Mark suggested.

"They would not be able to help you either, I'm afraid. Is there anything else I can help you with?"

"No, you've helped enough," he said with sarcasm.

Mark had no idea where Elaina lived, and the name Ruiz was common in Southern California. It was not quite 5:00 P.M. so he decided to try the school of psychology at UCLA.

"Psychology," Mark heard the receptionist announce in a distinctive New York voice. Grace, the sixty-ish "earth mother" to all psychology students, had answered the phones for untold decades. She had coddled hundreds of eager minds through the hallowed halls of academia.

"Hello, I'm trying to get in touch with Elaina Ruiz, a former student. Can you help me get a message to her?"

For the second time that day a receptionist choked on the name. "I'm sorry, who is this?"

"I'm Mark Lipton, a reporter for the Chronicle, but this is more of a personal inquiry. Her friend Jenny Barrett and I are trying to get in touch with her."

The mention of Jenny's name broke the ice. "I'm sorry Mr. Lipton. I think I remember you. I'm afraid I have terrible news. Elaina died three months ago."

"Jesus," Mark gasped. "How did it happen?"

"I wish I could tell you, but I have little information. We just learned of it last month. I know that she fell ill, was briefly hospitalized, and died unexpectedly. We hope to have a notation in the next alumni newsletter, but we can't get much detail from the family."

"Is the family in Southern California?"

"Yes, in Riverside. I'd have to ask permission to give out the number, but I'm sure you can find it."

"I'm very sorry, and I know Jenny will be devastated. Did anyone from school attend the funeral?"

"I don't think so. We found out so late. Dean Raulson sent a letter from the school."

"Thanks for telling me straight up. If I find out anything from the family, I'll let you know. Say, I just thought, since Ruiz is a pretty common name in Riverside. Is there anything you can tell me to narrow the search?"

"I suppose it will be okay. Look, I'll give you the number if you promise to let me know what happened."

"Sure Grace, I appreciate it."

***

As Jenny traversed the parking lot, she noticed the sky glowed with an eerie amber cast from a thick haze that hung over the valley. The cars around her were dusted with a light gray powder floating down from the sky, swirling across hoods and windshields. Another of LA's incessant brush fires had pumped soot and ash into the evening air, obscuring the sun while giving the world an unearthly glow. It was easy to imagine one had fallen into a science fiction movie, and the aliens were about to invade.

Jenny lived in the foothills and had been through two threatening fires in the last three years. She recalled how unnerving it was to sit on a roadside overlook and watch a turbulent fire march across a field toward your neighborhood, jumping from bush to bush like a swarm of combusting rabbits. Her townhouse was street side, facing a ravine across the road. Last year the fire had advanced to within a quarter mile of the road before the Santa Ana winds had finally diminished, giving the fire department a chance to knock the blaze down.

Jenny quickened her pace to her car, jumped into the driver's seat, and flipped the radio on to hear where the demon god of fire was striking today. She was relieved to hear it was ten miles west of her, stuck in a lightly developed canyon. "Looks like the ranchers win the fire lottery this week," she thought. Back home, in rural Oregon, brush fires had a different meaning. Everyone would pull together, coming from fifty miles away to man the fire line. In LA, you probably could not get through the camera crews to help out.

Jenny eased her gold Toyota Camry out of the parking lot and headed for the foothills of the Santa Monica Mountains. She had been raised on a ranch outside Grants Pass, Oregon, a heritage she desperately held onto in the urban insanity of LA. Her townhouse was surrounded by mountains, trees, birds, and the occasional coyote. For her it was a wonderful compromise: city by day, nature by night.

Her Toyota lurched into a supermarket parking lot, squeezing into a slot crowded by a garish steel and lacquer sculpture in the form of a Ford Bronco on stilts. The recreation vehicle towered above her, giving off a rubbery stench from its pristine, never-seen-mud tires. Jenny hated the pretentious owner, sight unseen. In the store she sped through the aisles to pick up some simple fixings for dinner and some cereal and low-fat Haagen Dazs, an oxymoron if ever she had heard one.

She was quickly scanned through the checkout and zipped her debit card through the reader, a wordless transaction save for the simulated electronic computer voice quoting item prices, final total, and the eerie "Have a nice day."

The checker smiled at Jenny, who must have looked like she needed a little human contact, so the friendly cashier said with a vacuous smile, "Do have a nice day."

Jenny reconsidered her position. "I guess it must be pretty easy to program the inner workings of a teenager into a microchip," she cynically reflected. She sailed into the parking lot and walked to her car. As she squeezed between the vehicles a booming voice suddenly thundered, "Get away from the car. You are too close to this vehicle. Please step away."

Jenny turned to see who was yelling, only to discover it was the voice alarm of the Bronco. The car was shouting at her, telling her to go away. "Now they're putting bullies on microchips," she lamented. She dealt with machines all day long and was in no mood to be harassed by some moronic car alarm. People walking by were eyeing her suspiciously, although a few offered looks of sympathetic frustration. The owner did not emerge and the damn car kept yelling whenever Jenny tried to open her door. She was soon overwhelmed with contempt for the owner.

A smile spread across her face at the absurdity of the situation.

She searched her thoughts for a way to prevail over this electronic bully. Then she saw them, scurrying around the shopping carts. Pigeons. The ultimate urban weapon. She sat the grocery bag on her car seat and rummaged for a second, withdrawing a jumbo box of Cheerios. She popped it open, scooped out a handful of the nutritious little "O"s, and threw them on the ground in front of her car.

The pigeons were exquisitely adapted to life in a parking lot, and thirty of them swooped to devour the cereal. The next handful landed on the Bronco's hood, followed by handfuls to the roof. The pigeon network was well-tuned, for soon over a hundred birds were flocking to the truck, eating and excreting in synchronous orbit. It was a guano festival. Jenny started her car and slipped away while the Bronco engaged in futile argument with the birds, "Please move away from the vehicle."

With the oaty smell of victory wafting through her car, she drove the seven miles up the canyon to her home. She couldn't wait to see Mark. He was fun and challenging and a great friend, as any thirty-year-old adolescent would be. It had taken them a year to get past the dating thing, but now the affection was largely platonic. He was still interested in getting sexual, and a couple of times in the last year she let it happen. But he was always respectful when she wasn't interested and would still give her a good hug.

The car bounced into the townhouse complex driveway and Jenny parked. She walked past the deserted pool and up the path to her two story townhouse. She had about an hour before Mark arrived. She checked phone messages on her computer, which served as her voice mail, fax machine, and remote Progressive system. She noticed she had left the voice recognition program on, so, from across the room, she shouted, "Daisy, play messages." Her computer had been named for the song sung by HAL, the maniacal computer from the classic sci-fi film 2001, after he got his lobotomy.

Daisy's screen switched to the message log, which displayed the callers by name and phone number from caller ID. Although her friends were always impressed with Jenny's verbal command over her computer, it was actually a simple technology available on most modern personal computers. She simply "trained" the machine to recognize a few words and phrases, and paired the phrases with an appropriate function. "Note" meant record from the microphone. "Call" meant launch auto dialer. Heck, it was no more complicated than training rats to push buttons for food.

The machine was an IBM Aptiva Pentium II running at 366

megahertz. Progressive had cut a great deal for interested employees. What Jenny liked most was the efficient arrangement of the hardware. On her desk was the monitor, keyboard, mouse, and a slim console that held a disk drive and CD-ROM. The rest of the machine, including the bulky box of computer guts, was tucked away in a fireproof file drawer in her desk, completely out of sight. This offered great security, for a burglar would probably just steal the monitor and disk console, leaving the important stuff behind.

As impressive as her system was, Jenny wanted it to be more human. She was hoping to get a fully interactive voice recognition program for the system, so she could speak more naturally, rather than in short, discrete words. Daisy could record continuous speech, like a voice message, but could "understand" only about forty commands. With a more sophisticated program Jenny could even play chess with Daisy while she cleaned and vacuumed on the weekend. Unfortunately, her budget couldn't manage such an upgrade right now.

As she changed into sweats, Jenny heard her mother's voice message and the excitement over Jenny's plans to vacation back home in Oregon next month. In the background she could hear her father threatening to "work the smog out of her lungs." They were trying to get her younger brother, David, up there too.

Everything she knew about technology she owed to her brother and his Radio Shack obsession as a child. He built everything from telegraphs to metal detectors to computers, and Jenny always helped, learning about circuit boards more from osmosis than interest. It was in software that Jenny excelled, the programmed interface between machine and human. Her logical mind and intuitive insight gave her a natural talent for navigating through computer programs. She thought of computers as very bright but emotionally detached children. Her job was to put the humanity in them. It had paid off handsomely in her career.

"Daisy," said Jenny, to get the computer's attention, "Take note. Remember to e-mail David about vacation. End note." Daisy dutifully stored the dictation as a memo.

***

Ezra Whitney was a frail figure skirting along the streets near Ohio State University. White hair, thin frame, his 72-year-old body moved painfully with a hesitant gait. A heavily creased face framed his sharp blue eyes that revealed a much stronger will than body. A quick intelligence glowed as he visually devoured the environment. He was in a cheesy area for a noble purpose. He needed to buy drugs.

The area was composed of academic festivity mixed with the poor and the homeless. It was probably the safest sleazy part of town in Columbus. Ezra went into a used-book store to complete the transaction. Although surrounded by millions of words on the racks and walls of this secondhand establishment, no words would be uttered by Ezra or his "supplier." He wove his way to the back wall, out of view of the front counter, which was manned only by a spaced-out college freshman with his nose in a dog-eared book. Ezra came upon another student, well-dressed and groomed, conservative, looking like a business major. The young man smiled in silent greeting, for he liked the old man and felt sincere sorrow for Ezra's situation.

Ezra was buying morphine for Nora, his wife of forty-six years. She had been battling cancer for more than three years. The cancer had started in her breast, but had been missed on two examinations at her HMO. By the time it was discovered it had spread to her neck and pancreas. The doctors suspected it had invaded her brain, though Ezra had only observed her to be a bit less confident in her activities. Nora was still clear and lucid in conversation.

Her pain was overwhelming. Nora had never been one to complain. At times in their life together, Ezra had seen her endure monumental pain with hardly a whimper, yet the tenacious spread of cancer seemed to attack every sensitive spot in her body. There was no hope of surgery or treatment. The doctors had agreed that the only meaningful strategy would be to make her comfortable until the end. That mostly meant pain management through powerful drugs like morphine and Demerol.

When Nora had adequate medication, she was fairly happy and active. It has long been known that most legitimate pain patients rarely become addicted to opiates. Nora tolerated the medication very well. Unfortunately, her health insurance company had taken an overcautious stand. Although Nora's level of pain had increased, her medication dosage did not. In fact it had been reduced because of the company's concern for her "addiction potential."

Ezra had vehemently complained to the company that his wife probably had less than five months to live. What was the point of their addiction concern when this 70-year-old woman had to endure an excruciating death? Still, they wouldn't budge. Ezra couldn't help thinking it was simply a money thing. They had signed over their Medicare cards to Great Health Benefit with the promise of comprehensive benefits. Now his wife was in severe discomfort and the company refused to approve increased medication dosages to deal with her pain-wracked body.

What Ezra didn't know was that MOM was driving Nora's treatment. Although he spoke with case managers and physicians, all data were fed to Woodland Hills, California. MOM searched through the details of Nora's medical history, compared treatment outcomes of similar populations, and calculated the acceptable care to provide for her.

Also unknown to Ezra, and the rest of the world, were all the elements of the treatment formula that MOM used. The computer worked in the best interest of its creator. It took a digital approach to all things medical. Money was always more easily calculated than such intangibles as quality of life or human dignity. Elderly sick patients consumed a tremendous percentage of healthcare monies. Yet MOM knew, from thousands of case examples, that pain saps the will to live. Statistically, each milligram reduction in pain medicine increased the death rate for elderly patients by five percent. In large populations, such manipulation of patient comfort had even lead to larger stock dividends.

Ezra tried to switch to another health plan, but they had signed a contract pledge for three years and it was illegal for any other company to provide care without GHB consent. HMOs can only make a profit if members stayed in for a few years. He would have to petition the US government to change plans, a process that took time and money. His many calls to Great Health Benefit had produced some sympathetic words, but no authorizations for treatment, and no legitimate places to turn. MOM's electronic grip reached instantly across the country.

His disappointment turned from dismay to anger. Ezra vowed his wife wouldn't suffer any longer. No more muffled cries in the night. He set about finding a source of medication on the street. Hanging around Ohio State University, he looked for signs of drug transactions. According to newspaper reports, drugs flowed around the campus as freely as beer, yet in a week he had not seen anything that looked like a drug deal. He didn't want to risk visiting a rougher part of town, but he felt increasing pressure to help his wife manage the tremendous pain. Finally, he spied what looked like a drug deal outside a sub shop. He saw money go one way and some small packets go the other. With the deal completed the two walked off.

The "seller" looked like a normal student. Ezra followed him for fifteen minutes, trying to think of something appropriate to say without causing alarm. "Hi, I'm an old fart looking to buy some serious drugs. Oh, they're not for me, they're for, ah . . . a friend." Ezra's anxiety shot up immediately as the young man seemed to sense he was being followed. He turned to eye Ezra with suspicion, then he zigged and zagged across the street a couple times to test him. Ezra followed in clumsy pursuit. The kid did not seem alarmed. More like curious. By the time Ezra reached the corner, the young man had disappeared down a side street. Ezra's heart sank as he looked up and down the bustling avenue. Tears welled in his eyes as he realized his failure. He turned toward a building to hide his eyes from passers-by, not wanting any attention.

Suddenly he felt an arm on his shoulder. A hot breathy voice whispered, "What's the deal, old man. Did you want something?"

Ezra turned to see the young man clutching his shoulder. The fright in Ezra's eyes put the young man at more ease.

"Can I help you with something?" he asked.

"I don't know. I mean maybe. I've never done this before," stammered Ezra.

"Never bought a lottery ticket," said the young man, offering a knowing smile and a raised eyebrow as a hint on how to pursue the conversation.

"Why, yes. I'm looking for some lottery tickets," said Ezra, trying to mimic the young man's smile to show he understood.

"Good, why don't we head over to the Brawny Bistro and talk."

Ezra let himself be lead gently along the street. They soon entered through the oak door of a German beer garden-themed restaurant. It was noisy and crowded inside. They settled at the far end of the bar and ordered beers.

"My name's Ezra," he said, realizing his first mistake in giving out his real first name.

"Call me Bob," said the young man. He stood about 5"11", blond with light skin, with a muscular frame, confident stride, and a very engaging smile. He hardly seemed like a drug pusher.

"So tell me what you want," said Bob as their beers arrived.

"I've never done this before."

"I can tell," said Bob, almost sympathetically.

"I need some help getting something to help a friend."

"A sick friend?" asked Bob.

"Yes, my wife."

"Cancer?"

"Why, yes. Very painful. She's a sweet woman who has always done the best for people. She shouldn't have to suffer this way."

"Medicare cut you off?"

Ezra was surprised at the blunt question. "Not exactly. We signed up with an HMO. They won't give her any more medication. Also, we can't go anywhere else for treatment right now. We have a binding contract with them. I want her to be comfortable."

"Hey, you're not the first. I have about nine other clients like you right now. Mostly cancer. It's a real shame."

"You have others like me?"

"Sure. This managed care thing is steering a lot of people my way. And, to tell you the truth, I'd much rather deal with trustworthy folk like yourself. You'd never try to rip me off. You've always got the money. And, hey, I like helping people out."

Ezra couldn't judge the sincerity of the drug dealer, but he felt encouraged by the discussion.

"So, do you want heroin?"

"God no," blurted Ezra, shocked at the suggestion. "This is not an addict. It's my wife."

"Hey, old man, don't get too excited. It's just that heroin is what most of the others use."

"For cancer?"

"Sure, it's the best. They use it in England all the time. It's legal there. Much more concentrated and effective than morphine. Fewer side effects. Actually cheaper."

"I couldn't do that. The word makes me sick. I'd like some morphine. In bottles. From a pharmacy. I'll pay well."

"Street price is about four times pharmacy price. Got to make a living."

Ezra expected as much. He was so excited that this conversation was happening that he jumped at the figure. "Yes, that would be fine."

Bob looked around. "Okay. Here's the deal. I run a clean business. You will have to trust me, but I realize I have to earn your trust. Then maybe you'll send some of your friends to me. If all goes well, we'll start doing bigger deals. Okay?"

Ezra flushed with excitement. "Yes," he said as he put out his hand to shake on the deal. Bob was taken aback for a second, then pumped the old man's hand like it was a car jack.

Bob initially moved the drop site around until he was pretty sure Ezra was legit. After a month they settled on the old bookstore because it was easy to set up and he could be in the store without touching the stuff when Ezra picked it up. Ezra would in turn meet Bob on the street and purchase some "tickets" from him.

Ezra didn't tell Nora where the medicine came from. He thanked God that this person had been delivered to him, then felt a wave of guilt for participating in this underground business. When he got to heaven, would God understand his motivations? It didn't matter. It was the only way he could live with himself. He had spent a lifetime protecting this woman as best he could. He wasn't going to stop now.

Ezra reached up to the book shelf and removed the book with the red sticker that Bob had placed there earlier. On the shelf he found the little morphine bottles. He placed them in his pocket, returned the book to the shelf, and wandered out of the store. The evening looked warm and inviting. He was glad Nora would be able to enjoy it with him.

Ezra sauntered up to the porch of his clapboard house, which sported a vinyl cushioned swing lounger, rusted but still serviceable. He and Nora had sat there countless times watching the world evolve. She rarely made it outside these days.

He entered the living room and caught a glimpse of Nora resting on the sofa with the TV ranting about a contestant winning holiday prizes. Even in sleep she squinted with pain, the lines around her eyes screwed up to restrain the agony. He was now getting over half the morphine she needed from Bob, yet he didn't let her know. She would never let him spend the money on high-cost pain killers. She was just that way. He was concerned about the bite the morphine was taking from their fixed income, but he would have to scrimp elsewhere. His wife would not suffer.

The old man opened the medicine cabinet and withdrew a syringe. The protective seal from the morphine bottle was quickly stripped away and he filled the syringe with liquid peace. Nora had not injected herself in the last eighteen months due to a slight palsy, so the task fell to her husband. He emerged from the bathroom, entered the living room and sat beside her. She barely stirred. He had looked at this now fleshy face for over fifty years, and she looked no different to him now than when he first laid eyes on her. He gently began stroking her forehead and she awoke, smiling up at his grizzly face.

"I got your medicine, love," he said. "Let me see that shapely hip."

Nora laughed at his sexual innuendo and rolled over on her stomach. Ezra efficiently injected the medicine into her hip and gently massaged the area to lessen the sting. Ezra still felt an excitement to touching his beloved, although much of their contact had become treatment focused. When the fires of the cancer were quiet, they still found time to snuggle. He then walked into the kitchen and dropped the syringe into a beaker of alcohol to use again. Maybe tonight he could get her to sit with him on the porch.

Chapter 5

Mark arrived a bit after 7 P.M. Jenny greeted him with warm hugs, but Mark seemed unusually subdued.

"God it's been too long since I've been to 'casa Jenny.' You look great," he said, handing her a wrapped bottle of red wine.

"Thanks, good to see you too. Come into the kitchen, I'm making stir-fry."

As Jenny sliced chicken and vegetables, Mark opened the wine. They talked about mutual friends and caught up on news of each other's lives.

"I got some bad news today," he finally told her. "I called Great Health to follow up on Elaina. They gave me the runaround and I finally had to call the school. Jenny, Elaina died about three months ago."

"Oh my God." Jenny was stunned. "How? What happened?"

"Don't know. I spoke with Grace in the psych department. She didn't have much information. There was a brief hospitalization, don't know why. Elaina died in the hospital. Couldn't get any more. Her parents live in Riverside. Did you know them?"

"I met them once, but they wouldn't think to call me, though Elaina and I were buddies for a while in school. I don't know what to do. She was so nice. I spoke with her about nine months ago. She was excited about some new project at Great Health Benefit. Sounded like it was pretty hi-tech. It's unbelievable that she's gone."

Mark draped his arm around Jenny's shoulders and held her close. "Why don't you give her parents a call tomorrow? Find out what happened."

"Yeah, I think I need to do that." She flipped open her address book and turned to Elaina's listing. It was odd how the name still looked alive, sitting there with other friends and acquaintances whom she could still call. It would be a while before she could drop Elaina's name. Two numbers were listed: home and work.

"I don't have her parents' number."

"I do. Grace gave it to me. On second thought, maybe I should call them. They might be embarrassed that you weren't invited to the funeral. May be easier if they speak with me."

"I hadn't thought of that. Sure, but let them know I want to speak with them."

The evening became one of mourning and remembrance. They sat on the couch after dinner, touching and consoling each other, even laughing briefly.

"I remember I was in the computer lab when Brian Ellis came in to print the final version of his dissertation. It was on the psychological problems of geriatric incontinence. Elaina was in the lab and jumped on another computer. She somehow intercepted the file on the network heading for the printer. She told the computer to replace the word 'incontinence' with the word 'intercourse' through the entire document. Fortunately she told the computer to print the correct version as well. We watched Brian walk out of the lab clutching his masterpiece. About five minutes later he came running back, white as a ghost, thinking his entire dissertation had been turned into porno. I'm going to miss her."

Jenny was glad Mark was there. His arm wrapped around her provided a sense of protection that she needed right now. Her hand stroked the soft hairs of his forearm, feeling the taut musculature under his skin. It felt good to touch, and be touched. Mark began gently rubbing the back of her neck while he rambled on about some people at work. Elaina's death had instilled a pressing sense of mortality in both of them. Where was each of them headed? Were they realizing their dreams? If they died today would there have been too many regrets, postponements, delays of their life goals?

Mark's other hand began moving in sympathy over her stomach. It soon began brushing the bottom of her breasts as he shifted his lips to her neck. Warmth spread over her as the question of intimacy arose. She moved to meet his lips as his hand crested her breast. They were good at sex, and she enjoyed the intense passion that always emerged from Mark. His desire was so focused, more on her than her body. She loved the appreciation in his touch as he seemed to celebrate every caress. He would often look deep into her eyes at the moment of his orgasm, as if wanting to join with her mind as well as her body. It was so tempting to open that erotic door. His hand drifted under her shirt, brushing against the bare flesh of her breast. A lightening charge of desire flashed through her, her legs melting apart.

Yet Jenny also had to protect herself from the pain Mark often inflicted. Not intentionally; in fact it was more her process than his. She was always surprised how quickly her possessive attachment grew when they were close, and he reflexively moved away. The tug-of-war had doomed their two-year relationship almost three summers ago, but the feelings were too easily reignited.

"Mark, I don't want to do this right now. I feel close to you, but with Elaina's death I just want to be held. Okay?"

"Sure, I'm sorry, it's a little weird for me too. I guess something like death just makes you want to grab big handfuls of life." Then he smiled, "I wonder if you'll ever lose your power to launch me into erotic meltdown?"

"Well, soon I'll be getting my early gray hairs. Before you know it, I'll be old, wrinkled, and toothless."

"Toothless! That might actually be safer," he said with a grin.

Jenny smacked him with a pillow. They talked easily the rest of the evening, intertwined as friends.

***

The whole merger story was broken to the executive staff at the Friday morning meeting. Jenny entered the second floor conference room and was immediately overwhelmed with the din of anxious chatter. The rumors had been building at a fever pitch. Larry Harrington had made himself unavailable for comment until this morning. His lack of response had confirmed everyone's worst fears, and speculation had grown so fast that the prevailing belief was that final checks were to be distributed this afternoon.

Although Jenny knew that was ridiculous, a faint fear arose as Larry approached the podium to speak. He had entered from the side door and it was evident to everyone that he seemed different. His gait was leisurely, his faced almost glowed with a curious peace, particularly amidst the chaos of this assembly. She noticed he took longer to shake hands with his staff: not the cursory acknowledgment of a typical business greeting, but a longer, more thoughtful exchange. She realized it looked as if he was saying goodbye. Her heart sank a little.

Another man was walking about five feet behind Larry, unnoticed in the wake of their leader. He had the bearing of a young executive, athletic build, wearing an elegant blue suit, light brown hair trimmed like an IBM lifer. His eyes appeared almost black as he scanned the crowd with mild interest. He paced Larry confidently and positioned himself behind and to the right as Larry took the podium. The assembly quickly hushed as the leader addressed the group.

"I want to thank you all for being here so promptly," he began. "I have some very important announcements. I know rumors are flying all around and I promise to clear the air as quickly as I can. As you know, Progressive has enjoyed tremendous growth and recognition in the last few years. I must thank all of you for making this company one of the most effective organizations in the field. I feel proud to have some of the best talent in town. We have expanded fourfold in just three years, taking on substantial national contracts. We have assumed responsibility for the mental health of millions of lives, yet we deliver personalized services to each and every client. The leadership in this room has helped pioneer modern mental health services, and we've done it primarily with and for the people of Progressive. MOM may help us out in the housekeeping department, but it is you and your staff that truly bring the humanity to Progressive."

"We have struggled through our birth, our childhood, and we are now just entering adolescence as a business entity. We are a part of the revolution in healthcare that has swept through the 1990s. Streamlined systems, economies of scale, clinical accountability, financial efficacy, these are the buzzwords of today, and we live and breathe them."

"The cottage industry of medicine is rapidly disappearing. Physicians and healthcare providers are no longer sitting in homey, Norman Rockwell-style offices giving tetanus shots. They're working as an integrated team in the management of health, ensuring that everyone gets the care they need. The next step in the development of Progressive is to become part of that integration. It has long been our dream that mental health be treated equally to medical health. Progressive has just been presented with the opportunity to realize that dream." The pause in Larry's speech was met by a vacuum of silence as everyone held a collective breath.

"I am pleased to announce that Progressive has agreed to join with Great Health Benefit to form one of the most sophisticated service delivery systems in the country. It is the next logical step in our evolution. Through the merger of our talents and resources we can become one of the most successful of the new breed of top to bottom, cradle to grave, healthcare systems. And it is all of you that will drive us there, and if I know you, it will be in the front seat with the pedal to the metal."

Larry paused for a second, letting the wave of inspiration roll across the room before he dropped the other shoe. "However, my days of racing in the fast lane are nearing an end. I will be taking a back seat in this new venture. I'll be turning over the reins of daily operations to younger, more capable hands. I'll still be around, sticking my nose into things, but more as an adviser than a leader, which is to say I'll be almost retired, living a schedule much more tolerable to humans, catching up on important family business." Audible gasps and sighs circulated through the room. Jenny slumped in her seat, feeling deflated.

"Damn, it's all true," she thought. "I just make it to the executive level and our leader bails. Now I suppose they're going to purge some staff, downsize us all." Just about everyone in the room had similar thoughts, which seem to be leaking through their plastic smiles like an infant's failed Pamper. The healthcare revolution was quickly losing its luster in this room.

Larry didn't give anyone much time to reflect. "Let me introduce the new driver on this bus," he said, turning to the gentleman behind him and gesturing for him to step forward. "Ladies and gentlemen, I'd like to introduce Carter Newton, Vice President of Network Operations for Great Health Benefit."

Jenny joined in the welcoming applause as she closely scrutinized the man stepping forward. His movements were sure and poised, a man who would have been raised and refined in a privileged family. His angular jaw and broad shoulders conveyed a jocular masculinity, but his hands moved with grace and gentleness, clutching the microphone from its holder on the lectern and cradling it like fine china. Unlike Larry, Carter would not be constricted to one place while speaking.

"Thank you, Larry," said Carter, briskly walking away from the podium, whipping the microphone cord like a snake handler. "It is with great pleasure that I welcome all of you to the Great Health Benefit family of companies. As you know, Progressive is renowned in the field for outstanding client services and excellent treatment management. You have earned the esteem of your colleagues and Great Benefit is proud of this new association. I want you to know that we plan for Progressive staff to continue in their traditions of excellence."

"I can understand that many of you may feel unsure of your future with us. The newspapers are filled with accounts of health services mergers and major layoffs. We at Great Health Benefit know that it is really the people that make the company and we want you on board. We'll need you now and in the future for this transition to work. Fortunately we are in an expansion mode right now, so we have no plans for cutbacks." The crowd had no reason to doubt Mr. Newton, and they desperately wanted to believe him. A rolling round of applause signaled their pleasure with his statements.

"Another reason your future is secure lies in your knowledge and skills with the MultiAxil Outcome Management system, which has been in use at Great Benefit for over two years. Our operation uses a major expansion of this state-of-the-art computer system, but all of you are clearly familiar with the fundamentals. You'll simply graduate from MOM to Super-MOM, our upgraded version. I think these will be very exciting times, indeed." Carter glanced around the group, offering his most engaging smile.

"I know you must have a million questions, and unfortunately we have very little time. Most of your questions will be answered in the next few weeks. You are free to share this announcement with your staff, and an official statement will be issued later today. The daily operations will remain unchanged for a time. However, some of you will be tapped to join us at our corporate offices, either here in town or in Connecticut."

A chill shot through Jenny as she envisioned sending her parents a Currier and Ives Christmas card of wintry snow and ice, with the message, "I'm living this." She had no interest in moving to Connecticut.

Carter postured for the conclusion of his presentation. "I realize these events are unfolding quickly. We plan to accomplish the merger in stages over the next three to six months. There will be some shuffling of positions, but we want to keep things much as they are. If it ain't broke, we don't intend to fix it. I ask that you hang tight, trust that you are an essential part of this admirable organization, and keep doing your excellent work. You have much to be proud of."

Brief applause emerged from the stunned staff and Carter turned the podium back to Larry. Jenny realized the winds of change were blowing like a tornado all around her and she needed to perk up her corporate survival persona. She consciously pulled back her shoulders, plastered a smile on her lips, and ignored the groans around her. Larry quickly dismissed the group from the meeting with the promise that more information would be coming soon. As he surveyed the mingling crowd, he caught Jenny's eye and beckoned for her to come up front. She was taken aback for an instant, for she had spoken with Larry only a handful of times and couldn't imagine his interest in her now.

"Jenny," Larry exclaimed with brimming enthusiasm, "I'd like you to meet Carter Newton." Carter whirled around from a gaggle of handshaking staffers and stepped very close to the two of them. "Carter, this is the woman I told you about. Jenny has done so much to make MOM work. She's an amazing blend of humanity and techno-smarts. She's been a de facto head of the project since it began and has seen to it that the computer bends to our will rather than people accommodating to it. She drove the programmer-analysts nuts making the system user friendly. Yet in the end our productivity has jumped through the roof and MOM is really taking care of people. I'm sure she'll be a real asset to you."

Jenny felt an instant blush on her cheeks, for she was unprepared for such high praise from the boss. Carter's face brightened and he engulfed her hand in both of his, offering a firm and commanding handshake. "It's a real pleasure to meet you, Jenny. I've heard some great things about you and I know we'll be working together soon." She smiled into his handsome face and raised her hopes that maybe these changes weren't so sinister after all.

"Are you going to be spending time here at Progressive?" Jenny asked.

"A little, but mostly I will be scouting talent to bring over to our corporate offices. In fact, your reputation precedes you, so you've already been targeted," he said, giving her hand a lingering squeeze.

"Targeted," asked Jenny, extracting her hand, a little put off by the term.

"Yes, but I mean that in a complimentary way. We're looking to fill some key slots and Larry gave us a list of talent. Recruitment has been a problem for us. Your knowledge and familiarity with MOM make you and your staff a real blessing. We want to get you into the saddle as soon as possible. Oh, I should say, I'm talking about the office here in the Valley, not Connecticut."

"Whew, that's a relief," said Jenny, trying to appear jovial while her mind spun with questions.

"Look, Larry's tugging at me to meet some more people. I want to get you over to Great Health Benefit next week to show you around and start getting your input. I'll have my secretary set it up for Monday or Tuesday. Okay?"

"Sure, if it's okay with Larry." She could have kicked herself for the comment. "Get with it girl, this is your new boss," she thought. He just smiled and was quickly drawn away to the eager crowd.

***

Back at her desk, Jenny's head still seemed in a whirl. This had been a most amazing morning. She felt almost detached from her surroundings. Fortunately her day didn't appear too demanding. Much of it would be spent relaying to her staff what limited information she had about the changes taking place. She scanned her desk and found her mouse semi-glued to the blotter by a half-eaten glazed donut. She freed the plastic rodent and checked her e-mail. Thirty-seven messages! A quick perusal found thirty-two of them to be questions or speculations about the morning meeting. She began to draft a quick summary for her staff and associates, knowing Larry would certainly put out a company-wide statement before lunch. Mostly she expected to be hand holding her staff today.

A memo from Laura Paine, her VP, appeared in her e-mail. "Now you know as much as I do. Sorry I couldn't tell you more," was the reply to the query of Wednesday. The memo went on, "I did hear Larry singing your praises to some Great Benefit reps. I heard they lost a key staffer a couple of months ago and desperately need a replacement. Could be you. Good luck." It was Laura who had delegated most of the MOM project to Jenny, which seems to have turned into a pivotal event.

The reality of the work-a-day world soon came rapping. The computer let out a chirp as Jenny saw the name of one of her staff paging her. She picked up the phone. "Maria?"

"Yes, Jenny, sorry to bother you. I've tried to deal with this provider in Florida, but he's getting pushy. I'm kind of new at this provider stuff and no one else is available. This guy's threatening legal action."

"Did you pull up MOM's protocol for handling touchy providers?"

"Yeah, but this guy scares me. Can you take it?"

"Sure, let me switch to provider screens."

"OK, but beware, you may need to play hardball with this guy," warned Maria. "He doesn't want to let go of the client."

"What does MOM say about his outcome stats?" asked Jenny.

"Not good. A new provider, always asks for the max sessions. Tries to get the clients to pay privately. Really builds up dependency in them quickly."

"Okay, but I want you to monitor the call, it's the best way to learn."

As the provider screen pops up on her monitor, Jenny greets the doctor in her most sunny voice, "This is Dr. Barrett of provider services, may I help you?"

"Yes. I'm Dr. Nick Wilkins in Plant City, Florida. I just evaluated one of your clients and I'm trying to arrange for her treatment."

"Yes, Ms. Estes passed me the call. I see you're recommending intensive treatment for an eating disorder," Jenny offered in summary.

"This is a rural area and few therapists specialize in eating disorders," Dr. Wilkins explained. "In fact I'm the only one in town."

"Yes, Dr. Wilkins, you're the only one on the panel, but Ms. McClane in Tampa has an eating disorder group," noted Jenny.

"But that's almost an hour away, which would be quite a hardship on the client. I would be willing to see her."

"Well, Dr. Wilkins, as you are aware, we require that assessment and treatment be separate processes, to avoid any conflict of interest. Since you have done the assessment, she must be referred on to another provider for treatment. Since she is under our managed care program, she must see one of our contracting providers. I'll have to recommend that she join Ms. McClane's group," countered Jenny with finality.

"Well I can't support that and I think it's a violation of practice standards to require a patient to travel so far for treatment," said Dr. Wilkins.

Jenny was of course ready for this, popping up a row of provider problem screens. "Dr. Wilkins, according to my data the Florida Health Security Act states that specialists need only be within two hours travel time. Our recommended provider is within that limit." Why didn't this guy get the message, Jenny wondered privately.

Dr. Wilkins was clearly frustrated. "I will have to go to the insurance commissioner if you don't provide a better alternative. Or I will simply recommend that the patient see me privately and complain to her employer about the shoddy care you're recommending."

Jenny popped up Dr. Wilkins' credentials screen. Malpractice, licensing, hospital affiliations. It was all there. Normally she might have tried to sweet talk him into accepting the treatment plan, but she felt he was becoming far too pushy and was starting to bully her. Jenny was amazed that these therapists, who were supposed to be sensitive, understanding, and persuasive, became raving lunatics whenever anyone questioned their treatment. Off-line Jenny muttered, "If this guy's gonna throw hardballs, he better have a big mitt!"

"Dr. Wilkins, you are entitled to pursue that option if you wish, but may I offer a word of caution," Jenny said in a sobering voice.

"Your contract with Progressive clearly shows your agreement with our policies regarding the separation of assessment and treatment. To see the client yourself would be to violate that covenant as well as many professional standards. We would consider it a dual relationship that exploits the client and promotes a dependency. We would be duty bound to notify your regulatory board, the Department of Professional Regulation in Florida, and the American Professional Insurance Company regarding potential malpractice. Depending on how adversarial your regulating board is, such a query might become quite troublesome. You would also be required to notify your professional association and any of the other managed care companies you have signed with, since you have probably agreed to alert them in the event of any professional complaints. Additionally, your actions with this client may trigger a retrospective review of your earlier cases with Progressive. You have already contractually agreed to abide by any retroactive denials with a refund of payments. I would recommend that you think very hard about what would be in the best interest of this client." Jenny had set up the transmittal forms to the respective agencies on her screen and now gently stroked the "send" key, awaiting final word from Dr. Wilkins.

After a lengthy silence Dr. Wilkins responded. "I see your point and agree that Ms. McClane's outpatient group is worth a try. Please fax me the referral materials and I'll help the client."

"Thank you Dr. Wilkins," said Jenny, a smile of clinical victory on her lips as he hung up.

"Wow, I guess you set him straight," said Maria, who had been listening in on the call.

"I hate doing that, but sometimes the providers forget they have a contract."

On dark days Jenny found it frightening to consider the power that sat at her fingertips. In years past the medical community ran the show, taking full responsibility for the patient and remaining unchallenged in directing care. In the decades after World War II employers increasingly offered health insurance as a cheap benefit. Within twenty years almost every working American was covered by a generous health insurance plan, most of which paid private doctors endless amounts of money for any treatment. Funded with such a blank check, medical costs skyrocketed. Eventually, only the insured could afford care. Employers screamed at the rising costs and a new arrangement was proposed, the managing of care.

The idea was to put someone between the physician and the money who could decide whether a treatment was "medically necessary" and worthy of payment. The contract was no longer exclusive to the doctor and patient. It now included the insurance company. American business loved the idea of controls, and it soon became the model of most health insurance as a way to control costs.

Unfortunately, the movement had some unintended consequences. The rise of managed care quietly shifted the balance of power from physicians and healthcare providers to the managed care company. Essentially, an insurance company was deciding who, when, where, and even if a patient would be treated, and not from a position of professional responsibility or knowledge, but for profit.

This is what troubled Jenny most after showdowns with pushy providers. It was clear the pendulum had swung far to the side of managed care companies. She could easily tighten a contractual noose around the neck of a provider in Florida, Nebraska, or down the block. The very ethical standards and laws which were developed to police an independent breed of practitioners could now be used to pressure them into contractual compliance. The information systems in the giant corporations could instantly blacklist a provider and cause them no end of investigative heartache, just by faxing a letter to a regulatory board. For the provider it was somewhat like being falsely accused of child abuse; by the time you're exonerated, you've already been ruined. Jenny was happy to be sitting in the office of the winning side, but she often wondered where it was all going.

The computer chirped again and Jenny was back on-line with her duties. She made a note to call Mark and confirm his lead on the merger. She wondered if he had found out anything more about Elaina's death. Suddenly she remembered Mr. Newton's invitation for next week. She would be walking in the offices of Elaina's last employer. "I wonder if Carter Newton knew her?" she reflected.

Chapter 6

Carter Newton walked into the glass cube of the Great Health Benefit building, just two miles away from Progressive. The eight-story building stood a block from the ever flowing Ventura Freeway. Carter's office faced the river of traffic from the fifth floor, an indication he still had much room to rise in the corporation. He actually preferred the view. Sometimes he relaxed by staring at the constant flow of life and commerce, sometimes slow and bumper to bumper, but always in motion, much like business.

Carter Newton was all business. He lived and breathed the challenge of business every day. It was poker, chess, and tennis on a playing field of money. He sizzled at cutting deals, gaining advantage. A professor once told him the purpose of an MBA education was to learn all the laws of business so you could figure out how to get around them. Carter excelled under that philosophy. Carter was raised in the Midwest by German immigrant parents, working in the small family bakery from the time he was eight. His brilliance in sports and academics brought him early fame and promise. He paid for most of his schooling himself, through scholarships and part-time jobs. He enjoyed tennis and chess, for there was little element of luck. It was you against another, survival of the fittest. Just like business.

He picked up the phone and called his superior, Thomas Baldwin, senior VP of Operations, currently in Connecticut. After speaking briefly with the secretary, he heard Baldwin pick up.

"How'd it go with the new recruits?" Baldwin asked.

"As well as can be expected," replied Carter. "Most were pretty shocked to be losing their leader. Apparently the rumors were well contained. Few had any clue. I think they'll work hard to stay with the ship, which would be a great benefit to us. They're smart, well-trained, and enthusiastic about technology. Much better than that Portland group we got last November. They couldn't collectively type their own names."

"Did you spot anyone who can slip into that development position vacated by, what's her name, Elaina?"

"Yeah, I called Harrington last week about our needs and he introduced me to his star project director. She's a psychologist as well and did a great job easing the staff into the computer-assisted care system. She should be an asset. I've invited her to tour our facilities next week. We could bring her aboard really quick."

"Great, Carter, you're staying well on top of things. How has the family reacted to the untimely death?"

"Elaina's family was moved by our generosity in creating a memorial fund. I put the company life insurance settlement on the fast track. Sent them a letter of gratitude for her service here."

"Tragic loss. So young. Has there been any clarification about how she could die while in a hospital?"

"Not to my knowledge. Coroner's report says it was a rare medication reaction."

"Just tragic, the whole thing. So have you found any links to the security breach on MOM? We've got to find out who invaded the system."

"No, sir. The IS Department can't find a trail. The hacker was pretty smart, though, could easily cover her tracks."

"So you think it was a 'her'?" asked Baldwin, commenting on Carter's choice of pronoun.

"Sorry, sir. I suspect it, but no one is sure. Anyway, we're trying to close the loopholes, but it's hard when you don't know which door he or she came in."

"Seal them all if you have to. I want this system bulletproof. When we turn over care management to the system everyone in the industry is going to want see the algorithm. They'll be storming the walls, may even try to buy the staff off if necessary. We don't need MOM's rules of treatment decisions being discussed in the local press."

"We'll keep at it, sir."

"You know I'm going to be called to testify before the Joint-Congressional Subcommittee on Health Insurance Reform. Senator

Gray's little annoyance. We've got it pretty well covered, but I don't want any surprises. We don't want to give them any reason to propose legislation to look inside our computers. If you do trace that program leakage, get back to me immediately."

"We're working on it, but I don't think you need to worry about Gray's committee."

"Have you found any dirt on him?"

"No, but MOM hasn't been unleashed on the problem yet. I'm sure an extensive search will turn up something dark in his medical history."

"Good. There's another matter, Carter. You know we lost big to the Federal Trade Commission with our life insurance and investment divisions. We've got six Attorneys General screaming fraud at our sales tactics. We've got to get these staffers out of the line of fire and make them happy so they don't squeal. See if you can absorb some in your division. You must need bodies for the new contracts. If MOM is as good as you say she is, these people don't really need to know much about medicine."

"I'll see what I can do. We're opening another floor to take on the new clients. Should be some space."

"Great. Well, see if you can get this gal on line as soon as possible. We're falling behind schedule on the new system and the work keeps piling up. Our new goal is thirty million subscribers by the end of next year. I don't want to hire and train gobs of new people to service the contracts. That's why we have computers. Let's get the system going."

"You got it. Talk to you soon," said Carter, hanging up.

***

Mark Lipton banged at the keyboard on his desk, making last minute corrections before putting his feature article to bed. His editor had given him a hard time about boring insurance stories on managed care. Fortunately, this time Mark took a David and Goliath angle about this poor guy who lost his wife to heart disease when the health insurance company refused to pay for adequate tests. The man had taken the company to court and won a judgement of 1.3 million dollars— not a big sum in the million-dollar world of personal injury, but obviously a statement by the jury that greediness will not be tolerated. Mark used the article as a forum to educate the public on the subtleties of managed care, which he saw as the new province of the robber barons.

Just before lunch he picked up a voice message from Jenny, saying the rumor of the merger was all true, publicly announced at a meeting this morning. Mark found her voice sounded pretty upbeat, which was surprising given her aversion to life changes. He made a note to check out the press release that would be coming soon. He also smelled a story about the chaotic merger mania that kept the healthcare field in a spin.

Since he didn't have a lunch date with anyone, he decided to pull up some research on Great Health Benefit to take with him while he gnawed through a submarine sandwich. He logged onto Nexus, the national research database, plugged in the name and asked for references in the last twenty-four months. The system dutifully displayed every news and periodical reference to the insurance company for the last two years.

The list was longer than he expected. Over 500 articles with references to Great Health Benefit were available. Mark scanned the headlines and was struck by how many were negative. "Great Benefit Investigated by Insurance Commissioner." "Insurance Company Salesman Accused of Fraud." "State Attorney Requires Health Insurer to Refund Premiums." "Court Tells CEO: Pay Claims or Go to Jail." Page after page detailed the constant litigation or state actions against the company. Mark wondered why such conflict would have gone unnoticed. A quick scan of the bylines found another oddity; California, New York, and Illinois seemed under-represented. Florida, Texas, and the Midwestern states were prominent.

He captured and printed some articles to take with him. He put a call in to Jim Witcomb, the business editor.

"Witcomb," was the answer on the phone.

"Jim, it's Mark. Can I get some time with you today?"

"Maybe, what's it about?"

"That Great Health Benefit thing. You were right, they're moving on Progressive. I did a little search over Nexus about the company. It seems like they're being investigated or sued by just about everyone."

"They do play hardball. Hey, my lunch date bombed out. Want to get together about 12:45?"

"That would be great. Sub Shoppe?"

"Come by my desk. We'll walk together."

Mark landed in the chair next to Witcomb's desk at 12:40. He gazed upon the sixty-ish, gray-haired man clad in a plaid sweater, shirt and tie. He was from the old school of reporting, a solid researcher, well-connected, enjoying some regional renown after thirty years at the keyboard. An air of tired wisdom surrounded the man, yet his perceptions were always current and relevant. It wasn't just that Witcomb had so gracefully moved into the new technologies, it was that he could always spot the human nature inevitably wired into new machines or systems. He believed that machines always pick up a little of the personality of their builders, or in the case of larger systems, the company CEO. Witcomb's writing often reflected the similarity of quirks between man and machine.

"Hey Mark," he said in greeting, "let me just log off and we'll be gone. I pulled up some old stuff on Great Health Benefit, remembering their origins." He scooped up some papers and the two of them meandered off to a local sandwich shop. They briefly glimpsed the sun and then scurried across the bustling street. Even the brown haze of smog couldn't hide the beautiful spring day. They quickly entered a sliver of a doorway in the center of the block. Like salmon they swam against the current of departing customers and secured a booth away from the entrance. Within seconds a waitress offered them menus. They quickly ordered without even glancing at them.

"So, you've developed an interest in GHB," opened Witcomb.

"I have to admit, when you bounced me the lead, I was actually more interested in talking with a friend who works for Progressive. I thought it would be pretty much routine, but she didn't know a thing about it."

"Not unusual," said Witcomb. "Mergers are taking place so quickly, sometimes senior VPs aren't sure."

"Well, it led to an unfortunate discovery. A friend from college who worked at GHB corporate just died."

"I'm sorry to hear that," Witcomb offered with a glint of perplexity.

"I don't know any of the details, and I'm going to try and talk with the family soon."

"You don't think GHB had anything to do with it? I mean they're ruthless competitors, but they don't routinely kill their employees," stated Witcomb.

"I know, but it's just that death hasn't touched me personally too often and I guess it shook me up. Then, when all this bad press turned up, I got a sinking feeling for my friend, who may be headed there."

"Is she more than a friend?"

"Used to be," admitted Mark. "She's a great gal, full of principles and ideals. I'd hate for her to get sucked into an evil empire. Am I taking this too far?"

Witcomb moved back as their sandwiches were delivered, taking the opportunity to consider his words. He wanted to dig out a story on GHB, and clearly Mark had some interest and motivation.

"I don't know how far it goes. I'll tell you, GHB has grown exponentially in the last few years, mostly by becoming the darling of big employers. They offer the companies some of the cheapest health packages around, which has gained them a large market share. The problem is they never seem to pay anyone. They have almost built a firewall between the client and the benefits; it's like squeezing pennies from a stone."

"So you think they're greedy and ruthless?"

A grave look came over Witcomb's face, as if he too had been touched by them.

"Mark, I think they're hurting people. Lots of people. Maybe millions of people."

"What makes them so different from any other greedy insurance company?"

"Size and success. They are rapidly becoming the model of health coverage. Not only are they signing up employers, they're pushing some stranglehold capitation contracts on physicians and clinics."

"What do you mean, capitation contracts?" asked Mark, making notes on his napkin.

"Capitation. It's the real revolution in healthcare, but no one seems to know about it. Capitation takes the basic doctor-patient relationship and turns it upside down."

"How?"

"Since the beginning of time, physicians, like everyone else, made money by providing a service. You go to a doctor, they examine and treat you, you pay your bill. The more doctors treat, the more money they make."

"Okay," agreed Mark.

"In a capitated contract, the doctor or insurance company makes money by *not* providing care. Basically, the physician or clinic is paid up-front to 'manage' the care of a group of patients. Let's say the local dairy company gives the XYZ Managed Care company $100,000 to provide all the care their fifty employees will need for one year. That's $2,000 the company can spend on each employee's healthcare needs. Now the XYZ company gets paid up-front. If no one comes for treatment, they get to keep all the money. If everyone comes for treatment, the XYZ company goes broke. So they have to control how much they pay out for care. Their profit comes from paying as little for care as possible."

"I thought physicians and such still got paid by the managed care companies," Mark stated.

"They do, but the companies are spreading the risk of capitation around. They'll either put a provider under contract or simply hire them as an employee. Then they'll build in bonuses for not hospitalizing patients, not referring to other specialities, or for not ordering expensive tests."

"They get bonuses for withholding care?" Mark exclaimed.

"Wake up and smell the cough syrup, Mark. This is the arrangement we have under *our* health insurance. See. Nobody knows."

"Well who's watching these guys? Who makes sure they don't let people die for their own profit?"

"That's a very good question. I'm sure in the near future you'll come up with an answer," said Witcomb.

"What? Wait a minute. What about all the licensing boards, the insurance commissioners, hell, the malpractice attorneys?"

"They're trying to figure it out too. All these new arrangements are very confusing. Doctors call up to get treatment approval. The managed care company says 'no.' Patient can't afford to pay, finally dies. Family sues. Doctor says talk to company, company says talk to doctor."

"Still, doesn't the doctor have to treat him, I mean ethically?" asked Mark.

"Well, my very bright student, you just found one of the flies in the ointment. There was a time when insurance companies essentially had to pay whenever the doctor said treatment was necessary. Doctors had a higher duty to the patient, but they also had the authority. That's all changed now. Insurance companies drive the bus."

Mark was stunned, mostly at his own ignorance. "So it would seem pretty clear that whoever denies care pays the piper," he said.

"That's why you're not an attorney. You think too logically. Actually, some companies have gotten smarter. They don't deny care, they avoid care. They make it impossible to follow procedures or to get a clear authorization. It becomes a game of hoops and hurdles. They put a line of case managers up front and pile on the requirements. They have stables of young and hungry attorneys to draft perplexing policies and contracts. Oh, they also have giant computer systems that help them find every little profit angle."

"Jim, your cynicism is showing. Certainly there must be some decent companies that are doing it right."

"Yeah, There are. They're just not winning market share. They'll have to bend or die, I'm afraid," replied Witcomb.

"You said Great Health Benefit is making a good profit."

Witcomb shuffled through some clippings and produced a sobering headline: "Managed Care Company's Profits Up 350 percent. Looking for Places to Put Swelling Cash Reserves." Other clippings told similar stories. GHB was treating its stockholders very well.

"Okay, I get the picture," said Mark. "These guys are ruthless, anal retentive, and extremely successful. So what do you propose?"

"According to a very good source of mine, GHB quietly launched a new program about five months ago. It was mostly an internal thing, no publicity announcements. There was a shuffling of executive management that I was aware of, but my source put it in a more sinister context. GHB wants to double its presence in the healthcare market without sacrificing profitability. It can win market share with lower prices, but that means it must spend less on care. They have reportedly restructured their claims processing and computer systems to accomplish this by the most draconian of means. I want you, Mark, to check it out."

"I'm honored that you asked me, but I don't know much about the insurance biz."

"I think you're the right guy. You've done some great work on medical stories and you're good at following money trails. You also do well explaining how the issues affect mom and pop, which is particularly important for something as dull as insurance."

"That's what worries me," protested Mark. "Medical stuff is one thing, insurance is another. I'm not sure what insurance angles would be interesting?"

"Take medical records. They're now housed in large, insurance industry-owned data warehouses. They sell lists of people's names, illnesses, and treatments to mass mailers. Medical data is flying all over the Net. Remember when Nixon's Watergate burglars wanted Daniel Ellsberg's psychiatric records? They had to actually go to the doctor's office to get them. Now, the burglars would just cruise in through the Internet and pick up the electronic records, all without leaving their living room. That's a mom-and-pop angle about the new healthcare that most people have missed."

"They can do that?" What about the protections? The federal privacy bill?

"Minor problems, Mark. If you read the fine print of the alleged privacy bill, you'll find out everyone and their Aunt Matilda has access to medical data as a "healthcare data trustee." Additionally, the managed care companies now give discounts on co-pays and deductibles if you agree to let them market some of your "non-sensitive" medical data."

"So they're doing it anyway."

"Mark, that's only the beginning. This medical revolution stuff goes deep. However, I'm sure your inside connection can tell you all about it."

"I don't know how much of a whistle blower she is, "said Mark. "If she gets pulled into their system, she may just go along. Don't make the assignment based on her," Mark cautioned.

Witcomb sat back in the booth, his food untouched in front of him. He absentmindedly moved the potato chips around on his plate, but it was clear he was in deep thought over something. His eyes avoided Mark's as if he couldn't be trusted with his thoughts, or the anguish they seemed to cause.

Finally, Mark braved the obvious question. "What else is going on, Witcomb? You look like this has suddenly become a life-and-death issue."

Witcomb's eyes widened in surprise, as if Mark had somehow seen his thoughts.

"It is in a way. I think GHB is eventually going to kill thousands of people."

"What!"

"Through neglect, manipulation, or intimidation, GHB is going to deny crucial care to thousands of people. And no one can stop them. At least not yet."

"What do you mean, not yet?" asked Mark.

"There is another big part of the picture I need to tell you. As I said, hardly anyone is regulating all this healthcare reform. Employers and insurance companies are carving out new arrangements that no one even heard of eight years ago. Regulatory boards are about ten years behind in understanding new policies. Here in California we've been trying to catch up, but the industry has too much power and momentum. In fact, they don't even have to tell us much about their internal policies and systems. That has been a great stumbling block to regulation. All these claims of 'proprietary' data. Everything belongs exclusively to the corporation."

"Then how do you know if they deliver on their policies," asked Mark.

"Bingo. No one does. They can say what they want about their great HMO care because there is hardly any way to check—which brings us to our own Senator Donald Gray. He's now chairing a joint congressional committee in Washington to look into the problems. He wants to peer behind the closed doors to see how the companies really work, not only the policies and procedures, but what the information systems actually do. These computers are making ever more decisions about care. He wants to see how they do it."

"He doesn't have the authority to demand the programs?"

"No one ever has had that authority. It's new territory. The computer is about the best place in the world for a corporation to hide anything today. It's very hard to legally get it out. You have to settle for what the corporation says is in there. It's more protected than a personal journal. Senator Packwood should have been more high-tech with his diary."

"So they can print one thing in the manual, but have the computer do things another way?" Mark asked.

"Right. Senator Gray has been pushing for authority to take that extra step in his investigations, but the legislature isn't convinced they need to open up the cabinets of a company's computers. The lobbyists are trying to gut any proposals, screaming 'proprietary information' and 'trade secrets.' Gray needs something dramatic that he can present. Some smoking gun. I'd love to help him get it."

"Why are you so bent on this, Witcomb?" asked Mark.

Witcomb hesitated as his face took on a harder edge, his teeth clenched together, anger welled up in his eyes. "This has touched me personally. I'm going to lose my sister-in-law to colon cancer within the year. I blame GHB. I don't want to go into it right now, but I'll tell you this. She did everything right, tried like hell to get early treatment. They stonewalled, misdirected, misinformed, and did everything possible to avoid paying for treatment. After six months of screwing around it was too late. She's going to die, which it turns out is cheaper for the company than saving her." Witcomb hissed the last sentence, rage streaming from his narrowed eyes.

"I'm sorry, Jim," said Mark. "I had no idea."

"I know. I'm too close to this to tackle it directly. That's why I want you to follow up. You're good, I trust you, and I know this will capture you as you wade into it. How about it?"

Mark thought for a minute. His eyes fell upon the clippings strewn about the table. This could be a very big story, particularly if half of what Witcomb suspected was true. "Well, hell, dinosaurs are still widely popular, so I may as well go after the Tyrannosaurus Rex of health insurance companies," Mark agreed.

"Thanks Mark," said Witcomb, handing him an overstuffed file folder, now covered with grease spots. He picked up his diet soda and offered a toast, "Just don't become dinner, little mammal."

"You know, Witcomb, I'm amazed that on Tuesday of this week I hardly knew GHB existed. By Friday I've brushed up against three dramatic stories, all seemingly out of the blue. I guess it's like Hollywood celebs dying in three's."

"You don't believe that superstition, do you," said Witcomb, rising from the table with the check. "The reason you notice the celebrities is that you care about them. No one cares about insurance companies. They're big, dull, and almost invisible to normal folk, but they touch everyone."

Witcomb rose and sauntered off. Mark sat in the booth, reflecting on the enlightening conversation. Witcomb was right; he didn't know anything about his own company health insurance. He liked it that way, it meant he was healthy. If he had used the insurance, he might have a different take.

Mark made a note to himself to come down with something non-lethal so he could check it out. Maybe just get an annual physical. "They still do those, don't they?" he thought to himself. His last was in . . . college, that's right. He smiled at his own lackadaisical attitude about his health. "If it ain't broke, don't fix it." The thought of getting probed and stuck was not appealing. But then, what if a garden of diseases was quietly growing within his body, diseases with no outward signs until they're terminal! His anxiety quickly melted into laughter as he realized how he and most people in the world avoid doctors. Denial is potent medicine.

Chapter 7

Senator Donald Gray (D-CA) was trying to verbally drill a hole through the skull of a pompous bureaucrat trying to get at the truth of her testimony. Muriel Estevez, MD, a senior scientist sent over from Health and Human Services Administration, was testifying before the Joint-Congressional Subcommittee on Health Insurance Reform, which Donald Gray chaired. He was originally vice chair, but when Republican Matthew Small of Ohio suffered a stoke and had to leave office, Donald was elevated to a spot few people wanted.

He was a first-term Senator, although he had served two terms in the House. At 48 years old he still looked fit, broad shoulders, olive skin with hardly a crease, black hair with silver temples, a hard and distinct jaw line. His dark eyes were somehow more peaceful than threatening. The friendly, ebullient lawyer was well known in the capitol and generally liked by all. However, his passion for consumer issues, from his tenure in California with the Department of Consumer Affairs, often put him at odds with corporate lobbyists.

The subcommittee was formed more to pacify concerns than to solve them. Healthcare reform bills again flooded the nation's Capital. The White House was trying to muscle through a major revamping of Managed Competition, although staff were forbidden from using those terms in any official descriptions.

Dr. Estevez from HHS was describing the agency's hopes for efficient data management in the Medicare and Medicaid programs, especially to reduce fraud and overspending. As the government hemorrhaged in red ink from mismanaged care, large insurance players had stepped up to the mound to pitch their solutions. Gray was concerned about the ultimate cost of these solutions.

"Senator, I want to make it clear that our country stands on the threshold of a revolution in healthcare," stated Estevez with a camera-ready smile. "We can envision a time when everyone will be guaranteed efficient, effective, and universal healthcare, delivered anywhere in the country with state-of-the-art knowledge. A diabetic child in the backwoods of Idaho will have access to the same professional care as if she lived across the street from Johns Hopkins Medical School. They will monitor and treat a boy with leukemia in the Everglades of Florida with the same technology as Sloan Kettering in New York City. The future is already here, Senator. We only need to tap into it." She paused to let the scope of her vision sink in.

The Senator grabbed the brief pause to redirect the discussion. "Dr. Estevez, we're all aware of the benefits of the new and wondrous technology that can deliver care to remote places. However, I'm concerned with some recent statements by HHS officials on the use of technology for a broader range of purposes. Some of this medical data is quite sensitive. People may not want to share it. What protections are there for this?"

Dr. Estevez smiled with a glowing confidence. Her team had anticipated this question. "Senators and honored committee members, information is what will get us out of the mess we're in. For eons, healthcare was delivered by individual practitioners who operated with little or no supervision in what was largely a cottage industry. This was fine when medicine was limited to bruises, bumps, and births. Today, medicine is a true science. No single practitioner can hope to understand it all. We can't leave it up to the vulnerable consumer seeking care to rely on the luck of the draw whether he picks a healthcare provider who is competent or negligent. Medicine is far too complex. We see our role, and that of information systems, as helping the right people with the right knowledge treating the right patients."

"What do you require to do this?" asked the Senator.

"A new understanding of healthcare. A larger sense of community. Not only does it take a village to raise a normal child, it takes an industry to cure a sick one. We need people to understand that we're all contributing to science, every time we're treated. The information from each and every treatment event should be stored, tabulated, compiled, and analyzed for the betterment of everyone. Universal knowledge will lead to universal healthcare."

"Could you elaborate on that last phrase?" the Senator requested.

"Certainly. We now have the technology to closely monitor the health of every living American, from cradle to grave. Imagine, every physician in the country contributing their individual knowledge and experiences, both positive and negative, into a system dedicated only to finding the best way to cure illnesses. Each provider can then tap into the most sophisticated healthcare database in the world for the correct solution to a problem. They too will contribute their data, aiding in the treatment of the next patient, and so on."

"What if they don't want to contribute their data?" challenged Donald Gray.

"Senator, it would be grossly unfair for a patient to use the contributed data of thousands of good people to fix a problem and then selfishly refuse to contribute their experience to the common welfare. To tap into the universal knowledge, one must contribute to it."

"So, am I to understand that, pardon my graphic example, my hemorrhoids will join with millions of others for the common rectal health of America?" Laughter circulated through the chamber, Gray hoped it threw Estevez off her soapbox, but he underestimated her skill.

"Yes sir. Even beyond that, your health data may be used to predict the risks for hemorrhoids, possibly saving many children from a similar life of discomfort, or even the greater risks of anal fissures, infections, and painful surgery. I'd consider that a worthy cause." She smiled demurely at the Senator in her little victory.

Gray smiled and silently cursed himself for losing the round, but he was just getting started. "Well, Madam, I'd be pleased that my personal experience could save a child from such suffering. Yet I, and many like me, would rather not have our personal discomforts available for public scrutiny, or government scrutiny. What assurances do we have that they have protected our individual data?"

"Confidentiality is one of our greatest concerns. All the systems proposed take great care in protecting the identity of individual patients. It is not their name we are after, Senator, it is their medical problem. Congress has already dealt with the security of healthcare data. Only official health information trustees, as defined in the Health Information Security Act, have access to sensitive data."

Donald Gray was waiting for this. "Dr. Estevez, I have in front of me the actual wording of the Health Information Security Act. Are you aware of just who is defined as a Health Information Trustee?"

"Ah, in general I am, sir. However, I couldn't recite it right now," she replied.

"I completely understand, for it is quite an impressive list. The Act states that the following are considered Health Information Trustees: hospitals, clinics, physicians, support medical personnel, laboratories, case managers, utilization reviewers, insurance carriers, managed care entities, employers, third-party health administrators, healthcare researchers, and on for 14 more categories. It seems that our country is full of Health Information Trustees. In fact, it would be hard not to sit next to one at a lunch counter."

"Senator, your point is well taken, but I assure you that the security of American health information is our top priority. Time does not allow for me to detail the many protections and barriers built into the system. However, be assured us it is more secure than the gold at Fort Knox."

"Dr. Estevez, I'd like to enter a contrary opinion into the record. Quote, 'The only way to guarantee privacy of medical records is to pay cash under an alias.' The former director of the American Health Information Management Association said that. I'm afraid it describes one hell of a way to start a relationship with a doctor."

"I've heard that quote, Senator, and I believe it was an overstatement."

"May I request that HHS submit to this committee a report on the specific safeguards that exist to protect this information? It would benefit this committee greatly if that report could be in our hands by the end of the week."

"With pleasure, Senator."

"I'd also like to ask you about your agency's campaign against fraudulent medical claims. It has been the subject of much discussion."

"Senator, insurance claim fraud is a tremendous expense, costing millions each year. It is essentially stealing from the truly needy. There is only a finite sum of medical dollars available, and many unscrupulous doctors are lining their pockets with public money."

"Yes, Dr. Estevez," said Gray, cutting off her speech. "You have made it clear that you want to stop these bogus billings. However, I'm also concerned about the many good doctors and healthcare providers who are trying to comply with your convoluted billing procedures. I have read procedures, published by your own office, that would drive a normal person mad."

"Senator, we've spent a great deal of time trying to streamline the claims process."

"I'm sure you have. However, I'm holding a study by the General Accounting Office on the real efficiency of your efforts. It seems it is getting next to impossible for providers to file a claim in compliance with your regulations."

" Providers also don't like to be questioned," Dr. Esteves said, "but it must be done."

"Well, according to this GAO report, it is done very poorly. In fact, workers with only a high school education made up to 90 percent of all decisions on medical necessity of treatments. Further, these workers processed over 400 claims per day, averaging just 72 seconds per case. And of the many claims that were denied, over half were overturned on appeal."

"It is a gargantuan job, Senator."

"My point is that you have minimally educated people deciding complex medical cases in less than a minute. That sounds like a breeding ground for negligence to me."

"These case workers do an admirable job, and in many of these companies state-of-the-art information systems assist them," Dr. Estevez insisted.

"I'd say these systems must be directing more than advising. These people aren't even trained in medical care. It must be terribly frustrating for the providers, who must explain complex medical data in simple, high school-level terms."

"We have experts available for consultation. It isn't that difficult, Senator. The doctor need only tell the case manager what the patient has and what needs to be done. Then the case manager either agrees or doesn't."

"Based on what?" asked the Senator.

"Based on their extensive, two month training program and the advice of our pre-programmed systems. They only need to punch in the right words."

"So, a physician with eight years of medical training must convince a high school graduate with two-months of training that a procedure is necessary?"

"Yes, although it's more sophisticated than your description."

"And if the treatment is denied?" asked Gray.

"Then the doctor can appeal the decisions," responded Dr. Estevez.

"Yet this GAO study found that over half of all denied claims are reversed on appeal. So over half the time, the physician was right, but couldn't convince the high school-educated case manager."

"We have steps to process all of this."

"Certainly, we should use our medical talent to argue with untrained case managers rather than delivering needed care."

"We need to be sure that the treatment is medically necessary," stated Estevez.

"Do you think this agency attitude may be somewhat condescending to the providers? It hardly seems a way to gain their cooperation."

"We are more interested in their compliance with established medical practice than their cooperation." As the words left her mouth, Dr. Estevez immediately regretted the comment. She hoped Gray would ask a follow-up question to dilute the statement, but he just let it hang there in a silent room.

"Any further questions of our esteemed visitor?" asked the chair. There was no response from the committee. Finally, he moved for lunch recess. "Then I thank you for your testimony, Dr. Estevez. I look forward to your report. The committee will take an hour recess before resuming the hearings."

Senator Gray slipped through the side entrance of the chamber and joined his staff in the office. He nodded to Joyce, his dedicated secretary, who waved three messages at him while she talked on the phone. They were snatched up as he sailed into the inner sanctum of his ample office and closed the door. He got two entire minutes free before his chief aide, Linda O'Donnell, pushed through the door.

"Nice going with Estevaz," she said, her billowy, red, curly hair framing her lightly freckled face. Her green eyes squinted with mock pain as she teased him, "Sorry, does the Senator need to stand owing to his unfortunate hemorrhoidal condition?" Her green wool business dress, buttoned from hem to bust, hugged the "zoftig" body of his most trusted aide. Linda was a woman of candor, confidence, and complexity. She had a quick wit and abundant street smarts. He knew that buried in her ample cleavage was a Phi Beta Kappa key. Although the two of them taunted each other with erotic barbs, nothing beyond honest affection had ever occurred between them. Linda loved Gray's wife, Emily, almost as much as he did.

"Yeah, yeah. So I lost that round. She still verified that everyone and their mother have access to medical records. It was the statement I needed as a lead-in for Thomas Baldwin, the Great Health Benefit Pooh-bah. We get him next. Say, did that gal ever resurface, the one who said she worked for GHB?"

"No," said Linda. "She dropped off our radar scope in February. I figured she got cold feet. I left a couple of messages after that one visit, but she never returned my calls. GHB must have made her a better offer."

"Too bad. I'd have loved to get an inside piece of that computer. What do they call it, MOM?"

"Dream on. I think you're wasting your time on Baldwin. He's a darling of this President. He's got the Administration's full support. GHB has saved more Medicaid and Medicare dollars in one year than every legislative effort over the last ten years. 'Turn it over to private enterprise,' that's what the President said in his campaign, that's what he did, and as far as anyone can see, it's working. A Democrat has reduced entitlement spending. Well, at least it's pissed off the GOP."

Linda sat on the edge of Donald's desk, her skirt drawn tight across her thighs, with the gaps in her buttoned dress showing flesh that beckoned the Senator to peek. Through high school and college Linda had been rather dumpy and awkward, suffering many social scars in her struggles with men, but she blossomed into an attractive woman of some stature after graduation. Linda took a perverse satisfaction in the discomfort she could stir in men, even those she liked.

"So what have we got? Hasn't anyone found a disgruntled employee who knows anything?" said Gray in frustration.

"They'd make the Pentagon envious with their security. Apparently, they've spread the access out so far that no low-ranking people have any idea what's going on. That Elaina woman was the highest source we'd ever found."

"What about that programmer who left?" asked the Senator.

"He only knew accounting stuff. Nothing about patient records. He's useless to us."

Donald hated missing such an opportunity. Fate had transpired to put Thomas Baldwin and his evil empire on the witness stand, where the nation's citizens could hear how their lives were being sold out. With no solid evidence, however, it would look like the Senator was just pointlessly badgering the man. "What do we know about their system?"

"Not enough, I'm afraid. We've got some people working on it back in Southern California. Still, no one has dropped by the office with any magnetic tapes," replied Linda.

The intercom buzzed. Donald pressed the button. "Yes, Joyce."

"Message from Senator Elway. Thomas Baldwin's plane was recalled to the terminal just before takeoff for some problem. He's stuck in New York for the moment. All planes are full for the weekend. Can't be sure when he'll get here. What do you want to do?"

"Shit. Well, maybe that is better. Give him our blessings and tell him we'll reschedule next week." Turning to Linda, he said, "Hey, this gives us a little more time. Maybe there is a God."

"Yeah, but I bet she owns stock in GHB."

***

Back at his desk, Mark Lipton spied the note on his monitor, reminding him to call Elaina Ruiz's parents. He fished out the number Grace had given him. He had never met her parents and was pretty sure Jenny hadn't either. He had to think about how to approach this, finally deciding to just express his sympathy and explain that a number of friends were shocked to find out about her passing so late.

The mother answered the phone, who spoke in simple words with a heavy Spanish accent. "Allo?"

"Mrs. Ruiz?"

"Si, who is this, please?"

"My name is Mark Lipton. I was a college friend of Elaina's. I just found out about her . . . that she died. I just called to express my condolences."

"Oh, my Elaina," she sighed with sadness. "Oh, she was so beautiful. Thank you, thank you." Her voice raised in pitch as she spoke, while trying to keep the feelings of sadness from overwhelming her. Mark felt guilty for disturbing her tenuous peace. "How did you know her?" she asked.

"I met her back at UCLA, about seven years ago. She was a wonderful person. You couldn't forget her. Beautiful, smart, very giving. Everyone loved her."

"Yes, Elaina was wonderful. It was too bad not many school friends got to come and say goodbye. Father Aldiva gave such a good talk. He had baptized her as a baby." Her tears were breaking through. "We all miss her so much, but God has her now."

"I'm sorry we didn't hear about the ceremony, Mrs. Ruiz. We would have certainly been there. It just seemed so sudden." Mark was hoping she'd volunteer some information.

"Yes, it was too fast. My Elaina was healthy. Very strong. It was her will that seemed to go. And that terrible place. If she had only come home."

"Mrs. Ruiz, I'm sorry, I don't know any of the circumstances of her death."

"It was a very sad thing, mister . . . "

"Lipton, Mark Lipton."

"Yes, Mr. Lipton. Thank you for calling. I know many people loved Elaina."

"Her friends out here don't really know what happened. I wonder if I could talk with you about it?"

"Not now, please, Mr. Lipton. Maybe you could come by. I love to see the people that were her friends, to hear about her from many voices. Maybe you have good stories to tell of Elaina."

"Yes, I do. So do the many people who knew her. I'd like to come by and visit, maybe with another of her friends, Jenny Barrett. Would this weekend be okay?"

"That would be so nice. Jenny, I think I remember her. Yes, Sunday after church would be good. We don't get many visitors now. Her sister is back in Virginia. Her father and I just work in the garden. Do come." She gave Mark the address and directions.

By 4:00 P.M. Friday afternoon, Progressive had quieted down considerably. More than the usual number of staff had bailed early from work, exhausted and disoriented from the morning announcements. Friday afternoon was not a typical time for people to call for mental health assistance. Most thought a weekend filled with sleep, escape, or inebriation would solve their problems. By Monday reality would have settled in like a hangover and the phones would start ringing again. Sometimes even late Sunday night.

MOM chirped at the arrival of a phone call from Mark.

"Hey Mark, got my message?"

"Yeah, thanks for the validation. How are you doing with the changes?"

"Well, I met my new boss after the meeting. Seems like a nice guy. I'm supposed to go over to their corporate offices next week. Some special project."

Mark restrained comment on his new assignment. "I spoke with Elaina Ruiz's mother today."

"How is she? What happened?"

"She's still pretty fragile. Didn't feel like talking much about it on the phone. She did invite us over to speak with her this Sunday. Wants to meet the people who knew Elaina. I said you might come. Interested?"

"Yeah, I'd like to come. I only met her parents once at a family barbecue. Nice folks. The mother is kind of old world, big heart, simple life. Lived for her kids. I don't think she understood much of what Elaina did professionally, but I know she was proud of her."

"It's about an hour's drive. Why don't you come to my house about 10 A.M., it's on the way. Unless you'd like to come Saturday night and get an early start in the morning," he said hopefully. "I'll heat up some muffins."

"Sorry, my muffins are hot enough. I'll see you Sunday," Jenny replied.

An hour later Jenny arrived at home, lumbering through her front door, sorting her mail and feeling completely drained from the challenges of the week. She dropped the pile on her desk with a smack. "Daisy, play messages" she shouted to her computer. Although the computer monitor was turned off, Jenny's Daisy was always running, acting like a digital secretary. Following a flash of the hard disk access light on the disk console the machine cued up the first of three voice messages.

"Jenny, a bunch of us are going to Coyote Junction tonight," said her friend Lydia, who lived on the other side of the condo complex. "Let me know if you want to come. We can drive there together." They would have to use Jenny's car, because Lydia never came home with her. She would always score with some guy and run off to a daring little tryst. They were mostly married men, which Lydia had come to believe reduced her chances of getting AIDS. She wouldn't listen to the obvious doubts about cruising husbands. Jenny decided to pass on the invite.

"Jenny, it's Mom. Dad and I are going to Medford today on some business. We'll be back Sunday if you want to call."

The last message was a telephone pitch on mortgage refinancing. "Not exactly the hottest social life," she thought to herself. "Daisy, check mail." The computer dutifully called up America Online and logged into the large commercial service. "You have mail!" was the announcement from the mindlessly happy generic announcing voice. Jenny sat at the desk to better view her e-mail, flipping on the monitor. The first was from her brother, David, currently selling banking software in Singapore.

"Hey, sis. This is a place you've got to see. Clean, beautiful, very user friendly. Just don't spit on the sidewalk or break one of their little rules. When these people say they'll whip your butt, they mean it. Anyway, I hope this finds you well. I spoke with Mom the other day and she's got me worried about Dad. Seems he's had some stomach problems for a while and old Dr. Shepard hasn't figured it out yet. I think they're going to see a specialist in Medford. I'm going to be very busy the next two weeks, so see if you can touch base with them. Talk with you soon."

The news of her father was a little alarming, for neither parent had mentioned any medical problems to her. Admittedly, they had become reluctant to mention medical concerns around her, after an unfortunate incident two years prior, when her mother had a cancer scare. Jenny overreacted and pulled every record she could find on her mother trying to help in her treatment. Her position at Progressive gave her tremendous access to medical information. Fortunately, it was a false alarm, but her mother was shocked and embarrassed by the stacks of records detailing her medical history. Now they only told her about an illness after it was cured. Jenny was dismayed that she'd lost their confidence and was trying to rebuild it. At their age she wanted open communication with them about their health concerns.

The second piece of e-mail was an obscene message from some obscure Internet site. A file attached to it contained a full color picture of two women in a sexual pretzel hold. Jenny marveled at the clarity of the hi-resolution photo. The message was a juvenile attempt to be sexually suggestive, but Jenny burst out laughing when the author wondered if she were a "cunninglinguist". "Heck, I'm not even bilingual," she countered. It was the modern day equivalent of an obscene phone call, kids using technology to be outrageous, complete with eight-by-ten glossies. Jenny figured the return address was useless. Some kids probably logged onto a server from home. On the bright side, this is pretty safe sex. Can't get anyone pregnant in cybersex. This was only the second time in two years she'd received a prank e-mail. Maybe she should shoot this picture over to Mark? No, she reconsidered, he was hungry enough.

Jenny decided a quiet weekend was in order, particularly with all the changes on the horizon. She'd watch some movies, surf the net to learn more about Great Health Benefit, maybe catch up on her mail. She thought briefly about Mark's offer to come over Saturday night. It always felt good being nestled in his arms, and she reflected how things hadn't been jumping in the sex department. Her e-mail was the hottest thing she'd experienced in four months. There was only so much a girl could do for herself, and she was wearing out her fantasies.

Ultimately, Saturday night was spent safely with Sergei Rachmaninoff, or rather, his Second Piano Concerto and the Symphonic Dances. Jenny treated herself to a live concert of romantic classical music at UCLA by the somber composer, who perfectly orchestrated her feelings of sadness and yearning.

Chapter 8

Dr. Alex Shepard hunched over the ancient oak desk in his consulting room. He glanced periodically at the computer monitor against the wall, awaiting an authorization from a distant insurance company to treat the fractured index finger of Harold Gross. The patient was a 24-year-old white-water raft guide who recently had a losing encounter with a boulder in the rapids. Dr. Shepard had treated thousands of broken fingers and toes over the years, yet now he sat and awaited permission from afar.

The Shepard clinic was a small, freestanding building on the southern end of Grants Pass, Oregon. A picture window in the waiting room proudly displayed a pastoral view of the Rogue River as it wandered through town. The building was thirty years old and would continue to function long after Dr. Shepard had quit practice. He was 66 years old and not a day went by that he didn't dream of retirement.

The good doctor had served the community of Grants Pass for thirty-five years. He could remember when the local economy flourished on the agriculture and timber industries. Sometimes many years ago, in very tough times, he actually accepted chickens or sides of beef in payment for his medical services.

The town had since matured far beyond that bucolic neighborly time. Tourism and retirement villages had taken over. Medicine had changed even more dramatically. Now it was all third-party reimbursement, prior authorization, case management, and prying eyes. He didn't like the "new medicine," but he had to keep working to make ends meet. He had gotten into deep trouble with a managed care company and the resulting fight had obliterated his retirement dreams.

It would be five or six more years before he could permanently hang up his stethoscope. It wasn't just that because one managed care deal went sour, for most of the managed care deals stank.

The knowledge that some physicians were in far worse shape was of little comfort. The pressure to sign capitated contracts often pushed small groups into risky ventures. He knew of three practices where the physicians were essentially indentured servants. They had agreed to accept financial risk for a group of patients and quickly became buried in debt as the needy patients accessed treatment. It was clear the negotiations had been completely one-sided and misrepresented, yet legal action was far too costly to pursue against the deep-pocket insurance company. The groups now worked under a mandated contract to repay the company for contractual failures. They were medical slaves to the master bean counters. Dr. Shepard counted his blessings in avoiding that trap, yet he had his own struggles with the insurance companies.

The State of Oregon was proud of its progressive approach to comprehensive care for the elderly. The poor, the needy, the indigent elderly were arriving in hordes every year. Families needed only to spend down grandmas' assets and then ship her off to Oregon and everyone was happy. Oregon had become a haven, or dumping ground depending on your view, for the elderly. The state mandated the standards of care for the treatment of the elderly patients. It did not mandate the standards for treatment of medical personnel, i.e., employment practices. This gave the insurance industry a great advantage. They used their significant clout to take over the state's burden of care. They promised to stretch the Medicare and Medicaid dollars and stop the "greedy" doctors from soaking the patients.

Soon, insurance company reps were signing on town-loads of clients. Dr. Shepard remembered the "men in 500-dollar suits" blowing into town. First they held razzle-dazzle meetings for the Medicare recipients, promising the retirees no deductibles, full insurance coverage, freedom of choice in providers. No more medigap insurance payments. True protection for your family. Within eighteen months, three large insurance companies, including GHB, had virtually sewn up the state.

Then they lined up every practitioner, sat them at a free lunch, and proceeded to scare the daylights out of them with talk of exclusive contracts, closed markets, and join-or-die provider panels. The healthcare providers in Grants Pass had seen the rapid growth of restricted contracts. All had already lost a few patients by failing to join the right provider panels. A gulf was growing between the very needy patients and the very capable doctors. "Join or die" was the rallying call.

The Oregon Medical Association tried to protest to the State Attorney General's Office about restrictions on free trade, monopolistic practices, and antitrust actions. However, the State had become overwhelmed with needy patients, exploding medical expenses and diminishing budgets. The governor liked the idea of turning over the problem to private industry with the promise of fixed costs and "managed care." It was his best bet, and the legislature agreed.

Dr. Shepard prided himself on being a "good ole country doctor." Throughout his career he stayed close to his patients, deferred payments, speaking honestly and directly but always with compassion. Nothing was more sacred in his mind than the doctor-patient relationship. He would look the patient directly in the eye to explain a diagnosis or treatment plan. He tried to make it a team effort. Whenever he entered the "temple" of another person's body, with a needle, a knife, medication, or just his words, he wanted to feel welcome. With this philosophy he earned the respect of hundreds of people.

Managed care changed all that. The restrictive contracts, intrusive case managers, and financial constrictions threw a body block on doctor-patient rapport. He soon learned that managed care didn't simply mean trying to convince a distant insurance clerk that a procedure was necessary and cost-effective. It really meant becoming an employee, losing autonomy, feeling the leash of a strict master.

It was at one of those free luncheons that Dr. Shepard saw the first of a new generation of managed care contracts. They contained the blueprint for the new medicine. The contracts were two inches thick and weighed close to a pound, dense with legalese that was largely incomprehensible. In total, it was more paper than Shepard had seen when he closed escrow on his own home. Doctors had long been resentful of attorneys for the explosion in malpractice litigation. It had ushered in the era of defensive medicine. This document went further. It was the era of combative medicine.

One advantage to this mass recruitment for the managed care companies was that all the contracts were the same. The local medical society had some respected local attorneys review the documents en masse and distribute memorandums to member physicians. A seismic wave of dismay spread throughout the state. The contracts contained the new terms of engagement, a new definition of patient care.

The AMA attorneys highlighted "gag rules," things the physician couldn't ever say to the client without first checking with the case manager. There was a danger that a recommended treatment might not be available under a patient's policy, and back-pedaling on recommendations was difficult. Dr. Shepard had a brief mental image of himself saluting the men in suits. "Permission to speak with the patient, sir," a vision from the military that was both amusing and frightening. Congress later "banned" gag rules from contracts, but with professional oblivion only a computer mouse click away, physicians were careful to sing the tunes the major companies requested.

There were "pretty talk" clauses, restrictions that the physician could never criticize the company or its policies. If the patient voiced frustration with the company or his benefits or even the procedures, the physician was to offer reassurance and hope, but never criticism. It was part of the new "salesman" role of the integrated team.

The pretty talk clauses lead to limits on patient advocacy. "No is no" when it comes from a case manager. Repeatedly challenging the decisions of the managed care company was grounds for termination. Although there were procedures for protesting a decision, they were not to be used too frequently. Reputations could be damaged.

The contracts spoke of credentialing requirements, a process physicians usually went through for approval to work at hospitals. But the insurance companies wanted more. They looked at the doctor's personal life, private medical history, and even required notification of anything that might affect clinical judgement. By joining the company the physician gave up his or her own medical privacy. If a doctor was put on any psychoactive medication, antidepressant, or drug that could affect performance, the company was to be notified immediately. A physician seeking personal psychiatric consultation was to be monitored closely.

Despite their best efforts, the physicians and care providers were no match for the insurance companies. They controlled the clients and the money—over 65 percent of the local patients were covered by one of only three companies. The few providers who attempted to thumb their noses at the new arrangement were soon begging for entrance. Some had to close their practices.

Another curious thing happened as managed care took control of the populace. The opinions and camaraderie of the local medical community became less important. Membership in professional associations, even the AMA, dwindled. It served little purpose to promote your services to a colleague if she or he had no ability to refer clients. All decision-making was centralized in the faraway land of Woodland Hills, California. The executives knew little of the local conditions, but held the power of making referrals that served their interests.

The medical community continued to seek local consultation and advisement, for they still wanted to provide good care. Dr. Shepard used the digital technology on his desk to send Harold's X-ray to a colleague, Dr. Alice Price, a radiologist he respected. This new technology allowed for innovative collaborations in medicine. Dr. Price's office would receive the scanned X-ray, pop it up on any computer screen in her clinic, and she could then read it on the fly. She could e-mail her impressions back to the Shepard Clinic in seconds. Dr. Shepard wanted a second opinion regarding the extent of the fracture to rule out a secondary injury. Within twenty minutes Dr. Price responded with "thumbs up" for the treatment plan.

Her opinion would be for his own edification only. Dr. Price was not on GHB's panel, so her opinion meant nothing to them. If her credentials were not in their database, she was not a doctor in their eyes. Yet Alex guessed that the eyes scanning the GHB copy of Harold Gross's X-ray may have never seen a real broken bone. The insurance industry was not required to credential their own staff for medical competence, at least not at the level of a practitioner.

What Dr. Shepard didn't know is that no person reviewed the X-ray. In fact, no human being made the judgement on care. Rather, it was an electronic amalgam of people and machines. After receiving the transmitted X-ray, MOM immediately scanned it for comparison against thousands of standardized X-rays stored in her files. Graphic resolution and scanning were so advanced that large computers could reliably recognize abnormal patterns in MRIs, sonograms, X-rays, and pap smears. The technology that was developed to have computers look for elusive subatomic particles in nuclear labs could also look for bone fragments or a vascular aneurisms in patients.

Though Dr. Shepard knew little of MOM's pivotal role in the treatment decision process, he did know from experience that the company would only determine if the X-ray supported his diagnosis. Yes or no. The company would add nothing to the diagnosis. Its computer would not use its digital eye to advance the diagnosis, to screen for complications or point out additional defects in the patient's hand. Instead, the company would claim it was not their job to diagnose, only to confirm a medical opinion for insurance purposes. MOM could only offer the equivalent of a thumbs up or thumbs down. If there was any doubt, MOM would route the matter to a clinical associate or on-line physician for a second opinion. Eighty percent of the time this wasn't necessary.

The computer issued an audible synthetic ring to announce an incoming call. Dr. Shepard heard the modem squawking and the electronic "handshake" between the two machines. GHB confirmed the diagnosis and approved the treatment plan. Doris, his nurse, had already set the hand in a flex cast. Dr. Shepard knew what the best course of action for the patient would be, despite the insurance company's take on the matter.

It was this attitude that had gotten him in so much trouble two years ago. Melba Bradley, a 42-year-old mother of three and a twenty-year diabetic, was having increased difficulty with her left leg due to poor circulation and some neuropathy. Like so many diabetics, there was a very good chance she would lose the leg. Fortunately, Dr. Shepard had followed the advances in vascular microsurgery at the University of Washington's School of Medicine. He recommended a consultation to see if early intervention could save Melba's leg.

Unfortunately, his contract with GHB had two provisions he had overlooked; the gag rule and a damages clause. Buried in the two pounds of contract was a stipulation that he could not advise a patient of any procedure or treatment that was not in general medical practice or approved by GHB. Officially this was to save the patient from false hopes and disappointments from unproven treatments. In reality, Dr. Shepard knew, it was to save the company from being pressured into spending more money than they wanted to authorize.

Melba, on the advice of Dr. Shepard, contacted the medical school and set up an appointment. When GHB got wind of it, the roof caved in. The company sent a young attorney from another town to sit and explain the trouble Dr. Shepard was in for practicing medicine outside of the "team" concept. They lectured him on what constitutes modern medical practice and how malpractice could mean giving too much as well as insufficient care. Since he had abused the trust of Mrs. Bradley's care, would he be good enough to advise her of his premature conclusions and the need to be followed for the next few months by another physician in town?

Dr. Shepard took pride in his restraint from surgically inserting the attorney's head in his ass. Fortunately few patients in the office heard Alex Shepard advise the chubby-faced kid what he could do with his contract. Some quick mental arithmetic told the doctor what he needed to know about this conversation. The surgery to save the leg would cost up to $70,000. The surgery to remove the leg could be done at a discounted facility for $6,500, including a prosthetic leg. If the company waited long enough, Melba would no longer be a candidate for the rehabilitative surgery. This, he feared, was what they wanted to run through their "team."

Few knew that most of the team was made up of a beefy computer named MOM. She needed only to display to the caseworker a bar chart graph comparing treatment expenses to convey the point. A short expense graph looked better than the long one. The case worker missed the irony that the vertical graphs of Melba's expenses also reflected her future leg length. MOM chose the short route.

Melba and her attorney raised a great stink. So fierce was the lawyer's attack that it threatened to make the short graph much longer with legal expenses. Melba got her surgery. She and the leg are doing fine.

GHB was not happy with that outcome. It took a very punitive attitude toward Dr. Shepard for his advocacy role in pointing out "inappropriate options" to the patient. In a larger town, with more competition, they would have simply removed him from the approved provider list, but that was not practical in this small town. Instead, GHB "fined" him 60,000 dollars for Melba's surgery. This was all inference on his part, for there were never any memos or letters to this effect. The company simply "renegotiated" his contract for the next year, reducing his reimbursement rate and withholding bonuses. They also dropped his referrals in half, as did the other companies in town.

Like the Hollywood blacklist of the 1950s, Dr. Shepard was targeted as managed care "unfriendly." There was no appeal process, no explanation, no one even to blame. Only the scarcity of doctors in town saved him from total ruin. Now, at 66 years old, this dedicated physician was on "probation." Not with a state licensing board, not even the AMA, but with a private corporation who could, from it's headquarters, with the click of a mouse, delete a needed professional service from a small community over a thousand miles away.

Dr. Shepard turned to the monitor on the desk and keyed in the information about his patient's hand. He also printed a hard copy of the authorization, never completely trusting electronics. Harold Gross left the office with a splint, a prescription for painkillers, and five dollars poorer for a co-pay. He was the last patient of the day. Dr. Shepard loosened his tie, said goodnight to his nurse Doris, and switched off the monitor on his desk. The computer remained running, for it would have a busy night. Three or four different managed care companies would trade data with his little machine: confirmations, payments, news, etc. He didn't know half of what his machine did when he was away.

That evening, while Dr. Shepard shared a bottle of Pinot Noir with his wife over dinner, another large managed care firm contacted his computer. The Axis Health System wanted to update the file on James Almanour, a troubling case involving potentially expensive treatments with little to gain; maybe five more years of life in a frail 60-year-old man. Dr. Shepard had learned from experience that Axis Health System's calculations put a cap on life value at $110,000 per year. This meant that any expensive procedure used to prolong life must provide a likely survival rate of one year for every $110,000 expended. It roughly matched the current "value" of life in the court system, as defined by recent decisions in negligent death and malpractice cases. Mr. Almanour needed a $650,000 procedure that would likely extend his life only four years, if at all. It took MOM only four thousandths of a second to compute the death sentence. However, before the company issued the letter of denial, it routinely reviewed the latest case material, which they assumed was sitting on Dr. Shepard's computer hard disk.

The good doctor had anticipated such an action. He had learned long ago how to "groom" a patient's record on the system to achieve needed medical authorizations. Unfortunately, there was little to encourage this case. The company had already sealed Mr. Almanour's fate last year when they failed to authorize sophisticated tests that would have detected his disease early. Dr. Shepard wouldn't put it past them to actually alter the medical record so they looked good, which is why he had another copy, handwritten, stashed in a file cabinet. The real record, the true account of the patient's treatment. He dreaded this part of the new medicine. He had helped this man for close to thirty years. Now, his hands were all but tied.

After retrieving Almanour's file, the company was satisfied with its decision and left an e-mail to Dr. Shepard regarding the futility of further advanced treatments. The duty to tell the patient fell to Shepard as part of his role in the managed care system. The company would talk in ambiguous terms, saying they weren't denying care, just not paying for it. The patient was free to cough up $650,000 on his own. Dr. Shepard had come to believe there were two types of patients today; the rich and the dead. Mr. Almanour was not rich.

Axis Health also covered William Barrett, Jenny's father. After calculating the remaining days on earth for Mr. Almanour, the computer searched Dr. Shepard's system for Mr. Barrett's records. Axis Health System had transferred Mr. Barrett's case to another physician, Dr. Majani of the Hubb Health Group. The rationale was contained in a brief letter about "redistributing patient workload." Yet the machine was sent snooping to collect tests, observations, and lab values to support Dr. Shepard's recommendation to remove Barrett's gall bladder. Axis Health's computer system was more primitive than GHB's powerful MOM. In a simple checklist fashion it confirmed the signs of fever, nausea, pain, and tenderness in upper right abdomen, with severe reaction to ingestion of fatty foods. There was little mystery here, the record was clear. The next morning a case manager would extract the data and e-mail an authorization for the common and routine surgery.

Unfortunately, since Axis Health didn't have any local hospitals under contract, Mr. Barrett would have to drive almost thirty miles to Medford to check into Langston Hospital. The procedure, a laparoscopic cholecystectomy, or lap chole in medical floor jargon, would require only an overnight stay. The drive to Medford would be uncomfortable, as Mr. Barrett also had chronic back pain, which made car travel challenging. Axis would save 200 dollars by requiring the trip, an easy calculation of cost-benefit for a machine that feels no pain.

Dr. Shepard would have eagerly assisted in the arrangements and recommended a competent surgeon on staff at Langston Hospital, but his services were limited to documentation of the condition. Axis Health would choose the physician, the time, the place, and the staff. They controlled this hospital.

Jenny Barrett, the patient's daughter, would hear the news of her father's proposed surgery on her own computer's voice mail the next evening, from the words of her anguished mother. Her father would be en route before Jenny picked up the message, taking a surgical vacancy created by the sudden death of another patient.

***

Crandall and Jerry were on a mission for God as they pulled up to Elliot Mears' townhouse complex. The four-day heat wave had ended last week, so the two of them bundled up in down jackets under a starless night.

Jerry briefed Crandall as they wandered through the complex.

"Elliot works as a computer project manager for a commercial Internet company. Used to have a big job at Microsoft, some kind of healthcare consulting. When his wife split and aborted their child, he kind of went over the edge. Sent automated voice and e-mail messages to everyone who had ever known her. Parents, college friends, roommates, past employers. 'Flaming' I think it's called. The police called it felony harassment, so did his employer. He left suddenly and did a stint in a mental hospital, but was never tried. The judge, a good

Christian, couldn't openly support Elliot's actions, but did agree to let the case go. But as you'll see, Elliot's still burning."

They approached a door labeled 43-145 and Jerry knocked loudly. It was opened by an overweight, balding man of about 35, with a face like a moon, bushy unkempt hair, and a perpetual look as if he had just smelled something terrible. A begrudging smile emerged and he waved the men in.

The two bedroom townhouse was crammed to the rafters with electronic gear. Cables spilled all over the floor, while lights blinked, disk drives hummed, and modems squawked throughout the home. Crandall could see five computer monitors from where he stood, and expected more would be found upstairs. One had a picture of Jesus as a screen-saver. Another had a crucifix bouncing around the screen. The room was mostly lit from the monitors, giving the place an inhuman air. Silicone prevailed at Elliot's home. Crandall could understand why his wife had left.

"Can I get you guys a beer or something?" said Elliot as he waded into the kitchen. He swung open the refrigerator to reveal: mostly death. Dead pizzas, dead sandwiches, dead milk. Along the door shelves were sodas and beers, more neatly arranged. To keep the evening focused, Crandall suggested sodas.

"Quite an astounding operation you have here, Elliot."

"My job lets me do a lot of work out of my home. In fact, I have software they can only dream of. Gives me more time for God's work."

A great incongruity was hearing these words from the person of Elliot. Beer, hardware, God. He does move in strange ways.

Elliot delivered up the sodas and returned to the "living room," which looked like the bridge of the Starship Enterprise after the crew's Christmas party. Elliot straddled a chair in front of a computer screen, then spun the chair to face them.

"Did you tell Mr. Bream what I had in mind?" he asked Jerry.

"Just a quick overview. It's a little over my head. I wanted him to hear it from the project manager," Jerry replied.

Elliot beamed at the reference. "Okay. Here's the plan. I have a way to obtain information that can produce reliable data on thousands, possibly millions of women who have had abortions. They think they can just steal away into the night and secretly dump our children in the trash. Throwing away innocent lives. Murdering . . . " He caught himself as the rage bubbled up, and quickly composed himself. "But there is always a record. Sometimes it's hidden in protective language or disguised as another procedure, but I've found a way to get it, to break through the veil of privacy. With about 96 percent accuracy."

"I'm intrigued, go on," said Crandall.

"The information is located in healthcare databases; hospitals, insurance companies, and at a special organization called the Health Information Database, a central depository of all medical information. It's all encoded in medical nomenclature or procedure numbers, but I've developed an algorithm, a computer program, that can seek out data, put it together, and find the markers of an abortion. It's highly accurate. Any woman confronted with the data would find it tough to deny."

"How does it work?" asked Crandall.

"We need to gain access to certain medical records, which is easy enough if we appear to be selling something, then we get a separate cache of medical data and merge the two. My program will sniff out connections and pop up the names of women who have been victims of abortionists."

"How many names are we talking about?" Crandall queried.

"Depending on which companies we access and our budget, we could theoretically identify a million women who had abortions over the last four years."

"A million women?" said a startled Crandall.

"Maybe more. Depends on your resources."

"Would you do the work here?"

"Yes, I have all I need. I have a lot of anonymous web sites and names. It would be hard to trace."

"What do you need from us?" asked Crandall.

" I need some front money to purchase lists and enough of a company shell that I can convince these people I'm really selling something of value," replied Elliot.

"I don't see any problem with that. We still have the alternative counseling centers," said Crandall. "Anything else?"

"Just some minor stuff I'll need along the way."

"How much do you think this will cost?" asked Crandall.

"I have connections in managed care, so I might be able to cut a deal. I hope we can do this for forty to seventy thousand dollars."

"How much is for you?"

"I'll look after myself. I'm part of the package. But, be assured, before God, you'll be getting a deal!" stated Elliot.

Crandall turned to Jerry. "Seems like a worthy project. Can we see a little of what can be done now?"

Jerry looked at Elliot, who recognized the challenge. A sly smile grew on the computer hacker's face. "You want a demo, is that it?" He spun in his chair and began typing at the computer. A prolonged belch emerged from the massive form at the computer, seemingly as a retort to the challenge.

Looking over Elliot's shoulder at the screen, Crandall saw his name scroll down the pages in dozens of listings. His radio and cable TV show, his media events, accusations of impropriety. Elliot mentioned the tonsillectomy Crandall had when he was nine years old. But then Elliot became somber, almost humble. He fired off some keyboard commands and then turned to Crandall.

"What you are about to see, Mr. Bream, will probably have no meaning to Jerry, but will show the capability of these systems to you. I offer this as a sign of power in the service of the Lord."

An image began to appear on the twenty-inch high resolution monitor. The picture scrolled slowly from top to bottom. First evident was the background, vaguely familiar to Crandall, a teal wall or backdrop. Then the parted blond hair of a woman. The eyes appeared and Crandall involuntarily drew a breath. His face became rigid, his eyes both pained and fearful. Elliot glanced at Crandall to assure himself of the intended reaction. Jerry had no idea who the woman was. She was finally completely revealed on the screen. Pretty, about 25 years old, somewhat buxom, yet almost athletic in physique. On the bottom of the screen was a caption; "Tetracycline 250 mg t.i.d. The price of love." Jerry sensed the stiffness in Crandall, but asked no questions. Finally, Crandall broke his silence.

"I understand. I am indeed impressed. You are a very gifted man. I do hope your talents are used for God's vision. You have my support. Let's begin the project."

Jerry looked perplexed. Crandall enlightened him. "It is a woman I dated after Sandra's death. She was wild and aggressive, and I was weak and angry. God had not yet given me a mission. But Julia ended up giving me the clap. Mr. Mears has apparently found the medical records for that incident. I thought it was all undercover. Paid in cash, no evidence. Apparently, I underestimate the power of medical information systems."

"Most people have no clue what is known and stored about them," said Elliot. "Until everyone went on computers, there wasn't an easy way to get at the data. However, as you see, we can get what we need."

"Can you just ask these companies to give you abortion information?" asked Crandall.

"No," replied Elliot, "it's much more complicated than that.

Maybe they code 25 percent of procedures as abortions, but most are hidden in vague medical procedures. To get the other data we'll have to request two or three lists of patients, then my program will cross-tabulate the data and apply the algorithm to identify the real abortions. The magic is that either list by itself is fairly harmless. Like nitrogen and glycerin by themselves are not dangerous. But put them together and you get nitroglycerin, which is highly explosive. We'll do that with the data. If I have your 'okay' I'll work up the plans and have it to you by Monday. We'll need to operate under an appropriate business license, so you may want to set up an appointment with your attorney."

As Crandall rose to leave he asked," Why would women allow such data to be disclosed?"

"A lot of reasons. Managed care companies get clients to sign global permissions slips to share medical data, then give them a little discount on their co-pay or deductible. Or they just fail to strip the data with personal identifiers and sell it in aggregate. There are lots of ways to milk the cow."

Elliot walked the gentlemen to the door and wished them well. Crandall's pulse was pounding with excitement. This was an intriguing plan, and it gave him hope.

Chapter 9

Sunday morning found Mark and Jenny blasting along the San Bernardino Freeway to Riverside. She had arrived at ten that morning, having chosen discretion over what would have been pure lust. The freeway traffic was quiet as the Camry cruised through the brown rolling hills of Southern California. A dry spring had muted the usual wildflowers that should have painted the hills with vibrant blues, yellows, and reds. Fortunately, the ubiquitous oleander was in splendid bloom, lining the roadways with frothy white, red, and pink flowers bursting from the dark green leaves of this particularly poisonous plant. CalTrans, the state agency responsible for the freeways, had chosen the hardy bush as the centerpiece of its roadway landscaping strategy. The fast-growing plant needed little water, minimal attention, and could almost survive being planted in concrete. All were essential skills for life in Los Angeles. Consuming even one leaf or flower could make a man ill, or kill a child. A few barbecue parties had been ruined when the leaves, used to start the briquets, imparted their toxin to the food, making the guests ill. The fact that oleander was highly poisonous seems a minor disadvantage in a county where over one third of the automobiles contained people packing firearms.

It was another beautiful spring day, made all the better by the company of the two friends. The windows were cracked to let in the scents of the life and bloom. The sun streamed in through the windshield, warming the interior. Mark reclined in the passenger seat, his head just outside Jenny's view, which allowed him to gaze at her exquisite profile without making her uncomfortable.

Mark recalled lying in bed with her, back when they were active lovers, watching her sleep on Sunday mornings. He would occasionally draw down the sheets, gently feasting his eyes on the slopes and curves of her body. After a night of exhaustive passion it was no longer a sexual gaze, but rather an aesthetic ecstasy of her form and shape. He would watch the morning light cast graceful shadows on her back while making the downy hairs of her shoulder glow in a golden arc. Jenny was his first mature love, growing from friendship rather than lust. As he looked at her now he yearned again for that closeness with her.

They had been good friends in college, meeting at UCLA when Mark took an abnormal psychology class as an elective. Jenny was strong academically, pulling a 3.9 grade point average because of her self-discipline and compulsiveness. Mark always took a minimalist approach to school. He realized the importance of book learning, but he was more interested in field studies. He was raised in Venice, California, the counterculture mecca and melting pot of all things "alternative." It was a city of transients, yet it maintained a curious sense of community. Mark had adapted well to the streets of Venice, swimming through a diverse soup of artists, crooks, retirees, and tourists.

The couple had dated sporadically through school, then became serious after Jenny completed her doctorate. As the relationship became closer, more of her things migrated to his apartment until she finally gave up her student hovel. Initially, the differences in their personalities were a nice complement; he wild and adventurous, she a firm reality check.

They gave each other ample space to pursue their careers and tried to maintain the relationship with few demands. Soon, the complementary differences increasingly became obstacles. Her career within the corporate world of Progressive had made her more pragmatic and concerned with her future. Mark stayed on existential time, living more for the moment and feeling no pressure to hustle down the road of life. He loved Jenny, in a way he had not loved anyone else, but he had some clear boundaries about how much he could give. Jenny was needing and wanting more. The demands of her job took much of her time and energy. Her social contacts with friends dwindled and she needed some close companionship. She pulled on Mark and he pushed away. They struggled with this ritual dance for six months.

Finally, Mark took a four-month assignment in Japan and Jenny had a chance to clear her thoughts. They agreed the friendship would only last if they split up, so she moved to her townhouse in Woodland Hills. Although both had since dated others and even had some brief relationships, nothing substantial had developed for either of them. They tried to get together about twice a year, mostly for fun, occasionally it included sex.

"Hey, Riverside coming up here, navigator," said Jenny, breaking his reverie. "You got the directions?"

"Yeah. They live a little outside of town," said Mark as he withdrew the crude map he had drawn from his pocket. "Get off at Orange Avenue, which should be along soon."

They were cruising through the outskirts of town. The landscape alternated between small communities, industrial sites, and orange groves. The "Inland Empire" of Southern California was an overlapping convergence of sprawling towns that had swollen by millions of people in the last twenty years.

"Is this where Elaina was raised?" asked Mark.

"Yes. I believe her parents moved here in the 1960s. They were into farming . . . avocados, I think. That was before the population explosion."

Jenny guided the car down the Orange Avenue off-ramp. Mark directed her through a series of turns until they found themselves on a sleepy street. It was filled with older ranch style houses sitting on two acre parcels. They stopped in front of a handsome white home, lavishly landscaped with bright flowers and ornamental shrubs. A carved sign on the mailbox announced "Ruiz."

"Are we ready for this?" asked Mark.

"No matter what, please stay near me. I'm afraid I'm going to lose it."

They walked up a brick path to the front door. A short, round woman with a wide smile greeted them, still in her church clothes.

"Oh, you must be the friends of Elaina," she said excitedly as she pushed open the screen door and took Mark's hand. "Jose, come and meet Elaina's friends."

"Hello, I'm Jenny Barrett."

"Yes, I remember you. You were at her school. Come in and sit."

They were shuffled into a large living room. The walls were adorned with paintings, mirrors, and dozens of family pictures. They passed a cluster of photos that caused them to pause. In its center was a photo of Elaina at her college graduation, looking vibrant and beaming, in marked contrast to the reason for their visit.

Jose Ruiz wandered into the living room and cordially greeted the visitors. He uttered few words and seemed to want to make a quick escape. He mumbled an offer to get everyone iced tea and retreated.

Jenny said, "It's so good of you to see us, Mrs. Ruiz. This has come as quite a shock to us. I'm very sorry for your loss. We'll all miss Elaina dearly."

The reference dampened the smile. "Please, call me Marta. Yes, it is a very sad thing. She was such a great spirit, but she is with God now. She will be waiting for me."

"When was the funeral service?" Mark asked.

"It was January twenty-fourth, three days after she died."

"I'm sure it was a lovely ceremony. I'm sorry we missed it," replied Jenny.

"There was so little time to prepare. We hardly knew any of her friends. I went through her address book to call as many people as I could."

"Many people loved her," Jenny assured her.

"I only wish she would have known that in the last days. Maybe it would have helped," said Marta.

"I don't think I understand. Was something wrong with Elaina? I'm afraid I don't know what caused her death," said Jenny.

"THEY KILLED HER," Jose shouted with fierce anger as he returned with the iced tea. "I'll always believe that."

"Jose," said Marta, "it was an accident. She was weak and torn with sadness. No one is to blame."

Mark and Jenny looked perplexed.

Marta explained. "She died in a hospital. She had a bad reaction to some medication. She went to sleep and her heart stopped. The medicine mixed with something else and she just slipped away. They tried to save her, but she was gone." Sadness spread over her face as she recounted the loss.

"Bah!," said Jose in disgust. "It was that company. I don't know how, but they did it. They made her go into that place."

"Did Elaina have a medical problem?" asked Jenny.

"No, it was a hospital for sadness. Pine View Lodge. A psychiatrist hospital."

Mark and Jenny stared in disbelief. "Elaina was admitted to Pine View Lodge?" exclaimed Jenny. "It sounds like she became depressed. Is that right?"

"Yes. It all happened quickly. In January Elaina seemed to become very nervous and unhappy. I think something changed at work. She began to talk mean about the company, which she never did before. She called us less and less. Then we heard that she had been admitted to Pine View Lodge for depression in January. Three days later she died in her sleep. They said she had a very rare reaction to her medicine. The company was so sorry. They even called to say that they had started a fund in her name to give to students. They really liked her," she said with pride.

"That is very unusual," said Jenny. "I've covered thousands of admissions and I've never heard of such a thing."

"Si," said Jose. "I think this is an evil company and they made our Elaina sick."

"Jose, please," pleaded Marta. She then turned to the visitors and said, "He has been crazy about her death. But the coroner said it was an accident. Jose wants to sue them. I'm not sure it will help him. I'm afraid it will just turn his heart black."

Jose scooped up the tray and moved angrily back to the kitchen. There was a prolonged silence as Jenny and Mark considered what they had just heard. It was an impossible story.

"It's so hard to believe that Elaina would have been so depressed she needed to be hospitalized," said an incredulous Jenny. "I remember in school she always seemed to weather the stress and pressure very well. She was so composed and in control. Even during her comprehensive exams she was confident. The only time I saw her get rattled was during a cheating scandal."

"Cheating?" asked Marta.

"Yes, a group of students was passing term papers and tests around. Administration did an investigation and suspicion briefly fell on Elaina because she associated with a member of the group. She was quickly cleared, but I remember her being very shaken up that people were thinking ill of her. It took a while for her to get over it."

"Yes, I remember that," said Marta. "She hated when people thought bad things about her. She never hurt anyone."

Jenny decided to move the topic elsewhere. "Was Elaina raised in this house?"

"Si, from about four years old. For many years the closest family lived almost a mile away. We had orchards here and at our farm. The girls would play in the trees. It was a good time. Would you like to see her room?"

"Yes," said Mark, "we'd love to see it."

They heard a door closing in the kitchen, suggesting Jose had gone outside. The trio moved down a hallway, passing many more photos, up to a door with a plaque on it displaying engraved Elaina's name. The room was large and bright, filled by the sun on the eastern window. A double bed with a brass headboard sat in the middle of the room. The wall was a ceiling high bookcase, with a built-in desk, and two Parsons chairs. It looked like the room of a high school senior, which was probably the last time Elaina lived here. On the floor next to the desk was a disconnected computer and a cardboard box full of personal effects. Jenny felt a chill blow through her as she realized these items must have been from Elaina's apartment.

"This is most of what I brought from Elaina's home," said Marta. "Some furniture is in the garage and some boxes upstairs. I gave some of her things to friends and the rest to the church for the poor."

"You've made it a lovely room. I guess Elaina got her excellent taste from her mother," said Jenny.

"Thank you." Marta moved across the room and hoisted a box on the desk. She rummaged through the items and withdrew a floppy disk. It had "MOM" written in block letters across the label. "I found this in her things. I thought maybe it was a message to me, although she always called me 'mama.' I don't know what to do with it. It's a computer disk, isn't it?"

"Yes," said Jenny. "It's used to store information, like letters, addresses, things like that."

"Do you think there might be a letter for me on this?" asked Marta.

"Maybe. Would you like me to take a look at it?"

"Please. We don't know what to do with it."

Jenny took the disk and placed it in her shirt pocket. She and Mark assembled the computer components on the desk. She connected the monitor and power cables, then plugged in the keyboard and mouse. Finally the power button was flipped on and a brief flash on the screen said the computer was alive.

"Oh, it looks like it works," said Marta with some excitement.

Jenny watched the screen carefully, reading the start-up information that flashed on the monitor. It was a little unnerving to be looking into the screen of her dead friend's computer, almost like reading her diary. Elaina undoubtedly used her machine regularly and Jenny had no way of knowing what items they would find: letters to old lovers, financial records, erotic adventures. She would have much preferred a little time to nose around before sharing anything with the mother. She didn't want to tarnish Elaina's image.

The computer suddenly stopped and displayed the message, "BOOT SEQUENCE FAILED. NO SYSTEM FILES. INSERT BOOT DISK AND PRESS ANY KEY WHEN READY." Jenny tried re-booting it.

"That's odd," said Jenny, "it doesn't have any start-up files on the hard disk. Maybe it was damaged when it was moved here."

"We tried to be very careful, but I don't understand these machines," said Marta.

Jenny placed the floppy disk labeled "MOM" in the floppy drive and re-booted. Again, the machine failed to start up. Jenny rummaged through the box until she found an old system disk labeled "MS-DOS 6.0." She inserted it and this time the machine completed the start-up routine. She told the computer to list the files on the hard disk. It reported, "NO HARD DRIVE FOUND." Curious, Jenny quickly typed a series of commands, scrolling information across the screen. There was no data of any kind on the machine. The hard disk was dead!

Jenny restarted the computer and pressed the DEL key to check the CMOS settings, the basic identity of the machine, which identifies the processor, memory, hard drives, etc. She told the system to find the hard drive. It reported, "NO IDE HEADER ON HARD DRIVE. DEVICE CANNOT BE USED."

"It appears the machine has been destroyed. There's nothing here. The computer can see the hard disk, but the manufacturer's information has been removed. I've never seen that before," stated Jenny.

"I know Elaina used the machine all the time. She told me she liked to talk with people on the interspace system."

"Yes, the Internet. I can see the hookup for the modem on the back of the machine. I don't know what could have happened," said Jenny.

"Maybe we weren't careful enough with it," said Marta.

"No, the hard disk isn't damaged, it's erased. That can only be done by actually typing in commands. Somebody formatted the hard disk, erasing all the data."

"So there's no messages," said Marta, disheartened.

"Oh, let me see what's on this floppy disk." Jenny inserted it back into the floppy drive and looked at its contents. Four files were listed. Jenny opened one of the files named MOM.TXT and saw the words "MultiAxil Outcome Management system." The disk was about MOM, the computer program. Great Health Benefit used the same program as Progressive. This was simply a disk from work.

"Well, that solves the mystery. This floppy came from Elaina's work. They have a program there called MOM. I'm sorry, it's just some material from her work," said Jenny.

Obvious disappointment washed across Marta's face. "I see. I guess I expected it. Elaina would never call me Mom, always Mama. I was just hoping there was something more from her."

Mark began speaking with Marta as Jenny poked around the computer. She wondered why the hard disk would have been purposely erased and who would have done it. Maybe Elaina's father tried to use it and accidentally formatted it. "Maybe I can unformat it," she thought. She picked up the MS-DOS disk and inserted it again. She started the unformat program that comes as a safety measure on the disk. She received the message, "NO MIRROR FILE FOUND, DISK CANNOT BE UNFORMATTED. LAST FORMATTED Jan 21, 1995."

"Mrs. Ruiz, when was Elaina admitted to the hospital?" Jenny asked.

"Let's see, it was January 19. Yes, I'm sure."

"And she never left?' Jenny asked.

"No, she died three days later."

Jenny checked the computer's onboard clock. It reported the correct day and time. That meant that the hard disk was formatted the day before Elaina died. Who could have done that? And why?

"The computer was in her apartment?"

"Si."

"Do you know if anyone else had access to it?"

"I don't think so. Elaina lived alone. Did someone break the computer?"

"Not exactly. It still works fine." Jenny decided to move off the subject so as not to alarm Mrs. Ruiz. "I'm sorry there was no message for you."

"That's okay. Tell me, is this a good computer?"

"Yes, it's fine, only about two years old. You can certainly use it."

"Well, why don't you take it, Jenny. No one in my family knows anything about computers. You know so much. I think Elaina would like you to have it."

"Mrs. Ruiz, I couldn't. It's a valuable machine. Maybe you can give it to someone else?"

"Okay, but I don't know anyone who could use it. Why don't you take it and donate it to some organization? I have no use for it. If it doesn't have anything of Elaina's on it, then it's just a pile of metal. Please, it would mean so much to me."

Jenny looked helplessly at Mark. "Okay. We'll find a good home for it, I promise."

Mark was peering into the box containing Elaina's personal effects. "Jenny, maybe there's something else in here for Mrs. Ruiz. Sometimes you store data in the strangest places, maybe Elaina did too."

"Doesn't look like it. Mrs. Ruiz, you said the other boxes are in the garage?"

"Si, mostly furniture and house things, a few records and tapes, some videos."

"May I see?" asked Jenny.

Marta led them into the garage from a kitchen doorway. It was stuffed with boxes, furniture, lamps, and books. Jenny recognized some pictures from Elaina's apartment walls. She rummaged through a few boxes, not looking for anything in particular, just wanting to touch some things she remembered.

"Jenny," said Mrs. Ruiz. "If you want any of these things to remember her by, please take them."

"Thank you. I'm just remembering some of our old times." A sharp sadness hit as she thumbed through some phonograph records, haunting tunes filling her head with images of Elaina in her UCLA apartment on Veteran Avenue. Suddenly the garage seemed to shrink around her, making her feel claustrophobic. She felt the need to leave. Jenny motioned to Mark and the two of them started for the door. She placed her arm across the shoulders of Marta and thanked her for allowing them to visit. Mr. Ruiz seemed to have disappeared. They loaded the computer components and the box of disks into the Camry. Amidst some tears and hugs they said goodbye.

"Please come back anytime," said Marta.

The couple was silent until Jenny entered the freeway. Mark saw the consternation in her face, as if she was wrestling with some enigmatic problem.

"It's such a tragedy that she died that way. I hope they sue the hospital," said Mark.

"You know, Mr. Reporter, there are some very curious things about all this."

"What do you mean? Do you smell a conspiracy on the Internet? You got a little weird on her computer."

"That's the biggest mystery of all. Why would her computer be sabotaged? Someone had to deliberately erase all the data on the hard disk so thoroughly that it can't be recovered. That's not an accident. And why was it done while she was in the hospital?"

"Jenny, how can you be sure about all this? Maybe the computer clock is wrong. Maybe it got spiked by lightning. Heck, it could be a virus, couldn't it?"

Jenny shot him a dark look. He knew not to challenge her on

technical issues.

"Okay, are you saying you suspect Elaina met with foul play?"

"Mark, I don't know. It's just too strange. Why would Elaina be so depressed she had to be admitted to a psych hospital? How could they mess up the meds so badly she ends up dead? Why did this beautiful woman have to die?" Tears erupted from her eyes, and she struggled to maintain good control of the steering wheel.

Mark placed his hand on hers. "I'm really sorry, Jen. Let's see if we can do something nice for her family."

She squeezed his hand. "Okay." They rode the rest of the way home in silence.

Jenny arrived home at 4 P.M. after declining Mark's invitation to dinner. The visit with the Ruiz family had been draining. Denying her need for companionship and snuggles was difficult, but she was still protecting her fragile heart. After lugging Elaina's old computer into the living room, she piled its components in a corner, next to her desk. At her query, Daisy reported one telephone message from her mother.

"Just called to let you know we're safe at home," announced the message. "Your father still has that stomach trouble so we went to see some doctor in Medford, Dr. Majani. He did some tests and decided to take out Dad's gall bladder. He about had a cow. Said he didn't want the surgery. Took us an hour to convince him it was for his own good. We have to go back day after tomorrow. The doctor says it's a simple procedure, just three little slits in his abdomen. Called a "lapicoly" or something like that. The doctor has a thick Mideast accent, so I'm not sure what he said. Dad will just stay overnight. Dad's okay, but still uncomfortable. He's gone to bed. I'm going to a church meeting this evening. I'll talk with you soon, dear."

"Daisy. Take note," she instructed the computer, "search MOM at work for medical information on Dad. End note." Even as she finished the memo, Jenny hesitated. It would be perilous to risk her parents' confidence again, even if she could help.

That evening Jenny assembled Elaina's computer and linked it to her own. She used some of her most powerful tools and utilities to search for any data on the hard disk, but it had been wiped clean. Even the operating system had been removed. It wasn't that the hard disk had failed. If that was true, she could probably have resurrected some data. Instead she found all data had been turned into zeros, suggesting a deliberate action by someone. Whoever did this had been very thorough. Was it Elaina? She couldn't imagine why, and it had apparently happened when her friend was in the hospital.

A bath and a glass of Cabernet were much more inviting. She was in bed by 8 P.M. Sleep came fitfully that night, with a splattering of dreams with disjointed themes. Some included her dead friend.

Chapter 10

Nora Whitney took a turn for the worse that week. Cancer was often like that—not a day-to-day deterioration. Disability came in sudden spurts, a ratcheting down in functioning, with distinct clicks signifying lost capabilities.

Ezra and Nora went to her clinic Thursday afternoon, but had to see the physician on duty, one they didn't recognize. In fact, they really didn't have one assigned doctor, despite the HMO's contention that Dr. Farrakim was their primary care physician. In two years they had only seen him once in twenty visits. They wouldn't have recognized him on the street.

The new physician, Dr. Corillo, was young and very business-like. He began to excuse Mr. Whitney from the examining room, but Ezra said, "I attend all my wife's examinations. I'm the caretaker here. I have to know what's going on."

"Mr. Whitney, I understand and appreciate your concern, but I think it best to give your wife some privacy for some of the exam. I'll fill you in completely."

"Doctor, I don't mind if Ezra is here, " said Nora. "He knows me better than anyone."

"I'm sure he does. Nevertheless, I'll feel more comfortable. Please excuse us," the doctor said with a firm voice.

Ezra didn't like being dismissed by this pompous young twerp, but he complied to hurry the process.

He sat in the waiting room for what seemed like a long time. In fact it was close to forty minutes before a nurse summoned Ezra back into the room. Upon entering he sensed Dr. Corillo was even less friendly than before.

"Mr. Whitney, your wife tells me she is taking morphine twice a day now. I reviewed your prescriptions and determined that we haven't prescribed anywhere near enough to support that frequency. Where is all the morphine coming from?"

"Well, doctor, we're just trying to make it last longer," replied Ezra.

"Do you mean by stretching it out? Giving her less?"

"Well, just trying to make her comfortable," he said nervously.

"Mr. Whitney, I've ordered a blood test on your wife to assess her serum level of morphine. From it I can determine how much she is taking and how regularly she's taking it. It would be helpful if you were straight with me. Are you getting it from somewhere else? Another physician or clinic?"

Ezra felt trapped. He couldn't fool the doctor for long. Maybe he should just be straight with him. Still, being straight hadn't gotten him anywhere. The new doctor-patient relationship required a guarded approach.

"No, sir, there isn't another doctor or clinic. I have a friend whose wife died from cancer. He had a number of bottles of morphine left over. I bought them to help Nora out."

"I'm very concerned that Mrs. Whitney is over-medicated. I understand your concern for her comfort, but you must understand the dangers of these addictive drugs. She may already be hooked. We'll have to gauge the lab results and make a determination." Dr. Corillo left the room.

"Oh Nora, I'm afraid I may have messed this up."

"Ezra, are we in trouble? Did you do something wrong?"

"No, hon, I did something right, but I hope they don't get too upset about it.

Dr. Corillo was gone for twenty minutes. When he returned he had a grim look on his face. "The lab tests show a high level of morphine in her blood. She cannot continue at this level," he stated.

"I never gave her high doses," said Ezra. "Just enough to cut the pain. No more than that. Just to make her comfortable."

"This amount of morphine will make her more than comfortable. I'm afraid I'll have to stop our prescriptions. I must also ask you to provide the name of the physician who is giving her even more. I'm sure he doesn't know about us."

"Please, don't punish her. There is no other physician. I told you

I just used the remainder of my friend's morphine. We're just about out. Please don't stop the pain meds for her," pleaded Ezra.

Dr. Corillo was paged to the phone. "Ah, there is the insurance company. I'll have to tell them what I found and see what they say. Please wait here." He spun around and left the room.

Ezra was sweating and trembling. How could his little plan have gone so wrong? Nora sat there with a look of perplexity. He tried to soothe her. If they cut her meds off, maybe he can get a little job to pay Bob for more medicine. Maybe they didn't need this stupid clinic. Who were these bozos in California who think they can run people's lives from across the country?

Dr. Corillo returned. "I'm sorry. I've spoken with a case manager from Great Benefit Health. They are also concerned with the addiction potential and they have recommended that we no longer participate in her morphine treatment. We will, however, continue with the radiation treatment."

"Doctor, please don't cut her off! She's in agony with these tumors. I'm the one who messed up the deal, take it out on me."

"I'm sorry. We'll support you in any way we can, but we can't risk losing a patient to a very addictive substance."

What Ezra wouldn't learn until later is that Nora's chart had been electronically imprinted with a code for "substance abuse: prescription drugs." This indelible warning would accompany any request for medical information or further treatment. MOM had scrutinized Nora's chart and calculated the action plan. The case manager had simply read the results off the screen. At 71, Nora was a newly diagnosed substance abuser.

The formula, or algorithm as it's called in computer circles, was a composite of many factors. This secret formula was considered the private property of GHB, so few people knew what factors went into the calculations. There was clearly one beneficial result for GHB in calculating any kind of patient non-compliance to treatment: Great Health Benefit automatically gained substantial control over a patient's medical procedures. Drug addicts had far less chance of winning judgements against the company for denied care. The company would be watching every delicate move of this fragile woman.

Ezra had one prescription for morphine left that he had not yet filled. After settling Nora back into her bed, he flew down to the pharmacy to fill it. He wasn't sure if the company would eventually stop all prescriptions, but he figured a company based in Los Angeles probably cannot act too quickly.

He entered the Buy-Right Pharmacy. He had previously shopped at Forman's, an independent drug store and community fixture since he was a kid. However, like much of the healthcare industry, the deep discount drug universes had replaced the mom-and-pop storefront drug store. Ezra just couldn't afford to pay much for medicine on his fixed income.

Rachel McGraw was the pharmacist on duty. She had served Ezra and Nora for over six years. She liked the old man a lot and was impressed with his dedication to Nora. She set aside an order and addressed Ezra.

"Morning, Ezra. How's Nora doing?"

"Fairly well, thank you. Rachel, I need to fill this prescription ASAP. You know, it's what keeps her going with all that pain."

"Sure Ezra, just give me a minute." Rachel punched in the numbers on her computer console, which automatically called Great Health Benefit for confirmation and authorization of the medicine. Within seconds a flashing message blipped on the screen. DENIED! Text at the bottom of the screen explained that the patient was no longer to receive this prescription and that GHB would not reimburse. She tried the authorization two more times.

"Ezra, there may be a problem with your prescription. Insurance company says no."

His heart sank. "How could they act that quickly," he wondered. "Well, can I just pay for it with cash? You know how important this is to Nora. We've been coming here for years. Can't you do something?"

"I wish I could, Ezra. Yet without the prescription there's nothing I can do."

"I can't just buy it myself? Her doctor prescribed it."

"Actually, Ezra, *their* doctor prescribed it," replied the pharmacist.

"I guess I'll have to go to another physician. Nora has to have her medicine."

"Aren't you in the Golden Seniors program through GHB?"

"Yes, we are."

"Well, I don't think you can just switch. In fact, no other physician can see you unless GHB authorizes it."

"What! You mean I can't just go see another doctor privately and pay for it?"

"Unfortunately, no. Doctors are required by law to submit bills for any Medicare patient they see, whether Medicare will pay or not. You can't see anyone else without their permission."

"My god, we're pariahs," exclaimed Ezra.

"No you're not, " said Rachel, but the more she reflected on his statement the more she realized it was true.

After a few more desperate pleas Ezra left the store. He was becoming frightened. For a few minutes he had trouble catching his breath, realizing he was panting as he walked down the street. He felt as if his world was suddenly shrinking around him.

***

On Tuesday Jenny got the call to come to the Great Health Benefit corporate office. Carter Newton had requested that she clear her schedule for the next three days while she became acquainted with the GHB computer system. He explained that behavioral care, the mental health part of the business, was undergoing a major revision, and he needed her on a special project to implement changes. Jenny was duly flattered and thankful that Larry Harrington had helped secure a valued spot for her.

Monday had been a blur of activity. All directors and managers were instructed to produce comprehensive status reports on all systems, procedures, projects, and budgets. Jenny, new to the job, had little experience with such reports, so she was happy to hand it over to Laura Pierce when called to GHB. The merger was on the fast-track. Lunch on Monday included a brief phone call with her parents. William Barrett grumbled about his stupid insurance company while her mom tried to reassure him that Dr. Shepard would prevail.

At 9 A.M. Jenny drove the two miles to the GHB building, a striking glass cube. The route cruised through commercial districts that were quickly becoming glass and concrete canyons reminiscent of Hollywood or Century City. The building entryway was more elegant than she expected. An upscale bistro sat off the main entrance, with servers running about in tuxedo-like uniforms in the garden atmosphere. The dark green marble floor of the foyer was intricately inlayed in a stylized floral pattern, reflected in the etched metal elevator doors. She checked the directions to the appointment location and entered a waiting elevator. The doors noiselessly glided shut and Jenny felt a gentle pressure of acceleration. Upon reaching the sixth floor the machine softly announced the floor and she exited into an reception area. She told a woman sitting at a long desk wearing a headset of her appointment.

Two minutes later Carter burst through the door. "Jenny, it's so good to see you. I can't tell you how happy I am you're on board. I'd like you to meet my assistant, Valerie." Four steps behind him appeared a stout woman lugging a video projector and a large leather satchel. "We're on the way to a meeting. If you'd like some coffee or a snack, there should be plenty at the meeting. We'll be working all morning, but I've arranged a tour of the facilities for you at 10:30. Follow me."

They maneuvered through hallways and cubicles until they entered a sizable conference room. One wall contained a darkened video screen flanked by large speakers. Red glowing LED eyes winked at her from electronic gear through smoked glass cabinet doors beneath the speakers. A thirty foot table surrounded by leather chairs stood in the center of the room. Three people sat at the far end of the table, engaged in animated conversation, which they barely interrupted to acknowledge Carter's arrival. Jenny took a chair at the other end, next to Valerie. Carter moved to the other three, who quieted instantly when it was clear Carter meant to address them. He queried them, shook their hands, and then he left the room.

As Jenny sat down she noticed that the table was inlaid with smoked glass squares at each seat. Valerie pressed a wood panel, which rotated to reveal a series of switches. She flipped a few and an eight-inch computer screen began to glow under the glass. She extracted a mouse from a holder in the panel and a keyboard dropped down from under the table. She also extended a small microphone and a two-inch plastic sphere, which Jenny recognized as a micro-video camera. The table contained thirty-two networked workstations carved into the black walnut finish, an intimate marriage of cellulose and silicon. Jenny was impressed with the style of Great Health Benefit. The room filled quickly as more staffers arrived.

"Can I get you some coffee, Dr. Barrett?" asked Valerie.

"Yes, black, thank you. Please call me Jenny. Maybe I could get a muffin as well."

Jenny realized one great advantage in moving to a new facility; she would begin as Dr. Barrett. At Progressive she would always be "Jenny, the almost-a-doctor," despite receiving the Ph.D. over a year ago. There was something distancing about the word "doctor" that didn't feel right to her at Progressive, but in the intimidating grandeur of GHB corporate, the term gave her a little boost in self-esteem.

Upon returning with the coffee, Valerie tried to set Jenny at ease. "Is this your first visit here?"

"Yes," said Jenny. "Carter said they wanted my input on some new project."

"Oh, you must be the psychologist for the Caduceus Project."

"Kadoo'sis?"

"Yes, like the symbol for medicine. They've been working on it for six months now. It's a major revision of our master outcome management program, which we call MOM 3.0. Some people are calling the new project 'SuperMOM' because it can do just about everything."

"Yes, we use MOM 2.0 at Progressive, though I guess it's a smaller version. We primarily do psych benefits, although we have to check on medical history as well. You do *all* the medical management, right?"

"Medical, dental, psychiatric, chemical dependency, worker's comp, you name it. We've only done the psych/CD part seriously for the last year, when we acquired American Behavioral Health. Progressive is the third behavioral care firm we've purchased. Our company is growing so fast we can hardly keep up," she said with pride. "We're the only company using version 3.0 of MOM. It's a giant step forward, really powerful, but the staff is having some trouble adjusting to it. That's why they need a person like you, Jenny."

A rush of excitement coursed through Jenny as she allowed herself to be swept up in Valerie's enthusiasm. "This could be a remarkable career move," she thought to herself. Progressive, as sophisticated as it was, had only updated to MOM version 2.0. Even at that, the company used barely 60 percent of its features. This was going to be a challenge.

Carter returned to the room and placed himself at a podium that extended from the wall. He pressed a button and the wall monitor flashed into life, displaying the GHB logo. The din of chatter quickly died and all eyes fell upon the VP.

"Let's begin," he said in a straightforward, business-like tone. "We'll be joined on the monitor by three members of the team in Connecticut: Jim Bryer, Chris Whalen, and Morris Scott. Valerie, could you set that up? I'd also like to introduce the newest member of the team, Dr. Jennifer Barrett, from Progressive. We are truly fortunate to have her talent on this project. I have it on good authority that she is a whiz at whipping systems into shape. We'll be giving her a tour shortly and she'll be visiting some of you over the next few days. Please let her know of your interface problems and concerns."

All eyes turned to survey the attractive woman seated next to Valerie. Many offered smiles of encouragement, others showed only detached interest. A few women seemed to painfully look away, as if Jenny represented something evil. As Jenny nodded in greeting to the inquisitive group, their collective gaze seemed to drift above her head. She turned in her seat to see three head shots of the Connecticut team members on the wall monitor. They were mirrored on the workstation monitor under her folded hands. Carter flipped more switches on the podium and the three heads appeared on yet another wall monitor at the opposite end of the room.

"Okay, team," began Carter, "let me bring you up to speed. Overall the project is moving well. GHB has purchased a controlling interest in HealthCode Software, Inc., developers of the original MOM software. We are now free to develop all the elements we want, and we can put our own proprietary stamp on the deal. We're actively bidding on some major national contracts, and we now include comprehensive psychiatric and chemical-dependency benefits rather than farming them out to other companies. That means our expert systems and appropriately trained personnel need to be able to deal with psych and substance abuse care by June 1st."

Carter let the date sink in, then continued. "The pilot project with Honda America revealed a number of weaknesses in the system, which must be corrected before we can safely bid on the big contracts, like General Motors. That contract alone would add up to 1.4 million lives to our rolls, bringing our total covered lives to over 23 million. We plan to undercut the other bids by twenty percent, but we can't possibly hire and train hundreds of new case managers and reps. We will be getting some staff from Great Benefit Financial division, which has had a setback with the FTC, but we need MOM to take over more of the assessment and treatment decision making. It's the only way we can get consistency. Every time we give the case managers too many treatment decisions our costs go up. I want them to trust this computer completely. They need to learn that MOM is now the expert."

The numbers were staggering to Jenny. GHB provided care on a scale she could barely imagine. Progressive in its best year covered only 2.1 million lives and that almost stalled their system; 23 million was an impossible sum. She began to have doubts about what she could really offer to such an immense system. She peered around the table. Most of the team members had begun working the computers at their seats, pulling data from their departments for updates.

"Okay, status reports please," said Carter to the man on his left.

From around the table Jenny heard each division sound off on such concerns as hardware, programming, legal affairs, contracts, quality improvement, training, and so forth. Jenny's head was swimming with numbers, systems, divisions, and people. She maintained a plastered smile on her face, but her head was pounding. "What the hell am I doing here?" she wondered.

The concept of medicine that unfolded was unlike anything she had heard of. A division called Claims Recovery seemed to be speaking of extensive litigation against anyone who contributed to a member's illness. Another division represented commercial products that were not covered under the policies. GHB was making a tidy profit selling discounted alternative medicines and equipment to fill gaps in members' policies. Yet another division discussed the profitability of selling their customer lists to third-party marketers. It was industrialized medicine on a scale Jenny could hardly fathom. The faces around the table were young, neatly groomed, and had most likely never before worked in a medical care facility. The room was full of MBAs and techies.

Carter continued speaking. "We need to convey to everyone on staff that every contact with a member is a marketing opportunity. The client may be calling for insurance authorization, but we must also see it as a sales opportunity. They want something from us, and we want something from them. If we can't sell them one of our services, we must find a service they need and sell that marketing opportunity to another company. The only way we can continue to underbid the competition is to turn every contact into a profit potential. So while MOM does the diagnosing, you can be gearing up the pitch. It's going to take a coordinated effort to revolutionize medicine, and we all need to work together." Finally, Carter interrupted the meeting for a brief coffee break.

"I think you're going to fit in fine, Jenny," said Carter as he placed a hand on her shoulder. "I expect it will take some time for you to learn the system. However, Harrington has great confidence in you, and so do I. Fortunately, you don't have to know everything. We just need a lot of help getting people to trust the system. As you heard, too many case managers are trying to do their own brand of medicine, as if they were floor nurses working with doctors. They need to know that MOM is the doctor. The system has been upgraded to know every treatment procedure, diagnosis, recommendation, and medication available. MOM is the expert."

"Am I understanding this correctly?" Jenny asks Carter. "It sounds like MOM has become a fully expert system that helps the case management team decide client care."

"Actually, MOM is designed to make the decisions, not just help people make them. We have spent millions of dollars making her the smartest medical computer around, smarter than most doctors. She's connected to the Harvard Medical School library, the Albert Einstein Medical Institute, and our own library of millions of case histories. No physician has that much knowledge immediately available when treating patients."

"Still, MOM isn't really seeing the patients. It's the providers in the clinics and offices. Don't we generally try to collaborate with them on patient care?" asked Jenny.

"Yes, that's true. But too often we've found the doctors are just making decisions based on their new Mercedes lease or their vacation plans. When you really look at the patient's symptoms it's a different story. I'd guess you have lots of fudging in the psychiatric world. Mental health providers are always exaggerating symptoms, saying a patient is suicidal when they're really just feeling a little lonely. We had a big problem with that last year when we took over the American Behavioral Health contracts. We tried to work with the therapists, but they just kept scamming us. We finally had to change our authorization procedure so that we talked directly with the patient and informed them of their rights. It cleaned things up pretty quickly."

Another team member briefly distracted Carter, which Jenny took as an opportunity to withdraw and compose herself. She was shocked at the attitude he had displayed. It seemed like he held the entire field of psychotherapy in total contempt. Admittedly, mental health had always been considered an odd child in the family of medicine, but rarely did she encounter such hostility. She too had lost some of her idealism about therapists in the last few years, and had even pulled clients away from a few abusive practitioners. Still, those were few; most therapists were helpful.

Jenny's identity was still as a psychologist and she took offense to the wholesale dismissal of the field, yet he was her new boss. She was wise enough to recognize a losing battle. "Don't rock the boat while you're just getting on," she thought to herself. Taking a deep breath and focusing briefly on the peaceful image of the creek flowing by her parents' ranch, Jenny re-engaged reality. Carter returned his attention to her, but seemed to have moved on to another subject.

"Valerie, call Hepman and see if he's ready to give Jenny a tour. Thanks. Jenny, I want you to take your time in the next few days getting the lay of the land. I've arranged for Greg Hepman from information services to take you around. He's a chief consultant to the Caduceus team. Kind of a techie, but he's worked with us on the mental health module, so you'll have some common ground. I'll check in with you toward the end of the day."

Chapter 11

Greg Hepman was a lanky, slender man who slipped through a narrow crack in the conference room door. Although dressed in an ill-fitting "power suit," his entrance drew little attention. His dark brown hair was deceptively long, yet combed back and trimmed at the collar, as if in reluctant compliance to a corporate standard. A skinny face with a protruding nose and large teeth made him look like a rodent. His eyes darted around as if checking to see who was watching him. He did not appear comfortable in the crowd of people and walked straight over to Carter.

"Greg," said Carter, "I'd like you to meet Dr. Jenny Barrett, a new psychologist on the team. She comes from Progressive and has lots of experience with MOM."

Jenny shook his flaccid hand. "Nice to meet you," was his non-committal reply.

"I'd like you to give Jenny the grand tour for the rest of the day. Introduce her to the staff and set up her workstation." Carter glanced at Valerie, who wordlessly confirmed that the workstation was available. "Good, start there so she can feel like she has a home." Carter sent them off with a good-natured smile.

Jenny followed Hepman as he meandered through the cubicles. "They devote this floor and the fifth floor almost exclusively to utilization review and case management," he said. "We handle treatment authorizations nationally from Chicago to the West Coast. Connecticut takes the rest. There are over 400 terminals operating here. When we get fully up to speed we'll centralize all authorizations here."

They walked past cubicle after cubicle. Each contained an

employee sitting with a headset in front of a computer screen. So much pain and suffering flowed through these electronic networks. Doctors, nurses, and practitioners of all kinds called to tell of their patients' breaks and sprains, heart attacks and hemorrhages, neuroses and addiction, births and deaths. Every treatment action was authorized, monitored, and recorded by Great Health Benefit. Each discrete treatment event was electronically etched into a massive computer hard drive. Billions of electrons were aligned in regimented rows, creating a parallel universe of people's lives on a magnetic disk. The men and women who took the calls would digitally pump the identities, diagnoses, and treatments of their members into the great machine. Once magnetically stored, the lives could be tallied, compared, compressed, aggregated, duplicated, and transmitted to interested parties. The electronic medical record had made confidentiality passé. The data was too important, too profitable, too powerful to keep quiet.

The scale of the operation made Jenny dizzy. As she moved down the hallway, the din of conversation from the case managers drifted up from the cubicles.

"No, Dr. Hirsch, that is not a covered benefit. The only treatment I can authorize for impotence is a penal implant."

"Madam, I know your little girl is ill, but your name does not come up on the computer. I can't verify your coverage."

"We can authorize three days of detox for alcohol withdrawal."

Jenny had to smile. "Geraldo would kill for some of the tragic stories that sail through here," she thought.

Greg led her to the elevator, then up to the seventh floor. It looked much like the sixth. They walked past the reception desk that greeted people at each floor and started for the door when a security guard hailed them.

"Mr. Hepman. I can't let your friend enter without clearance."

"Oh, right," said Greg. He fished in his pocket and produced a laminated name tag labeled "Visitor." "Jenny, put this on. You can't enter here without a security clearance."

"Why's that?"

"We have a lot of managers and executive staff on this floor. They can access vital hardware and records. You know, security. I'll have one with your name on it tomorrow."

They entered through the door. Despite the allegations of upper echelon staff, the floor looked like any other; cubicles in the center, offices along the walls. So much for prestige.

They finally arrived at an empty desk on the end of the row. It backed up to an exterior window overlooking the Ventura Freeway. Jenny dumped her purse and briefcase on the desk. The cubicle was clean and barren, the drawers empty. Along the overhead shelf were a few procedure manuals and benefit books. Greg withdrew a small manila envelope from his pocket and extracted a set of keys, inserting them into the desk lock.

"You can store your stuff here. It should be safe, particularly on this floor," he said, handing her the keys. "Do you want a few minutes to get oriented?"

"Thanks, I'd like that. I should call Progressive and see if there are any fires to put out."

"Phone's here, or you can use the computer. Inside the key envelope is your user ID and log-on procedure and initial password. Passwords are changed weekly on this floor. We know it's a hassle, but we've learned from experience. I hear Progressive uses MOM as well, so it should be easy for you. I'll be back in about fifteen minutes."

Jenny called her voice mail at Progressive, but found no crisis messages. She decided to log onto the GHB computer and establish her identity with the new system. She powered up the monitor and waded through the screen prompts. The graphics of this system were more colorful and textured than Progressive's, resembling realistic real world objects like tape recorders, file boxes, buttons, radio dials. It had a friendly, even inviting appearance.

She put on the headset and heard little sound bytes and tones that were played with the varied computer functions. Speakers stuck out like ears from the sides of the monitor, and a small slotted hole identified the microphone, but they were silenced when the headset was plugged in. Jenny's fingers settled on the home keys of the keyboard, a familiar sensation which helped her feel more at ease. The beauty and elegance of this machine was enticing. It might be exciting working with it.

MOM began the new user set-up interview. Jenny was prompted for some minimal information on her name, location, e-mail address, a brief physical description. She was asked to repeat a few phrases into the microphone as MOM recorded her voice patterns. Many of the questions on the screen required only "yes" or "no" answers, so she plowed through them quickly. Curiously, the questions would alternately appear on opposite sides of the screen, as would the squares for the mouse-clicked answers. A few times she was asked for information that should have been obvious to the machine, like station ID and cubicle number. "You're not smart enough to know what machines are attached to you," she wondered aloud. Then she winced at the thought that MOM might still be recording her voice, but she restrained the urge to apologize.

Jenny became slightly frustrated when a number of typing errors appeared on the screen. She'd reposition her hands on the home keys, but soon errant letters popped up on the screen again. For someone who communicates via a keyboard for much of the workday, it was the equivalent of stammering. Jenny was considered a power computer user, and she took pride in her keyboarding. "It must be the excitement of the day," she concluded.

At one point the computer appeared to get stuck, repeatedly asking her the same question. The program clearly had a glitch, so she tried some work-arounds. Her frustration grew as she used increasingly advanced techniques which didn't seem to help. Finally the machine progressed to the next question, then it got stuck again. As pretty as the computer was, MOM definitely had some problems. She finally used a little-known command a system engineer from Progressive had taught her. Suddenly, the session ended and her screen went black.

"Hey! You just shut down the whole system," explained a robust feminine voice from behind.

Jenny turned to find the beaming face of an older black woman. She appeared to be in her sixties; with salt and pepper hair, a large, round face, enormous eyes and an infectious smile. She had been peeking around the corner of the cubicle, then sauntered up to Jenny with her hand out. "Hello, I'm Mable Jackson, one of the UR nurse supervisors. I was just kidding about you shutting down the system. Just trying to get you going on your first day."

"Rats, Mable. I thought my virus had taken hold and crashed the system," Jenny retorted with a smile as she shook her hand. "I'm Jenny Barrett, a psychologist from Progressive. You guys just bought us. I come with the deal."

"How nice. Are you going to be working in psych/cd?"

"Actually, Carter Newton brought me over to work on some new project. Caduceus?"

"Wow. I'm impressed, little lady. That's a top priority around here. The suits have been jumping through hoops to get it working. I've seen a bit of it and it looked 'awesome," as my grandkids say."

"Well, I wasn't especially impressed by what I just saw. The machine kept messing up."

"You mean getting stuck on questions, repeating itself, stuff like that?" asked Mable.

"Yeah."

"Sorry, honey. It was no error. The machine was checking you out."

"What do you mean?"

"Little game they like to play. The Hitman will tell you about it."

"The Hitman?"

"Yes, Greg Hepman. We call him the Hitman," said Mable.

"Why on earth would you do that?"

"Well, just between you and me, he got the name because one of his jobs is eliminating staff who can't adjust to computers. Unfortunately, he's the touch of death. If they send the Hitman to help you, you're dead. There's a lot of medical people who have trouble adjusting to computer-supported therapy. They need more than the regular company training we all get, so the company sends the tough nuts to Hitman and his group for help. He's truly brilliant at computers. He was one of those child computer hackers, using his home computer to break into systems. Really clever, but he has zero people skills. He couldn't teach a fish how to swim. No one has survived on the job after visiting the Hitman's department. It's pretty sad."

"Why do they keep him around?"

"Like I said. He's brilliant." said Mable. "And too often, he finds a way to get MOM to do the job that medical people once did. He's a big project manager, hired right out of college. He built the company's original computer system to manage the General Motors contract. But it had a big problem. He was supposed to design some bulletproof security around it so no one could get unauthorized medical data, but he was a hacker at heart, and a little too clever. He designed a very tough system, but he left himself a little back door so he could get in. I guess programmers do that all the time. Anyway, some on-line computer bandits found the door and breached the computer. They downloaded the medical records of 250,000 GM workers and sold them to malpractice attorneys. They screened the cases for potential suits, first against physicians and later against GM. It was a big mess. Very ugly."

"I never thought about that. I guess there are a lot of people who would like to browse through those records. I'm surprised I didn't hear about it at a computer conference," stated Jenny.

"To avoid too much press, they dealt with it quietly. However, since all this electronic medical record technology was so new, they couldn't replace Greg. They didn't want him going to work for the competition."

"So now he's building an even bigger mouse trap," said Jenny.

"You got that right, honey. I probably shouldn't be tellin' you all this, but I'm too old to be scared anymore. I got three years to go to retirement. They won't be messing with me. Say, did Hitman tell you where the important stuff is, like the coffee and bathrooms?"

"No."

"That's just like him. Here, let me show you around." Mable gave her the survival tour, chattering all the way. As they walked along the hallways, workers occasionally looked up from their screens, often breaking into smiles when they saw Mable. She introduced Jenny to many of the staff and to little bits of benign office gossip. She treated everyone like her children, even one woman of fifty. Jenny sensed a seasoned professional nurse behind that folksy persona. Mable explained that she had been with the company for twelve years, and had worked with one of the founders, William Bendi. Mable assured Jenny that she would learn more than she wanted to know about Bendi at the company's orientation meeting.

"You must have seen some amazing changes in the last twenty years."

"I sure have, honey. I'm not sure they're all so good. Some of the youngsters around here have never worked in a hospital, never gave a shot or had to hold a little girl's hand before surgery. Seems like they mostly want people with book learning, 'cause that's what computers know best. Rules and procedures. These machines don't know nothin' 'bout tears or pain. That's supposed to be our job."

"Well said, Mable," Jenny responded. "I hope I can bring some of that to the new project."

Mable gave a broad smile and put her hand on Jenny's shoulder. "Now don't let on that you know the Hitman's secrets, even though everyone does. Deep in the hard wires of his soul beats a heart of stone." She let out a hearty laugh and returned to her desk. "Let me know if there's anything you need, Jenny."

***

Hepman returned to find Jenny cruising through the computer system. She had read and filed the e-mail start-up instructions and was now looking through the directory of employees. The machine was working flawlessly now. Her skillful and confident navigation through the system impressed him.

"So what do you think about our MOM?" said Greg with a hint of a pride.

"Very impressive. I'd say you're one or two generations ahead of Progressive. Is all of the line-staff's equipment this sophisticated and current, or only the ones on this floor?"

"This is pretty much what you find all over the shop. GHB really believes information technology is the future of medical management. The more the computer can do, the less we have to worry about inconsistent care. We're trying to make the system as friendly as possible."

"The graphics are beautiful. I've never seen a corporation invest so much in such a stunning computer interface. It must cost a fortune," observed Jenny.

"Well, no matter how much a pretty monitor costs, people cost much more, especially medically trained people. That's one of our biggest costs, hiring professionals to manage the care of our members. Unfortunately, the older ones always want to do it their own way, like they did it in the hospital or doctor's office. We find the younger ones are more adaptable. They're more willing to follow the rules and protocols we establish. In fact, some tell us they appreciate how MOM makes so many decisions for them. They're starting to trust MOM as an expert. That's what the Caduceus project is all about," said Hepman.

"To make MOM the expert? You mean to help the frontline staff research decisions?"

"No, I mean to have MOM make the decisions. We've already shown that MOM is as good as UR doctors and nurses in recommending treatment, and that was last year. We're scheduled for another trial in October and I know MOM will win."

"Win what?" asked Jenny.

"Win the reliability trials for medical care. She'll be better than medical people."

"You seem pretty confident," said Jenny, desperately wanting to find the error in his thinking.

"Look, medicine is getting too complex to be left to one person in an examining room. There's too much to figure out. A doctor can't keep all this in his head, but MOM can. In about three nanoseconds the computer can check a patient's entire medical history, look at 10,000 similar cases, review the medical literature on the matter, then recommend a diagnosis, and even find treatment within ten miles of the patient's house. The machine never has a bad day, doesn't have to finance a BMW, isn't sending kids to college, and never gets tired of reading medical journals."

"But you're taking the human element away. Computers don't act like people," exclaimed Jenny.

"Actually, we're keeping people in the equation, but we're taking away the drudgery. Think about the space shuttle. Computers run the whole launch. There's no pilot guiding the blast-off with a joystick. Humans can't think and react that quickly. It's the same with illnesses in people, who are certainly much more complex than space shuttles. If a doctor flubs two or three diagnoses out of a hundred, that's three people who are in trouble. I know MOM can help save those people."

It was clear Jenny wasn't going to have much impact on this true believer. Hepman was standing taller now, his chest slightly puffed out. He was in his element. She wasn't sure if this was simply the view of a computer head or the party line for GHB. She decided to back off from the conflict and accept an informative tour of the system.

"I see," she said, "so you're trying to make the system friendlier so people will follow its advice?"

"That's part of it. The sad reality is that we have found the more it looks like TV, the more readily people will accept it as authority. Heck, if TV can turn Ricki Lake or Sally Jesse into an authority, it could do wonders for MOM," said Hepman with a smirk.

Jenny reluctantly agreed.

Greg shifted gears for the tour. "Let me sit at the console for a few minutes and I'll show you some nice features of our system," he said. He plopped into her chair and began looking around the monitor. "Where's the video ball?" he asked. Under the rear of the monitor he found a two-inch plastic ball with a small lens in one side, like the ones she had seen in the conference room. He fixed it on top of the monitor and suddenly a two-inch-square moving image of Hepman appeared in a window on screen. "There. Most of the managers and supervisors have these, so you can see who you're talking too. It's a great way to get known around the company."

"How do I know when I'm being viewed?" asked Jenny.

"You know, a lot of people asked the same thing. They're worried that management could be spying on them. We programmed the system so it always shows the viewer's image and pops up the terminal address here in the corner of the screen. Actually, Legal said we had to let people know for privacy reasons."

"Can I store the image if I get Mel Gibson on the line?" Jenny asked with a smile.

"Absolutely. We've been storing images from the providers for a few months," replied Greg.

"What kind of images do you get from providers?"

"Only a few have the active video. Mostly they send in scanned images of medical problems. They take a digital picture or an X-ray of the problem and send it to us by modem. Here, this section is doing the dental authorizations," said Greg as he walked into a nearby cubicle. He was greeted by a young woman at the terminal, who briefly looked at the two of them while continuing to speak in the headset. A three-inch pixie-like ceramic figure sat on the edge of her monitor with a sign saying "Happy Birthday Beth." Jenny looked over Beth's shoulder to see an image on the monitor of the interior of a wide-open mouth. It was obvious to even her untrained eye that a molar had split in two. She could see severe reddening around the gums. Beth drew a square on the screen around the molar and pressed the "save" key to document the injury. She then authorized the dental work needed to reconstruct the tooth.

"Greg, this is amazing," said Jenny, duly impressed. "Where is this provider?"

"Omaha," said Beth. "The client came into the office with the injury an hour ago. Fortunately, this is one of our HMO sites, so we're set up with the digital camera. Next year they'll have the video, right, Mr. Hepman?"

"Yeah, like some clinics have now. At about half of our medical clinics we can get live-action video during the examination. Our advisors can confirm the diagnosis and lab results, or even ask to take another look. Then we can save the image in our centralized medical chart here. That way, no matter where the client goes, we can call up their entire medical history, with pictures."

"Don't the doctors feel like someone is looking over their shoulder?" asked Jenny.

"They're all under contract with us," said Greg. "They get used to it pretty quickly though. OB/GYN had some problems with the camera. They wanted to know who was reviewing the images, so MOM directs all those queries to female staff."

"God, I don't know how I'd feel about images of my private parts being beamed all over the country," said Jenny.

"Well, if we're gonna pay, you gotta play. Do you know how much money we lost to unnecessary surgery by greedy providers last year? This keeps them honest."

"What about the urologists, didn't they complain?" asked Jenny.

"Not a peep," he said with a grin.

Greg led Jenny out of the cubicle and down the hallway to board the elevator. They exited at the fifth floor and marched passed the reception desk to an expansive work area. There were few offices along the walls, so the view out the windows made the area look immense. Again, the din of medical talk drifted up from the cubicles as hundreds of staff fielded thousands of calls each day. GHB was a very centralized organization, and all information roads lead to Woodland Hills, CA.

"The fourth and fifth floors house the bulk of the medical phone reps and case managers," Hepman explained. "The clients of course have an 800 number to call, which generally connects them here. The client will navigate through the voice mail, which does a great deal of our processing. In fact, the clients can either press an option, like "one" or speak the word. MOM will recognize it 98 percent of the time. In the process MOM establishes identification, confirms benefits, and directs them to a specialty area. If it's a simple procedure, like getting a physical or any generously covered benefit, MOM will provide the authorization and note it in their medical record. About 12 percent of our clients never even need to talk to a human being."

"Doesn't that make it a little mechanistic? I mean, especially for a medical care firm," asked Jenny.

"The clients seem to really like it. The voice menu includes assurances of confidential communication. They report it feels like a private conversation that no one will know about."

"No one but the 10,000 people who have access to the record," said Jenny, sorry for the comment when it left her mouth.

"Is it any different at Progressive?"

"No, I'm sorry, I didn't mean that to sound so negative. I guess I was raised in the old cloak of secrecy model of medical records. You'd think I'd be over it by now."

Hepman stepped into the doorway of another cubicle. A young woman on the phone looked up and smiled in acknowledgment. Hepman grabbed a pencil and wrote "Giving a tour. We're just watching," on the pad. The woman nodded in agreement. Her badge said her name was Belinda Smart.

"Ms. Arnold. Your fertility clinic has been working with Mrs. Sherman for almost two years and she has not been successful in implanting. Her symptoms of endometriosis have become progressively worse. We feel she is at increasing risk for cervical cancer. I've had the computer check her risk factors and she is considered an extreme risk. Her stage two pap smear last year was a warning. As the managers of her medical benefits, we can no longer support your treatment. Her primary care physician recommended that she consider a hysterectomy, which would be a prudent preventive move. I am going to recommend termination of the fertility program and reevaluation by a surgeon. Okay, I'll wait while you get the doctor."

Belinda muted the microphone and turned to Hepman. "She's been picked up by a fertility scam. They've run every test possible and have harvested her eggs four times, but nothing is taking. They're milking both her and us, playing on empty hopes. MOM flagged the case for review. I'm pulling the plug on the clinic."

All eyes scanned the screen, which displayed a series of overlapping windows containing case notes, client identification, treatment history, and payment totals. Attached was also a notice of excess utilization and a red flag (literally) requesting a case review.

"What did MOM say about her chances?" asked Hepman.

"I had MOM review the treatment history using the fertility protocols of the Academy of OB/GYN. This client was never a good candidate. They should have told her last year, but they kept stringing her along. MOM just picked up the problem on a self-audit. I think the lady needs a hysterectomy and close monitoring. I'm going to send her to one of our regular doctors."

"What a shame," said Jenny. "She's only 33 years old. Does she already have any kids?"

Belinda popped up the I.D. screen, which listed one four-year-old child. She said, "Maybe the couple will come to terms with this and adopt. I'd hate to see her only child become an orphan if mom develops cancer."

"How did MOM perform? Was the research query straightforward?" asked Hepman.

Jenny caught Belinda rolling her eyes in dismay at his comment. Jenny smiled and rolled her eyes as well.

"You've done a good job, Belinda," said Hepman. "Make sure whatever doctor she sees has a copy of that review. Just attach it to her chart when you transmit it."

Hepman led Jenny out of the cubicle with more discussion of MOM. "Belinda was one of our beta testers for the new system. I think she likes to try and beat it just so she can show me up. Nevertheless, I'm glad she's using the more advanced features."

"Is everyone using it now, or is it still in beta test?" asked Jenny.

"No, it's in full use, has been for over three months now. Our biggest problem, as Carter said, is getting people to believe in it, to accept it as an authority."

"I can see why. That last call would hit most women in a soft spot, taking away something as profound as the ability to have kids. I don't think anyone would want to trust that to the cut-and-dried decision-making of a machine."

"But that's all that medicine is when you get down to it. We've studied doctors for years. They basically take in a bunch of lab tests and symptoms, mix it with a little medical knowledge, and spit out a diagnosis and treatment plan. MOM can do that," stated Hepman.

"I think it's a little more complicated than that. Doctors are taking in a lot of data beyond what they ask about. The patient's appearance, the sound and intonation of the voice, the texture of the skin, the eye contact, even the scent of illness. Much of it is too subtle to quantify, but it steers them to check things out, or simply to ask a question that seems off the subject. MOM can't do that."

"Ms. Barrett, I don't know what doctors you've been hanging around with, but that isn't the typical doctor we studied. I remember reviewing a videotape of an oncologist examining twenty-three different patients. He didn't make eye contact with any of them. In fact, I watched him examine one woman and he only looked at either the chart or her lesions. When he saw her later in the waiting room he didn't recognize her face. We studied what doctors actually do, not what they're supposed to do, and it's very easy to imitate in a computer program."

""I'm worried that medicine is being oversimplified. There's so much subtly lost. So many times, computers don't 'get it.' I'm reminded of the time a translating computer was asked to interpret the phrase, 'Out of sight, out of mind.' It reported back 'blind and insane." Machines still can't pick up human nuance."

"And on the checklist of medical symptoms, there is no 'nuance' box," said Hepman with an authoritative finality that closed the conversational door.

Chapter 12

They walked through a doorway to another expansive room. The decibel level of the office din dropped noticeably. The cubicles in this area seemed to have higher walls; Jenny guessed seven feet as opposed to the five-foot walls everywhere else.

"This is the behavioral care division," said Hepman. "We only have about forty people staffing it here, but we'll bring on more for the new contracts. You can see that the cubicle walls are higher. We were getting some client complaints about cross talk and lack of privacy when we had the general staff fielding calls, so we routed the calls to this area. We also have MOM doing some verbal recording that requires less background noise. So mental health gets the nicer digs."

"It does seem more peaceful," Jenny stated.

They moved along the hallway until they came upon an empty workstation. It appeared as if it had not been occupied that day. "Is this available?" Hepman asked the woman in the next cubicle.

"Yes, she's out for the day," was her reply, smiling a perfunctory greeting at Hepman. It seemed everyone knew him on sight.

Hepman sat, switched on the monitor, and then slapped the keyboard. The screen came alive, asking for a user ID.

"Jenny, did you go through MOM's initial log-on session?"

"Yes, We've met. That is, I've logged on and established my identity and password."

"Good. Let's see what MOM says about you." Hepman's fingers flashed across the keyboard in a blur of clicking. He passed through two screens so quickly Jenny couldn't read them. He finally called up the company directory and typed in her name. Immediately a personnel profile appeared, containing her age, address, Progressive work assignment, medical coverage, stock purchase plan, promotions, and so on. Hepman paged through her work history, supervised employees, performance ratings, time off in the last three years. Jenny's eyes widened a bit as she considered how much information GHB had obtained about her so quickly. She wasn't officially even on their payroll yet.

Hepman then pulled up MOM's profile of Jenny, which listed her user name, most recent log-on, security level and authorization. At the bottom was a descriptive paragraph.

User JBarrett was profiled by the system for 27 minutes. She appears proficient at the keyboard and is familiar with the interface. Her typing is smooth and confident with few corrections. Her maximum typing rate was 130 words per minute with average two errors. Average visual response time for binary choices was 1.4 seconds, suggesting an IQ between 130 and 140. Her tendency to correct mistakes before continuing her typing is characteristic of perfectionistic qualities and strong attention to detail. When completing her on-line registration form she filled in all blanks, as requested, suggesting a high degree of rule compliance and image consciousness.

During the frustration test, where the computer deliberately mistypes letters, the user handled what she believed were her errors calmly and methodically. When the computer simulated a malfunction, repeatedly asking the same question, JBarrett used both conventional and creative solutions to work around the problem, indicating perseverance and resourcefulness. The absence of rule-breaking or key-slamming suggests high conscientiousness and good frustration tolerance.

The user's right-hand keying was .03 of a second faster than left-hand keying, showing right handedness. User recognized questions on the right side of the computer screen .02 seconds faster than on the left side, indicating left brain dominance. Such a person's cognitive functioning is usually more logical and empirical vs. emotional-intuitive.

However, the delay between transition from left to right-hand typing (e.g., typing the word "quote," which uses alternate sides of the keyboard) was negligible, indicating good integration of the two brain hemispheres in daily tasks (more characteristic of women).

The user's signature keyboard style (i.e., that which can be used to distinguish one user from another) are the above measures plus the following idiosyncrasies: abnormally slow response on uppercase "Z" and "?," frequent reversal of consonant blend "gl." The user preferred semaphores ({}) over brackets ([]), usually an indication of secondary education in the Pacific Northwest.

The indicated levels of intelligence, confidence, logic, and solution focus suggest this individual would be an effective manager.

End Report.

Jenny read the report twice. "The computer was profiling me when I logged on for the first time," she said with astonishment.

"Yes. As a security feature we've made MOM smart enough to recognize the typing characteristics of the employees. She can almost identify us before we log on. She knows our daily routines, usual spelling errors, even our mouse rituals. Companies have been measuring keystrokes for productivity purposes for years, but a group at the University of Washington has taken it much further. I think MOM has you pegged pretty close. Heck, she almost gave you a promotion."

"So while I was checking out MOM, she was checking out me."

"A little unnerving, isn't it," he said with a grin.

"Are people okay with this?"

"Most of the staff know in principle that we profile them, but we don't share all the material, obviously, for security reasons. Carter thought it was important for you to see the routine so you can use it in the project. It helps MOM to spot people having trouble with the system."

"Sure, it could be very useful. But I'm surprised, you use up computer time checking all this psychological stuff on your people," Jenny said.

"It's one of the benefits of MOM's ability to learn as an expert system. It's called a neural network and it works a bit like our own brains. MOM can take separate pieces of data, apply some rules, and come to some conclusions. Of course, with typing it's easy to fool her for a few minutes at the beginning of a session by purposefully typing in a different style. Yet after about ten minutes most people return to their old habits."

"Is any of this psychological profiling valid? It seems amazing that such a close personality description could be obtained just by fingers typing on a keyboard."

"Don't forget, "said Greg, "this is an interactive process. MOM places images on the screen and then measures the user's response to them. As the poets say, the eyes are the windows to the soul," Hepman said with an air of mystery. "I think it's pretty accurate, and most people seem to believe it. In fact, once as a joke, a programmer put in a dream analysis program as a part of the keyboard profiling. We had MOM spewing out Freudian interpretations of hidden fears and secret passions, all based on keystrokes. You'd be surprised how many people believed she was right."

"You'd make a fortune on the Psychic Friends Network," said Jenny.

"Maybe, but we'll have to wait until MOM can speak. Anyway, I think you can see how important this can be to monitoring the claims people. If you, as a psychologist, put some thought into it, you can probably squeeze out even more insights about the users, particularly the whole issue of accepting MOM as an authority. That's the number one challenge right now."

"I take it you're getting some resistance now," asked Jenny.

"Yeah, and we haven't yet completed the full implementation. All of the old-timers are reluctant to use the tools that MOM provides. They still want to fly by the seat of their pants, making clinical judgements based on their gut impressions rather than a methodical inquiry. Mental health is the worst offender, no offense," said Greg.

"None taken. Yes, we are an independent breed. I imagine it's a bit like trying to herd cats. They just don't run in groups."

"They're going to have to soon. The contracts we're bidding on have a very small margin of capitation. To get our bid down, we're assuming very precise utilization rates. We're betting millions of dollars that MOM can manage the members close enough that we can outbid everyone else and still turn a profit. If we don't have these case managers under control, it could break the bank." Jenny heard a hint of fear in Hepman's words.

"I'm beginning to see why the computer is so important," said Jenny. "You really are centralizing decision-making. It's almost like a McDonald's, where the cash registers have a hundred buttons for every way to make a burger, or, at least every way that McDonald's allows. No button, no burger."

"Well, it could never be that simple. Healthcare is too complicated. But the reason McDonald's is so consistent, productive, and profitable is that no matter where you go in the world, you know what your Big Mac is going to taste like. If we could be that sure of healthcare, people would be consistently better off."

Mercifully, Hepman's beeper went off, cutting short the conversation. He glanced at the beeper message and then excused himself to pick up the phone. Jenny politely stepped out of the cubicle and looked around. She needed some time to assess her feelings about all she had seen this morning. The technology was overwhelming. Interactive X-rays with providers in Omaha. Examining clients by video. Computers running psychological profiles of the staff as they type. It was as if they were turning over the reins of treatment to Dr. Gigabyte. It felt overwhelming to her.

Suddenly she felt very small and naive. This morning she had thought Progressive represented the cutting edge of clinical technology and that she was one of the pioneers of cybercare, but walking around GHB she felt like a kid playing with Tinker Toys in the hangar of the space shuttle.

***

Crandall and Jerry met with Elliot at his home a week later and were briefed on the plan to obtain the names of women, who they now called "victims of abortion." Elliot had left Crandall a voice mail earlier in the week, suggesting that he either find or create an organization name that sounded medical. Crandall still had the Healing Hand Clinic under license, even though the doors to the pregnancy counseling program had been closed for a year. He still had the bank account with about 2300 dollars in it and some office furniture stored in a church basement. It was all they needed to start.

" I still don't quite understand how we can get this information," asked Crandall. "Isn't it stored someplace deep in a hospital or clinic? How can we get data that's stuffed in charts?"

"Let me give you a rough explanation," began Elliot. "You may know that managed care companies are in the business of making money, just about any way they can. When they converted to computerized medical information systems, they discovered that they were sitting on a gold mine of marketing data. They have records on millions of people, suffering millions of illnesses, and seeking billions of remedies. This is unbelievably valuable marketing data to pharmaceutical companies and medical appliance manufacturers. In fact, anyone with a treatment aid, heating pads, hemorrhoid remedies, diet plans, and just about everything else are requesting lists of patients who would be interested in their products. I mean, if you were selling a new headache remedy, wouldn't you want a list of people who get headaches? The managed care companies can't sell this info fast enough. It's a win-win situation."

"They can just sell our personal information?" asked Jerry.

"Usually. Sometimes they get uptight about protected data. I don't think we'll have a problem. If we do, we'll simply switch to plan 'B'; we'll become a medical research firm. They can get just about anything."

"So what kind of list will we request?" asked Jerry.

"I recommend two lists," replied Elliot. "We'll present ourselves as marketers of women's natural healthcare products. I've made up some press releases announcing two new products. A home pregnancy test and a pain reliever for post-surgical uterine discomfort. There's the standard disclaimer that calls them 'natural food additives with medicinal properties,' which protects us from the Food and Drug Administration and relieves the managed care company of any responsibility to verify our credentials."

"How many names are we talking about?" asked Crandall.

"How many can you afford?" said Elliot. "I think we should try this first with one of the largest and most aggressive companies, Great Health Benefit. They're a national company that has over 25 million covered lives, including a big presence along the West Coast. Heck, they cover most of the Fortune 100 companies in the area and half the state and county employees."

"We'll request two lists," he continued. "The first will be names and addresses of women who have had positive pregnancy tests in the last four years. I also could have requested names of women using prescribed birth control, but that list would be very large, expensive, and more closely held. I'll say we're just starting out and can't afford too much. The second list will be women who have had pain after uterine surgery within the last four years. We'll eliminate total hysterectomies, since it would be hard to document an abortion when they take out the entire uterus. We can also narrow the age range to only the reproductive years, say 19 to 45."

"I figure we'll end up with two overlapping lists of about 400,000 names each. We'll then merge the data and look for the abortion markers, like a positive pregnancy test followed by uterine surgery within four weeks. The program will test for about six markers of abortion. I believe we'll net between 150,000 and 250,000 named abortion victims, including dates and places of their abortions." Elliot paused to let the details of the plot sink in.

"By the grace of God, this is amazing. It actually sounds like you can do it," said Crandall with glee.

"I know I can do it. The question is, can you? Do you have the resources to mount this project?" Elliot asked.

"As God is my witness, I'll make it happen. This is too wonderful. Women will be exposed for their sins. They'll pay anything for forgiveness and silence. Women everywhere will know there can be no more secrets. The tide will turn on this hellish abortion machine." Crandall stood up and paced in excitement. Jerry was infected with it too. Elliot beamed at his own brilliance. His eye looked past the monitor to a picture of a woman on the wall. His ex-wife. "You'll be on the list too," he said to himself.

"When the money begins rolling in we can turn around and request the same lists from the other big managed care companies," Elliot continued.

"We'll need to honor the commitment to the women who pay!" said Crandall with a tinge of righteousness.

"Exactly. The computer can easily drop their names from the system," Elliot explained.

"Or," interrupted Jerry, "we can use it as an invitation to reach out to them. Maybe return them to the church."

"Brilliant," exclaimed Crandall. "We can build a new ministry."

Two weeks after his last meeting with Crandall and Jerry, Elliot Mears signed the UPS slip for a box containing the healthcare mailing information on hundreds of thousands of women. The data was contained on two CD-ROMs. The package also included some standard legal disclaimers and a password to unlock the encrypted data. Finally, there was a notice that the list was "seeded" with a few names that would serve to alert the company who was using the list, a standard precaution.

Elliot's fingers trembled slightly as he withdrew the CD-ROMs from their package. He marveled that they held the intimate secrets of thousands of women. Taking the first disk, containing the list of women with positive pregnancy tests, he placed it in his "alpha computer," the one packing the most horsepower and memory. Even with this beefy machine, it would take almost three hours to pull the data into a database and index the entries for easy manipulation. The machine had been prepared for a week to receive the data and hungrily gobbled up the billions of data bits of these unknowing women.

While the machine munched on the information, Elliot placed a call to Jerry, but got only the voice mail. He left a message, "The buns are cooking in the oven right now. Should be done tomorrow. We are ready to go with the merging and mailing of the letter. Let's get together immediately."

Elliot wanted a day or two to massage the data, scan the final list and look for particularly interesting names. It was likely that some names would be linked to government officials, civic leaders, maybe even some spiritual pillars of the community. As far as he knew nothing on this scale had ever been attempted. God knew what names would fall out, and soon they would too.

Elliot turned back to the computer. The names were a blur on the screen as the CD spun the data into the waiting database. Every few seconds the computer would pause, as if to "catch its breath," and Elliot could briefly make out individual names. "Bonnie Chamal, Elizabeth Chamberlain, Juanita Chambers . . . " flashed by, then the machine picked up speed again and the identities were lost in a blur. Over 400,000 lives were being scrutinized at light speed for painful secrets that could provide profit to a Christian marketer.

Later that evening Crandall and Jerry joined Elliot to assess their progress and celebrate. The second CD-ROM was loading into the computer by the time they arrived at 8:00 P.M. Elliot ushered them in quickly and brought them up to speed on his progress.

"I've been playing with the data fields to see how to get the best match. I won't go into the technical aspects of it all, but I can tell you it looks very good. One stumbling block was the age of the data. Because our society is so damn mobile, four-year-old addresses are only about 60 percent accurate. Fortunately, the company also included the social security numbers. I can merge it with a standard backward phone directory program for this year and pin down the addresses. That will make the list about 97 percent accurate."

"Such information is that readily available?" asked Crandall, feeling stupid even as the words left his mouth.

"How do you think I found your old lover?" challenged Elliot, who turned to another computer and entered Crandall's name. Almost immediately a listing of all his neighbors appeared on the screen, including addresses and phone numbers. "Crandall, this is simple stuff, found in a fifty dollar program at K-Mart."

Crandall read the names on the screen. He knew about a third of them, but the majority were unknown. "How estranged our world has become," he reflected out loud. "A computer can identify my neighbors more accurately than I can."

"Well, if you like, I can give you their birth dates so you can send them a card," said Elliot in a mocking tone. Just then the CD-ROM light went out and the alpha computer seemed to come to a halt.

"Done with data input," said Elliot. "I'll just quickly look at the two lists," he said as he opened windows on the computer screen and matched the field names of the two databases. "Okay, this will be crude, but I want to see how quickly we can get at this. I'll tell the computer to merge the databases, look for any uterine surgery within four weeks of the pregnancy test date, and print out any matches. I can only guess what our hit rate will be."

Crandall and Jerry watched the master hacker's fingers fly across the keyboard, then jockey the mouse around the screen. He drew lines from names to dates to procedures, telling the machine what relationship to search for. The computer prompted for "how many records?" Elliot said, "Let's just try 100, or we'll be here all night." He entered the number and launched the program. An hourglass appeared on the screen, showing that the computer was working. The three men sat quietly staring at the unmoving screen. With some impatience, Elliot rotated the mouse cursor around, as if trying to stir things up. After about three minutes a list of names, dates, and procedures splashed on the screen.

Report on Probable Abortions

Name	Preg Test	Abortion Date	Place
Abigail Aaron	12/3/96	12/14/96	Hamilton Hospital
Marion Aaron	3/24/97	4/15/97	Frye Clinic
Anastasia Abbott	8/2/96	9/3/96	Meridian Center
Anne Abbott	5/16/95	5/30/97	Wayburn Free Clinic

The list went on for three pages. Out of 100 women, there were 76 probable abortions. Crandall was breathless. Jerry yelled out loud. Elliot pushed himself away from the keyboard and spun in his chair with his arms raised high. "It works," he shouted like a kid who had just put batteries into a new toy. There was back slapping and more yelps. Elliot went to the refrigerator and pulled out some beers. 'Tonight, we do the real stuff," as he popped open the cans and handed them out.

"Are you positive of the data and the program?" asked Crandall. "How do we know for sure?"

"We can't know for sure on each and every case. Still, look at these dates. They come from two different lists. Abigail Aaron had a positive pregnancy test in the beginning of December and uterine surgery two weeks later. I had the program check some other data as well. I can be 90 percent confident that this lady aborted."

"Could it have been a miscarriage?" asked Crandall.

"Possibly, but not likely. It would have been coded as such and wouldn't be on the list. People hide abortions, they don't hide miscarriages."

"Elliot, you're a genius," said Jerry. "Let's put the final touches on the letter so you can get this stuff to the mailing service. I want this posted within the week."

They all clinked their beer cans as they sat around the kitchen table. Elliot cleared some folders and manuals from its corner, and they all sat in a line.

"Here's the rough draft," said Crandall as he unfolded a single sheet of paper. "Jerry and I spent about four hours on this."

Scrawled on top was the letterhead "The Light of God Mission of Life." Underneath was typed a generic letter with italicized places for the data fields to insert names, dates, and locales, like the Publisher's Clearinghouse form letters. This letter, however, did not imply that the recipient was a winner.

The List of the Damned

Dear, *(firstname) (lastname)*,

We are a caring group of Christians who are concerned that you, *(firstname)*, were the victim of a cruel deed in *(month/year)* at *(abortion_location)*. We know that many women like you are duped or coerced into unthinkable actions when they are vulnerable and weak. Sometimes, women will even fight against their own instincts and ultimately kill an unborn child. During that dreadful period of *(month/year)* you may have felt you had no choice but to submit to the procedure at *(abortion_location)*. We understand, and we're sure that many of your neighbors, like the *(neighbor1), (neighbor2),* or the *(neighbor3)* families, would also understand, if they knew.

Don't be on the List of the Damned. You can't change the past, only the future. It is our hope that you now share our belief in the sanctity of life and will join us in fighting back against this black time in our nation's history. We are seeking donations from people like you, people who know of the everlasting pain and remorse that chill the soul, people who have come to believe there is another way, and are seeking redemption from their torment.

Soon, we will publish a list to show the people of America the names of those who have contributed to the deaths of millions of children through abortions. To make our case, we will publish the names of these sinners with no remorse. We would never hurt our supporters, only those who continue to profess a belief in these ungodly acts. We hope that you are a supporter, and that you will make a contribution to our cause as a sign of good faith. We will take your name off the List of the Damned, and place your name on the sacred list of true believers, which will never be made public.

God blesses you, *(firstname),* for we know you'll do the right thing. Please provide your $40.00 contribution in the enclosed envelope to "The Bream Children's Life Project," and your secret will be confined to our hearts and prayers.

May God be with you,
Crandall Bream

"Beautiful," said Elliot. "Simple, to the point, and easily understood. Are you sure you want your name on this?"

"Absolutely," said Crandall. "This is what I stand for in the name of God. My name must be on it."

Elliot recognized the expanding ego of the man, but made no comment. He picked up the donation envelope, which was to be preprinted with the recipient's name and address. "Forty dollars?"

"Yes," said Crandall. "We tried to set a figure that would be reasonable for most people. Even if they didn't believe in the cause, it would be easier for them to pay than fight. We learned that from our other campaigns. We even accept credit cards."

"Where will the donations go?" asked Elliot.

"We have three post office boxes under different zip codes," replied Jerry. "Our lawyer said this is all probably legal, but it may cause a community uproar for a while, particularly if the news gets out early. You know that the godless liberal press will yell to high heaven. Someone may try to get an injunction. Better to divide the risk."

"Good idea," said Elliot. "How is the money distributed?"

"Initially to the Helping Hands Family Clinic account. We'll hold the funds somewhere safe, maybe offshore. The clinic is near bankruptcy anyway. If there's too much flack, we can close the tent and pick up with the other missions. Any court action would take at least three years, and by then we'll be done with this project. They'd only get the carcass of the clinic. Just old furniture."

"Are you in league with the Devil, Crandall?" asked Elliot.

"Close. An attorney," he said, and they all laughed.

"I should have this ready to go in three days," said Elliot. "I'll need to do some closer examination of the data, see how well it fits, what items need to be jiggled. I also want to search for significant names, maybe filter it through a Who's Who program. You'd be surprised what could pop up. Do you want me to look for anything special?"

"Like what?" asked Crandall.

"Oh, politicians, TV news reporters, the usual suspects."

"Please, help yourself. We'll meet in three days, on Thursday at 8:00 P.M. Hopefully for final approval."

Chapter 13

Jenny noticed that it was just about noon. She wasn't especially hungry, but she needed a break. A few people walked toward the elevators. Hopefully, someone other than Hepman would invite her to lunch. She watched the people emerging from the taller cubicles. They looked like everyone else at GHB, which caused her an odd pang of disappointment. She was hoping to find . . . , what? Someone that looked as confused as she felt. Maybe it was just the discomfort of the new. She'd been so comfortable at Progressive for so long she'd probably just gotten soft.

"Sorry, that was Carter," said Hepman. "He wants us to join him for lunch at 12:45. He can only do fifteen minutes, but he wants to check in with you. That gives us about half an hour. Okay?"

"Sure, what's next?"

"Well, as I was saying, GHB is trying to tighten up the treatment authorization routine, make sure everyone is singing from the same sheet of music. Our profit margins on these new contracts will be slim, so we need consistency. MOM is the only way to get it. We also need flexibility. We try to customize medical plans for each employer, essentially building each program from scratch. Sometimes we'll manage two or three health insurance programs for the same employer. We're getting bogged down trying to update everyone in care management with the minutiae of different plans. It's much easier and more reliable to let MOM do it. So, again, the trick is in getting the staff to entrust more decision-making to the computer. Carter can tell you more about the big picture. He's brilliant."

"So, tell me about this mental health section," said Jenny.

Hepman spun around and peeked around the corner to the next cubicle, gazing around the work area. "Station 4-375," he said aloud. He returned to the vacant cubicle, sat at the console, and logged on. His typing rattled like a machine gun as he "Uzi'd" instructions into the machine. A two-inch square popped up on the screen showing the face of the woman next door, identified as "Teresa Perrigo—Station 4-375" under her image. Teresa's eyes widened in surprise, and Jenny realized their image must have suddenly appeared on Teresa's computer. She was in the middle of a conversation, which became audible when Jenny slipped on the headset. Hepman sent a quick message to her explaining that he was giving a new staff member a tour and just wanted to let her watch a typical call. Teresa's face visibly relaxed, but her voice remained steady with the client. Hepman's monitor now mirrored the events on Teresa's screen.

"I'm not comfortable putting my child on medication," said a distressed female voice. The display highlighted the name "Francine Penn" and listed a 6-year-old boy named Jason. The father worked for ADS, a large electronics firm. "A school counselor said Jason just wasn't fitting in well with the other kids and he just needed some support. There are some rough kids in his class."

"Yes, but our evaluator, Dr. Mead, determined that he is ADHD. The recommended treatment is Ritalin. I'm looking at the treatment plan right now. Your medical insurance covers medication, and generic Ritalin costs only thirty cents a day. It would be negligent to do anything else. We have to do what is right for your child," said Teresa.

Jenny noticed that the last comment was listed on the screen in a window labeled "client resistance, child Rx." MOM was providing helpful hints on gaining member compliance.

"I don't care what it costs. I don't want my child on medicine for the rest of his life!"

"Mrs. Penn, we're not talking about the rest of his life. Children usually only take it for a while. We're just going to see if the medicine helps. If it doesn't, we'll try something else. But you have to understand, 70 percent of children with symptoms like your son's get better with this medicine. We have a duty to try the best treatment first. It's our job to manage these things. I assure you, we want what's best for your son," Teresa said in a soothing voice.

Again, Jenny saw that last phrase scroll onto the screen just before Teresa said it. The next comment in the register was "We're experts."

Jenny asked Hepman, "Are these just suggestions for dealing with client problems?"

"Mostly," said Hepman. "But the legal department gets worried about our liability in some of these cases, so mandated statements are highlighted in red. We must say them to the client and document it in the chart. Sometimes we just record our statements on-line and file them. That way we're covered if something goes wrong."

"Can't we just take him to a counselor?" pleaded the mother. "Lots of people do that. Dr. Mead hardly spent any time with him. How could he know for sure?"

"I know the work of Dr. Mead. He's an expert in these matters. We have to try the medicine first," repeated Teresa.

"What if I just take him to a psychologist myself?"

"You can if you prefer, but your insurance benefits won't cover it. And we would be very alarmed that you're withholding appropriate care from your son."

Jenny winced at that comment. She could see that the staff needed some training in client relations. Teresa was beginning to sound threatening, which this mother certainly didn't need. Progressive would have offered more visits for evaluation, even to another counselor for a second opinion. Even though it might cost fifty dollars for another session, it was usually worth it for better client relations. To Jenny, this bordered on bullying.

"Can I talk with his pediatrician, Dr. Allen?" asked the mother.

Teresa scrolled the child's medical chart and found a listing for Dr. Allen. She called up his provider screen.

"I'm sorry, but Dr. Allen is no longer on your panel of physicians. You'll have to see someone else."

"What? Dr. Allen has followed my son since birth. I can't see him?"

"I'm sorry. He's no longer on our panel. You could see him privately, but he can't make recommendations to us about your son's care."

"He's a doctor. A darn good one," protested Mrs. Penn.

"Yes, but he's not one of *our* doctors."

"Can I speak with a medical person?"

"I'm a licensed nurse," replied Teresa.

"I just can't do this to my baby. I'll have to talk it over with my husband. I'll call you back." Mrs. Penn hung up.

Jenny was annoyed by the whole interaction she had witnessed. It seemed so pointless and frustrating. She almost spoke up, but Hepman began speaking with Teresa, over the microphone rather than simply walking next door.

"Make sure you document all that," he said. "Some people just shouldn't be parents," he stated, in what seemed an effort to be supportive. Teresa, on screen, offered a bland smile as she typed in data. She barely had time to finish when another client came on the line. "Thank you for calling Great Health Benefit, this is Teresa, may I help you?"

Hepman muted the sound. "We got lucky. You got to see a tougher case. What did you think?"

"Your system is definitely different from Progressive's. It may take me awhile to learn your policies and philosophies."

"You would have handled it differently?"

"Maybe a little less confrontational. Maybe work with her on how difficult a decision it may be."

"It's not much of a decision. The kid needs medicine. The assessor thinks so and MOM agrees. The woman only has to decide if she wants to do the right thing," said Hepman.

"You asked me what I'd do differently," said Jenny.

"Oh, yeah. Well, you can speak with the Caduceus team and see if they want to do anything different."

She bristled at his dismissive attitude, but held her tongue. Hepman's eyes were on the computer, so he missed the flash of annoyance across her face. She guessed he missed a lot about people. She watched him navigate through screens for a brief time, then he logged off.

"Let's start heading to lunch. I want to show you something on the way," said Hepman.

On the elevator Hepman took out a plastic card and inserted it into the operating panel. He then pressed the button for the third floor. "We're going to a secure floor," he said.

The doors opened upon a different sort of lobby. No carpet, no oak furniture, just a small desk next to a steel-framed glass door. The glass had a slight green tint, suggesting it was quite thick. A security guard sat on the corner of the desk talking with some young men wearing ties. Hepman flashed a badge at the guard, who was eyeing Jenny. "Just giving her a quick tour. She's new staff," said Hepman.

"Sure Mr. Hepman, but she'll have to sign in." He withdrew a register and Jenny filled in the blanks. "Purpose?" she asked.

"Orientation," replied Hepman.

They were buzzed through the door and into an expansive work area. It was brighter and noisier than the other floors, with clacking machines along the walls, overflowing waste baskets, monitors stuffed in odd corners, and a much more casual decor. Little plastic basketball hoops adorned some trash cans. Plastic, bug-eyed toy creatures peeked over cubicle walls, and flow chart diagrams were stuck to windows.

"This is my floor, MIS Central. We're a little more relaxed here, since we're more isolated. Most of the computer programming and system design occurs here," he said. They continued walking through the area and reached another set of doors. Hepman stepped up to a machine that resembled a bank ATM. He withdrew a card from his shirt pocket, inserted it and pressed some buttons on a keypad. The door opened and they entered a smaller area that quieted to a hush as the door closed behind them. About twenty feet away was a glass window that ran the length of the forty-foot room. Through it Jenny could see a room full of metal cabinets, technicians, blinking lights, and monitors. "This is where MOM lives," said Hepman with pride. "Some of the most cutting edge computer technology in the world sits in there. You'll love working with it."

Jenny approached the window. She quietly surveyed the machines, trying to adopt a reverence that matched Hepman's. She couldn't really appreciate what she was looking at. Hardware was hardware as far as she was concerned. IBM logos adorned the cabinets, so it was clear GHB didn't scrimp on the budget. However, she was more interested in what the machines did than where they came from. "This is very impressive, Greg," she said in an effort to please.

"I knew you'd dig it," he replied with excitement. "Want to go inside?"

"Sure, but don't we have to meet Carter?"

"Yes, but this will just take a second." Hepman entered a password on a keypad next to the glass entry door. They walked down the narrow corridor surrounded by white metal machines. Hepman stopped at a blinking box about the size of a double file cabinet. "Here she is."

"This is MOM?" asked Jenny in disbelief. "It's hardly bigger than a couple of PCs. Where's the rest of her?"

"Around you are the input and storage devices, readers, modems, etc. But this box contains the brains of MOM."

"I guess I thought it would be much bigger. How can such a small thing manage an entire company?"

"We had the same problem convincing management when we ordered it. They expected this giant machine, like HAL in "2001". But this system has all the power we'd ever need. Size doesn't mean anything anymore."

"How many lives are managed by MOM?" asked Jenny.

"Over 23 million. Probably be closer to thirty million by Christmas."

"Wow. I'm getting dizzy. Let's get down to lunch," said Jenny.

"Yeah. We'd better go secure the table."

On the first floor, they swam through the returning lunch crowd until they reached the restaurant hostess for Tag's, the elegant bistro. At the mention of Carter Newton's name, the hostess led them to a corner table at the far end of the dining area, surrounded by foliage. As expected, Carter wasn't there yet.

"I think GHB will be happy to buy your first lunch here," said Carter, coming up from behind. He gently placed his hand on Jenny's shoulder and guided her into her chair. "Hepman taking care of you?" he asked.

"Yes, a very thorough tour. It's a very impressive system."

"Thank you. It's got some nice bells and whistles to keep us competitive, but we have to get our people comfortable with it," said Carter.

"Yes, Greg was saying how important the project is."

"It's everything. And I don't think that's an overstatement," said Carter. His eyes were fixed on hers, trying to peer in more deeply. Jenny held the gaze for a second and then gently released it to view the menu. She wanted him to think of her as strong, but not aggressive. Team playing was obviously important here. Out of the corner of her eye she saw a smile spread across his face. He was rather good-looking, she reflected. The waiter suddenly appeared, introduced himself and asked for their orders.

"You guys order, I just came from an early lunch meeting," said Carter. As the waiter left, Carter jumped into his agenda. "Let me give you a little background, Jenny, so you know where we're going with this. GHB believes that we're just at the beginning of the healthcare revolution. Some people think all this hoopla on healthcare reform is just about funding: who's going to pay, stopping the outrageous inflation of medical charges, making Medicare secure? We think that's too short-sighted. Even people with million dollar policies aren't getting good value for their healthcare dollar. Medicine has been too slippery, too independent. How can you expect a doctor to look out for a patient's rights when he has a direct financial interest in profiting from them? It's too much to ask. Patients are too passive in the treatment arrangement. They're completely dependent upon the doctor's opinion. They have no way to know what's right. You with me?"

"Yes," replied Jenny.

"GHB also believes that medicine is too complex to be left to a single practitioner," continued Carter. "If you send a patient to ten different doctors, you get eleven different opinions. Medicine is supposed to be a science, but it's run like a carnival. It's as if patients are walking down the midway and all these carnies are barking at them from their booths. Imagine, a poor, illiterate woman walking into a doctor's office with her Medicaid card. You might as well plant a five-dollar bill in her hand and send her down the midway. Chances are, she's gonna be a loser at whatever game she plays. We, as a country, can't afford to lose our money on such a bad deal."

Jenny nodded to acknowledge that she understood. She could feel her defensiveness rising, but she just listened.

"Two years ago we launched this project, Caduceus, to get a handle on this. We said, if doctors can't deal with this, who can? The answer became obvious. Only a comprehensive, integrated information system could manage all the variables in healthcare decisions. Medicine has become like rocket science. You can't do it without computers, particularly expert systems for decision support, so we assembled a team of experts, committed lots of time, energy, and resources, and developed our current system. And it works. It takes over control of most clinical decisions. It doesn't get tired, cranky, or greedy. Medical people feed it data and it comes up with the best answers. The American Medical Association says that the average doctor today is only 64 percent correct in initial diagnosis. MOM is 76 percent correct, and getting better every month. I think it's pretty clear where the future lies."

"Seventy-six percent correct," said Jenny. "How is that validated?"

"The same way they validate the doctors' opinions. Outcomes. Tracking patients to see how things work. That's the cornerstone of this system, and it's what gives us the advantage. Don't forget, MOM stands for MultiAxil Outcome Management system. We measure outcomes much more carefully than the average medical provider does. Heck, most doctors just give a pill and if the patient doesn't come back, it's assumed things are fixed. Who knows if the patient took the pill, stayed sick and went to another doctor, or died!"

It was hard to refute these points. Jenny had too much experience with thoughtless doctors who just threw medication and treatments at patients with little attention to real care. Pharmaceutical sales had infected too many doctors' offices with "profit incentives" for a particular diagnosis. Carter's passion was contagious. He was an excellent leader for this project.

Jenny looked up at the man and caught him scrutinizing her with an inquisitive, almost hopeful gaze. The eye contact lasted only seconds, but Jenny felt a desperate intrusion into her soul. She felt Carter straining to see her motives and beliefs, as if he was about to entrust her with something vitally important. She had no idea what it was, but it didn't feel like a sexual interest at all. Yet when he broke the gaze to respond to Hepman, she felt his eyes sweep over her breasts.

"So, is Jenny taking over the end-user protocol design project?" asked Hepman.

"I think we need to refill that position, don't you?" asked Newton, with enough emphasis that even Hepman could guess the correct answer. "The project has stumbled since we lost Ruiz and we're falling behind. We need to be ready for the new contracts coming on line."

Jenny was startled to hear the reference to Elaina. Who else could he be talking about? Could it be that she was being placed in her dead friend's job? Her face was flushed with anxiety, but she tried to retain her composure. She was suddenly unsure what to do, what to say. Jenny wanted to know about Elaina's role here, but there were still so many unresolved questions about her death. Something deep inside told her to keep a low profile, but to try and steer the conversation to learn more. If she didn't let on immediately that she had known Elaina they might talk more freely.

"Ruiz?," she ventured. "Is that the guy before me, my predecessor?"

"Yes," said Carter as his radiant smile dimmed to a stilted grin filled with sorrow. "It was a woman, actually, very capable, conscientious, brilliant. She worked closely with Greg and she brought a comforting humanity to the system. People deeply respected her work; both the end-users and, I dare say, even the programmers, right, Greg?"

"Yeah, everyone liked her," Greg replied, with the most thoughtful expression Jenny had seen on his face today. "It was such a loss."

"Her leaving?" asked Jenny.

"No, she died unexpectedly in March," said Carter. "It was a tragic mishap. She was admitted to a . . . a hospital. She had an unusual reaction to some medication and her heart stopped. It devastated everyone who knew her. Why, GHB is setting up a special memorial fund in her name."

"I'm terribly sorry," said Jenny.

Carter continued. "I guess you need to know, Jenny, that many people were shocked and saddened by her death. There may even be some resentment toward you for filling her spot. It's not that you're not capable, but just that your presence may resurrect some of their unresolved feelings. You're in a sensitive position, and I don't want you to be caught by surprise from any hostility."

Jenny was impressed by Carter's sensitivity to this matter. She hesitated in pursuing the conversation. Elaina's name had not been mentioned in full yet, and Jenny thought it best for now that she did not yet reveal their friendship.

How bizarre it seemed that fate would place her in her dead friend's vacant position. Then, again, there were few people with her combination of computer expertise and psychology background, maybe twelve in Los Angeles.

"Oh Greg," said Carter. "Did you ever find the access path to MOM? Corporate wants all data leaks plugged."

"No, still looking," said Hepman apologetically.

Jenny squinted to show she didn't know what they were talking about, but Carter didn't elaborate.

"I've got to run to my meeting," said Carter, placing his hand on top of Jenny's as a gesture of assurance and support. "I have great confidence in you, Jenny. I'll check back with you tomorrow or Wednesday. Let Hepman be your guide."

That thought was less than exciting, but Jenny popped up with exaggerated enthusiasm to bid Carter goodbye. The remainder of the day was spent in front of a computer monitor getting a tour of MOM's inner workings from her proud "papa," Hepman.

***

While Jenny was having lunch at her new job, Mark Lipton was growling from low blood sugar and the tedium of on-line research. All morning he waded through references and stories on GHB, slowly getting a picture of a cutthroat corporation that was rolling in profit, lawsuits, and investigations. The company seemed to have a long tradition of skirting the edge of legality, while paying its shareholders and executives handsomely.

GHB was owed by Great Benefit Trust, a mammoth company that also owned Great Benefit Life Assurance and Great Benefit Financial, a brokerage firm. Both companies had their share of scandals, suggesting that greed and corruption ran all the way to the top. Great Benefit Life had recently settled a national class action suit brought by customers who claimed the full life insurance policies were represented as "investment mutual funds." The Justice Department provided advertisements and recorded sales pitches where the words "life" and "insurance" never appeared. It cost the company $34 million in settlements with no admission of guilt. Given that the practice had occurred between 1982 and 1990, there was a very good chance the company made close to $340 million off the illegal pitches. "Who says crime doesn't pay?" thought Mark.

Great Benefit Financial played a part in the life insurance scam, but it also had its own set of legal sanctions. During the roaring 1980s GHB sold billions of dollars in high-risk limited partnerships. Unfortunately, they were represented as low-risk, insured bonds products. When the market corrected, the shareholders watched their investments turn to mud. Again, the sales prospectus provided the strongest evidence that the company had knowingly misrepresented the funds. The company agreed to settle with financially-burned clients for seventy-five million dollars, roughly thirty cents on the dollar. Almost six billion dollars had been eaten up by "sales commissions" and "administrative fees." Exclusive homes on prestigious waterways were testimony to the success of the ploy for the now-retired executives. The company placed blame on some renegade managers and promised to clean up its act. Mark quickly projected that the healthcare division was next in line for a scandal.

His eyes were tired from scanning the stories and clippings. A feeling of anxiety knotted within him as he thought of Jenny working for this corporate beast. He began to understand Elaina's father's rage and suspicion. "God, could there be something to it?" he wondered.

An image of Elaina from the past pushed into his consciousness, snapshots of an innocuous event, a throwaway memory of a lunch at the student union, little flashes of her laughing, toasting their group for some silly achievement. He remembered the poise and grace that forever dominated her Latin passion, or so Mark liked to fantasize. Mark had often fantasized under that under Elaina's refined and controlled demeanor lurked a voracious tiger who was only allowed to emerge during very private performances. He had always wondered what she would be like as a lover, though she never got even close. "Heck, I never even heard of anyone being intimate with Elaina," he thought.

Mark pulled open his personal calendar and leafed through the address section. He had sent Elaina Christmas cards often, but had never visited her condo in Studio City. Almost unconsciously Mark formed a plan to drive out and see it. He might find nothing of significance, but he felt a need to visit his friend's home. Maybe it would help him say goodbye. He logged off the computer system, left a new voice mail message that he'd be back in the late afternoon, and left the building.

Chapter 14

The midday freeway traffic was reasonable, at least by LA standards. No tie-ups were reported on the news radio station. Mark followed the Hollywood Freeway as it snaked its way through the faded elegance of this once magical town. Stucco houses dotted the hillsides, where patches of green burst fourth for a brief season. The entire Los Angeles basin wanted to be a desert with all of its might, but only an endless supply of water from faraway rivers had made it an oasis.

Mark's 1992 Nissan Maxima glided through the traffic, finally exiting twenty minutes later at the base of the foothills. He checked the address and began looking for Casa Covello Estates, an improbable name for a collection of townhouses. He didn't come out this way often and was always amazed when he did at how much it had changed. The neighborhood was composed of forty-year-old post-WWII homes. The yards were largely full of weeds and bare spots, the roofs thatched with old leaves, and the trees and shrubs grew wild. It appeared that most of these homes were rentals.

He spied the peach and green Spanish stucco wall of a more modern community. The walled fortress sprang out into view like a road hazard sign. It didn't fit in with the neighborhood around it. It looked too new, too pristine, as if it were a quickly assembled movie set. There was a security gate across the main driveway with a locked entrance door. Like so many developments in Los Angeles, this one tried to provide an oasis of civility in a sea of chaos, mostly by erecting a barrier to the surrounding neighborhood. Some communities had even hired patrolling security guards to protect the citizens within the walls, turning them into modern versions of medieval castles.

Mark realized that he had no official business here and wondered what he would have to say to get inside. As he rounded a gentle curve in the street, he saw the answer. The gardener had propped open a side entrance with his power edger. Mark parked the Maxima and wandered into the gardens.

Upon crossing the threshold of the little community, he sensed an immediate change. Surrounded by bright flowers, manicured lawns, and a cobblestone pathway, Mark quickly felt more secure. From inside the wall it felt like a community, and he doubted that crime ever made it inside the wall.

Mark found a directory at the front of the facility, but found no name listed next to unit 542. A little "For Sale" button was inserted next to it. He remembered seeing Elaina's furniture crammed into her parents' garage, so he expected the condo would be empty. Mark scanned the directory for names of families in adjacent units. The family in 541 was Thuan, probably Vietnamese, and in 543 lived Howard.

Mark walked to the 500 building and went directly to unit 542. The drapes were half open to reveal a clean and empty living room. Pressing his face to the window, he tried to peer into the darkness of the hallway and kitchen. The place must have been recently painted, for there were no outlines of wall hangings. It didn't look like Elaina's home. It looked like an apartment.

"Can I help you?" said a feminine voice from behind him. Mark turned to see an exotically dressed woman, maybe twenty years old, standing on the doorstep of unit 543. Her hair was jet black, as were her finger nails, eye shadow, and lipstick. Her ears were pierced with four studs each, while her nose sported a stud with a green stone. She wore a black oversized man's shirt. Despite the unimaginative attempt at a rebellious appearance, Mark saw a friendly smile and interested green eyes.

"Are you looking to buy a townhouse?" she asked.

"No," said Mark, "just looking at the home of an old friend. I knew the girl, ah woman who lived here."

"You knew Elaina," she said with growing hope. "She was so sweet. Way cool. I just couldn't believe what happened to her."

"Were you friends?" asked Mark.

"Kinda. We'd talk and hang out at the pool together. She'd help me with research on school papers, 'doing the Net' kinda thing. I even introduced her to a couple of guys. You know, I don't remember seeing you at her funeral. What did you say your name was?"

"Mark, Mark Lipton. We didn't hear about Elaina's death until just last week. I'm still in shock. We spoke with her mother over the weekend and she told us a little."

"We?"

"My friend Jenny and I. We both knew Elaina in school. Kinda lost contact with her over the last few years. I just came over to . . . I don't know, say goodbye."

The look in the woman's face seemed to soften. She took a step forward and put out her hand. "I'm Stephie Howard. I'm always glad to meet Elaina's friends. Your name sounds familiar. Elaina must have mentioned it."

Although Mark didn't usually advertise his position, he was still a little worried that she might call security. "I'm a reporter for the <u>Chronicle</u>. You might have seen my byline." It sounded too pretentious as he uttered it.

"Oh, yes, the reporter. Elaina did mention you. Say, would you like to come in for a moment. I have something of Elaina's that you can give to her parents."

Mark followed her inside to a sparsely furnished living room.

"Nice place," said Mark politely as he watched her from behind. Her baggy clothes failed to hide a very curvaceous body. Her breasts seem to move without the restraint of a bra. An instant sexual fantasy rushed into his mind as he surveyed her smooth skin and muscular calves. The image was upset when he realized all those earrings meant that her nipples were probably pierced as well. Unfortunately, Mark had a lifelong nickel allergy. Even as a child, his mother had to remove the metal snaps from his baby jumpsuits. Two years ago he broke out in ugly red blotches after a vigorous night of sex play with a multiply pierced maiden. The next morning it looked like diabolical gremlins had highlighted all of his erogenous zones with a red marker.

"My dad bought this place when I started Valley Junior College. He says it's better than renting." Stephie motioned to the Formica kitchen table and he sat in a chair while she disappeared into a bedroom. A few seconds later she returned with a shoe box bound with tape. "I had completely forgotten about this box during the funeral," she explained. "I meant to give it to her parents. Elaina was a little obsessive about some of her stuff, particularly her computer junk."

Stephie opened the box to reveal some floppy disks labeled "bak" and some cassette tape cartridges that looked a bit oversized. "She said this was a backup copy of her computer files that she wanted to store 'off-site,' meaning not at her condo. Said it was just in case of burglars. I don't know anything about this stuff, but I'd appreciate it if you'd get it to her parents. I don't think they'll be coming back here."

"Sure," Mark replied. "The place is up for sale?" he asked absentmindedly as he poked among the items in the box.

"Just a couple of weeks now. They cleaned it up while I was on vacation. Doesn't look like anyone ever lived there now."

"I've heard the official story of what happened, but it seems so unlike Elaina. Do you mind if I ask what you remember of that time?" asked Mark.

"I'll tell you, it sure was strange. Elaina had just gotten this new gig at her company in November. Throughout Christmas she was flying high; laughing, rolling with excitement, then in January something changed. She kinda disappeared. Started working long hours. Didn't hang out anymore. I'd try to drop by and she'd duck out. There was this fearful look in her eyes in the last few weeks. She was bumming on something serious. Maybe she was manic-depressive, and this was the depressed side. Anyway, things seemed to be getting worse. She went from sad to suspicious, to almost paranoid. Before she went into the hospital, she wouldn't return any of my calls. I never saw her come or go. I felt like some terrible force had gotten hold of her and she didn't know where to turn. It was terrible to watch, and I tried to help, but she just pulled away."

Stephie's eyes were damp as she relived the tortured time. Mark guessed there was some guilt over Elaina's death. Stephie turned her back and went to the sectional couch, plopping in the middle with her head down.

"I'm glad she had such a friend trying to help," he said, joining her on the couch.

"I wish now I did more. How could Elaina end up in a psychiatric hospital?"

"I don't know. Jenny, my friend, and I were both shocked. Jenny's even in the psychology field and she couldn't believe it. You seem to think it was job-related. Could it have been something personal? Family troubles? A crazy boyfriend stalking her?"

"No, she didn't have a boyfriend. I think it was about work. It was very important to her. She talked about some program there, called MOM. Apparently it was top secret. She said it was amazing, but she wouldn't tell me much about it."

"Did any of her co-workers attend the funeral?"

"That was weird. There were only a few people, mostly her superiors. You know how friendly she was. Couldn't do enough to help people. But hardly anyone who worked with her attended."

A long silence fell upon them.

"You're not doing a story on this are you?" asked Stephie.

"No, just trying to fill in the gaps for myself, although I am curious about Great Health Benefit."

"Can't help you much there. Say, I'm sorry, can I get you some coffee or something?" He followed her eyes to the end table, where a rose-colored bong stood next to a crystal box containing loose green leaves. Her eyes were inviting him to stay, maybe even find some comfort. A flash of sexual excitement shot through him as he realized where this might be going. Could he really have her that easily? If he was twenty-something he wouldn't have given it a second thought. But Mark had done enough health-related stories to know the risks of unprotected sex, and he hadn't come prepared. If only he could get the rest of his body to listen to reason.

"No thanks. Just a couple more questions and then I must get back to work."

"Mind if I have some? This talk about Elaina is bummin' me."

"Go ahead," said Mark. She automatically filled the bong, lit the bowl, and took an extraordinarily long "hit." There was a long silence as she held her breath. Mark remembered from college that it wasn't polite to ask questions at this moment. The smell of marijuana took him back to his days at UCLA. Actually Jenny, Elaina and a few other friends had partied with "grass" on a few occasions. It seemed an eternity ago.

"Anyway," began Stephie when she resumed breathing, "I don't know much about GHB. A company representative came out after she went into the hospital, said he was picking up work stuff. I don't think anyone else from work ever came by."

Mark watched Stephie's face relax as she held her second hit. Her eyes openly wandered over his face, boldly exploring his appearance. She inhaled a third time and offered the bong to Mark. He wasn't sure if she wanted him to indulge or simply set it on the end table. She moved a little closer to him and let her body sink into the billowy couch. A playful curiosity seemed to replace her anxiety.

Mark felt another stab of excitement as Stephie's warm smile invited him closer. Although Mark had grown more cautious in the pursuit of casual sex, this opportunity was hard to dismiss. He put the bong to his lips and covered the top with his hand, showing Stephie that he knew the drill and was willing to join in. His lungs were unaccustomed to smoke and he could barely restrain a cough.

After the token hit, he set it on the end table and returned to her gaze. He leaned forward, placing his face within an inch of hers, testing the waters. Stephie rose and met his mouth with hers, forcing his lips apart and thrusting her tongue deep in his mouth. The act melted away any resistance he had, and they stretched out on the cushions. His hand gently caressed her firm breast, then he opened the buttons to her shirt. Nipple rings. A few minutes later his hand had slipped down her pants where he discovered more hardware. Labial rings. He knew tomorrow his face would look like he'd been wrestling in poison ivy. But for now the passion roared on like a locomotive.

Few men believe they met their <u>Playboy</u> inspired quota of college sex. Everyone else on campus did, but somehow their individual luck with twenty-something peers was embarrassingly poor. That made it easy to feel entitled to make it up after college. As the years crept past thirty there was a yearning to revisit those women, to use money, position, or simple maturity to "poach" from the next batch of undergrads.

An hour later they lay exhausted. There were warm cuddles and gentle strokes with this girl he hardly knew. He looked at his watch and rose to leave. She pulled him back.

"No," said Mark, "I should really get back to work. God, I can't believe this happened. You're amazing."

"I hope you won't be writing about this."

"No, but I'd like to see you again." Yet even as he said it, he felt the event fading. Blitz-sex was far more delicious in fantasy than in reality. By the time he was fully dressed, the aura of having been fucked was almost gone. It was as spiritually nutritious and satisfying as cotton candy. The naked girl on the sofa was the only real evidence that sex had occurred. She cooed as he placed the black shirt over her and kissed her gently on the cheek.

Mark scooped up the shoe box and departed. At 2:30 P.M. he walked out of her apartment, staring straight at Elaina's front door. Love and Death, like the title of the old Woody Allen movie. It had been a strange day. The smell of lawn mower exhaust and new-cut grass brought Mark fully back to the present.

He fiddled among the items in the shoe box as he approached his car, but they looked quite uninteresting. There were six floppy disks with some cryptic descriptions in "computerese" and two of the strange-looking tape cassettes. There was also a newspaper clipping with Senator Donald Gray's name highlighted. "Not exactly distinctive keepsakes for such a special woman," he thought. He dropped the box behind the driver's seat and placed a newspaper over it to hide it. He was back at his desk by 3 P.M. There was a tingle around his lips. The rash was already spreading.

***

Ezra began calling every physician he could find listed in the Columbus Yellow Pages. He started with oncologists, but exhausted that category the first day. Rachel was right; no one would take on Nora unless GHB released them from the contract. One office manager said one of their physicians had bent the rules once for a hardship case and was eventually fined $25,000. There was nothing anyone could do to help him.

After three days and over eighty phone calls Ezra was devastated. Nora's supply of medicine was running low. He had arranged a meeting with Bob to see if there was any way to get a price break on the deals.

Bob watched the old man enter the Bistro and was surprised how much older he appeared than just last week. For a few minutes Ezra just stared into the pale brew in the glass.

"Thanks for seeing me, Bob."

"Mr. E, you look terrible." Bob had a habit of cryptic speech, a survival skill in his business.

"It's my wife. She needs more medicine. I messed up big time. The clinic found out she was taking more morphine than they had prescribed. I had kept it all secret from her, so she didn't know not to tell them. They cut her off," he said with a hiss.

"Tough break, Mr. E. It's happened to others on my client load too. These companies watch things pretty closely. Do you have a binding contract with this HMO?"

"Yes. They won't let us go."

"I was afraid of that. So what can I do for you?"

"I have to keep Nora, my wife, on the medicine. I can't watch her suffer. But it's so expensive through you. I'm not complaining, mind you, and I'm glad you've been there, but I don't know how long I can continue."

"Well, there might be something we can do. But you've got to be willing to work with me."

"Anything," pleaded Ezra.

"Okay. I can give you a break if you bring me some more customers. You know, people like you, with medicinal needs. I know there are lots of people in your situation, and I like working with you folks. You're easy, safe, and much more appreciative than other . . . users."

"I'm not sure I know anyone else. We've been pretty isolated."

"May be time to get out into the world. Maybe attend a support group or hang out at the senior center. I'm just trying to give you some choices."

Ezra suddenly realized what was happening. He was being solicited as a drug pusher. The thought revolted him, and a dark look crossed his face. Bob had anticipated the reaction.

"Look, Ezra, I know this is against your principles, but so is the way you're being treated by the medical establishment. They've taken all your rights away. You can't even go to another doctor. They don't care about you, so you have to take care of yourself."

"But, God, pushing. I don't know."

"Ezra, wake up and smell the painkiller. Doctors used to work for *you*. Now they work for big corporations. They used to push drugs for the benefit of you, now they push drugs for the benefit of the corporation. Things have gotten all crazy." Bob was very good at his trade. All those marketing courses at Ohio State were paying off.

"Okay, let me think about it," said Ezra. "What else can I do to get a break?"

"This is a touchy subject," said Bob, leaning closer and speaking under his breath. "You may want to consider a more powerful drug. It's stronger, cheaper, and actually much safer."

"Heroin," said Ezra, with a look of desperation.

"Yes. It's very pure, pharmaceutical quality from Great Britain and the Netherlands. No bad stuff. I can give you some articles on its use in Europe if you want. America has been positively puritanical about it, but it's one of the best medicines there is."

Ezra was anguished over the idea of giving Nora such a dirty-sounding drug, but he had seen a few articles on the subject and new what Bob said was legitimate.

"Will my wife know the difference?"

"It feels pretty much the same. I assume your wife doesn't really get high on the morphine, she just relieves her pain."

"Yes."

"She may notice that the quantity is less, unless you add some water to fill it up. The color may be different too. You can just tell her it's from a different company. Who draws up the syringe?"

"I do," said Ezra.

"Piece of cake. I can give you a little sample with your next purchase. I promise you it won't hurt her. It's basically the same thing as morphine, just more refined. Heck, the library is full of studies on it. Check it out."

"Okay, I'll give it a try. Is there anything else I can do?"

"I know a doctor who works outside the system. He's completely trained and skilled, but is frustrated that he can't practice medicine the way he'd like to with all these managed care companies looking over his shoulder. It's something like an underground network, almost like the old abortion days, but now it's geriatric care."

"But they're still treating my wife at the clinic."

"But they're not giving her the right stuff," countered Bob. "Anyway, I'm just mentioning it if the other things don't work out. Just keep it in mind."

"Bob, how do you know so much about all these medical scams."

"Mr. E we're in a revolution, and where there's revolution there is profit. Just ask Bill Gates."

They said goodbye and Ezra headed for home.

"I found a pharmacy that would let me pay cash," Ezra lied to his wife as he filled the syringe. She stood at the kitchen sink mashing potatoes. Her palsy disrupted her fine motor coordination, but gross motor activities were still possible, and even good therapy for her.

"Are you sure we can afford this? I'm afraid we're going through money too quickly. The pain isn't so bad right now," said Nora.

"Don't you worry." The syringe was filled with a fluid that was darker than usual. "It's a generic product from Europe. Somehow it's cheaper to import it."

Nora didn't question him further. She steadied herself on the sink and he quickly injected her with the new drug. His hands, usually rock steady, trembled slightly. He asked God for forgiveness and understanding. The validation of the medical journals couldn't help erase 70 years of war on heroin. Ezra watched her closely for the next four hours, playing gin rummy and helping in the garden. She seemed no different. Her smile returned quickly. Her eyes twinkled signs of love. At dinner she even scrambled some eggs. Bob was right. This damn stuff worked great.

It was one of the most difficult days of Ezra's life. He had taken what to him was a staggering risk with someone he loved more than life itself. It seemed to have worked. The angel of his life was peacefully asleep, her head surrounded by a halo of gray hair. It had been a good day together. He cradled her soft breast in his hand, as he had done for four and a half decades, and drifted off to sleep.

Chapter 15

For the remainder of the week, Jenny received a thorough orientation to GHB. This included classes on its history and founder, video messages from the CEO and president, and reviews of policies, procedures and computer security requirements. Unlike Progressive, the roots of GHB were not planted in the soil of medicine, but rather, in the insurance industry. Although the GHB historians spoke of the importance of clients and employees, it was clear that profits were the primary commitment. The language and philosophy of the two companies were different and this created some anxiety for her. Could she really fit in here?

Jenny used the breaks between the meetings to keep in touch with Progressive. The chaos reportedly grew after the final merger agreements were approved. Resumé s were flying over the Internet as her colleagues tried to secure a future. A few had left voice or e-mails for Jenny to gain some sense of GHB's plans. Since she had been gone all week Jenny was already seen as one of "them."

Fortunately, the demanding orientation schedule limited her time with Hepman. She felt he was coming on too strong as a "buddy," like she was being groomed for induction into some special club and he was her sponsor. His face often registered surprise or disappointment at her responses, as if she was not acting as he expected. In fact, she wasn't at all sure what the expectations of her were. She vowed to talk with Carter at the first opportunity to clarify her new role.

Thursday was the first day she made it back to her assigned desk at GHB. Jenny brought some items from home to personalize the area a bit. She logged on from her workstation at 8:35 A.M.

"Good morning, Jenny," was MOM's reply, displayed as text on her screen, followed by a listing of her day's scheduled events. Her heart sank for a minute when she saw Hepman's name dominating her appointments, but was pleased to see a meeting with Carter listed there. Maybe she'd get some direction.

Since viewing MOM's profile of her, Jenny felt a little odd typing in requests. She had long appreciated Progressive's reluctance to install keystroke counters to measure worker productivity. Somehow, MOM's abilities were more sinister.

"Jenny," said Hepman as he entered her cubicle. "Good to see you again. How'd they treat you in orientation," he asked, but did not wait for a reply. "We got a full day ahead of us. Carter gave me a list of special jobs, which will give us an opportunity to work on the system. You up for it?"

Jenny could glean that there was only one correct answer. "Yes, I'd like that."

"Good. First off, Olde and Byron have asked for a profile on a troubled employee."

"Who are they?"

"A big accounting firm in the East. Our sixth largest account."

"So what's troubling the employee?"

"No one knows," said Hepman with a shrug. "Refused a referral to the company doctor. Said he was okay. Company thinks differently. Anyway, it'll give us a great opportunity to familiarize you with the new system."

"Do we have an authorization for release of information? Did the client sign one?" asked Jenny.

"Doesn't matter. He signed a global release when he started the program."

"I don't think that applies here. Doesn't he need to specifically sign a release for every access to his record?"

"Jenny," said Hepman with impatience. "We're here to service the client, who happens to be the employer. They're paying for the info. Let's get it."

"Okay. What do they want to know?"

Hepman scrutinized a handwritten note. "Seems that Olde and Byron have some suspicions about one of their directors. They think he's skimming funds to support a cocaine habit. They want to know what the medical records show."

Shock registered on her face, but Hepman missed it as he looked at the computer screen. There was no doubt this was a blatant request for private information. Jenny was sure this was way out of bounds for any reasonable employer request.

"Mark, we can't do that. Won't that put GHB at great liability if someone finds out the source of the information?" Jenny insisted.

"Don't worry. We always put it in a statistical report."

"I don't get it," admitted Jenny. "How do statistics on an organization prove someone is using cocaine?"

"Watch and learn," said Hepman. He sat at Jenny's terminal and logged on under his own name. He moved through a few menus until he reached one Jenny had not seen before. The heading on the screen said "Caduceus – Beta Version 3.8".

"This is the Caduceus program," he explained. "It's really a more advanced version of MOM. State-of-the-art. It's a hyper-relational database with an intelligent search engine. The cool thing is its ability to learn from experience. If it figures out a retrieval problem on one mission, it will remember that solution on the next mission. After a few queries, it can anticipate your requests."

"Now let's see," he continued. "The company is concerned about Roy Dahl. First, I'll get his personnel records from the employer." Hepman pulled up the employer's files from Oshkosh, Wisconsin. "We get access to these when the company signs on for health benefits, of course. Here's our friend Roy now." Displayed on the screen was Mr. Dahl's personal information: date of birth, demographics, work history, salary, dependents, etc. Hepman used the mouse to highlight all the information on the screen.

The screen displayed a question from Caduceus, "Desired process?"

Hepman typed in "Exhaustive search for treatment of mental health, chemical dependency, related physical problems or any risk markers for same."

They watched as MOM sequentially highlighted each word in the sentence, interpreting the words and phrases against her vast dictionaries and language databases. A few seconds later the screen displayed:

"TASK: Search for any treatment suggesting chemical abuse in subject Roy Dahl.   (Y/N)"

Hepman looked up at Jenny with a smile. "Is she smart or what?" he said with pride smeared all over his face.

"A nice interpretive algorithm," said Jenny, trying to subdue her awe of this machine.

MOM replied, "What databases?" and listed every known medical, insurance, judicial, and even credit databases.

Hepman scrolled to the bottom of the list, clicking on "ALL".

"Place search results in. . ." and Hepman created a folder in his virtual file cabinet on the computer.

MOM announced that a search had been launched. Hepman explained to Jenny, "It's a specialized program that will search out every occurrence of Roy Dahl's name, or even that of his wife or children, in every relevant database in the US. His personnel data is used to verify the identity."

Jenny was astonished. This was far beyond any technology she had seen at Progressive. It made her uneasy to witness the casual merging of clinical, personal, and financial data. In graduate school they had drilled into her the sanctity of the medical record, which should never be opened to prying eyes without full patient consent. But to computers, it was all just data: billions of single bits and bytes that could be instantly traded, calculated, and distributed in a nanosecond. Cyberspace had no boundaries at GHB.

She risked a question. "Why would a health insurance company have links to credit and judicial computers?"

"Because we have access to anything that affects health. Criminal activity places a client in a higher risk category for injury and certain stress-related illnesses. We also need to know about financial status, particularly when someone claims they can't afford the co-pay of treatment. We can check it out."

"How long will this take?"

"We should have the data in an hour or two. It can take up to four hours to complete a search, depending on how much it finds and brings back."

"Brings back? You make it sound like it ran off somewhere to get the information," said Jenny in an attempt at humor.

"That's exactly what it did. We created an intelligent agent, a software entity that will independently jump from one computer to another looking for Roy Dahl's data. There is no direct link to MOM right now. It's kind of like a computer virus, in that it embeds itself in systems and looks for important data, but all it does is collect data and return home. The little critter is off on its own in cyberspace." Jenny imagined a furry little animal with electric white fur wiggling through the data lines.

***

Hepman's beeper began chirping. He plucked it off his belt and examined it. A smile grew across his face. "Time to check out some more bad guys."

"What's up? Is your critter back already with Mr. Dahl's data?" asked Jenny.

"No, another job for the cyber-detectives. I told MOM to page me when this provider comes on-line. Carter wants us to check him out. She's letting me know he's logged in."

"You going to chat with him?"

"Not him. His computer. Here, check the memo." He handed Jenny a handwritten page. "We've got to check on some records to see if this provider is violating his contract and putting our clients at risk. This one's a psychiatric group, right up your alley. Hey, maybe you know him. Dr. Wakefield, in Pittsburgh."

"Yeah," said Jenny in disbelief. "He has a small clinic practice, works with kids and families, some county victim referrals. He's on Progressive's provider list."

"Well, we've had some reports that he may also be seeing pedophiles. If he is, we have to worry about the waiting room mix. I don't want child-molesters sitting in an unsupervised waiting room with children, and neither does GHB," cautioned Hepman.

"I can agree with that. So why don't you just inspect his records?" asked Jenny.

"Well, they're not our clients. In fact, they are reportedly mostly cash clients, maybe even using aliases. We don't know who to ask about."

"So what do we do?" asked Jenny, not really understanding her part in this.

"We're going to investigate. Just work together and figure this guy out."

"You mean, go to Pittsburgh?" Jenny asked with a start.

"No, we can do it from here. Hepman jumped into the chair next to Jenny. She noticed he had a box labeled "ProviderLink–PC", which he opened. He took out a manual and started to browse. Hepman said, "Dr. Wakefield uses our ProviderLink software to do claims billing with us. His computer transmits the claims data after hours. We'll intercept the transmission."

"Why? What can you do with billing information?" asked Jenny.

"It's the computer link that I want. We'll be able to take a little look at his system."

"Are you sure we can do that, I mean legally?" asked a dubious Jenny.

"To use the ProviderLink software Dr. Wakefield had to agree to some terms about swapping information. He has also contractually agreed to allow GHB to inspect his files. Since his files are on the computer, that's where we'll look. I told MOM to flag us when he calls," said Hepman with a hint of pride. He was in his element.

Jenny was examining the box. "So what does this ProviderLink program do?"

"It's a pretty good package for personal computers. The company sells it cheap to the providers. The software gives them an accounting package, a communications program, and a clinical notes database. As an extra incentive, GHB promises to pay claims within two weeks if they're electronically billed through ProviderLink. The providers can even use the software to manage their other clients. I helped write the program," beamed Hepman.

"But it also lets you invade the other computer from here?"

"Yes, it's what we call an 'undocumented feature'," Hepman said with sarcasm. "The next version of ProviderLink will be even more powerful. We'll be working interactively with the providers directly through the computer, day or night."

"This package says that the program data is password protected, with up to four million possible letter combinations. What do you do about that?" challenged Jenny.

"It will take MOM about five minutes to try all four million combinations. If that doesn't work, there's a master code-breaker upstairs, but it requires special authority. Don't worry. Mom can take care of a little PC."

"This doesn't feel quite right. I wouldn't want someone snooping around my home computer," Jenny protested.

"Hey, Dr. Wakefield agreed to these terms when he installed it. Oops, here comes his link." MOM had flagged the transaction and Hepman jumped on the keyboard. "OK, let me just suspend the transmission here. Now I'll access the main program."

Over 2,500 miles away, a personal computer in Pittsburgh prompted Hepman for a password. With the flick of a key, MOM began sending a storm of compressed digits over the connected phone line, as if drilling through the armor of a safe. After four anxious minutes the password was found and they were in control of Dr. Wakefield's computer.

"All right!" exclaimed Hepman, "now we can cruise around." He scrolled through the financial and client data. "Yikes, this guy was getting about 120 visits a month from the Gray Alliance Steel company employees."

"Hey, didn't GHB just lose that contract?" asked Jenny.

"Yeah, and we're set to trim the provider list in that area fast. We ... Oh my God, this guy's got over $130,000 in outstanding claims with GHB. No wonder Carter wanted to check. . ." Hepman abruptly cut off the sentence and quietly probed deeper.

"Now watch what we can do, Jenny. First I'll have MOM compare all of the logged cases on Dr. Wakefield's computer with her own matching files to see if he incorrectly billed anything."

To Hepman's disappointment, everything corresponded perfectly. He then looked for names not known to MOM. Again, nothing unusual. "So, Wakefield doesn't use our super-cool client tracking system for his cash clients," Hepman observed. "Let's see where the other clients are stored."

Jenny saw letters and codes scroll by on the screen, which she recognized as files and directories. It gave her great discomfort to be looking into Dr. Wakefield's machine. She felt like she was secretly wandering around in someone's house, like a burglar peeking into drawers. Hepman looked like he was getting excited.

"Is it that easy to break into any provider computer?" asked Jenny, with a note of disbelief.

"Well, as luck would have it, our own federal government has made it fairly easy. The Justice Department was afraid that sophisticated data encryption coding would make it impossible for them to access the data they wanted, so they made the stronger codes illegal. Now, any corporation can buy the code-breaker on the open market. Made life much easier for hackers." Hepman had the smile of a kid playing with a new video game.

Suddenly the screen announced "WordPerfect."

"I didn't know MOM had WordPerfect in her," said Jenny.

"She doesn't," said the Hepman. "We're running Dr. Wakefield's computer from here."

Hepman was awfully good at what he did. She was also a little frightened by the ease of this intrusion.

"I couldn't find any other financial or database programs," Hepman noted. "If these are cash clients, Wakefield may just use his word processor to manage them. What I'll do is ask WordPerfect to see if any files contain the word 'pedophile,' as would be the case in any reports he had written up for the county."

The program began searching through all of the files in the computer, one word at a time.

"Is this legal? I mean, walking all over his computer," asked Jenny.

"There are very few laws about this. Dr. Wakefield agreed to let us examine the relevant files on our clients when he signed on with GHB. Our legal department said a file may be defined as whatever we think it is, which might include the entire hard disk. Besides, it's for a 'noble' cause. We don't want pedophiles mixing with kids, do we? I promise I won't leave any footprints. To tell the truth, though, I could leave a dead elephant on the hard disk and these computer-phobic doctor types wouldn't see it."

At the end of the search, the program had flagged thirty-seven files containing the word "pedophile." Hepman began looking at each record, which revealed several "pedophile assessments" sent to the county court.

"There they are. This guy is history," said Hepman in triumph. "I just had MOM copy all of the files to memory. Dr. Wakefield can say bye-bye to GHB."

"What about all that money owed him?" asked Jenny.

"Carter will probably have a little discussion with him; maybe cut a deal. He may just threaten him with legal action. That often sways negotiations. $130,000 buys a lot of lawyer time," said Hepman. "Hey, we had to trim the Pittsburgh provider panel anyway."

Jenny sat in awe. Experienced as she was with computers, it was always a wonder to see a true master at work. Hepman flowed through the circuitry like electricity itself, yet the outrageous invasion was too great a violation of professional ethics. What kind of company was this? It seemed so predatory. If this was the way GHB treated its healthcare providers, it was no wonder they were so profitable. She recalled her conversation with Al Friedman in the lunchroom at Progressive. "They'd eat their young if it was profitable." Jenny felt a wave of paranoia pass over her, as if every monitor on every desk was watching her. She couldn't shake it off.

"I wonder what there is on me," Jenny wondered with hesitation.

"Don't ask unless you really want to know," warned Hepman. "One woman who was testing the search engine made a query on her daughter. It came back with documentation of an abortion at a college clinic that the mom didn't know about. You just never know."

"Notice that MOM can take immediate control of the client contact," continued Hepman. "She's smart enough to respond to key words and direct the interaction to a positive outcome. That's one of the reasons we tend to hire nurses and medical personnel with little experience, particularly recent grads. They're much easier to train and are more willing to accept the idea of medical authority on-line."

"Yes, it is very impressive," replied Jenny. "Yet, I wonder about the other things MOM considers in computing appropriate care. As I understand it, MOM also directs the financial administration of care plus that of the company. That's the part that makes me a little uncomfortable. For computers, it's always simpler to calculate money than, say, quality of care. It's easy to add up fees, daily rates, and item costs. But how do we calculate patient comfort, successful response to treatment? What exactly are the formulas that MOM uses to compute care?"

"Sorry, that's proprietary information. Company secret. Those formulas are what make us competitive in the marketplace. Only a few of us have seen them," he said with a smile suggesting he was one of the chosen few.

"At Progressive we had to have the computer program, the actual coding, reviewed by and independent auditor before we could run it. Didn't you go through the same procedure?"

"Sure, everyone does, but that's just to get started. Do you think there haven't been any changes to your program since that audit?"

"Well, sure," said Jenny trying not to appear naive.

"I think they reviewed Caduceus version 1.1. We're now operating version 3.8. Caduceus version 4.0 is to be launched next month. There have been major program rewrites and I've overseen much of it."

"So, only the company really knows how the computer decides things?" Jenny asked.

"Yeah. It's better that way. Got to keep the competitive advantage. If we opened up the program to inspections, our secrets would be all over town."

Hepman checked his list. "Carter wants me to accelerate your training on MOM to prepare for the big roll-out next month. We've been sitting on a big revision that will be started in five weeks, when the new contracts come on line. Gotta get everyone up to speed. We're meeting with Carter later today, as well as some other division heads, who you'll be working with on occasion."

***

Jenny spent the morning beside Teresa Perrigo, whom she had met on Tuesday during her tour. Teresa recalled Jenny's friendly manner and felt comfortable with the new shadow. Jenny watched Teresa field call after call. Sick children. Broken bones. Elderly alcoholics. Sports injuries of weekend warriors. With each contact MOM provided the script, the data, and the decisions on care.

Teresa spoke with confidence and authority. Although she was of slight build and almost adolescent appearance, her voice was deep and commanding. Jenny closed her eyes and imagined a burly Germanic nurse, decked out in whites and nurse's cap, using decades of wisdom to make the patient comfortable yet fulfill her necessary tasks. This vocal image probably helped the young woman in dealing with medical personnel in clinics and hospitals across the country, as well as with the patients.

Much of Teresa's time was spent with case managers and utilization reviewers requesting care for patients at their facilities. By the time Teresa answered the phone, the caller had been routed through four or five levels of voice mail. The entire case history was present on the screen when Teresa addressed the query. She would click on treatment options, be prompted for additional information, and even request more data from the facility. Faxes and electronic images were sent immediately, and MOM could read and interpret most of the information. Occasionally, the GHB staff would need to clarify a point for MOM, for she wasn't yet "human," yet Teresa felt more like a secretary to MOM, not a trained clinician.

Jenny studied the interaction between Teresa and the computer in great detail. MOM had something of a personality. It was gentle yet firm, intelligent, but not pedantic. There was an element of caring. When Teresa's typing rate slowed, MOM asked if she needed a break, and offered to reroute her calls for fifteen minutes. Teresa agreed with MOM and hung up her headset. Jenny wondered if MOM could tell a joke or get pissed off. "Hey," she thought to herself. "She's just a bunch of digits."

While Teresa relaxed with a cola extracted from her desk drawer, Jenny continued her interview. "When do you graduate from nursing school?"

"Hopefully, in September. This is my internship. It's taken me almost three years because I've been working part-time. It's nice that they pay me a little. If I'm lucky, I'll come on-board full time after my state board exams in November."

"I didn't realize you weren't licensed yet. You sound very professional on the phone," said Jenny.

"MOM helps a lot. It's like I have a whole medical staff at my fingertips and almost like MOM is listening in on the conversation. In the last year I've only had to call on a supervisor twice for help with a patient."

"Have you had much floor duty in a hospital as part of your training?"

"Six weeks last summer, at the VA in Brentwood," Teresa said proudly. "Then three weeks at Northridge Hospital."

"Do you feel prepared?" asked Jenny, wondering how such an inexperienced student could be placed in the critical role of treatment authorization.

"Yeah, it's cool. The whole thing seems fairly simple. I don't have to know everything right off the top of my head. It's all in there," Teresa said, pointing to the monitor. Curious how people seem to identify the monitor as "the computer," as if, like a person's eyes, it was the "window" to the soul.

Progressive would never have placed such an inexperienced practitioner on-line. What did this recent teenager know about healthcare?

"Do you get much flack from the physicians on the phone when they're pitching a case?"

"Not really," said Teresa with a flick of her hair. "I use a virtual voice."

"Say again?" said Jenny.

"The virtual voice. It's this awesome feature. MOM ages my voice so I sound about 28 on the phone. Something about lower bass registers and terminal phonics." Teresa tapped some keys and an icon appeared on the screen. It resembled a graphic equalizer for a stereo, a collection of sliding scale knobs at different sound frequencies. She used the mouse pointer to highlight a number in a box. "See. This number here is the estimated age. If I increase it, you can see the buttons shift position." As her "age" crept up to forty years old, the equalizer adjusted her frequencies. "Heck, if I kick it up to 60 years old I can order stuff on the phone at a senior's discount."

"So the patient feels more confident and accepting of your advice," said Jenny.

"Pretty cool, huh. The more experienced staff know how to tweak it to sound more compassionate, or nurturing, or whatever they need."

"So the patient is really dealing with a virtual person," Jenny thought to herself.

It was clear Teresa was enamored of the system. It was equally obvious she couldn't function without it. Jenny found it hard to imagine this young woman running down the hallway of a hospital with a crash-cart, ready to dive into a life-and-death emergency.

Chapter 16

An hour later, Hepman collected Jenny and took her to the fourth floor.

"We'll be meeting with Carter later, but first you need to see the CR section. He'll ask you about it," said Hepman.

They entered guarded double doors, over which a sign announced, "Claims Review and Recovery Section; Security Area." They were waved through as the guard inspected their badges.

"This is our most profitable area right now, part of the retrospective review process. We review approved claims and find ways to get paid back," said Hepman.

"From whom?"

"Anyone we can. Client deductibles that weren't collected. Physicians who didn't follow the rules. This department uses the new capabilities of the Caduceus program to minimize our claims payments. MOM and the staff review treatment histories to assess responsibility for injuries or illnesses. If we find a person or firm responsible, we go after them to recoup our expenditures."

"You mean like Worker's Compensation or job disability?" asked Jenny.

"Yes, at least that's where it started, but we're able to take in much further. We've been able to collect on a broad range of claims. Slip-and-falls, household injuries, even sexually transmitted diseases when a lover didn't inform the patient of his or her condition."

"What? You sue people over sexual diseases? How does that work?"

"As part of our health benefit package. Clients sign an

authorization allowing GHB to pursue any parties responsible for an illness or injury. We explain that it saves them on premiums and co-pays. Why should they pay for someone else's negligence? Then we collect from that party's insurance company. Saves us millions of dollars a year."

"Why not do it up front, when you approve care?" asked Jenny.

"Too much hassle. We were getting a lot of flack for denying treatment authorizations, so we switched to denying payments."

"I guess it makes sense," said Jenny with a doubtful look. "I find it hard to believe this would be such a big deal."

"It started with AIDS cases. We were getting clobbered with expensive care. Sometimes it involved a lover who didn't tell a member that they were HIV-positive. Eventually the courts held that this was negligence and held people liable for causing damage through the sexual exposure. Since the insurance companies were picking up the tab for these expensive AIDS cases, they became partners in the suits. When they won a few cases they realized these claims were not just limited to AIDS cases. If they could prove that anyone was responsible for an injury or disease we could recoup some expenditures. Now it's a full-time division."

They walked over to an empty workstation, sat down and logged on. "Let me show you how it works. I'll tap into a conversation." He told MOM to follow the next incoming call. Within a minute the screen lit up with the face of one of the staff. He was identified as Maurice Brown, by the caption under his image. Hepman alerted him that they would be monitoring for instructional purposes. Hepman flipped on the speaker phone.

"What the hell are you doing to my mother!" shouted an irate male member. The screen noted it was Benjamin Seidman, who had recently been treated for a broken leg. "She called me up today saying I was suing her," he screamed. "I'm not suing my mother, and I didn't authorize you to sue her. What's the deal?"

Maurice pulled up the record of Benjamin's treatment. Attached to the electronic file was a letter from the Review and Recovery section. It read . . .

"In the matter of *Benjamin Seidman vs. Grace Seidman*, we are seeking recovery of damages to our client for injuries sustained on your property and paid for by his healthcare insurer, Great Benefit Health. Mr. Seidman reported he was cutting the branches of a tree on your property, using a step ladder provided by Mrs. Seidman. Through no negligence of his own he fell from the ladder and sustained a broken leg. GHB incurred a treatment expense of $1,261 for doctors' examination, setting the cast, and medication. You are hereby served notice of our intent to recover these expenses from your homeowner's insurance policy, underwritten by State Farm Insurance of Illinois. Please contact them for any additional information.

Thank you for your attention to this matter."

"I see the letter you're talking about, Mr. Seidman," said Maurice. "Seems you were cutting down some branches on a tree at your mother's home. You sustained an injury from a fall and broke your leg, is that right?"

"Yes. I do most of the yard work for her since Dad died three years ago. She can't do it herself and we can't afford a gardener. What's that got to do with anything?"

"Well it really shouldn't concern you or your mother, Mr. Seidman. This is a routine matter between insurance companies. It happens all the time. We're just trying to get the other insurance company to pay their part. That's why your mother has insurance, isn't it?" asked Maurice. Hepman and Jenny watched these words scroll by on the screen as MOM provided the script to deal with the customer.

"What do you mean, it happens all the time? I've never sued anyone, particularly my own mother. This has upset us both. I never authorized any suits," explained Seidman.

"Oh, but you did when you signed onto the program. I'm looking at section 24b on your signed policy. You agreed to allow GHB to act on your behalf in pursuing claims against anyone responsible for your illness or injury. It's a standard contract agreement."

"But my mother didn't do anything! I'm the one who fell out of the tree. Take it off *my* insurance."

"It's not that simple, Mr. Seidman. We already checked into your homeowner's insurance plan and this circumstance is not covered. I'm afraid your mother is considered at fault."

"That's pure nonsense. She didn't do anything. Just pay the claim like you're supposed to."

"We have, Mr. Seidman. Now we're trying to recover those expenses. I know this seems odd, but let me assure you, it's routine procedure now. It's just a formality within the insurance industry. Your mom shouldn't be mad at you. Just put it out of your mind. We'll take care of it."

"Wait a second. What if the insurance company refuses to settle."

"They almost always settle."

"What if they don't?"asked Seidman.

"Then we'll go to court."

"Does that include my mother?"

"I guess it would, but none of these ever get to court, Mr. Seidman. They're always settled."

"So I should just tell my mother it's okay that you're suing her, it's just a formality, and there should be no problem."

"Exactly. I know it sounds weird, but it happens every day," said Maurice, trying to be supportive.

"I can't stop it?"

"Only if you want to pay the damages yourself."

"Then why would I be paying for health insurance?"

"For the sake of you and your family."

" I think I'll need to run this by my attorney. I want to make sure my mother's assets will never be at risk."

"I think that's a good idea, Mr. Seidman. Oh, by the way, how's your leg?"

"Fine," he said curtly, and hung up.

Jenny was speechless for a moment. "Suing his mother?" she asked in bewilderment.

"Tough break," said Hepman, unaware of the pun. "But when you get right down to it, it makes perfect sense. People have to be more careful. Hey, we gotta go to that meeting now with Carter Newton."

***

Hepman rose so quickly that the wheeled chair moved out to the hallway. Jenny collected her things and followed. A quick ride to the fifth floor took them to and into the waiting room for Carter's office. The secretary's desk was vacant, but papers scattered about suggested she was near. Hepman motioned for Jenny to sit.

"I've got a couple of things I need to touch base on quickly with Carter. It'll take about five minutes and then we'll bring you in. There's coffee against the wall. Make yourself comfortable. Amanda, Carter's secretary, is out to lunch."

Hepman left Jenny, quickly knocked on Carter's office door, then let himself in. Carter was on the phone, jotting down notes. "Yes, Tom. Hepman is joining me now. He's been with her this morning. I'm going to speak with him now to see if she's appropriate for the position. Talk with you soon." He hung up the phone.

"She's waiting outside," said Hepman.

"Well, what do you think?"

"I'm not sure yet."

"Damn it, Hepman, we've got to get someone on-line now."

"I just can't get a good take on her. She's got lots of techno-smarts. Seems comfortable with the system. I think she's excited about how sophisticated the program is. But I'm not sure."

"Can she be trusted?"

"I think she's pretty trustworthy. Maybe too much so. She's trying to hide it, but I've caught her reacting negatively to some of our policies. Admittedly they're different from Progressive's, so maybe she's just feeling intimidated by all there is to learn."

"That's why Progressive is history, replied Carter. "Couldn't run with the big dogs. But she's got to believe in our mission and policies if she's going to train our people to accept MOM's authority. More importantly, she'll know a lot about MOM's treatment paradigms and decision processes. That's the guts of our program. We can't have another turncoat."

Hepman reacted with a grimace. "Mr. Newton, is it fair to call Elaina a turncoat? We're not even sure she's the one who breached the system."

"Get real, Greg. I know you liked Elaina. Heck, just about everybody did. But you were had. She used you to get into the system. I just know she was the one. I don't like speaking against her after her unfortunate death, but we can't make any more mistakes. There are millions of dollars riding on this. Our goddam formulas might be in the hands of our enemies, or the press, or the government. We've got to find the leak. By the way, have you figured out how she got into those critical files?"

"Not yet. Whoever it was," Greg corrected, "they knew how to cover their tracks. We know it was probably someone inside the company with high-level security. Could have been any one of forty people. And we now know the password used."

"Whose?"

"Mine," said Hepman with embarrassment.

Carter's eyes widened, then a devilish grin spread over his face. "I'll be damned. That little bitch. Probably got it looking right over your shoulder."

"Corrected now, sir,"

"Good. So you're not sure if Jenny will play on our team?"

"Not yet," said Hepman. "We haven't even looked at her

personnel files from Progressive. We took her on Harrington's recommendation."

"God, please don't let Jenny wig out on us! Okay, get the personnel file today. Have MOM check it out. Exhaustively! Cross-check everything. All of her medical history, every pap smear, credit history, FBI records, Health Information Databank, school records, traffic tickets. Maybe we can have MOM follow her closely for a couple of weeks. Can you have MOM check her out psychologically? I mean, without alerting her. She is a psychologist. Don't make it too obvious."

"I already showed her the profiling program. I think she believes that's the most MOM can do. We've got to keep her on-line, so I'll have MOM watch her reaction to tough clinical decisions, maybe even throw some ethical dilemmas at her to see where she stands. Can I use a Rat?"

Carter was taken aback for a second. "A Rat?"

"Yes, a Rat, you know, the polygraph mouse? It would help get a quick read on her."

"Tell me more about it."

"It's a mouse that looks like any other mouse, but it has a special metallic coating. It can take readings from a person's hand and tell about their psychological state, kind of like a lie detector. The thing measures skin temperature, pulse, and galvanic skin response, which is basically the electrical conductivity of the skin. All of these measurements are associated with a person's stress level. They've been used in biofeedback for years. We can essentially measure her mood. MOM could have a hot wire lead to Jenny's emotions to gauge her reactions as case material was presented. If she was uncomfortable with GHB's treatment decision system, she wouldn't be able to hide it, hence the name. The mouse would "rat" on her."

"Good idea. Are you sure she couldn't detect it?"

"No way. We'll have a graph of her emotional responses within a few days," said Hepman.

"Is it legal?"

"Well, we already monitor the employee's e-mail, voice mail, and even their video appearance. I can't see how it's different. But no, Carter, I haven't checked with legal."

"I'll make a note to do that. Anything else, Greg?"

"Are you going to let her attend the meeting with the team?"

"Sure. Only way to get her feet wet is to let her swim around."

Three people arrived at Carter's office at 11:00 A.M. Jenny

recognized them from the staff meeting on Tuesday, but couldn't remember their names. Thankfully they introduced themselves and made small talk, asking about her impressions of the place and comparisons to Progressive. Soon, Carter's door opened and the group filed in. Carter and Hepman sat on a sofa next to the office window. The others filled chairs around a coffee table.

"You all remember Jenny," said Carter. "We haven't scared her away yet. Jenny this is Dave from IS Security, Angela from Client Products, Norm from Legal, and Rich from Claim Recovery. I wanted to have a brief meeting to touch base with you all and let to Jenny hear what we're working on. Her job is to help make it work with the rest of our staff."

There were brief smiles and polite nods. Jenny still felt a curious distance from them.

"Dave, whatcha got," said Carter, trying to generate a more relaxed tone.

Dave glanced at his yellow pad. "System integrity seems strong. We've reinforced the barriers to MOM's decision algorithms and compiled the code with more protection. Since we think the breach came from inside, we've double-encrypted the passwords, which are now changed weekly for anyone with level-four access. On the plus side of the investigation we have the list of suspected machines used for the access trimmed down to twenty-four, all on the principal suspect's floor. We don't know yet, and may never know, how much was actually copied. All searches of personal disks and tapes were negative. It appears she . . ." Dave hesitated, glancing first at Jenny and then at Carter. The executive nodded for him to continue. "It appears the suspect acted alone," Dave finished.

Carter hurried to explain for Jenny. "We had a security breach to the system a few months ago. Very critical data. Not sure how it was done, but we're pretty sure who did it. The employee is no longer with us." His understatement clued Dave to move on to another topic. There were a few more minutes of technical details on new hardware and procedures. Jenny got a cold feeling as she put together who they might be talking about.

"Rich, how goes your end?" asked Carter.

"Very well. Our department revenues have increased 35 percent since February, however, some clients are starting to kick up a fuss about double deductibles. Seems when we sue the homeowners or small businesses, the owner has to pay the deductible, which is often $500 to $1,000. Our department is being swamped with negative calls. Some members are even talking to Senator Gray's group. I think the protests are going to increase and it will take a bigger bite out of my staff's time, as well as their morale. We're going to need more people," said Rick.

"The Caduceus Project should help when it's rolled out in full next month," said Carter. "Also, we're getting a bunch of people from Great Benefit Financial. They had to release over 500 people because of that FTC investigation about false sales pitches on securities. We've been asked to absorb them. They don't know much about medicine, but they're good at marketing. And remember, every client contact is a marketing opportunity."

"We're also going to shift control back to the front end of treatment during the authorization process," Carter continued "You just need to hang on for a bit. And don't worry, Senator Gray's wackos aren't getting anywhere."

"Mr. Newton, there are reports that they are talking to disgruntled employees," said Rich. "I know of two."

"Fine. Not to worry," replied Carter. "We have the Feds right where we want them," boasted Carter, aligning himself with the lobbying team of GHB. "They're desperate to get a hold on the Medicare and Medicaid costs. We've saved them over two billion dollars already. The reason this is being played out in the Senate is because that's our turf. Medicine has become politicized, which is all to our advantage. We don't have to waste money on laboratories and research. Let the universities do that. The AMA is a nickel-and-dime operation against our lobbyists. They don't call the shots in medicine anymore. We've made medicine a truly efficient industry."

"Didn't that new bill just require health plans to add more days to postoperative care for mastectomies? We just reprogrammed MOM for that."

"Rich, you're absolutely right, but we added two days of care for just one procedure that costs us very little. It took Congress two years to push that through, and we let it happen. Two years before, we had to add a couple of days recovery to childbirth. So what? These are incredibly small dollars, but because the issues are about motherhood, breasts, and apple pie, they garner all the attention. Cancer, heart disease, stroke, and all the big-buck diseases are unregulated. No one wants to even talk about them. We, as the caretakers of millions of people's lives, know that heart disease kills ten times more women than breast cancer. And, thank God, there are no mandates about cardiac care. We can still be as creative and resourceful as we want. We can keep Congress busy just talking about one body part at a time."

"Isn't Senator Gray's committee supposed to be looking at the whole issue of managed care?" asked Rich.

Carter was getting impatient with this discussion. "Look, Senator Gray is going to have his own problems very soon. He's in the pocket of the doctors, who probably just want to squeeze more money out of us. In fact, there may even be a scandal brewing that will keep Donald Gray occupied for a while. That's all I can say for now. Who's next?"

Norm took the opportunity to speak. "Well, there's another Senator Gray issue that's cropped up. The Titty Tax."

Carter shot a frown at Norm and glanced sideways to Jenny, alerting him to be more professional.

"Sorry," Norm said to Jenny. "I know that must sound terrible, but that's the way Senator Gray and the ACLU are approaching it."

"Bring us up to speed, please," said Carter.

"Well, about six months ago we started a new benefit for women at very high risk for breast cancer. MOM can easily identify these women from their medical histories. It's in their best interest to consider bilateral prophylactic mastectomies. By removing both breasts before there's any sign of cancer, their risk is reduced by 91 percent. It's a whole lot cheaper than treating someone once they get cancer, and it saves lives. We thought it was a win-win deal. So as an incentive, we offered to reduce the co-pays and deductibles of those high-risk women who elected to have the procedure done."

"Sounds pretty generous," said Carter.

"Well, you're not the ACLU. Turns out this woman in Nebraska was a good candidate, but she was also poor and a single mother trying to support three young kids. The co-pays and deductibles were tough for her, so she opted to have the surgery to save money on her premiums. Well now, the ACLU says that to give her a discount is the same as charging someone who didn't have the surgery more. They claim it's coercive, and discriminatory. They've gone so far as to say if women who don't have the surgery must pay higher fees to keep their breasts, it amounts to a "Breast Tax," said Norm.

"That's a crock," exclaimed Carter. "It's a private decision between a woman and her insurance carrier."

"Well, Senator Gray says we have no business mixing our business interests with women's bodies. He's looking for an investigation. Anything that will get him into our computer," Norm replied.

"As I said, Senator Gray is in for some tough times. This issue may disappear with him." Carter turned to Hepman. "Greg, how's the implementation going?"

"We're in the final beta test on about 20 percent of the case management machines. The final program coding of Caduceus should be completed and compiled in two weeks. We're on schedule."

"How many machines have access to the source code, the stuff that all our competitors want?"

"It's down to ten. Most of the programmers only work on small sections of the project. It would be difficult for anyone to get any of it, and nearly impossible for someone to get all of it. Heck, there are over three million lines of coding. You'd need a tanker truck to haul it away," Hepman said with confidence.

"Good," Carter said. "Jenny, you're going to be working with this new system very closely. As I told you earlier, and I want everyone to hear this, MOM is about to become the most powerful medical expert decision-based computer in the industry. She's tapped into all the major medical databases, the Health Information Database, the National Practitioner Database, and all the teaching hospitals. Only MOM is sophisticated enough to integrate a patient's health record, current medical treatment standards, and the financial realities of the patient's insurance benefits. Your job is to help our staff learn to completely count on MOM for treatment decisions. No human can manage all of this. Medicine is too complicated. I want to know where the greatest psychological resistance will be and how to work though it. We can't have staff arguing with MOM all day. We're counting on you."

"Yes sir," said Jenny, as if she were about to salute.

"All of you should help Jenny in any way you can. Greg will be arranging her training and demo schedule. Give her anything she needs," said Carter.

All heads nodded. Soon the group was dismissed. Carter asked Jenny to stay for a minute. Hepman hesitated in his own departure, but Carter shooed him out.

"Coffee?" Carter asked.

"No thanks, I'm wired enough," replied Jenny.

"What do you think of the team?"

"Good group of folks. Seem very dedicated to the project, and your leadership." A little test of ego?

"Thanks. This has been an immense project. It's hard to believe we're so close to full implementation. The company has hundreds of millions, maybe over a billion, riding on this project. We have to make it work, and we have to keep it private."

He motioned for Jenny to sit on the sofa next to him, and she complied. He leaned toward her, his arm on the back of the couch, his broad smile not twelve inches from hers. His face beamed with health and virility. She had only seen him in his executive persona, but now she saw him as an attractive man. His smile was infectious, and a little mischievous.

"I just want to say how lucky I feel to have such a talent on board," he said, as his gray eyes peered into hers. Jenny wasn't sure what this was about. She appreciated his vote of confidence, but she felt drenched in his exuding masculinity. Was he making this personal?

"Thanks, it's all a bit overwhelming. Things are different over here. Bigger than Progressive, faster, more sophisticated."

"It's all glitz, Jenny. You can handle it. I've talked with some staff and they're all impressed with you. Even Mable, who is both a joy and my biggest irritant, thinks you're okay. I just wanted you to know. We're so deep into the project I didn't want to overlook you."

"Thanks."

"Is Greg treating you well? Giving you what you need?"

"Oh, yes. He's like the IS guys at Progressive. They must all come from the same school. A little too focused on the bits and bytes to realize that those are people's lives in the memory banks."

"Well, if you can make him more human, I'll give you a promotion. Feel free to check with me on anything. Greg is more knowledgeable than anyone, but I want you to get whatever you need."

"Will do," Jenny said, trying to avoid his penetrating look. She felt his hand on her shoulder as he gently invited her to stand up.

"I'll check with you tomorrow. If we're that close to final testing, I may need your input fast." Carter stood over her, his hand dropping to the small of her back, and he guided her to the door. The mixture of power, closeness, and attractiveness took Jenny by surprise. "Girl, "she thought to herself, "you've been too long between lovers. Time to get back in the saddle." She left the room and joined Hepman, waiting in the lobby.

Chapter 17

"Looks like we're gonna spend some time with MOM today," said Hepman, as he took Jenny down a stairwell to the third floor. They emerged into the secure area and a soft but persistent alarm went off. A nearby security guard put down a clipboard where he stood and immediately walked over to Hepman. Although he must have known Greg Hepman like a brother, he requested his ID card. This area was under the heaviest security Jenny had so far encountered, for it contained most of the computer hardware that was MOM. If the grand electronic matron had a heart, it was somewhere in this room.

They approached the glassed-in enclosure she recalled from the other day. A couple of technicians walked around the array of a cabinetry and monitors, checking on the machine's vital signs. Hepman again seemed to become more reverential, not wanting to turn his back on the machine for fear of offending it. He led her to an office on the perimeter, letting himself in with a key.

The office might have been spacious if it weren't for the piles of junk strewn about. There were three computer monitors winking from under racks of software manuals, floppy disks, and flow charts. There was no art on the walls, just scheduling boards and some product posters from Microsoft. Jenny imagined a little sign saying "nothing biological allowed in this room."

Hepman shoved some manuals to the corner of his large, utilitarian desk, revealing a keyboard. He punched in his log-on passwords and a slightly different version of MOM's logo appeared on the screen. "This is where we write the code for MOM," said Hepman, tapping a metal box with varied lights and cables next to the monitor.

"This is where the final version of Caduceus is stored. We're polishing the final product this month, working out all the bugs." Hepman absent-mindedly massaged the metal box containing millions of lines of programming code that was the new incarnation of the master program.

"This is your baby?" asked Jenny.

"You bet. If it runs as well as I know it can, the company's profits will explode and I'll get my own department."

"Pretty heavy guard around here. Is all of MOM sitting on this desk?"

"Actually, a very good portion of it," Hepman said with a obvious pride. "Certainly the most important part, the medical decision formulas and algorithms for guiding treatment. I don't think any other company has the depth and resources of this program. MOM is probably the best doctor on earth."

"But she has very cold hands," said Jenny, trying to lighten the conversation. "I'm really interested in these expert decision systems. We didn't have much at Progressive. Could you run me through the process?"

"Sure. It's fairly simple on the surface. Essentially, MOM has stored billions of medical facts, opinions, probabilities, and outcomes. Every patient who is treated for a cold, a broken nose, lung cancer, stroke, or even leprosy is stored in this giant, networked database. When you access MOM with a description of the patient's symptoms, or the physician's observations, MOM churns it around, compares it to millions of cases that have come before, and develops a treatment recommendation."

"For every patient?" asked Jenny in awe.

"Basically. In fact, each new patient becomes a statistic in the new database. Everyone is contributing their data for the good of the whole. If we find a cost-effective treatment that works for you, we'll start using it on patients like you."

Jenny understood the fundamental idea behind expert decision systems, but she also knew that the programs were at the mercy of their inventors. The computer could certainly add up millions of pieces of data in a nanosecond, but there was so much more to calculating healthcare. Who decided what data to consider? What was important? And to whom? Did MOM use only medical data to compute a decision? Not likely. Financial factors were equally important, maybe even more crucial to the company. How was that worked into the system?

"Greg, this is powerful stuff. Can I see how the decision algorithm works?"

"Ah, but then I'd have to kill you," he said with a grin.

A chill shot down her spine as she eyed the programmer. But she quickly recovered and said, "Well, if I'm going to get the staff to trust it, I'll have to know that it's trustworthy."

Hepman was clearly torn between pride in the system and caution at prying eyes. "Well, I guess Carter trusts you. You have to understand. This is the highest security in the company. Not even the Feds get to look at this."

"I feel honored," she said in deference.

Hepman walked to the entrance to his office and hailed a colleague at a nearby workstation on the main floor. "Jeff, what Caduceus version have you got loaded now?"

A shorthaired, Asian man in his twenties looked up from the console. "Beta 4.4."

"Good," said Hepman, then to Jenny he added, "We'll take a look at the decision process as it moves through the program. I can even show you some actual programming code, that is, if it will mean anything to you."

"Sure. I don't know much about programming, but I'd love to see it," said Jenny. She knew a little about programming, and she wanted Hepman to believe she could appreciate his genius. Besides, she might learn something about MOM.

Hepman sat at his console and logged on.

"We'll use one of our sample patients. I like Veronica Sigma." Veronica was one of seventy composite patients invented by the staff. She was thirty years old and presented to a GHB clinic with frequent headaches, dizziness, some nausea, a rash on her buttocks, and fatigue. She was also irritable, tearful, had a history of endometriosis, and was infertile.

Jenny watched as MOM prompted for questions on the screen, as if speaking to a nurse or doctor. What is her white blood count? Enter her temperature, gait, visual disturbances, dietary history. Current medications, checked against what the computer knew was prescribed. The patient's past medical history was displayed for confirmation. It included some family history: her father's alcoholism, her mother's herpes. At each question a list of options was presented, showing normal and abnormal values, much like a standard laboratory report.

The depth and intricacy of the detailed history seemed to bring the patient to life. Jenny marveled at the efficiency of the program. It would have been easy to believe that there was really a physician on the other end of this terminal, typing in the correct responses. That this was the work of a computer, born from the mind of this geek next to her, was unfathomable. Suddenly, there appeared on the screen the spread legs of a naked woman, her genitals completely exposed. A cloth was draped over her hips and her buttocks seemed to be on the edge of a seat. Jenny realized she was looking at an image of a pelvic exam of the mythical patient.

"Notice that the rash spreads all the way around from the buttocks," said Hepman, with a self-satisfied smirk. Jenny felt his intense gaze upon her as if to measure her response to the image. "I can rotate the image for a better look," he offered. Hepman clicked on a screen button labeled "rotation" and spun the three-dimensional image around. He zoomed in for a close-up of her labia, delicately pointing out a part of the rash to make this all seem to be about medicine. Jenny tried to remain dispassionate and clinical.

"Yes, that is quite an aid to remote diagnosis. Can MOM actually use those images?"

"She does much more with the X-rays and MRIs. These images are mostly for confirmation by doctors and nurses. They're stored with the chart, just like in the doctor's office. Eventually computers will be able to interpret any image you can photograph and these pictures will be invaluable for research. They can also help to document the need for treatment."

"Isn't it expensive taking these pictures and transmitting them around?"

"Cheaper than dirt," said Hepman. "We don't have to deal with film and developers anymore. Just about every physician and dental office now has a hundred dollar device that will stuff images into the computer with a cheap video camera. Thousands of images. From here we can see just about anything we want."

"No kidding," said Jenny with a nod to the spread-eagled woman on the computer screen. "I hope you have some protections on this."

"Hey, we're all professionals here," countered Hepman, with a look of mock innocence.

Turning back to the screen, Hepman pressed the "Diagnosis" button. MOM munched on the data for a few seconds and then flashed an assessment on the screen:

> Probable diagnosis: Pregnancy, with secondary posterior dermatitis. Recommend: pregnancy test, topical cortisone based cream applications to rash. Loose clothing. Reassess after pregnancy test.

"Pregnant! But it said she was infertile!" exclaimed Jenny.

"Yes, that's what her medical history showed. That's the beauty of MOM. It's like working with the best physicians in the world. Because you are. MOM embodies all those scientific procedures that make for accurate diagnoses. This was an actual case, from Harvard I believe. Turns out she was pregnant. MOM saw through all of the distractions and false signs, coming to the right decision. This case example really shows what she can do."

Jenny watched as Hepman continued with the example, reading the results of the laboratory tests, confirming the pregnancy. A form came on screen asking if the client elected to continue the pregnancy. Hepman clicked "yes" and MOM scheduled the client into a prenatal program, prescribed some vitamins, and arranged for follow-up visits. Within a month MOM would know the sex of the child. The patient would have to pay extra for that information.

For the next hour Hepman guided Jenny through case examples. The Caduceus program made MOM a superior diagnostician. Time after time the medical data would be entered and MOM would correctly diagnosis the illness. Jenny even went back and changed some of the lab results on the patients, giving them different diseases or additional problems. MOM seemed to work flawlessly, recommending tests, referring to specialists, suggesting medication. Mouse Medicine, a point-and-click affair.

"This is very exciting, Greg. You've done a wonderful job. I can see the value in this expert system. Does it ever make mistakes?"

"Sure. Who doesn't? But it only makes them once. It has the ability to learn from its mistakes, which is more than you can say for some medical practitioners. That's why feedback and close monitoring is so important. MOM gets smarter. Want to see some coding?"

"Sure," replied Jenny.

Hepman ended the program and called up the written computer program language that runs the machine. Jenny noticed he entered no passwords as he entered this highly protected part of the system. That meant he used a log-on script that automatically entered the code words for entry, at least at this terminal.

Hepman's beeper went off. He glanced at the message on the display and quickly swapped out the computer code screen to the more customary MOM screen.

"Our agent is back with the data on that guy, Roy Dahl. I want to take a quick look," said Hepman.

He clicked to open the folder he had created earlier. Seventeen files listed in chronological order documented the recent activities of Mr. Dahl and his family. Hepman scanned and peeked through them. There were medical visits, pharmacy prescriptions, MasterCard listings of over-the-counter medicines purchased at Wal-Mart. These included a large number of nasal sprays and Benadryl, very popular with hay fever sufferers and cocaine users. The Dahl family medical records showed no history of allergies. Most of the purchases were made by Mr. Dahl, despite the fact that his wife did the grocery shopping and used the ATM card.

One listing from the wife's charges stood out. The cyber-agent found a book purchase on her credit card at a drug treatment facility. It was entitled " When Someone You Love is Addicted," published by Narc-Anon, a nonprofit support group for the families of narcotic-addicted individuals.

"I believe this is called Bingo," said Hepman. "I think our boy is going to be having a little chat with human resources."

"How can you be sure it's him?" asked Jenny.

"Well, it ain't his eight-year-old son or six-year-old daughter. The guy's drinking enough Benadryl to dry up Lake Tahoe and his wife's buying books. I think we have enough to proceed. This is our client. We have a vested interest in his healthcare."

"Do you investigate many claims like this? I mean, it's like a private investigation. Must be expensive?"

"It's actually pretty cheap. The problem with private investigators is that you have to pay someone to nose around to dig up a couple of facts on someone. With MOM, we just tell her the facts we're interested in and she'll launch a search. Computers are great at matching stuff up. And electricity's pretty cheap."

"So you just tell this little cyber-creature to go scurrying around the Internet, dropping into databases, and hauling back incriminating data."

"Pretty much," said Hepman, missing the subtle outrage in her voice.

Hepman transmitted the Dahl information to Carter, who would relay it back to the company. A couple of mouse clicks brought the computer code back to the screen.

Jenny spent an hour looking at the flow charts and coding of Caduceus, how it interpreted symptoms, branched to diagnostic subroutines, retrieved medical data, and searched for community resources. She was sufficiently familiar with computer coding to get an overview of how it all worked. Yet, her head was spinning by the end of the day. It was like walking through some fantastic futuristic ride at

Disney. But this was real. Too real.

"Greg, I'm getting close to overload for today. I think I want to just digest this for a little while. In fact, it'd probably be a good idea for me to just run these samples through a few times to get the feel of the system. Then I can start to make some recommendations. Can I get access to these case examples?"

"Consider it done. I'll give you access to this folder." Hepman updated the authorizations. "I might as well give you level-four access. You can log on from Progressive or home if you need to. Just be sure you read the rules on passwords."

"What level of access do you have?"

"We go up to level six. I have level seven," he said with a conspiratorial grin.

Around four o'clock she returned to her desk, waving to Mable Jackson while passing her cubicle. Mable motioned that she wanted to talk when she was finished with a call. Jenny checked her personal GHB mailbox to find three e-mails, a fax, and a voice message from Hepman. The e-mails were standard human resources welcome messages with directions to policy and procedure manuals. Nothing from Progressive. Out of sight, out of mind.

Jenny called home for messages. Daisy, her computer, played a message from her mother that bore anxiety about her father. Another was from Mark, wanting to get together. She didn't want to use the company phone to call long distance, and she was leery of using her credit card after this morning's adventures with Hepman, so she instructed Daisy to call on her data line over the Internet. She reached their voice mail and left a message that she'd call in the evening.

Mark picked up his phone on the first ring. "Lipton."

"Barrett," was her mocking reply.

"Hey, Jenny. How goes it in the belly of the beast?"

"I need a big hug. And some Thai food. And someone to feed me."

"You know, I got a lead on a guy that might be interested. Busy tonight?"

"Hopefully. I'd love to see you and unload some burden. Mark, this place is amazing. It's like they're in Lear jets and everyone else is on bicycles."

"Meet your new boss yet?"

"Yeah, he seems okay. Haven't got to know him yet. They've been rushing me into this new project."

"Caduceus?"

"Wow. Good reporting. I thought that was all an in-house secret."

"No, it's in the trades as their new secret weapon. God, they act like Microsoft hiding a new operating system. Everyone knows all the details a year ahead of release."

"I've got to call home tonight. My dad's sounding ill and mom's concerned. I may need a friend and some TLC."

"Sure, I'll bring a liter of good times. Say, I've got some Elaina stuff. I visited her old apartment, just sniffing around, and ran into a neighbor. She gave me a little box of junk. Some tapes and things."

"She?"

"An old grandmotherly type," he lied.

"I'll bet. Sure, I'd like to see it. Maybe we'll play some of Elaina's music."

"I don't think they're that kind of tape. These are not like any cassette I've ever seen. Kinda square, with a metal bottom."

"Backup tapes."

"What?"

"They sound like computer backup tapes, Mr. Technology. Every week or so you're supposed to copy all the data on your hard disk to these tapes, then store them in a safe place. That way, if a burglar or lightening zaps your computer, you can recover quickly."

"So this might be the missing data from her computer, Ms. Detective?"

"That's right. Maybe we'll check it out tonight."

"I'll put it on the priority list, right next to cleaning the grout. I don't get to see you that often, and I don't want to play computer."

"Okay. Be at my place at seven. Maybe you could stop at the Siam Orchid for take-out."

***

Nora continued to deteriorate as the cancer ravaged her body. Within two months she could hardly stand up for five minutes. She would struggle to find a comfortable position on the couch. The injections came more frequently. Ezra could see the light fading in her eyes. The stress was beginning to overwhelm him. He called upon neighbors to help watch her while he ran errands. He avoided calling his insurance company for assistance for fear they would run another test and discover her use of heroin. Yet she was needing care beyond his ability.

"Ezra, maybe we should get a nurse to come in. I'm sure the

insurance pays for that," encouraged Nora. She was upset that he rarely seemed to smile anymore. He was becoming obsessed with her comfort, yet there was little he could do. "And you look like you're losing weight," she'd scold.

Ezra called GHB to see about getting some help. He'd heard about Hospice care for the terminally ill. He asked the case manager if there was such a program for Nora.

"Sure is," said the young man brightly. "I can have one of our home health team come out to help. The aid can help with meds, personal hygiene, and IVs. I see that Nora's on some hefty pain medicine. Our staff can help administer it if you like."

"No, I think she likes it better when I do it. She trusts me."

"I understand sir. But if we have a medical professional at your home we might as well use her."

"Is this an aide or a nurse?"

"An aide."

"I think I'll just continue giving her the medicine."

"Mr. Whitney, I see in the record that there has been a concern for substance abuse with your wife. I think it better if our staff follows this closely."

Ezra could feel the rage building inside him, but he restrained any outburst. "Do I need a referral from her doctor?"

"Yes. All you need to do is call him or her and mention that you've spoken with me. They can order the home visit."

Ezra felt relief that the ball ended in his court. He didn't need any agents from the insurance company coming in to enforce their will. She'd be right back to being undermedicated, with a watchdog to see she doesn't cheat.

Ezra lost about ten pounds from anxiety and reduced calories. He looked gaunt and frail. The illicit medicine took an increasing bite from their limited budget, so he had to economize somewhere. He dropped his food intake to about 900 calories a day, mostly pasta and peanut butter.

Nora fell on a Thursday, while Ezra was redeeming a McDonald's coupon for a senior's meal. She stumbled while rising from the commode and pitched her head into the faucet on the sink. When Ezra found her an hour later, there was dried blood on a gash over her left eye and a heavy bruise on her arm and shoulder. She was disoriented at first, calling to their long dead cat. Then her eyes cleared and she gazed at her husband. They both knew this accident signified a new chapter in their lives. Although she had no broken bones, her spirit had been shattered. Looking into the tired face of Ezra, she wanted to leave the man in peace. This was too big a responsibility now. Ezra wouldn't admit it, but she could. It was her turn to take protective action.

"Ezra, I'm scared to be here alone. I think we need some real help, maybe a nursing home. I love you to death, but we're going to have to face this."

While she napped, Ezra called GHB to ask about assistance. MOM had queried the benefits before the case manager said "Hello." Like most Medicare HMO programs, the quality of the resources had to be measured against the feared rate of utilization. To keep costs down GHB had aggressively negotiated some bottom-line contracts with nursing homes. There were now 230 nationwide that bore the title Great Benefit Extended Care Network. Ezra waited while MOM coughed up the names of some contracting facilities. He winced when the case manager identified the only two available in his area.

"Rosselet Gardens and Laurel Springs Manor. Mrs. Whitney will have to have a thorough examination to be sure she's qualified. Your primary care physician can do that. The homes are covered at 95 percent, so your out-of-pocket should be small . . . actually thirteen dollars a day."

"A day," roared Ezra. "For how long!"

"Uh, as long as she's there. Well, only to a $2,500 deductible each calendar year."

"I don't know if I can afford that."

"If you don't have any money or any significant assets, you might get Medicaid supplements."

"Welfare?"

"Supplements."

"Who sets the prices on these establishments?"

"Well, Laurel Springs is a GHB subsidiary and Rosselet Gardens is under contract with us."

"Are those my only options?"

"Well, you can go to any facility you want, but there is a substantially reduced benefit. Only $70 per day."

"I thought when we signed with your company all of this would be taken care of," Ezra shouted in frustration.

"Every medically necessary treatment is provided for in your contract," said the female voice reading from the screen. "I can also refer you to our extended care financing department. They have some really great deals on low-interest loans." A flag on her screen instructed, "A customer can 'hear' a smile on your face." She grinned.

"What can you tell me about it?"

"Do you own your home?"

"Yes."

"Well, many of our members find that, even with our great coverage, sometimes all the expenses are not covered. You can go to a bank to get a loan, but we try to make it easier. It's a special annuity program. We guarantee to cover your healthcare expenses in return for a mortgage on your home."

Ezra was livid. "You want my home now?"

"Oh, no sir. We would just take out a portion to cover any expenses that could put you in a financial bind. I can put you in touch with that division. They can explain it better than I can."

"So what you're saying is that I sign my house over to my health insurance company, who then promises to keep me healthy until I die, at which time they get the house."

"Something like that. Sir, that department can help you understand this. May I connect you with them?"

"Honey, I've been dealing with your company for a couple of years now. All they've done is cause me pain. I'm sure not going to trust them now."

"Well, if I can be of any more assistance, please feel free to call," said the unperturbed voice on the phone.

As Ezra hung up Nora groaned, "They seem to contract with some pretty bad places."

Both establishments had tarnished reputations in Columbus. Rosselet Gardens had been near bankruptcy for years. Laurel Springs had been only provisionally approved for occupancy by the State Board of Health Institutions to ease the crowding of the elderly.

"Snake pits," cried Ezra. "You're not going to either of them. We'll make it work. I'll hire an assistant or even a secretary if necessary. I won't have you smelling of urine."

Nora took his hand. She was fearful of her own weakness and couldn't bare the anguish in his face. They were running out of choices. She knew the money was a great concern. Retirement had been so expensive. Now Ezra seemed panicked much of the time. Nora began to suspect that the medicine must be costing them extra. A shiver shot through her as she thought of leaving her home, leaving Ezra, going somewhere else to die. She looked at Ezra's tired eyes. "It'll work out," she said to soothe him. A warm peace radiated from her hazel eyes. "Let's go sit on the porch swing."

Chapter 18

Jenny checked her Progressive voice mail and retrieved a message from Laura Paine, her Progressive boss. Or was she still even employed at Progressive? She got Laura on the line quickly.

"Jenny, how's it going over there?"

"Pretty well. Their technology is amazing. And the place is so big. I miss my family back at Progressive."

"Did you hear? Larry Harrington is gone."

"Gone?"

"Outta here. Sent out a memo about personal family needs and turned over the reins to GHB. Everyone's running scared."

"Any word on layoffs?"

"Nothing clear. Seems you're the only one whose been welcomed into their ranks. Nice going."

"We've got some really good people over there. I'm sure they'll want to tap that talent pool."

"I'm not so sure. Two of our staff went to interviews and were treated like burger flippers. Got the impression GHB wants 'em young, dumb, and easy. Talked a lot about their 'corporate culture' and need for technological team playing, whatever that is. Fortunately, I got a headhunter talking to Blue Cross."

"Sounds like it's pretty hectic over there."

"Panic is a better word. It's also kind of sad," said Laura in a revealing comment. "Like our family is being broken up. Our guardian father is out, the family is being split up. The new foster parents are big and scary. We've all suddenly realized it's the end of an era."

"Maybe more than you know," said Jenny. She wanted to tell Laura about the new medicine at GHB, but she could see it would only add to her grief. "I hope I'll get back there next week to see you guys."

"Mums the word on my job searches, okay?" said Laura.

"Sure. If I hear of anything, I'll give you a call."

"Thanks. You sure lucked out, girl."

Funny, she wasn't feeling very lucky. In fact, Jenny had an overpowering desire to become a mindless checker at a fast food restaurant.

A gentle hand caressed Jenny's shoulder. She turned to see the beaming face of Mable Jackson.

"How they treatin' you, Jenny? Is that Hitman trying to turn you into a robot?"

"Me and everyone else. He sure loves that machine."

"Don't he ever. I swear that man has silicon running in his veins. If they did brain surgery on him they'd find an old microchip, with a few bent pins, if you know what I mean. But don't worry, honey, medicine will always be about people helping people. This computer stuff is just somebody's new toy. Makes 'em feel important to say they got a big computer. I see my grandsons fighting over the Nintendo. Same thing with these execs."

"Thanks, Mable, I need to know I'm not crazy. I have to admit, though, Hepman showed me some impressive things in Caduceus, things that could really help people."

"Dog and pony show, honey. They just bring that out to impress government officials. That ain't how it works. You seem like a bright girl. Maybe you should run some cases on the real system. I know you're supposed to be helping us poor techno-phobic medical staff come up to speed on this. Take a look at what we see. Try running some cases tomorrow." Mable gave her a squeeze on the shoulder and returned to her cubicle. Jenny logged off and went home.

***

The pungent aroma of curry and garlic filled the interior of Mark's car. Bouncing on the passenger seat were bulging containers of Thai food, one of Mark and Jenny's favorite culinary adventures. Many good times in their relationship revolved around rice, noodles, and meats in such exotic dishes as chicken *musamen*, *pork moo kem*, and *plah lad prig*, a sinus-clearing spicy fish. From his long history with Jenny, Mark had come to believe there was an aphrodisiac quality to this food. He hoped the effect was still potent, for he would love to be close with Jenny tonight.

The rash on his lips from the nickel reaction had quieted down. The emptiness of that experience had caused a mild awakening in him. Man cannot live on a diet of plastic food or plastic relationships. There is a time when a responsible person must take better care of spirit and body.

Elaina's death illustrated how precipitous life could be. He wanted the touch of a woman he respected. A woman he could love. Shit, a woman he did love. And it scared the hell out of him. Jenny represented all the good things he should do for himself, and of course he rebelled against it like a misguided teenager. Every time she moved closer to capturing his heart, he ran off. He felt as if he hadn't matured a day since the tenth grade. Everyone else had moved on down the road of life. Mark was still taunting girls from a distance, not wanting anyone to get so close they would see his fear.

Though the Thai food initially spawned a reverie of some of their great sexual moments, he soon found the images turned to more poignant times. When his father died. When he was fired from The Daily. Jenny keeping him in school. Her believing in him as a reporter of substance when he was assigned to cover fluffy social events. Why was he still chasing twenty-something flesh pots? Because they're there? No, because you're a jerk, he corrected.

The on-again off-again relationship with Jenny was not entirely his doing. He was wise enough to know it played into her needs as well. But there was little doubt he limited the relationship more than she. The few times she tried to talk with him about her struggles with other male relationships, he could feel the dragon of jealousy rising quickly within him. He'd sidetrack the conversation, offer some stupid one-liner advice, and move onto another topic. No matter what their official status, Mark wasn't comfortable with images of Jenny in the arms of someone else. He knew the only way to prevent such images was to step up to the plate. But he'd already been at bat with her three times. How many shots would he get? The freeway exit to Jenny's home loomed up, and Mark guided the Maxima off the artery.

***

A series of fierce crimson brush strokes slashed across the paper suspended on an easel, violently portraying the thermonuclear origins of the sunlight that gave life to the garden depicted. The pastoral scene was virtually splattered on the paper, then pushed and smeared into a semblance of order. Emily Schuster-Gray's watercolor paintings were selling faster than she could produce them. It was heartening to know that her art works were popular on their own merits, not just as a vehicle to support her husband. People were clamoring for her pieces.

The petite, 43-year-old brunette with almond eyes was clad in a paint-spattered flannel shirt that hung down over tattered denim shorts. She sipped an iced tea as she considered another blend of color. Red-tipped, manicured fingers nimbly manipulated the brushes from paint cup to paper. At that existential moment, there was only her and the earth. She was trying to capture it on canvas.

After Donald's election to the Senate two years ago, Emily had taken a well-needed 18-month hiatus from all commitments, primarily to re-bond with the family. The extreme pressures and scheduling of the Senatorial campaign had exhausted everyone, including the two children. Katy, the 14-year-old, was pulled into the campaign through Nickelodeon and the Disney Channel, making appearances at celebrity charity events and competitions. Brian, the 12-year-old, always shy and reserved, had a harder time with the spotlight and finally withdrew to private school. This created a painful gap in the family that Emily resolved to repair when the last ballot was counted.

"Mom," yelled Brian from the upstairs bedroom. "Where's my cup for baseball?"

The earth was moved off its pedestal as the spell was broken. "Probably in the laundry room, where it fell out of your jock, AGAIN." She was quite sure testosterone impaired the brains of young men, certain they couldn't find a hat on their head with a mirror and a flashlight.

"When's Dad getting home?" asked Brain.

Their Southern California home sat high in the hills overlooking the city of Anaheim, the home of Disneyland and the bad bond deals of Orange County government. The sun was slipping into the Pacific Ocean at 7:30 P.M. Donald had called her as his plane took off from Washington, DC at 2 P.M. PST. After a five-hour flight, the trip from John Wayne International Airport to their home in Anaheim would take only half an hour. "Probably within an hour or so. He'll meet us at the game." Her comment was answered by the grating metallic crash of the washing machine lid. "Of course, Brian," she thought to herself with a smile, "I hid your damn cup in the washing machine like any normal mother."

"Found it," he finally proclaimed, speaking from somewhere near the family room.

At around 8:45 P.M., as Brian slid in a cloud of dust to steal home plate, Donald Gray wrapped his arms around Emily as he joined her in the baseball stands. "Hi, sexy."

"Hello," she answered, moving into his grasp. "I've missed you, big boy. We've got some catching up to do."

Brian was scanning the crowd as he dusted himself off on the walk to the dugout. His face exploded into a dimpled smile when he saw his father waving. "Did you see it?" he mouthed. His father gave him a thumbs up.

"How goes the battle? Did you get to skewer Baldwin?"

"No. Thank goodness his plane was delayed. Rescheduled him for next week. We still don't have much to open him up with."

"Oh! Barry called, from the local office. He said a reporter from the Chronicle wants to interview you while you're in town. May be doing a piece on Great Health Benefit."

"Sorry, I just want a quiet weekend with my wife and family." The Senator wove his arm around her back, inside her jacket, gently cupping her breast in his hand. "Is this spot taken?"

"Forever and ever," she said, clenching his arm even closer. "But I do think you should talk with him. Maybe he's dug up something you can use."

"Those interviews are usually a one-way street."

"Well, if you got nothing now, you can't lose any more."

"How's the painting going?" he said to change the subject.

"Very well. I feel completely refreshed and inspired. I think the kids are in a good place too, which makes it easier to take the time to paint."

"I'm glad you took that time off. You were such a trooper during the campaign. I felt so self-absorbed, so selfish. You had to sacrifice so much."

"It wasn't that bad. You had to focus on you. You were the candidate."

"You know what I mean," he said with a somber look.

"Oh, that. It wasn't your fault. It was our decision. It was the best decision. Let's put it out of our minds. Please Donald, you'll make me cry."

Emily Schuster-Gray stared out to the baseball diamond, not seeing a thing. Donald gazed at the profile of his wife, marveling at her strength and dedication.

Three years ago, then–Congressman Gray was diagnosed with prostate cancer during a routine physical. It took a few weeks to narrow down the specific type and spread of the cancer, but he soon discovered it was an aggressive, fast-growing type. Fortunately, it was still contained locally in his groin and radiation treatment was deemed appropriate. There was concern about a press leak to the public. The word "cancer" was likely the death knell for a political candidacy, even if the disease could be completely controlled. The medical records were sanitized under an alias, and Donald paid cash for the treatments.

For twenty weeks through the spring and into June, he received chemotherapy and was blasted with cobalt-60, five times a week. The doses were so small and focused that there were few side effects, other than some reddening of the scrotum and swelling of his testicles. Emily joked that, with a green jock, he'd make a great Christmas tree ornament. Fortunately, the symptoms were so mild it hardly interfered with his campaign schedule, and had no effect on their sex life.

A few weeks after the therapy ended, and while the household was sharing a wretched flu bug, Emily noticed some breast tenderness and thought she detected a lump. Her personal physician, Ellen Grosner, advised her to wait until after the flu passed, which took two more weeks. During her physical exam the doctor made a most astounding proclamation. Emily was almost ten weeks pregnant. Her diaphragm had failed her, despite her doubts about her own fertility in the last few years.

"Well, young woman," said the doctor. "I see you and yours are still sexually active. Unless there's something you need to tell me."

"No, it's Donald's all right. I'm just so surprised. I didn't think it was possible, particularly after his treatment."

"Treatment?" asked her gynecologist.

"Yes, he had prostate cancer. He received radiation and chemo-therapy treatments. Apparently it did the job."

"How long ago was this?" the doctor asked.

"Through most of the spring and into June."

"That's about when you became pregnant."

"Is there a problem?" asked Emily.

"There might be. We'll need to do some tests. But I'm concerned that the radiation treatments to the groin could have a major impact on the genetic integrity of the sperm. I'm afraid there's a chance some were damaged. We'll have to monitor this closely," replied the doctor.

Confusion and anxiety set upon Emily and Donald. It was clearly not the best time in their lives to be having another child, what with the impending campaign and all. She and Donald accepted it quietly while they waited for some test results. They didn't tell the children right away, for there was no telling what the tests would discover.

Abortion had never been seriously discussed as a personal issue between the couple, only as a social–political issue. They instinctively avoided the topic.

The lab results, including Alpha-Fetoprotein test and Trisomy 18, were unusual, but inconclusive. Emily was nearing the point in the pregnancy, 15 weeks, where an amniocentesis, the most definitive test, would be appropriate, but then the pregnancy faltered. First spotting, then serious bleeding. The amniocentesis was postponed until she stabilized. At 19 weeks the procedure was done, but it still required a two-week wait for the results. Emily's protruding abdomen was easily seen, even through baggy clothes. She greatly reduced her social calendar and stayed close to home. The physicians were expressing grave concern about the few lab results that were clear.

At 21 weeks Emily received the horrific news. The fetus had multiple and serious chromosomal deformities. Donald's irradiated sperm's genetic package had been severely damaged. It appeared that the child's brain was outside the skull. The chest cavity wasn't expanding for normal lung capacity. The child would likely experience grave pain upon birth from its exposed nerves, and then die in agony within the week. The couple decided that their Christian values wouldn't allow such a crime against nature if it was in their power to stop it.

Because of the campaign and their fear of a media leak, the procedure was masked in the records as a common D & C for uterine fibroids. Emily quietly underwent an abortion in the middle of the week, on a Wednesday morning. Donald was beside her, gripping her hand, commanding her attention over the hideous sound of the vacuum device. And then it was over. Hormones flooded her in the absence of the fetus, rocking her emotions. Donald held fast, reassuring, calming, clutching her close. "We did the best thing for the child," he said. "And God *knows* we did."

A week later Emily gave a speech to the National Library Association in support of her husband's candidacy. Donald was overwhelmed by the strength of his petite wife.

It was this sad recollection that Emily pushed aside at the ball game. It was over. Painful history. She held onto Don's hand, but she didn't stop staring into the outfield. Their son appeared in left field, massaging his mitt, a healthy, strapping boy, with a popular and accomplished sister. The pain was eased as Emily counted her many blessings.

The final product from Elliot Mears' computer was a list of

287,433 women in the western US that had likely had an abortion within the last four years. Incredibly, all the data, including names, addresses, and the beginning and ending dates of their possible pregnancies, were contained on a metallic tape cartridge no bigger than a box of crayons. Elliot's computer had transferred the data to streaming tape, the same type of cartridge that held the secrets to Elaina Ruiz' computer. He had three in hand, but two were merely copies of the first, to be placed safely in storage. The master copy was destined for the mailservice bureau, where its contents would be transferred to individual letters and envelopes and then mailed out in search of the original owners of the data, the many women whose collective pain had been captured and tabulated by immense, yet unseen, machines.

"Crandall, here it is," said Elliot, without giving up the cartridge. "I hope you have a check for $57,000 to handle this bulk mailing."

"Right here, Mr. Mears." Crandall had exhausted all of his resources and maxed out his home equity credit account to come up with the funds. The mail house wouldn't extend them any credit. Elliot took the check and dropped it and the cartridge into a padded, oversized envelope.

"In about three or four days the letters will start arriving. I'd expect in some households it will create a lot of conversation, but in others, it will hardly see the light of day. Silence for forty dollars seems a reasonable deal. Maybe the little woman won't get her hair done next week. It's such a nominal sum, easy to hide, yet it will forever corrupt their sense of privacy. None of these women could advise a sister to follow in her footsteps without remembering these ghosts."

"Good job. Oh, was there something else you mentioned on the phone?" said Crandall.

"Yes, I held one back for you to consider mailing personally. It might be an ace in the hole, or a "get out of jail free card," depending on what game you're playing. The name emerged while I was screening the data. It took a while to realize who it really was."

"Well, who was it?" asked Crandall.

"Emily Schuster," said Elliot, with raised eyebrows.

"The name sounds familiar. Schuster, Schuster," he repeated, trying to make the connection.

"Crandall, you need to spend more time with <u>People</u> magazine. Emily Schuster-Gray. The California senator's wife."

"His wife. She's on the list? You're sure?"

"I checked it three times. Then I examined some old news stories. Sure enough, three years ago the Senator's wife was reported ill.

Couldn't attend a few civic functions in June, during the height of the primary season. Reportedly had a virus. The records say different. Crandall, she was pregnant in June and un-pregnant in October. Maybe the public has a right to know about the self-serving morality of the dear liberal Senator from Southern California."

"Thanks for holding the letter back. This is going to take some extra thought. What a marvelous program you have, Elliot. Seek the truth, said the Lord, and it shall be revealed. Your computer has done that for us."

Crandall wrapped his arm around Elliot as a show of affection, but the computer hack was uncomfortable with real human contact. Elliot needed to keep things theoretical, or "virtual" as he liked to describe them. Silicone, the primary substance of sand and computer chips, was the only medium he trusted. Flesh was too real, too risky, too painful.

Crandall left with the letter to Emily Schuster-Gray tucked in his sport coat. He knew this was important, but he sensed that it was much bigger than he could imagine. This was out of his league. A Senator's wife, and so recent. What did he remember about Senator Gray? Wasn't he the man on some committee that was causing headaches for the insurance companies? Oh, yeah, the Joint-Congressional Subcommittee on Health Insurance Reform. They were proposing some changes to healthcare.

He bet the insurance lobby would love to have this little piece of cake. Maybe they'd cut Crandall's group a deal on more mailing lists. Hell, expand this project to fifty million women. Make them all pay. Crandall was starting to get excited, yet a cautious wind quickly swept through him. "Don't fall off a cliff while you're looking at a pie in the sky," his mother always said. He needed some consultation on this. Talk with Jerry, maybe take it to an insurance lobbyist. His head was swimming.

"Oh, God, please guide me through this," he prayed.

Chapter 19

Jenny arrived home, plopped down her briefcase, swung a grocery bag onto the kitchen counter, and dropped her coat over the back of a chair. It was 6:15 P.M. before she left GHB, barely enough time to get home with some groceries before Mark arrived. She had so much to tell him about this behemoth machine called GHB, but she'd have to get his sworn statement to silence, first. He was a reporter, after all.

"Daisy, messages!" she shouted to her computer as she flew to her bedroom, wrestling her sweater over her head. Daisy's screen sprang to life.

"Three, messages. Message one."

"Honey," she heard the voice of her mother. "Please give a call when you get in. Dad isn't cooperating, and I think he's getting worse." A click signified the end of the message.

"Message two," said Daisy.

"Hey," said Mark. "I'm bringing some saki to add to our Asian mood. I think you have some of those little cups you're supposed to serve it in. Or we could just guzzle it. See you soon."

"Message three," said Daisy.

There were a few seconds of silence, followed by some scratchy modem sounds and beeps. The series repeated twice and then abruptly cut off. Jenny figured it must have been an errant fax machine, though Daisy would have automatically detected a fax and received it.

"Checking e-mail" announced Daisy. "None on service."

Jenny pulled on some sweat pants and a tee shirt and then sat at her desk. The display usually provided the caller's name and phone number, but there was nothing listed for the errant call. She clicked on the listed item to play it again. Squawks and hisses, distinctly a modem. Daisy, like any modern personal computer, could receive modem commands from other computers, but this feature was not currently active, since Jenny rarely needed to access Daisy from work. It was unusual that a modem connection would have been attempted.

Jenny clicked on the call from her mother and Daisy dialed the number.

"Hello," was the hopeful response.

"Mom, hi."

"Hi, honey. Thanks for getting back to me so quick. Maybe you can talk some sense into Dad. He just won't do anything about his stomach pains. Been that way ever since that stupid surgery in Medford."

"Whoa, Mom. What surgery in Medford? You guys haven't been keeping me up to date. What's going on?"

"He's been having this gall bladder problem," said Mrs Barrett. "You know, feeling sick, gets a stitch in his side, can't sit still. The new doctor, Majani, says the gall bladder has to come out. But they send us all the way to Medford to some contract hospital. Said it was a new, safer procedure. They had this scope thing looking inside him. Just made some little cuts to his tummy. Said they took out the whole thing through this little hole."

"His gall bladder?"

"Yes, through this little cut. It couldn't have been wider than my thumb."

"This was Monday, Mom?"

"Yes, honey, we came back on Tuesday. The doctor said Dad was doing fine, but he's been swelling up something awful. I don't like it. I want to see Dr. Shepard, but they have him over a barrel. He can't tell us anything without their okay."

"Whose okay?" demanded Jenny.

"Our insurance company, Axis Health."

"Let me talk to Dad."

Jenny heard her doorbell ring. She picked up the cordless phone, walked over to let Mark in, giving him a kiss on the side of the mouth, close, but noncommital.

"Dad," she said, eyeing Mark with a look of frustrated concern, "How do you feel?"

"I feel fine, for a guy who just swallowed a triple pepperoni pizza and a handful of thumb tacks. For a normal guy, I feel terrible," he quipped in a weak voice.

"Is it just from the surgery? What does Dr. Shepard say?"

"We're not seeing Shepard. They switched us to a new doctor, Majani over at Hubb Health. We protested, but Dr. Shepard can't see me without insurance okay. Since I'm under a Medicare contract, I can't even just see him on my own and pay cash. Jenny, I don't know what this is supposed to feel like. They told me next to nothing. All I can say is it hurts like hell and I look like I'm about to give birth to a Holstein. I knew I shouldn't have set foot in that hospital. I hate doctors."

"What's wrong with Shepard? We've been seeing him for years," said Jenny with increasing impatience.

"I don't know, hon. It's like he can't tell us anything. Like he might say the wrong thing. I have to get my diagnosis through a case manager at Axis Health. Never get the same person twice."

"Well, just go to someone else. Get another opinion, Dad."

"Not so easy. Grants Pass doesn't have that many docs. They all work for Axis Health. They call the tune up here. Besides, the insurance contract doesn't allow us to see anyone else."

"Dad, if it gets worse, I want you to go to a hospital. An emergency room. They'll have to look at you."

"It isn't that bad. But I'm sure not getting any better."

Jenny looked for encouragement from Mark.

"Dad, Mark Lipton is here. Yeah, that's the one. Pretends he's a reporter."

"Hi, Mr. B," said Mark, sharing the phone with Jenny.

"Hi Mark." The weakness in the voice was startling. Mark had always known the man to be strong and resilient. He looked at Jenny and motioned for her to fly up to be with her parents.

"Dad, I'm coming up there to see how you're doing. Mom probably needs my help."

"You don't need to do that, Jenny, I'll be fine. Just have to slap some people around up here."

"Okay, the exercise will probably do you good. But I want to see you two, and I have some time off. Heck, I was planning my vacation up there anyway. I can leave a little early."

"Okay, hon. Here's your mother. She'll talk to you."

"Mom, he sounds terrible."

"I know, dear. What can we do? No one's helping."

"I'll be up there Wednesday."

"Can you take time off from your new job?"

"I sure can. See you then. Call me tomorrow and let me know. Call the insurance company and demand some follow-up."

"Sure, Jen. I'll keep on top of it. I'm so glad you can come up.

You always handle these matters so well. Never get rattled like me. It gets hard up here alone."

"I know, Mom. Love you. Gotta go."

Jenny put down the phone and threw her arms around Mark, holding him tight.

"That man is going to drive me crazy," she said.

"The apple doesn't fall far from the tree, my dear."

"I'm sure he's okay. It's a pretty routine surgery. I just can't believe they had to go all the way to Medford to get a simple lap chole."

"A what?" asked Mark.

"Sorry, they took out his gall bladder. But these days they do it with just three small incisions and a laparoscope. They call it a laparoscopic cholecystectomy, or lap chole. No surgical scars. In and out procedure."

"Sorry, I'll skip that one, thank you."

The couple moved about the kitchen in a graceful dance as they spoke, grabbing plates and silverware. Jenny retrieved the little Oriental cups for the saki, which Mark opened and placed in the microwave to warm slightly.

"Dad hates doctors and surgery. Probably just kicking up a fuss because he had to relent. Hates to lose an argument."

"Said the apple to the tree."

"Stop it," she yelled in mock anger. "I'll make you kneel on this rice with bare knees, an old Chinese torture."

"Doesn't work with cooked rice."

Together they unpacked the cartons of earthly delights. Soon the table was covered with steaming platters of exotic food. They rolled their eyes and moaned in blissful unison as the pungent sauces and tangy vegetables spun magic on their palates.

"Sorry about your Dad."

"He'll be okay," replied Jenny.

"So how's the new job?"

Her face turned sour. "Pretty overwhelming. Lots of high-tech stuff. Different philosophy than Progressive."

"Hey, I noticed. I've been doing some research on the GHB for a story. Not exactly a family friendly company. It seems they're being sued or investigated by everyone."

"Mark, I don't want you dragging things out of me for your story. But I also don't know if this is the right place for me to be working. They're doing some weird stuff."

Mark poured another round of saki, which they both promptly

downed as if they were drinking tequila shooters. The warm rice wine acted quickly to lighten their mood.

"Do you want to just vent, or can I use any of this in a story? An anonymous source, of course," said Mark.

"Sorry," said Jenny as she downed her fourth saki, "I'm no longer responsible for my actions. Anything I say should be considered unreliable and I will deny it tomorrow."

"Okay, I'll just be a friend. But I do worry about you over there. These guys look like they play pretty rough. I don't want you getting squished."

"You know what's really weird. I think I have something like Elaina's job."

"Like I said, how many computer-wise psychologists are there in town? Do they know you were friends?"

"Well, no. I haven't let on that I knew her. They've just mentioned her by her last name."

"Why the secrecy?"asked Mark.

"I don't know. I'm not sure how they felt about her. Hepman, this guy I'm working with, didn't seem to like her. And with her death and all, I just didn't think I needed to bring it up. The staff acted strange when Carter, my new boss, mentioned her in a meeting."

"I'd polish up that resumé kid," Mark said as he began picking up empty cartons of food. They moved over to the sectional sofa and spread out to relax, saki in hand. Mark picked up the shoe box of Elaina's things and handed it to Jenny.

"Anything good?"

"Oh, look at this," she said, holding up one of the tapes. "This is definitely a backup tape." She tried to move in the direction of Elaina's computer, but her body wouldn't allow it. "Over there, that big slot in the front. You stick these in there and it will restore the data on the hard drive."

"From when?"

"From the last time it was backed up."

"When was that?"

Jenny turned the tape over in her hands. Elaina's printing was all over the cassette. "It looks like the last date was January 18, 1995."

"When did she go into the hospital?"

"The next day," said Jenny. "And the computer was erased two days later."

"Think you can restore it?"

"I'll give it a try," she said, reluctantly beginning to rise.

"I didn't mean right now."

"Look, it will take hours to transfer this data from the tape. Let me just get it started."

"Oh, please don't do it. That evil machine will consume you. I'll never see you again, at least this evening. Besides, it's rude to do computer stuff while young men are visiting."

He knew it was hopeless. He'd opened his big mouth and raised her curiosity. Jenny took the two tapes over to her computer and plugged them into the tape slot on her machine. Mark grudgingly slumped next to her on a chair to watch.

"Look, we'll get back to talking in a minute. Let's just see what we've got. I'll have Daisy check the format to find out what kind of backup program will work."

Jenny's fingers raced over the keyboard, then clicked rapidly at flashing dialogue boxes. The tape began moving in the slot and Daisy flashed a message, "Tape Identification in Progress" on the screen. Within two minutes a report appeared on the screen. "Great, it's compatible with my system. I'll just copy over my program to her computer and start the restore process." Jenny clicked away as Mark's gaze drifted from the screen to the back of her neck.

"Saki and soft skin. What a great combination," he thought, gently moving her hair aside to begin massaging the tight cords of her neck muscles. Jenny cooed, but continued working.

Jenny loaded Elaina's computer with the basic programs to begin the restoration process. She switched to the keyboard on the other computer and began to configure it for restoration.

"Oh, we have to run a test tape to be sure it's working. Could you grab one of those tapes on the third shelf, in the silver box?"

Mark tossed it to her. Jenny unwrapped it and shoved it into the slot. There was a flash of light, a small sizzling explosion, and the acrid smell of melted plastic. Jenny was knocked backward to the floor.

"Jenny, what happened?" shouted Mark as he hurried across the floor to her side.

"Jesus, the damn thing exploded. Gave me a shock."

They approached the smoking computer, which now had black marks from the explosion painted on the front panel where the tape was inserted. Jenny pulled the power plug from the rear of the machine. She grabbed some tissues and withdrew the still smoldering backup tape cassette. It was completely ruined, for the tape was fused to the casing.

"Let's see what went wrong," said Jenny as she grabbed a screwdriver.

"Are you sure it's safe?"

She didn't reply. With her power screwdriver she had the computer cabinet off in seconds. Smoke billowed up as she removed it, and she fanned it away with her hand. She then grabbed a small flashlight and started searching around.

Mark looked inside the open cabinet of Elaina's computer with apprehension. "So you know all about these computer parts?"

"Yes, thanks to my brother. Actually, it's all pretty simple. It's really only about ten parts stuck together on a circuit board. People are just intimidated by how complicated these things look. They're easier to fix than a toaster."

"Ah, the great secret is out," said Mark.

"Sure. Here, this is the power supply, the video card, and the floppy disk drive. This big square chip is the brains of the computer. If you want it brainier, you can just pull it out and stick in another. I wish guys were like that."

"Sorry, our brains are soldered in."

"Yeah, soldered right to your favorite digit, I might add," she said, gently squeezing the bulge of his penis through his jockey shorts. "Anyway, to finish your tour, this is the memory, where it does its thinking, and this is the hard drive, where it stores everything it thinks about."

Jenny was following a wire to the tape drive.

"Holy shit. It's booby-trapped! Someone ran a high power wire to the tape drive so that anything plugged into it would be incinerated. Someone didn't want this machine restored. In fact, it seems like they set it up so that if anyone inserted these backup tapes they would be ruined. Pretty clever."

"Why?"

"I don't know why, and I don't know who. But they're damn clever."

"Do you think it was Elaina?"

"I can't imagine why she would want to destroy her own backup tapes. It's more like someone knew the tapes existed and wanted to be sure they couldn't be used."

"But why? What's supposed to be on these tapes?"

"Maybe the answer to the booby trap," said Jenny.

"Can you fix her machine to restore it?"

"I don't want to trust it now. There may be more booby traps. What I'll do is back it up from Daisy to another disk. A Jaz drive. I'll create a virtual computer, using Daisy. That way I can restore her machine to one simple disk and use Daisy to run it. I can use the tape drive in my system with her tapes. We'll restore her drive, check it for viruses, and take it from there. Whoever did this was sneaky."

Jenny instructed Daisy to restore Elaina's hard drive files to the Jaz disk. After a few breathless seconds, files began flowing onto the disk. The restoration was working.

"How long will it take?" asked Mark.

"About three hours. Think we can find anything to occupy our time?" she said with a new cup of saki, toasting to her victory.

They left the computer whirling and clicking on the desk and returned to the sofa. The talk was soft and inconsequential at first. Jenny flipped on the TV to American Movie Classics. Gary Cooper was running around the town in High Noon, looking for bad guys. Grace Kelly was hiding in a store, about to shoot one.

"Ah, the pistol-packing princess is about to save her man," said Mark. "Would you do the same for me?"

"You never stay around long enough to be my man, you bonehead. As soon as I saved your skinny ass, you'd be moving out of town."

"Well, they're married. Would you stay then?"

"If we're playing in fantasy land, sure. I'd stay and gun down the bad guys for you."

"And I would protect you," said Mark, toasting with more saki.

Mark leaned over and kissed her, gently on the lips at first, to test the waters. Jenny responded aggressively, opening her mouth and invading him with her tongue. His desire was launched like a rocket. His face was buried in her hair and the scent of her seemed to rush through him. As he began to break the kiss, Jenny pushed him over on the couch, ending up on top. Mark knew they were about to make love, but he still felt a bit ashamed about the earlier experience with the pierced neighbor of Elaina. He wanted this to mean more, not just their usual, lustful sex. After years of experience together, they were familiar with each other's "hot" buttons and turn-ons. Mark wanted more than gymnastics. He wanted to feel loved by Jenny.

She straddled his waist and pulled off his polo shirt, stroking the light curly hair that spread over his well-defined chest. It felt so good to laugh with Mark, to get a little drunk and wrestle around. She was feeling starved for skin-on-skin contact. She needed both an affirmation of her womanhood and a rousing good orgasm. It was also nice to nestle into the crook of Mark's arm and feel a primal fantasy of protection. Too much was happening in her life and she felt very much alone. Mark was safe and secure, a known quantity, a trusted friend. If only he could stick around for the love part.

Another swig of saki and she stripped off her shirt and bra. Mark seemed to quiver with anticipation, yet he didn't just reach up and grab her breasts. His hands slid slowly up her back, lightly drawing his fingernails along her skin. She shivered with excitement and felt an urgency in his hands as they pulled her toward him, squeezing her tight. Their mouths met, tongues darting in and out, lips rubbing lips. His hands finally made it to her breasts and he gently stroked her nipples.

Passion took over quickly. They were so hungry for each other. She quickly slid off his shorts, then stood up on the couch and slipped off her sweats and panties. Mark had seen her body hundreds of times, but he always gasped a little when she presented herself to him. He fished in his pants pocket and brought out a flavored condom. Pina Colada. She took it from him, opened it and slowly unrolled it over his penis, followed by her lips. Her tongue explored the latex sheath on his now throbbing penis. She straddled his hips and lowered herself onto his erection. They stared deep into each other's eyes, grinning with fun and familiarity. She brushed her breasts against his mouth and felt him stiffen even more inside her.

For the next two hours they played each other like fine instruments, caressing, teasing, enticing, and exploding in lustful orgasms and spiritual unions. Midway through the evening they moved to her bedroom, Jenny stopping only to slip the second backup tape into the computer. After another hour of passion they lay exhausted, sweating, and shamelessly satisfied.

Jenny finished the fantasy by snuggling into his arms. "Is this the part where you leave?" she asked.

"No, this is exactly where I want to be. Maybe for a long time."

"You talk like you're getting serious. I don't know if I'm ready for that again."

"I know. I've been a jerk about it. I forget how good it can be with you."

"Right, as you lie there with that self-satisfied, post-orgasmic grin. But will you love me tomorrow?" Jenny asked.

"If I do, will you take me back?"

"Sorry, my trust comes at a steeper price than that."

"Okay. I'm ready to pay up."

"Let's talk tomorrow when we're more sane and sober," suggested Jenny. "Presently, I'm not responsible for my actions."

They fell asleep together, something they hadn't done in years.

Chapter 20

Jenny awoke around 2 A.M. and headed for the bathroom. Returning to bed, she noticed the living room aglow in the bluish light of her computer screen. Daisy flashed a message on the screen: "Restoration Complete, no viruses detected." She removed the backup tape and placed it in the fireproof box near the bookshelf. Jenny switched to the Jaz drive and carefully ran it through the boot-up sequence. The computer reset itself to become Elaina's computer just as it had been on January 18. In a few seconds the start-up cycle was complete. Jenny was staring at a picture of Xenia, Elaina's cat, that served as wallpaper on the machine. As it turned out, Mark spent the rest of the night alone. Jenny poked and probed into the wee corners of the computer, looking for answers.

At the press of the first key the system requested a password. The screen security window bore the name "Ft. Knox Disk Security," a special program Jenny had never heard of. She'd have to get through it to find anything useful. She could try and guess the password, but that would be mostly luck. She could have Daisy fire millions of passwords at it, much like Hepman did at GHB, but that would take too much time.

"Daisy. Internet," she said out loud to her machine. Daisy launched the necessary communications programs and logged onto the Internet. Jenny typed in an obscure Web-site address that led to a computer in Utah. It belonged to a radical hacker group headed by a fellow named Dwick. His name, developed in adolescence, was originally an acronym for Demon Warlord Invader and Code Killer, but it stuck through the years and was now his signature on the Net. Jenny met him on-line years ago through her brother and was welcomed into the "club" as a techno-chick, a rare commodity in hacker circles.

Dwick's group kept a virtual warehouse of "secret" tools and programs in a guarded, members-only, directory. Jenny entered the required passwords and found herself in a hacker's K-Mart. At the "search" icon she typed the words "Ft. Knox Disk Security." A second later a window appeared with a cartoon character sticking out its tongue in a gesture of disgust. It was Dwick's rating on the quality of the Ft. Knox software, equivalent to a Siskel and Ebert "thumbs down" on a movie. Hackers take great joy in defeating security systems and then offering scathing criticism to the creators. Jenny read the review.

> This commercial software security package is an insult to hackers. A novice could defeat it with his mouse tied behind his back. Below are listed three separate hacks to get through Ft. Knox. If the nation's gold supply was protected this poorly, we'd be in big trouble.
>
> —Dwick

Jenny downloaded the information and left an e-mail "thanx" message. She had helped Dwick out once last year when an insurance company was refusing to pay for his four-year-old son's ear tubes to reduce recurrent ear infections. Jenny advised him of some choice words and threats he could use that eventually motivated the insurance company to approve the procedure. Dwick was very appreciative.

She was just signing off when a message scrolled across the screen, "Where you been, Jenny? It's cold up here without a friendly face."

"Dwick, are you up at this time of night?" It was 3:00 A.M. in Utah.

"Always, only time I can get some decent access speeds on the net. Hey, can you switch to voice?"

"Sure," said Jenny as she switched from data to voice communication . . .

"All right," said Dwick, with such clarity and fidelity she could hear papers shuffling on his desk."

"How about video, Jenny."

"Not now, my camera's in the shop. Besides, I'm not dressed for the occasion."

"Okay, I'll put up a naked Cindi Crawford picture to look at. She's almost in your league."

"You letch, I'm not sure if that qualifies as a compliment."

"It's great to hear from you, Jen. How's your brother?"

"He's cool. Selling software in the Far East."

"Everyone's working for Bill Gates. Jesus, Jenny, I just checked the speed on this connection. It's clocked at 140,000 baud. You running a T1 line?"

"Sure am," she said boastfully.

"How can you afford an industrial strength modem connection like that? Hell, my group pays 300 dollars a month for our connection."

"There's a lot of technical people who live in this complex. We got tired of poking along with 56K modems. The homeowners' association decided to spring for a T1 for the community, paid out of dues. Only costs me twenty bucks a month. Not bad for a light speed connection."

"I'm impressed. So, what brings you up to hackers paradise? Decide to leave the bosom of corporate America and come work for the radical cyber-militia?"

"Sorry. I like my 401(K) baking down here in the South. But I'm trying to get through a computer security program."

"Oh, yeah. Ft. Knox. Real lame program. My kid can get through it. Want me to do it for you? I can piggy back into the system on this connection."

"Sure. Have at it. I've got it linked to Daisy, my computer. A Jaz drive named Elaina."

"Yeah, I'm looking at it now. Elaina, who's that?"

"A friend. I showed her your site a few years ago." Jenny heard rapid key clicks on Dwick's keyboard in the background.

"Got it. Oh, yeah. I'm looking at her registration. She joined our group a few years ago. Referenced you as a referral source. Elaina Ruiz if it's the same person."

"That was her."

Code words flew by as Dwick undid the security from 1,000 miles away. "Hey, I keep in touch with all you straight-laced types, particularly the ladies. You know you're a very small club."

"That's right, and we're here to keep you slobbering male techno-dweebs in line," she said in jest. "This is her computer."

"Okay, Jenny, I'm through it. The system will now open up like a clam shell. The passwords are stored in a little file called SECRET.TXT, in case you need them somewhere else. How come you're hacking her computer?"

The levity of the conversation vanished. "She died, Dwick. Last January."

"No shit! I'm sorry, Jenny. Seemed like a nice gal. We helped her a couple of times." There were sounds of keystrokes on another computer, as if he was checking something. "Last January, in fact."

"You spoke with Elaina, last January?"

"Well, we didn't speak. Just e-mail. Said she needed a way to get into some big mainframe computer system, under cover. Wanted to scope some data. I sent her Waldo."

"Waldo?"

"Yeah, you know, like 'Where's Waldo', the puzzle where you try to find the guy in the middle of all these pictures. We have a program that wanders around in big systems without being detected by the master program. It's like a virus, only it doesn't cause damage. It can collect data, trace network systems, copy programs, and then it returns home, like a secret agent. In fact, it's called an intelligent agent."

"Yeah, they have them at GHB," said Jenny.

"How' d Elaina die?"

"Psychiatric hospital. Bad medicine. I'm not completely sure."

"Psych hospital! That's completely bogus. What's the real story?"

"I don't know, Dwick. I'm trying to find out."

"I tell you girl, those big companies are taking over the world. You think they killed her for finding out something?"

"Dwick, we don't know that it wasn't an accident. With all due respect to your chosen radical viewpoint, I don't think Great Health Benefit is killing their employees."

"GHB. They're the worst. Those money-grubbing animals are selling out old folks just to make a buck. They're probably auctioning off body parts to the Royal Saudi Arabian Organ Donation program. I'd just love to get something on them. Just to choke their computer."

"Dwick, settle down. You're getting too far out there. We don't know the truth of any of this. But tell me again. Elaina got a program from you in January?"

"Sorry. Yeah, she seemed kind of scared, though. Again, I only communicated through e-mail. Here, let me see if I can pull it up."

Jenny heard some rapid fire typing, a little swearing, and some drawers shuffling. "Let's see," she heard him say to himself. "December, November, March . . . Why doesn't anyone keep anything in order around here? Oh, got it. January. It's all compressed on a zip drive. Let me pull it up."

"Take your time," said Jenny, with barely contained excitement. She knew that Dwick wasn't the most organized guy in the world, but he did save everything. He said it was much easier to have a computer go look for something than for him to try to remember it. So he just stored his entire life on magnetic medium. Every note, every phone call, maybe every conversation, then he just looked it up. If something existed electronically, Dwick could find it.

Jenny could just imagine the world Dwick's little girl was growing up in. It appeared Nancy, his wife, was more of a down-home country type. She had mellowed him out. Most of his rantings were limited to his on-line newsletters and the chat forums he ran for a small subscription fee. His paranoia also got him jobs setting up computer security systems in many Rocky Mountain high-tech firms. As radical as he tried to be, Jenny suspected he had some fat contracts with aerospace companies.

"Got it, Jenny," he announced. "I'm looking at it. Not much here. Last e-mail was the 16th of January, 7:15 P.M. local time. Said Waldo worked well. Wanted to encrypt a really big file, 1.3 gigabytes. Also wanted to know if the encryption would survive being backed up and restored. I say yes to all. Recommended PGP, Pretty Good Privacy program. Attached a copy to the e-mail reply. She asked if I'd found out anything on the guy."

"What guy?"

"Ah," Dwick stalled for a few seconds, looking at an earlier transcript. "Oh, yeah. On January 3 she asked if I could look into a guy named Newton, Carter Newton. I guess I never did. Name mean anything to you?"

"He was her boss. Now he's my boss."

"Uh-oh. Are you next on the list?"

"Don't be silly. Why did she want him profiled, Dwick?"

"As I recall, this was all about some new program they were working on. She didn't like it, said it was going to hurt some people. Maybe trying to decide if she should blow the whistle."

"She told you all this?"

"Well, some of it I'm guessing. But I'm sure she was worried and didn't like this guy."

"Come on, Dwick, You'd find conspiracies in your sock drawer. I bet you feed your wife green M & Ms so you can get laid."

"And your point?"

"I'm sorry. It's just that this might be important stuff and I'm trying to figure it out. She was my friend."

"You're right, Jenny. Sounds like she got hold of some big stuff. What can I do to help?"

"Well, since you're still attached to her machine, see if there's anything on her computer. And try to find out something about Carter

Newton."

"Yes, Captain."

"Dwick! Stop it."

"Hey, let's check the computer, together."

Dwick's program informed them that Elaina's password was "Xeniass," which might be used elsewhere on the computer. Jenny liked the password. It was simple, quick to enter from the "home" keys on the keyboard, and not an obvious variant of the cat's name. It certainly wasn't high security, but good enough for a home computer.

What unfolded on the screen was a view of most of Elaina's life. Jenny and Dwick were staring at her financial records, her letters and notes, lists of friends, investments, recent e-mails, even the computer games she enjoyed. Elaina had migrated her life to the computer years ago, and it now held it all. There was an electronic Rolodex, her daily calendar, voice mail messages, faxes, even old birthday cards. With enough time, they could assemble a detailed picture of Elaina's daily life for the last couple of years.

Jenny told the machine to sort its files by date, so they could work backwards from the most recently opened documents. Among the lists of files her eye caught the icons for some photographic images. A few clicks and they were staring at Elaina's laughing face. The snapshot showed Elaina's arm draped around a fellow in a skimpy sailor outfit at a party. There were other pictures in the collection, mostly of people Jenny didn't know, but a few showed Elaina carousing in a festive atmosphere. The files were dated in January. A few weeks later her friend was dead. Jenny started to cry as she looked at her friend's face, so full of life on the screen.

"I didn't know she was so beautiful," said Dwick.

"She was a special person, to everyone. I'm sorry I lost contact with her."

"How did you end up with her machine?" he asked as he cruised around the hard drive.

"Her mother gave it to me. It was completely erased. Dead. Mark, my . . . friend, was given this backup tape by a neighbor. I just got around to restoring it today."

"Was the machine erased, or damaged?"

"Completely erased. Not even bootable. In fact, I had to do a low-level format. There was nothing."

"A low-level format. I'm impressed. Was the BIOS messed up, too?" Dwick asked, referring to the computer's most basic set-up information.

"Yeah, and it was booby-trapped. Someone ran a full power lead to the tape backup. I inserted a test tape and it got smoked."

"Jenny, it sounds like someone tried to "kill" the computer. They must have hit it with a 1,000 watt degausser to destroy every trace of magnetic data."

"A degausser. You mean what they erase magnetic tapes with?"

"Yeah. It's a killer on computer systems."

"But why would anyone bother. What does it mean? "

"I don't know. It's pretty weird. The only group I know of that is that paranoid, besides myself, is the Defense Department. They degauss their computers so no state secrets can be lifted. Erases everything permanently and irretrievably in four seconds. Why would someone do that to Elaina's computer? You know, GHB is on everyone's shit list. Pure corporate greed. Maybe Elaina got something on them. Jenny, this is sounding very suspicious," Dwick said with the bubbling excitement of a paranoid who has been blessed with a real conspiracy.

They continued through the files, with Dwick issuing commands from his console in Utah. There were some intimate letters to a guy in Colorado whom Elaina seemed to have met on a ski trip. Jenny read other letters to friends and family, and some communications with civic organizations. There was an article dated in December for the GHB newsletter, all about the new Caduceus project.

"Hey, that was the project she mentioned. Caduceus! Isn't that like death or something?"

"It's the symbol for medicine."

"So, I was right."

In a separate folder, Jenny found a letter to Senator Donald Gray, dated January 12. It was short and cryptic, basically saying she "agreed" with him and would seriously consider helping on the "project." Jenny copied it over to Daisy to print it out later. She also copied a few of the pictures, since her last picture of Elaina was about five years old. Something caught her eye in one of the party shots.

"Hey, Jenny. Do you know anyone in those pictures?" asked Dwick.

She examined the people in the background. Who were they? Maybe they knew something about what had gone wrong. Maybe she could find them.

The pictures were poorly lit, taken with a simple flash. She copied them over to Daisy and called them up in one of her advanced graphic programs, so she could manipulate and enhance the images. Zooming up on the background faces, she enhanced and sharpened the images of the shadowy people. Then she saw him. Leaning on the stereo cabinet. That unmistakable rat-faced grin. Hepman was at this party.

"Ah, found somebody, did we?" asked Dwick.

"Maybe. These are pretty bad pictures. But that looks like Greg Hepman, a computer nerd at GHB. Know him?"

"Not off hand. But I'll check our international computer directory of dweebs. Maybe he was at the last nerd convention," replied Dwick.

It was hard to imagine what circumstance of life would put Elaina, Hepman, and a male stripper at the same event. Maybe these were all co-workers, at a company function. Jenny couldn't imagine a friendship between them. Elaina was too refined for Hepman. Another mystery.

Jenny skimmed the files, but found little more of interest. She instructed the computer to search for any files with the words MOM, Caduceus, Newton, Hepman, or GHB in them. It was a disappointment to her when only eight files were displayed, and they contained only general information. Jenny worked her way back to files dating from August, long before there were any signs of trouble. Nothing!

"You know, "said Dwick. "There's a whole lot of disk space that isn't accounted for. We're missing about a billion bytes somewhere."

"You know, you're right."

"Hey, look at this. I just found out she had voice mail on this computer," said Dwick. "It's in the VOICEIN directory under the MODEM system. Check it out. Let's see who called her."

Jenny found the voice mail program, launched it, and played the main greeting. Elaina's voice sprang from the computer, pleasantly asking the caller to leave a message. Jenny listed the calls left in the queue. The computer was equipped with caller ID, so most message files were stamped with the phone number and name of the caller. She clicked on each message and heard the usual calls from Elaina's mom, some friends checking in. Then she clicked on a GHB number and heard Carter Newton's voice. It was cold and commanding.

"Elaina, it's essential that you be in my office tomorrow at 9 A.M. We must bring this matter to a close. Please bring any materials you have acquired that belong to the company. I asked that you not contact an attorney yet. If, after our discussion, you feel it is necessary, I'll understand. Neither of us wants to open up needless legal problems if this matter can be settled amicably. Please call to confirm with my secretary and I will see you tomorrow at nine."

The call was logged the day before she was admitted to the hospital.

"Is that the boss?" asked Dwick.

"Sure is. Doesn't sound too happy. I wonder what he wanted from her."

Carter's message sent a chill through Jenny, for it was delivered in an ominous and uncompromising tone of voice. It also sounded as if Elaina was about to be dismissed from GHB, as if she had stolen something and they wanted it back. Jenny was perplexed.

There were two more messages as of that date, but they were hangups. The caller ID captured number looked familiar. She chanted it to herself a few times, then she grabbed her notebook. It was Hepman's number. He had called Elaina at home, but left no message. Why?

Suddenly Jenny felt a hand on her shoulder and jumped. It was Mark, smiling down at her. "Hey, didn't you hear me say good morning. It's light outside, you know. How long have you been hacking at this machine?" he asked.

"Gees, what time is it? Six thirty!" God, I've been at this for over three hours, Mark. Oh, this is Dwick. Dwick, this is Mark."

Mark spun in perplexity, looking for another person. Then Dwick said from Jenny's computer speakers, "Glad to meet you." Mark still didn't get it, and looked around.

"Mark, Elaina was in trouble at GHB," said Jenny. We've restored her computer files and were able to track what was going on the last few days of her life. Here, let me play this message from Carter, my boss, and at the time her boss."

Mark listened with bewildered curiosity. "So, he wanted to meet with her."

"Can't you hear the tone of his voice? He's not happy with her. He's so threatening," said Jenny.

"You think that's bad, you should hear my editor. Sounds just like an annoyed boss, Jenny. So what?"

"I. . .I," she stammered. "Maybe you're right. Maybe I'm trying to make something out of nothing. I just don't understand how all this hangs together. It's so weird," she said to Mark. Then addressing the hacker still on-line she said, "Dwick, maybe we should hook up later."

"Sure thing. I've got what I needed. Look around for that Waldo file. Maybe she hid it somewhere. I'll check out your guy. Call me tonight." A click signified a break in the phone line. Mark still didn't know where the sound was coming from.

"That's what you restored on Elaina's system?"

"Right up to the day before she went in the hospital."

"So where did you hide that guy I was talking to?"

"Dwick. He's a little cyber-elf. He lives in that tiny green thing there."

"Jenny, this is very close to interesting, but I've got to get to work.

I did want to tell you what a great time I had last night." He looked deep into her eyes. "It's so good sleeping with you, even when you're not there," he said in jest.

"Sorry. It was great for me too. It's been a long time."

He put his arms around her and drew her close. "I mean it was really good being with you. And staying the night. And waking up to find you being a little nutty about this computer. I want to do it more. Can I come back tonight?"

"What are you saying, Mark?"

"Can I come back, again?"

"I don't know, Mark. Let's not talk about it now. You're going too deep too fast. I don't want to get hurt again. And you always talk like this after we've been together. Let's cool off, okay."

"I'll give you till noon, then I'm calling. We can move into deeper areas of our relationship. Like Indian food, *tandoori*."

"See you, Jenny."

They kissed at the door. She expected a cursory hug and butt squeeze. Instead he held her tightly, swaying slightly, lingering in the moment. She let herself forget their checkered history for a moment. This was a softer, more sensitive side of Mark that she rarely saw. "Little boy, are you growing up?" she wondered. She knew to remain cautious. He was always so good at asking her to come out and play, but he never stayed around for the work part. Why would this time be any different?

Chapter 21

The curious thing about bulk mail is that not only is it mailed in bulk, it also tends to arrive in "bulks." Some zip codes get it quickly, neighboring zip codes can be delayed for days. The individual pieces arrive at their destinations by some mystical formula known only to the post office and God, and God wasn't telling Crandall Bream when the first jaws would drop open from reading his, "solicitation," as he now called it.

Brenda Kominski received her solicitation letter on Monday morning, around eleven. She had to read it twice to really understand what it was talking about. It started off friendly enough, then something caught her eye. That date, April 1995 at Slatemore Clinic, underlined in red. She suddenly felt as if eyes were staring at her from across the street. This letter seemed to say so much about her. How could it be? How could anyone know about "it?" Such a little event, it seemed so long ago. A mistake with a man now gone from her life. She was alone. How could such a thing come back?

Brenda had put her life together well, working in a supermarket, living near her parents. She didn't need this aggravation, but for forty dollars she could make it go away. It hurt a little financially, but the promise of simple redemption was too seductive. Crandall Bream got his check.

The jaws and hearts of thousands of women dropped that day, and the next, and the next. The staggered arrival of bulk mail spread the misery over the week. The letter was greeted by each woman differently.

Heather Bracken's mother sorted her college-aged daughter's mail into a separate pile on the kitchen counter, then she left for work. Heather scooped it up as she dashed out to a biology class. While the instructor lectured about the process of photosynthesis, Jennifer's eyes fell upon her own dark history. The clinic name and the date slapped her into reality. This letter was about her abortion. They knew everything. The date. The place. Why were the neighbors' names on this letter? Did they know? Would they know? Jennifer shuddered as if someone had stepped on her grave. It wasn't that this was so shameful. It's just that she didn't want everyone talking about it. Or guessing who the father was. Or even knowing that she ever had sex. It was awful. She wanted it to go away. Fortunately, the letter provided an easy solution, which she complied with that very evening.

The solicitation found Mildred Beck as she plopped down on the couch after a long day taking tolls. She worked on the Bay Bridge to San Francisco, talking, or at least nodding, to thousands of people a day as they zoomed across the bridge into the great city. In fact, that was the only human contact available in her sheltered life. Outside of work she snuggled with her cats and read biographies. Thumbing through the mail, she anticipated a quiet evening when the letter caught her eye. She opened it and spied her name in the text. Then the date, which was two years ago. Then the hospital. Soon the pain was flowing all over her again. Anguish escaped her lips in a small cry.

How cruel this letter was! What was its purpose? To get money? Was that what it boiled down to? Money for pain. Extortion by medical history. Outrage filled her chest and exploded in a ferocious yell. Her Siamese cat jumped under the foot stool for safety as her master exploded in a rage. Books and magazines went flying through the air, driven by Mildred's anger. But with all the emotion and energy the letter generated, she vowed it would not produce a contribution. Mildred didn't give a damn if anyone knew. Crandall Bream would see no profit from this home. It was of little consequence, since there were thousands more women.

Sunlight radiated off the buffed oak kitchen floor of Linda Green's home. The breakfast nook had been featured in <u>Architectural Digest</u> as an efficient blend of function and French country charm. Her husband, Dan, now a judge in Sonoma County, had encouraged her to go all out in decorating the place, ever since she had given up her pharmaceutical sales position to pursue motherhood. The marriage still felt new as they celebrated their third anniversary. Much of their respective pasts remained, not really hidden, just undiscovered.

Crandall's letter hit like a glass of cold water in her face. At first, Linda couldn't be sure that it wasn't a common blackmail threat regarding some case her husband was judging, though it cited the specific dates, the hospital, and her neighbors.

Even Dan didn't know about this sad passage in her life. The pregnancy was the result of a stupid and desperate attempt to save a cold, exploitive relationship that needed to die. But in its death throes, it produced a small life. A month after the relationship was cleanly severed, she found they had created one last string. Dan had just entered her life and was moving quickly to intimacy. It was so easy to sweep this issue aside. Her doctor took care of everything and assured her of secrecy.

Now this was threatening to spoil everything. She sat on the edge of the sofa, crouched over as if protecting herself from a blow. Her hazel eyes welled up with tears, making it impossible to search the letter for some sign of authenticity. Her breathing was shallow, her head dizzy. What about the election next year? What if Dan's opponents got hold of this? How could anyone have found this out?

Linda closely examined the letter, its envelope, and the return envelope, as did hundreds of thousands of other women over the next week. Forty dollars was all they were asking. Could they be trusted? Was this just a con game? Forty dollars was such a small amount to end the issue. Even if it only stalled them, that would be good for now.

Was this just about her, or was this a form letter mailed to lots of women? There was no way to know. If it involved many women, the press would eventually get a hold of it. That would stop them. But then, some tabloid might publish the list anyway, just for a circulation boost. She had to get off that list right away.

She withdrew her checkbook and scrawled out the name. "The Children's Life Project." It could be easily explained as a donation. Who would question such a small act of charity?

Leona Mitchell, a computer programmer for Transamerica Credit Services, received the letter with bland curiosity. Being an employee of the computer age, she was not surprised that someone had obtained the information. She was annoyed that they should try to manipulate her with it.

As she read, the left side of her brain was activated into programmer mode, reviewing the computer instructions and resources needed to complete this scam. She smiled a little at its simplicity. Her experience in sifting through millions of credit records and producing mass mailings had numbed her to the social significance of the letter. She cared little who knew of her miscarriage. "It wasn't an abortion, for God's sake, " she thought. Then she realized how the group must have obtained the information. They must have used a "sniffer" program to find abortion evidence in medical records, just like she did with sniffers for credit risks. However, the program wasn't clever enough to reliably distinguish between abortions and miscarriages. That got her thinking about a new way to search credit histories. The topic of abortion left her mind.

Crandall's letter quickly became a napkin to hold Leona's egg salad sandwich. The threatening data had been delivered, sifted for useful information, and was now being used for one final purpose: protecting her carpet from mayonnaise.

No one saw the shock spread across Sondra's face as she read the letter for the third time and came to believe it was legitimate. The shy, anorexic, preacher's daughter clutched the letter to her breast and flew into her bedroom. The words "God Knows All" rocketed around in her mind as if bouncing in a racquetball court. A vile feeling of filth filled her body. She sensed the wetness in her vagina from her menstrual period. It too was filth. She condemned herself as wicked and foul for killing that child, and God, in the form of Crandall Bream, was never going to let her forget it.

Images flooded her mind's eye. A year ago, at age 17, she had been allowed to date only the "meek" boys that her stern parents approved. Despite these precautions, the prom had been a madhouse, and many strange things happened that evening. Max Schumacher, a burned-out football hunk, had taken an interest in her. Randy Wales, her "approved" date, had quietly slunk away in the presence of Max the Magnificent, a slogan on his football practice jersey. Schumacher had run the course through many girls at her high school, but he had succumbed to heavy drug use and was of little interest to anyone. Max's crushing embrace and musky scent were unfamiliar to Sondra, yet strangely exciting. She felt that special tingle in her loins, a sensation no one had ever explained to her.

Max had convinced Sondra to leave the prom with some of his friends. It turned out there were no friends, and soon she was involuntarily inhaling the fumes of marijuana that he billowed into the cramped, sealed car. Maybe it was the contact high, or her naiveté in dealing with men, or her curiosity about the growing excitement at his touch. He had made her feel special. He worshiped her frail, scrawny body, and idolized her tiny breasts. No one had ever taught her anything but shame for her body. This was a new feeling for her.

The sex was over in an instant. Sondra wasn't even sure it had really happened. Max left her that evening, never to speak with her directly again.

Two months later the morbid realization of her pregnancy couldn't be denied. She tried to talk with Max, but he just sent a friend over with some money and the name of a clinic. She sulked around her home for days, until her parents became alarmed, then she dressed up her face with a synthetic smile, gritted her teeth, and did what she felt must be done. She graduated from high school still sore from the procedure, but no one ever found out.

Sondra, reading the letter again, looked up and squinted out the narrow slats of her vertical blinds, feeling the neighbor's eyes upon her. She was about to bring a great shame onto this house. Her parents would be ridiculed by the church, just like the parents of Amy Land had been when she got pregnant. Her mother would cry and scream at her. God would never accept her again.

Sondra knew the price of taking a life. Her father had spoken of it often enough. "The murderers must die," he would shout to the congregation. She knew what she had to do. Grandpa's little gun was in daddy's sock drawer. The bullets were kept in the drawer under that. When Uncle Martin had committed suicide, she had asked her dad if it had hurt. He assured her that it hadn't.

Sondra had only shot a gun once, when she was 13, but the device was simple to figure out. She loaded the gun, but realized she still clutched the letter from Bream. She crumpled it up as she ran to the kitchen, placing it upon the gas stove burner, then set it aflame. Ashes floated about the kitchen as the message of death was consumed in flame, just as she imagined she would be for eternity. Sondra then went to her own room and stretched her thin body across the bed, her head on her fragrant, scented pillow. "Lilac" was the last thought she ever had.

***

Jenny showered and dressed for work, then plopped in front of

Elaina's computer to poke around for a few more minutes. The numbers were not adding up correctly. There were over a billion bytes of disk space she could not account for on the computer. Even if the backup tape was damaged, there should be some accounting for the missing storage space. Using the more exotic programs and utilities on Daisy, she poked and probed, tested and retested, looking for the missing data.

Then she saw it, the tag end of a folder with a nonsense name, as if written in some foreign language. It was a secret directory. She clicked to open it. It contained one file called WALDO.TXT, which was over one billion bytes in size. She attempted to open it. It said that all data was encrypted and needed a password. She typed "Xeniass," and the file was un-encrypted for her to view.

At first it was just a jumble of words in crude Courier style type. Headers, directory references, half-formed words, as if it was just a part of something larger. Indents, parentheses, and brackets. Jenny zoomed out and she recognized the structure of the text. It was the scripted language of a computer program. Jenny scrolled down a few pages to see if it changed, but it just went on and on. She scrolled down halfway through the document. The page counter indicated she was on page 1832 and still she saw nothing but code.

She scrolled to the top again and began examining line after line of the cryptic code. Jenny was looking for comments within the margins that programmers leave as helpful tips. She spied a reference to Caduceus ver. 0.97 beta. December 18. This was something about a test version of the new super-program.

There was half a page of disclaimers, showing that this was top-secret proprietary code, for the eyes of executive management and direct project personnel only. "Any other viewing, copying, printing, or transmitting of the code would be grounds for immediate dismissal and civil action for financial loss." Jenny began to wonder if this was the actual program that the company was staking its future upon. If it really was a beta copy of Caduceus, it represented the fundamental operating policies and decision-making rules for all the company's medical care, what the company valued, how it calculated risk, where it put its resources, how much it valued life itself. In the hands of GHB enemies it could be worth millions.

Why would Elaina have a copy of it on her computer? Even in her role of interface architect or principal trainer, Elaina would not have needed the code. Changes were made by highly trained programmers. She probably couldn't understand it. It wouldn't run on her personal computer, so she wouldn't be testing it. Jenny couldn't imagine Elaina stealing it, or planning to sell it to a GHB competitor, yet there it sat on her machine.

The telephone rang. Daisy flashed "Francis Barrett" on the screen.

"Hi Mom," answered Jenny.

"Honey, I'm so glad I caught you," her mother said in an unsteady voice. "Dads getting sicker, Jenny. We don't know what to do. They don't seem to want to do anything. I'm getting frightened."

"What does Doctor Jamani say?"

"It's Majani. Says this is all normal," replied Francis.

"And you can't see Dr. Shepard?"

"Dr. Shepard says there's nothing he can do without Axis Health approval."

"Mom, I'll fly up there tonight, will that be okay?"

"Yes. That would be wonderful. You handle these things so well. I'll pick you up in Medford, that's the quickest connection."

"Will do."

"Jenny, they sent us home last night. Wouldn't even admit him to the hospital. Insurance company refused. He was up all night in terrible pain."

"I'll make the arrangements from work and call you later. I'll leave instructions on the machine if you're not there. I'll also leave it on Daisy. Just enter the last four digits of your phone number and Daisy will play the message."

"Thanks, honey."

"Have you talked with David?" asked Jenny, referring to her brother.

"I tried, but he's in some remote village. I did leave him e-mail this morning."

"I'll do the same."

"Can Dad talk now?" asked Jenny.

"I think he's asleep. I'd rather not disturb him."

"Sure. I'll see you tonight, Mom. Love you."

Jenny dashed out to work. She'd pack this afternoon, then get over to Burbank Airport. She hit her desk at 8:45 A.M. Fortunately, there was open time scheduled this morning to become familiar with MOM and Caduceus. She logged on to establish her arrival time. Five e-mails were waiting. The two most important were from Hepman wanting to get her input on the diagnostic program and from Carter wanting to set a meeting for Thursday with the Caduceus team. One was from human resources, welcoming her to the company and inviting her to share a little about herself for the upcoming company newsletter.

The first priority was her father. She called Carter's office and explained her needs to the receptionist. A few seconds later Carter was on the line.

"I'm sorry to hear about your father, Jenny. Is it serious?"

"I don't know. No one seems to know anything. My mom's trying to manage this alone. I think it will just be a couple of days. I'm really sorry about this, Mr. Newton."

"No need to be, I completely understand. Your input is very important to us though. Let me make a suggestion. Have Hepman fix you up with a laptop computer with a security login. That way, if you end up with a lot of sitting-around time, we can send you some work. But just use it at your convenience, not ours. Okay?"

"Thanks, that's really thoughtful."

"Hey, you came highly recommended. I can't wait to see your sterling personnel file."

"Thanks. I'll probably be leaving around 3:00 today. I'll get with Mr. Hepman and see if we can work a little ahead."

"Great. And keep us posted."

Jenny booked a flight through Renee, the Progressive travel agent she had used for years. The flight left Burbank Airport at 4:10 P.M., arriving in Medford, Oregon at 5:50 P.M. It was about a half-hour drive to her parents' home in Grants Pass. "Home," what a good feeling the word produced. Spring would be intense about now. Blooming wildflowers, dogwoods, rolling grass hills. The Rogue River would be surging. She felt a strong need to touch her roots.

MOM flashed a message on the screen. Phone call from Hepman.

"Hello Greg," she answered, trying to appear like a friendly team player.

"Jenny, I heard you have to fly home. Sorry about your dad's illness. Can we get together around 11:00, at my office?" The words were almost devoid of emotion, fired in rapid succession, as if from a script.

"I think so. Let me try a few test cases and then I'll have something to talk about."

"Great. I have a laptop computer per Carter's instructions. You must rate pretty high to get one with a security linkup. I'll show you how it works when you get here," said Hepman.

***

The elevator plopped Jenny in front of the security desk leading to Hepman's office. The guard looked at her badge and waved her through, making her feel a little privileged. All the rooms and cubicles appeared vacant at first, then she heard a burst of laughter down the hallway. As she approached, she heard the unmistakable guffawing of men, in a style usually heard when they're leering at either naked women or abundant beer. The look and feel of this floor of the building was unmistakably masculine. Jenny wasn't sure if she had even seen another woman in the midst of these techno-brats.

She passed Hepman's office and continued toward the source of the rowdy laughter. In a cubicle at the end of the hallway about eight men were huddled around a 21-inch monitor. No one noticed Jenny approaching from behind. She skirted the outside of the circle until she got a clear view of the computer screen. On it appeared a naked woman, lying on an examination table, legs apart. A gloved hand was pulling back a heavily swollen labia, apparently infected.

"Hey, Walt, how'd you like those thunder lips smacking up against you," said an unidentified voice. Laughter circulated around the group.

The screen changed and displayed another woman, same compromising position, who had an overly large clitoris that actually looked like a very small penis.

"Now that looks like something Frank could compete with," said another voice. There next was a picture of a young women with astoundingly large breasts that were weighing her down.

"Now, she says she wants a breast reduction. Hey, I know some women who would love to have a piece of those. Maybe we can start a breast donation program," said a tall blond man.

Jenny was disgusted by the immaturity of these alleged professionals who were in charge of designing a healthcare system. She let out a cough to bring attention to herself. A silence swept through the crowd, then the men scampered off to suddenly remembered tasks. Hepman was up front, next to a young, very red-faced man who was busily closing down the screen windows.

"Hi, Jenny. We're just checking out the enhanced screen resolution for diagnostics. What do you think?"

Jenny struggled for a second, between indignity and realizing that she needed these adolescent tech-heads. To err on the winning side, she replied, "Don't I get to see the guys with testicular elephantitis?" It was humorous and made a few of the men cringe.

"Sorry, hope you weren't offended," said Hepman.

"I wasn't pleased. I mean, you have the whole damn Internet full of beautiful, naked women. Why would you want to look at diseased organs?" asked Jenny.

"Because we can," blurted Hepman in a bold challenge as they walked back to his office. "We're going nuts living in these walls, punching fifty to sixty hours a week. The guys were just blowing off steam."

"Does Carter know that this stuff goes on?"

"I don't think so. Hey, I'm sorry. We've got too much to do. Look, no one was hurt. The guys need a laugh wherever they can find it." Even Hepman could see that he wasn't winning her over with this approach. "They really have been working to improve the graphics for the doctors to diagnose remotely. It's a problem that came up while running the beta version, that's a test version before the final implementation."

"Thanks, we had betas at Progressive," said Jenny with a hint of sarcasm. Hepman
fidgeted, trying to recover.

She followed him into his disheveled office. There was a sleek-looking laptop computer next to the monitor on his desk. An Axil Laser 9000. Extremely fast and powerful, fully equipped, more powerful than Daisy, her desktop computer at home. A large cable connected the machine to the rear of Hepman's computer.

"I'm loading some special access codes onto this machine so that you can log-on from anywhere in the world. But it can only be done with this machine. There's a 56K modem built in with a customized log-on script. It can't be duplicated and it records any attempt to modify the script. If it gets messed up, you're dead. I can't fix it while you're on the road, so keep it simple. Follow the procedures." said Hepman.

"Are you sure I can't inadvertently do something wrong? I don't know anywhere near as much as you do about these things." The flattery softened Hepman. He was so hungry for acceptance.

"No, it should be okay. Let me show you the procedure."

Together they ran through the remote log-on process three times. It allowed Jenny access to her main account with MOM as well as special access to the training computers in this secret cavern, Hepman's lair.

"Can I just unplug it now and go?"

"Just a minute, Jenny. It's still set up to log onto my computer. I'll need to change that script to your system. What is your station number?"

"Sorry, I don't know," said Jenny. "I've hardly had time to even sit at my computer."

"Damn, my computer's off-line for security. I'll have to go look it up. Wait here and don't touch anything!"

Hepman left the room. Jenny curiously looked around the cubicle, but her eyes quickly fell upon the laptop screen. The log-on window still flashed with Hepman's name and number. It was the access script to his computer. He would come back in a few seconds and erase it. Jenny wanted it. She didn't know why, but she suddenly felt an irresistible impulse to get his password and log-on script.

She looked up from the desk and saw Hepman bent over a colleague's computer. Almost involuntarily her right hand moved to the keyboard and pressed the "Save As" key. She couldn't just save it in the same directory, Hepman would see it. Her finger tapped the "\" key to place the file in the root directory. She couldn't think of a name off hand, so she simply called it "m" when prompted. The program saved Hepman's log-on script in the root directory as file "m." She saw Hepman stand up from the other console. The window still registered the new file name. Jenny casually pressed the close button, returning the screen to what Hepman had seen when he left. Her heart pounded. This was a breach of security. If he discovered it, she could get in real trouble. Additionally, he might realize that she was much more sophisticated about software than he realized.

Hepman reentered the room and sat next to her. "Okay, station 7-202. Log-on name, Jbarrett. Password. Want me to put that in?"

"Sure. It's 'Ripley,' after the character in the movie <u>Alien</u>."

"Cute," said Hepman. "Remember, at your security level you must change your password every week. All done with the set-up. Now I'll obliterate my script with a bunch of zeros. We always do that so it can't be un-erased. Security, you know. I'll just do a final check on the system."

She watched nervously as he peeked and poked around the directories. Finally he shut the system down, closing the laptop like a clamshell. Jenny breathed easier. There was something exciting about getting away with this little scam. It was very unlike her, but she was surrounded by so many unusual events in her life.

"Hope your father's well," said Hepman with all the emotion of a floppy disk. Hepman plopped the laptop in her hands and bid her a good trip.

Chapter 22

Jenny wove through the giant glass cube of GHB with great efficiency, arriving back at her desk five minutes later. She stored the laptop in her near-empty file cabinet and locked the drawer. She was glad to tuck it away. It seemed dangerous now that it possessed her little indiscretion. She'd feel safer when it was outside the GHB building. Maybe she should just fire up the machine and erase it, she thought, but some deep inner part of her wouldn't allow that. She pushed the thought out of her mind.

"Clear your mind," she commanded herself. Grabbing the mouse at her computer she logged onto MOM and checked her e-mail. There was one message from Carter, expressing his sympathy for her father and encouraging her to take as much time as she needed. It included a PS to please stay in touch as much as possible. He advised her to take some procedure manuals with her to learn the system.

It was about 10 A.M., so she had a few more hours to spend at work. Might as well dig deeper into MOM, she thought, so she selected some sample cases Hepman had suggested and began to track the diagnostic procedure. Hepman had created about one hundred dummy cases to run through the system. Trainees were free to mix up the symptoms and lab readings and test MOM's ability to suggest a diagnosis as well as a treatment plan and available community resources. The recommendations were computed with "live" data-sets, meaning actual on-line information. For example, MOM knew the location of every kidney dialysis center in the USA, so changing the address of the sample patient would instantly change the dialysis resource list for that area.

Through the morning Jenny marveled at MOM's precision in clarifying problem cases. The Caduceus team used a masterful blend of two primary resources: medical research and case examples. The system tapped into the most sophisticated healthcare databases on the planet: Harvard Medical School, Albert Einstein Medical, Sloan-Kettering, Johns Hopkins, plus facilities in Europe and Canada. There was learned discussion on every medical condition known to man. MOM could synthesize the data like no single human being. It was as if every GHB patient was an invited guest to the American Medical Association's national meeting, and was allowed to present the entire assemblage with their symptoms.

The other major component to MOM's care, and the part many physicians adequately considered, were the millions of case examples stored in her database. They were cross tabulated by physician, location, symptom profile, treatment facility, types of intervention, costs, successes, and outcomes. There was no guesswork about whether a physician's reputation for, say, heart transplants or allergy treatments was valid. MOM could exhaustively examine any treatments and treaters in any state in 22 nanoseconds. MOM knew the average cost of the last 500 procedures in the state, the complication rate, the average length of stay in the hospital, and the success rate of the individual physician. Every imaginable lab value for healthy and unhealthy people was available for instant comparison, and MOM could provide this data in seconds to any contracting facility anywhere in the world. One of the company's most popular slogans was, "No Matter Where You Go, We'll Be There."

Jenny pulled up a sample case and laughed at the name. Heidi Dudy. She could easily imagine Hepman and his tech team dreaming up that name. The five-year-old Heidi suffered from recurring symptoms of the flu: nausea, vomiting, abdominal cramps, fever of 103°F, headache. She had missed twenty-one days of school in two months. Heidi's mother, a single mom, shared the first bout of flu in September, but her daughter never seemed to fully recover. A nine-month-old son was currently symptom free.

MOM examined the profile and quickly suggested a lab test for salmonella. Accompanying the suggestion were epidemiology studies from the local hospitals, showing a higher than normal occurrence of the food-borne disease. MOM expressed "concern" that repeated exposure would weaken the child's immune system to other opportunistic infections. The case manager was instructed to closely follow the patient due to risks of more serious illness and unnecessary expenses. Three panel specialists in the area were identified.

By manipulating the data, Jenny could observe the impact on MOM's recommendations. She moved the client to Boulder, Colorado. Spotted fever was added to the possible diagnoses, but salmonella remained the primary concern. Jenny increased Heidi's temperature to 105.4°F. MOM responded with a boldface message on the screen requiring immediate action, warning of possible infections starting with meningitis and ending with typhoid. Had the case not been tagged with the inhibiting code of "sample," MOM might have proactively alerted the local authorities.

Cases of liver disease, impetigo, ectopic pregnancy, and bone cancer followed. Jenny studied the way MOM made suggestions. The actual recommendations were products of GHB's in-house staff. At Progressive, MOM 2.0 sounded like a learned and concerned physician, who was consulting on a case. It "respected" the case manager's opinion and discretion. However, most of the on-line staff at Progressive were licensed mental health professionals who had previously worked directly with clients.

MOM 3.0 at GHB was much more authoritative. The statements were more like commands and directions. The staff at GHB was younger that at Progressive, less experienced, and new to medicine. Many were unlicenced. It was part of the strategy to standardize medical care. MOM would cut out individual variations in treatment. In theory, it made sense, but only if one took an extremely mechanistic view of patient care. Broken arm: apply cast, give pain medicine. Jenny was impressed that MOM could consider many variables at once, but she wondered could, or should, the machine replace humans? Or, more importantly, was there any way to stop the process?

"They let you visit your desk again, girl?" a warm voice from behind said with a laugh. Jenny turned to see Mable Jackson entering her cubicle.

"Hi, Mable. Yeah, I've got a couple of hours to play with this thing, then I'm out of here. Taking a trip to see my parents in Oregon. My dad's just had gall bladder surgery and he's driving my mother crazy."

"Sorry to hear that, honey. I had mine out five years ago. Best thing I ever did. He'll be fine. You know those men folk hate to lose body parts. They have to nurse their wounds like old soldiers."

"Thanks, I think you're right."

"So are you putting MOM through her paces young lady?"

"Yeah. It's much more sophisticated than the version at Progressive. I'm amazed at how quickly and thoroughly MOM diagnoses problems. I was just thinking, as much as I hate giving the machine so much decision-making power, she really does do a great job."

"You must be testing the new Caduceus module that Hepman and his team installed," Mable said with a hint of skepticism in her voice.

"You don't sound impressed."

"Oh no! I was part of the beta testing team. I was thrilled to see what the machine could do, medically. It was far better than any team of physicians could ever hope to be. It saved my butt a few times, reminding me to ask particular questions or cross checking on some obscure symptoms. If the clients can get to the medical part of the program, it's great."

"What do you mean 'if?' Doesn't every client go through MOM?"

"Yes," said Mable, lowering her voice, "but not necessarily for medical clearance. Remember, MOM manages every part of this operation, including finances, eligibility, capitation, and ultimately, profits."

Jenny muted her speech as well. "What are you saying?"

Mable suddenly looked a bit apprehensive. "Say, let's go over to the coffee machine. I need a jolt." While en route Mable continued talking. "Jenny, this old nurse has seen it all. I was working in the field when doctors had their offices in their homes. I've seen so many changes I can't begin to tell you, but what I've seen in the last three months is scaring me to death. I'm taking a chance telling you this, but I think your heart is with the patients."

"Mable, you can trust me. I'm a little overwhelmed myself. I want your input."

"Well, you know how competitive the health insurance market has become. All these giant companies are trying to underbid each other for big contracts with major employers. The HMOs are taking on millions of Medicare and Medicaid clients while lowering the amount of money spent on patients. That's the only way they can undercut the competition. It's getting ruthless out there. And now, they're using MOM to get even more ruthless. After they installed the new system, they had a major cutback on case management personnel, even though they increased the number of insured lives. But my workload didn't change. It wasn't like the usual downsizing, where the remaining workers pick up the slack for those who left. There was no slack. The call volume actually dipped, despite the company adding almost six million more subscribers to their rolls."

"So what happened? Was MOM just more efficient at directing traffic to medical care?" asked Jenny.

"No. She was telling them to go screw themselves, if you'll pardon the profanity. Most of subscribers never got to information on medical care. Mostly they got run around in circles. By the time they reached me, they were livid. I kept hearing these horror stories of denied care, refused payments, lost eligibility, reversed decisions. A few of us brought these issues to the staff meetings, but we were politely thanked for our comments and dismissed. Two of my colleagues were soon let go in another downsizing. They were ten year employees. Gone. We all got the message to shut up. But then," Mable hesitated in a moment of restrained emotion, "I lost a kid."

"What do you mean?"

With an undercurrent of anger, Mable hissed, "I lost a child. It was a case that I was managing. An eight-year-old girl died of meningitis. For all of this technological wonder, she never had a chance. We never used any of it. MOM spent ten days playing the eligibility and referral game. We were in the middle of overhauling the physician panel. No single doctor was allowed to take action. MOM never looked at her symptoms. She died of administrative botulism."

"I'm sorry, Mable. Those are tough cases."

"This was more than tough. It was neglect. I couldn't let it go. I hollered at Hepman for his stupid program, but it wasn't him. The program only reflects the Godforsaken values of this company. I pulled the complete contact history of Sedra Knight, the dead little girl. The family had called us twenty-seven times in two weeks, trying to get help. First MOM denied she could find the family on the eligibility rolls. Then they were referred to a physician who had died ten months earlier. When the family wanted to take the child to an emergency room, MOM threatened them with a $500 co-pay, which was more than this poor family's rent. By the time Sedra was finally seen, the disease was ravaging her. Nothing could save her. And the truth was, all of MOM's advice was bogus. In my research I saw all the documents in the database. MOM knew she was eligible, knew the doctor was dead, knew there was no co-pay. I tried to tell the Hitman, but by that time, the case had been sealed. He passed it off as some unfortunate glitch and promised to correct it."

"Maybe that's all it was," said Jenny.

"But it keeps happening. That computer is doing exactly what it's supposed to do."

"Mable, wouldn't that get the company sued?"

"That's the scariest part. No one is allowed to see the program. Who are you going to cross examine? MOM? Jenny, there is no requirement that any of this computerized decision program be regulated or reviewed. It's all 'proprietary' secrets. Sure, GHB submitted a copy for an initial audit last year, but that's not what's running on this computer. And no one, not even the government, is allowed to look at it. GHB is a big contributor to political candidates and has promised to keep Medicare and Medicaid from going bankrupt. The Feds will let them do just about anything to save their butts, and there's no one to check on the system."

Jenny looked into the dampened eyes of Mable Jackson. This seasoned nurse was no stranger to death, but this callous outrage touched her deeply, because she was a part of the company. They stopped at a water fountain where Mable got a drink and composed herself.

"Sorry," said Mable. "Thought I was tougher than that. Maybe I've been in the trenches too long."

"No, you're just too human. Does anyone else know about this?"

"Well, upper management, and my supervisor. And I talked poor Elaina's ear off. She was here before you, a psychologist like yourself. She listened patiently to me and a few others, particularly the two employees who left, then a month later she was gone too. She died."

"Did she try to talk with management about these issues?"

"She was having a big problem with the system. Lots of people were talking with her about their concerns. It was her job to get everyone's input, so they could adjust the computer to our staff. Except the company thought she was supposed to adapt people to the machine. They were not interested in changing the program itself. I think she had a big struggle with the Hitman and Carter Newton over this. Even told me once she might want to take it outside the company. But then she got sick. Maybe it was too much for her."

"Did Elaina work closely with Hepman and Carter?"

"Not at first. Still, toward the end she spent more time upstairs. Hardly ever saw her at her desk. Didn't look too happy either. Those two kept her on a short leash. Everyone got all quiet and secretive. I thought maybe she was looking for a new job. Then she was gone."

Unsure how much to reveal about her knowledge of Elaina, Jenny just nodded sympathetically. A coldness seemed to grip her soul. She was discovering too many points of convergence between Elaina, GHB, and MOM. It was beginning to seem sinister.

"Jenny, I'm sorry, I talk too much."

"No, I want to know about this. I consider this an important part of the job," Jenny offered in support.

"Well, if you really want to see what MOM does, don't just look at the medical part. Follow some cases through the system. See what people go through. Maybe they'll listen to you."

Mable wrapped her arm around Jenny's shoulders and gave her a sideways hug. Both returned to their desks. Jenny would be leaving in two hours, but she had enough time to run some cases. She selected three more case examples and told MOM to run them through from initial contact and eligibility screening. All went well. Each case was efficiently assessed, qualified, and authorized, using real-time criterion. Maybe the bugs were fixed? No, she thought, as she recalled the pain on Mable's face. Something's wrong.

A thought occurred to her about how these sample cases were programmed. The case ID number was well known to MOM, so of course everything would go well. As an experiment, Jenny created a copy of some case material and then gave it a new name and case ID number so that MOM wouldn't recognize it. Immediately, MOM rejected the case, denied eligibility, and refused further access. Jenny asked for clarification of status, but MOM merely referred the case to the Claims Resolution Department.

Jenny dialed Hepman from the console. A secretary answered and transferred her to the project director.

"Greg, this is Jenny. I've been running some cases through the system and I'm really amazed at how well it works. This is a cool system."

"Thanks, Jenny," said Hepman, hoping she had forgotten his earlier transgression.

"However, I do have a little problem and I'd like to see what happens with some real cases. If MOM is as smart as I think, then her artificial intelligence has overlearned the routine on these sample cases. I'd like to track the whole intake process with some live data."

"You mean to get a diagnosis?" asked Hepman.

"No, I mean the whole process. Eligibility, correspondence, financials, everything. I want to see all that MOM manages in client care."

Hepman seemed hesitant. "Well, that's pretty much what you're looking at. There are a couple of administrative checks MOM does, but mostly it's standard medical care."

"Greg, some of the cases I've seen on-line seem to take those administrative considerations pretty seriously. Aren't they part of the formula for care?"

"No, no, no. We only look for cost-effective treatment. We don't consider financials for anything else. That's why we keep everything separate."

Jenny thought he was protesting just a tad too much. "Well I think that seeing a more global picture of MOM's operation and decision process would be very helpful for me. Besides, while testing the system, I tried creating an original sample case with a new ID number. MOM just kicked it out for lack of eligibility, even though I gave the case good insurance coverage."

"Jenny, I really don't think this would be a good use of your time. Besides, only people with level six clearance have access to what you want. Part of security is that people are limited to parts of MOM. You only have level four access."

"Greg, I don't want total access. I just want a good understanding of MOM's decision process so I can figure out the best training approach."

"Okay," he said reluctantly. "I'll check with Carter to see what he thinks, but we need you up front getting the case managers swimming with the program."

Jenny realized she had bumped against a firm wall of security. Progressive had similar protections on their system, but at her level knowing how the computer "thought" was essential, at least on a global scale. She couldn't hope to understand the actual programming code. A flow chart, showing graphically how things are weighed and decided, would help her convince the on-line staff to trust the system. There was also an element of curiosity about how MOM was implemented in this more competitive, money-driven environment.

Finally, there was Hepman. She had to admit that this was just a power play. She didn't want him calling the shots. This system needed a dose of humanity, and Hepman was not likely to provide it. Deep inside MOM there were life and death calculations being made at the speed of light. In traditional medicine a physician would be accountable for those decisions. The doctor would consult with peers to explore decisions and could even be cross examined about the decision. MOM stood alone, guarded by a fortress of proprietary patents and trade secrets. Where was the accountability? She shivered as a dark thought intruded. "Maybe it died in a psychiatric hospital?"

***

Three months earlier, on a crisp cold day in late January, Elaina Ruiz slipped into a deep sleep from which she would never awaken.

On that wintery evening, a Filipino man, wearing a white lab coat and carrying a plastic container full of vials and syringes, walked unnoticed into the adult ward of the Pine View Lodge psychiatric facility. He had a round face, lightly sprinkled with acne scars, black close-cropped hair, a stocky build, and a vacant smile.

It was 6:50 P.M. Thursday as he glided almost unseen down the faded linoleum hallway. Groups of adults mingled in private huddles scattered around the hallways during these visiting hours. Conversations emerged from the patients' semi-private rooms. The nursing staff was busy answering questions, finding patients, arranging snacks. The technician's appearance was a masterpiece of professional anonymity. His uniform was different from those of the staff, suggesting that he was an outsider, yet his demeanor suggested that he was focused on an immediate task. He was of no interest to anyone on the ward, particularly during this hectic period. The "invisible" man.

Entering the nurses' station, he casually scanned the area. He was accustomed to modern medical centers, where the medical staff sifted through data at computer terminals. This creaky old facility sported only one computer monitor in the corner, which was most likely used for billing rather than patient care.

He approached the central chart wheel, a lazy Susan of patient records, and slowly spun the wheel until the name "Ruiz" reached him, then he withdrew the chart and backed away. Adhesive stickers on the front cover alerted the staff that this patient was allergic to penicillin, was a moderate suicide risk, and was to have no visitors until further notice.

The face-sheet noted that Elaina Ruiz had been admitted early yesterday for severe agitation and depression, possibly with paranoid features. She had been heavily medicated to facilitate a regimen of bed rest. The chart was labeled bed 12B. A quick glance at the chart wheel showed that bed 12A was unoccupied. She was alone in the room. Her last medications had been given an hour ago, an anti-psychotic, a tranquilizer, and sleeping medication. She was out cold from sedatives and sleepers. Things were as his "employer" said they would be.

A nurse brushed by the technician while retrieving some charts. "Whatcha need?" she asked.

"Blood gases," was his evasive reply, but it was enough to satisfy the nurse, who nodded and left with a stack of charts.

He replaced the chart, picked up his plastic box and left the nursing station. In times past, security and privacy on a psychiatric unit were closely guarded, but managed care's iron grip on insurance benefits for the last decade had contributed to the closing of over two-thirds of psychiatric hospitals. Beds were no longer filled with insurance-rich, middle-class workaholics needing peace and quiet. Now these hospitals scrambled to fill beds with anyone: from private drug detox admissions to publicly funded homeless schizophrenics. Staff was cut in half. Privacy amidst such chaos was low on the list of priorities.

The man walked down the long hallway to room 12, swung open the oversized hospital door and slipped inside. The room was dimly lit and became instantly quiet as the two-inch-thick wooden door closed, sealing the room like a vault from the frenzy in the hallway. He heard the gentle breathing of the woman, and soon he could make out her form on the bed. She laid on her side, her back to the door, knees pulled toward her chest. The bed was by the window.

The technician moved past the unoccupied bed and pulled the privacy curtain, which blocked the view from the door. He did the same as he reached Elaina's bed. If anyone came in, he might need a few seconds of "privacy." The sleeping woman didn't move at the sound of the sliding curtains. Her breathing was slow, deep, and regular. His eyes became more accustomed to the darkness and he could make out her features. Brunette, slender, late twenties. Attractive face with Hispanic features. He couldn't remember the last time he'd "done" a young woman. He was usually hired to kill older family members who weren't dying quickly enough. "Kind of like Kevorkian," he would joke, "except I put the *family* out of their misery." This young woman was something of a novel treat.

He pulled back the sheet covering her. She wore a simple, oversized flannel nightie buttoned up the front. It was important that she not awaken when he stuck her. While he carefully watched her breathing, he first touched her shoulder and then gently rolled her over onto her back. The soft body was limp and yielding, with no hint of responsiveness. Testing further, he placed his hand on her forehead, then circled her ear with his finger, and finally lifted her eyelid. The woman remained motionless, breathing regularly.

The technician relaxed a bit, secure that things were going as planned. He noticed her beauty and wondered why she had to die. "You certainly got somebody mighty upset with you," he whispered to himself. "Must be carrying some executive's baby from an illicit affair." He pulled up the nightie, exposing her panties and stomach. "Doesn't look pregnant," he thought. He pulled it up higher to reveal her breasts. He took the liberty of stroking the lovely body of a woman more beautiful than he could ever have without payment.

The distraction lasted only a minute. Voices in the hall passed the doorway and brought him back to his task. Removing some vials from his box, he withdrew a prepared syringe filled with a dark fluid. Upon raising the sleeve of the nightie, he found the bandage in the crook of her arm from a routine blood test at admission. He removed one side of the adhesive, pulled a small flashlight from his pocket, flicked it on and gripped it with his teeth to light her arm. He detached the syringe cover and carefully positioned the needle over the puncture mark from the earlier lab test. "Don't need any more holes in you, little lady," he quipped to add levity to a grim task.

The jab into the arm produced only a slight twitch in the woman. He pushed the liquid death into her vein. The chemical would mix with the other medications in her bloodstream and quadruple their potency. Normal side effects would be multiplied many times and become lethal. Ms. Ruiz would slip into a coma. Her blood pressure would drop to zero, a rare but well documented complication of chlorpromazine, and she would quietly slip away. The substance was only detectible for five days after death, and only by an expensive test. Los Angeles County's financial troubles would insure that the test was not done by the Coroner. Actually, it wasn't a bad way to die, he reflected. He just hoped it wouldn't happen to him.

The moon emerged from behind a cloud and the room noticeably brightened. Quickly the technician removed the syringe, replaced the bandage on her arm and repacked his box. He saw her face more clearly now, almost angelic in the moonlight, free of stress and fear as she swam through the dreamland of chemical sleep. For an instant he felt tempted to have her, to be the last to enjoy her lovely body, but he knew she would soon lose control of all body functions as her systems shut down. Very messy. Besides, the only sex that excited him anymore left deep lacerations and internal tissue damage. No marks were allowed on this body.

He gently placed the sheet back over her, almost as a comforting gesture of goodbye, and then left the room. The entire episode had taken only eight minutes. No one would remember a faceless technician drifting through the ward. She would be dead by the change of shift at 11:00. He had no idea why she had to die, and for $5,000 he didn't need to know. His business was as brisk as the January night air that swallowed him up as he left.

It was the season of "insurance death." The turn of the calender quickly shifted medical financial burdens back to the families of ailing patients, particularly through insurance deductibles and co-pays. Grandpa's nest egg began shrinking dramatically. The families were usually thankful that the old fart had made it through the holidays, but now the kindest thing to do was to pull the plug.

A great irony would emerge from this hit that would never be realized. The technician had just killed the one woman who might have saved his own mother's life the following year. A Nigerian clinic scam out of New York would obtain his mother's social security number and use it to bill for thousands of dollars of bogus treatment under three false names. His mother's medical records would become so confused and contradictory that case managers could not figure out her real medical history.

Elaina Ruiz was an expert in computerized medical records and would have sorted it out. Instead, a naive new graduate nurse would be called from a Dallas, Texas emergency room to confirm the mother's insurance eligibility and medication allergies. Trusting the flashy computer screen, the nurse would make a tragic error. Like Elaina, the hit man's mother would die quickly.

Chapter 23

Crandall Bream was completely unprepared for the staggering response to his letter. Although he often preached of "eternity and infinity," he had little conception of earthbound numerical figures, like millions.

Within a week, Crandall had received almost $687,000 in "contributions." It was far beyond his most celestial expectations, yet this represented a mere six percent response rate from the 267,000 letters mailed. Elliot, the consummate number cruncher, did some demographic market studies on the respondent's addresses. His analysis found that it represented about a 24 percent response rate among those who had received the letter. Because bulk mail was so slow, many women still had not yet received the letter. Although Crandall's spirits hardly needed a boost, Elliot advised him that a 24 percent return rate of all the letters mailed would yield $2.7 million in cash. The ministry was saved!

Crandall, Jerry, and Elliot planned the next steps carefully. Jerry had the foresight to open an offshore bank account in the Carribean, to safely store most of the money. That way, if things went terribly wrong, there was a fall back position with secure capital. Secondly, they agreed to purchase more and larger lists from managed care companies, this time hoping to top out at close to three million names. There was no telling how many mailing cycles they could complete before other competitors imitated the scheme or the Feds shut them down with an injunction. Additionally, they hoped a few more "sensitive" names of government officials or wives would emerge, to be used as a bargaining chip if things got too hot.

Surprisingly, none of the three conspirators had heard or seen any media coverage about the solicitation. It was curious that such an explosive issue, presented in such a bold fashion, would not have surfaced publically yet. Some of these people must be reporters. Crandall took it as both a sign of God's good will and of the shame these women felt about their horrible acts.

Unknown to Crandall was the anxiety and confusion the letter created on both sides of the abortion debate. Feminist and women's groups were furious, but hesitated to speak out in a public forum without some assurance that the women's names would be protected. The activist groups didn't want the blame for spilling the beans, particularly when many women would willingly pay forty dollars to assure their privacy. "Outing" had chilled the gay movement, and they had no desire to repeat that mistake now by publishing the names of these women.

The major news services were stunned by the audacity of the act, but needed to confirm that it was not another set-up for their own ridicule. Editors were still wary of the Olympic bomber fiasco. Confirming this story wasn't easy, for few people would admit receiving the letter, as it was an instant admission of guilt. It was one thing to be pro-choice, and quite another to have personally executed that choice. Caution miraculously prevailed in investigative reporting. Two supermarket tabloids got wind of the plot, but decided to embellish it with a mad-clinic-bomber-for-God spin, making the story unrecognizable to any recipient of Crandall's letter.

The letters also reached many women in the anti-abortion movement, including some who had secrets in their own medical histories. It was brought to the attention of the many anti-abortion leaders, who were as exhilarated as Crandall Bream that the veil of secrecy was pierced, but were concerned that too much revelation would frighten off their supporters. They were also alarmed about the aura of blackmail that cloaked the solicitation, fearing the media would turn it into a feeding frenzy on the Christian Coalition.

The Christian communities were initially silent on the matter, for Bream's soured reputation generated caution. Crandall's answering service collected 14 calls from the leaders of religious groups in eight states that day. By the end of the week, the proprietor of Waverley Phone Services would need to dedicate three operators to handle the incoming calls to Crandall.

***

Jenny's forehead was pressed flat against the plastic window of the

Boeing 737. Her eyes strained through the haze at 26,000 feet to make out the backbone of the Sierra Nevada mountains. She was headed home on a flight that would first stop in San Francisco and then continue to Medford, Oregon. Her mother would pick her up for the drive to the ranch outside Grants Pass. As the commuter jet soared though the puffy clouds, her eyes scanned the craggy mountain tops below, drinking in the majestic spires, the green carpet of evergreens, and the occasional jewels of blue lakes.

Images of family camping trips filtered through her mind's eye. She and her brother had spent countless summers in the mountains as children, either during family vacations or on scouting retreats. Even in the hermetically sealed aircraft, she could remember the feel of alpine air, dry and cool, mixed with the scent of pine and fir, accompanied by the sounds of a child's rubber soles scuffing on stone while racing along a hiking trail. The aircraft emerged from a cloud and Jenny saw the unmistakable glacier-carved valley of Yosemite. Even from this vantage point, Half Dome stuck out like a tumbleweed on a golf course. El Capitan's monolithic face rose out of the valley floor, standing guard over the Merced River. Jenny recalled running along the banks of the frigid river, daring her brother to dive in. She recalled her father wading downstream in his hip boots, whipping his fly-fishing line back and forth in giant arcs, until finally launching it to an inaccessible pool near the opposite bank. These were some of her most valued memories of family life.

The plane shook her to attention as it passed through some turbulence. Reluctantly, she allowed the reverie to disappear with the terrain below her. Images of her father in the woods lingered on. He was always so big and powerful, and so wise about the wilderness. His love of nature had infected both of his children. Jenny prayed that she wasn't about to lose the giant teddy bear. His hair had turned white in recent years, but he still moved with the stealth of a deer. She was grateful that he had shown no favoritism toward his son during her upbringing. She was always invited along on "manly sports." Her father even took some kidding about this from his friends, but he had a lot to give and wanted his children to share every bit of him. At 12 he had lost an older sister to pneumonia, impressing on him forever the fragility and blessing of life.

Forty minutes later the pilot announced preparation for landing. The late day sun peeked through the Cascade Mountains, casting long shadows from the volcanic buttes surrounding the valley below. Excitement rushed through her body. The grass covering the ground was still green, and patches of wildflowers painted the land with brilliant colors. She always felt more human in these surroundings. It was so far from the concrete cacophony of Los Angeles.

Jenny grabbed her single carry-on suitcase and laptop computer and scampered off the plane. Her mother was waiting at the single gate that serviced all flights into Medford. Gray, curly hair framed a cherubic face. Blue eyes, tinged with red from tears, sparkled at the sight of her daughter. Her mom had always been stocky, but now she looked like a stout grandmother, wearing sneakers, jeans, and a flannel shirt. Both embraced and rocked as they hugged.

"Oh, Jenny, I'm so glad you could come."

"Mom, you look great."

"I feel like I've been run ragged. Your poor father is getting ten different stories from twelve different people. I've been trying to make sense of it, but it's all beyond us."

"Is he still in pain?"

"I'm afraid so. The doctors are willing to give him pain medicine, but they won't let him go back to the surgeon for follow-up till Friday. They say it's just normal recovery. I'm getting worried about how many painkillers he's taking. It's not like him. You know that."

They climbed into the Barrett pickup truck and headed for home. Jenny listened to her mother recount the events of the last three weeks, mostly to let the woman vent her anxiety. The trip up the Rogue Valley was beautiful and filled with nostalgia for Jenny. The road repeatedly crossed over the Rogue River, and at each turn Jenny could remember some adventure from her childhood or the three summers she guided raft trips. Eating wild blackberries while floating down the river. Camping overnight at Waltman's Bend. Throwing up drunk after the high school prom at the bat cavern. Jumping off a 60-foot-high train trestle in a terrifying plunge to the cold river, just to show the courage of a 15-year-old.

As a river guide, Jenny had learned to respond with a clear head in a crisis. Things happened quickly on the river, and all the forces of nature could be working against you. The guide job required the ability to navigate through turbulent, rocky rapids, guiding a boat full of naive kids, sometimes while looking for a passenger who had been flung overboard into the swift current. It was not a time for panic and the river experience helped her develop nerves of steel in the face of danger.

As they traveled west, the canyon deepened and the sun was hidden behind a mountain, making it prematurely dusk. Yet the air was still warm and heavily scented with blooms of a hundred varieties. A half hour later they took the Grants Pass exit off Interstate 5, passing the famous Grants Pass gas station. The town looked much as it always had. They drove through town on the three lane, one-way boulevard, crossed the Rogue River again, then continued out of town for about two miles. Francis Barrett turned onto a dirt road, lined with oak trees. Another half mile found them at the entrance to the Barrett ranch. The driveway was guarded by two stone monuments that once held a swinging gate. The one on the left was Jenny's, the other dedicated to her brother. It was one of the first real laboring projects Jenny could remember doing. Her father offered to name the columns in exchange for the kids' help. Jenny remembered it taking a week to complete, but that was a child's perception of a mammoth project. It actually took three days, most of work completed by the father, but he let them tell their own story about it.

Jenny eyes fell upon the house as her mom stopped the pickup beside a giant shade oak. She heard the brook that flowed beside her bedroom window. It was a low house in a sprawling ranch style. Window box flowers hung in the front. It was good to be home.

Jenny's father was clad in pajamas, standing hunched over next to the couch in the family room, holding on to the padded arm, hailing them as they entered. Jenny left her suitcase in the hallway and approached her dad. He looked like a sick man. His cheeks were scraggly with a white two-day growth of beard. His arms were thin, yet his belly seemed immense. Pain was written all over his face as he moved; involuntary twitches and grimaces told of the torture. He seemed worse than she had thought. He kissed her and patted her shoulder in a hesitant, cursory way. Traditionally, he'd squeeze her tight and swing her around as if dancing.

"Dad, sit down, you need to take care of yourself," Jenny scolded.

William Barrett half sat and half fell back on the couch. He seemed to have aged ten years since Christmas. His abdomen was grossly distended from the surgery and she could see bandages through his tee shirt. Jenny grasped his forearm to reassure him. The flesh was withered and flaccid, and very warm. It was as if all the fluid in his body was congealing in his abdomen.

"What's your temperature?"

"It's been creeping up since yesterday. Staying around 101 to 102 degrees," said Francis.

"Damn doctor said I'd be feeling better right away," said Bill. "Now my back is killing me, my stomach is hanging over my shoes, and

I can't stand up without getting dizzy. I wish they hadn't dropped Dr. Shepard from the list of doctors. That Majani doesn't know shit. None of them do."

The venom was a surprise, for Jenny's father rarely cursed. The hospital had provided a post-op instruction sheet, which described a wide array of vague symptoms, so broad that there was no way to tell if Bill's recovery was normal.

"Can I get you more ice?" asked Francis.

"Sure, honey. I'm sorry for all the bellyaching, but my damn belly is aching," said Bill.

"Dad," said Jenny, "I'm worried. I think we should call Majani again. You shouldn't be this uncomfortable."

"Damn doctors got me into this. Probably want to take something else out. Just give me some of those pills and let me rest. I'll be okay."

"Dad, this could be serious," said Jenny with a raised voice.

"I'll be fine. Besides, we haven't been able to get the doctor. Just the answering service, and some other doctor that doesn't know anything."

Francis entered the living room with the ice. "If you want to call, the number is next to the phone. We also have the insurance company number. They're the ones who switched Dad from Shepard."

"Let's see, it's 7:15. Might as well start calling before it gets much later." Jenny called the Hubb Health Center, where Dr. Majani worked. After a brief discussion with the answering service she convinced the operator to page Majani, not the doctor on call. She hung up the phone to wait.

"Can I get you anything else, hon?" Francis asked Bill.

"No," said Bill, "I want to get off the subject of me and hear what's new with Jenny."

For 15 minutes Jenny updated them on her new job, Mark, and the death of her friend. Then the phone rang.

"Hello," answered Jenny.

"This is Dr. Majani. I understand you called," said a male voice with a Pakistani accent.

"Thank you for returning my call, doctor. I'm Jenny Barrett, William Barrett's daughter. I just arrived from Los Angeles and I was very concerned about my father's condition. I know he just had surgery, but he is in a lot of pain and his abdomen is quite distended."

"Yes. This is all normal. He just had surgery, you know. The procedure went fine. There should be no problems," replied Majani.

"But he seems to be very uncomfortable."

"I think he is scheduled for a follow-up visit day after tomorrow.

If you like I can call in a prescription for a stronger pain medicine," said the doctor.

"No. I don't think that will help. I'd really feel much better if he were seen tomorrow."

"This is not possible," replied Majani. "Our office is completely booked. We have many patients who need serious care. I also think the insurance company requires a certain recovery period. They don't like too many visits for no reason. Why don't we wait until tomorrow and see how he does?"

"Maybe I'll call the insurance company and see if I can get permission?"

"Okay, do that if you wish, but I'm telling you this is all normal. We do these all the time. Never a problem. There is no need to bother the insurance company. Let us talk tomorrow."

"Certainly, doctor," said Jenny with a complacent tone and hung up. "Well, that was close to useless," she hissed in anger. "I see what you mean, Mom."

"I don't trust this guy," said Bill.

"This is the insurance number?" asked Jenny, pointing to a scribble on the notepad.

"Yes, dear," said Francis. "Here, let me give you the insurance card with all the ID numbers."

Jenny dialed the 800 number. The line was answered by an automated computer attendant that listed eight options for services. Jenny selected medical benefits and was presented with another voice menu. She was prompted to enter her father's member number and other coded information from the card. Six layers of voice menus later she heard what she believed was a live human voice. Jenny realized that GHB clients went through the same frustrations.

"This is Andrew. How may I help you?"

"Andrew, my name is Jenny Barrett. My father, William Barrett, just had a lap chole two days ago. He's in a great deal of pain and has some abdominal distention. I think there's something wrong, but his doctor, Majani, says he needs to get approval for a visit from you."

"Yes, Ms. Barrett. Let me just pull up the screen on that. Yes, I see he had surgery on Monday. No reported problems. Hubb Health has a contract with us and they are responsible for follow up. It's up to them."

"But they said it was up to you! Don't you have to approve an early visit?" asked Jenny.

"Actually, no, unless there is some special problem. We don't manage the case from here. They have a contract with us that allows them to make their own decisions."

"Then why did he say you had to approve it?"

"I'm sorry. I have no idea. Why don't you just call them in the morning," said Andrew.

"But my father is uncomfortable and ill right now! He also doesn't feel confident in the doctor. Can he go to another physician? Dr. Shepard used to be on the list and my father has seen him for years."

"Yes, I understand your concern," said Andrew, as if reading it off the screen. "Let me check on a few things. I'll have to put you on hold."

Jenny was getting angrier by the minute. She listened to a bland synthesized rendition of "I Will Survive" while on hold as the minutes ticked by.

"Ms. Barrett?" asked a new, female voice.

"Yes."

"I'm Maxine Healy, a supervisor. Andrew was telling me about your concerns. As I understand it, you're afraid your father is not recovering well from his surgery on Monday."

"Right."

"Well, I examined the contract with Hubb Health and there really is little we can do. I'm sure they're doing the best thing," assured Maxine.

"Can my father go back to his original doctor, Dr. Shepard?"

"Let me check. No, I'm afraid your father was transferred to Dr. Majani to relieve Dr. Shepard's caseload."

"May I ask," ventured Jenny, "does Hubb Health have a capitated contract with you?"

"I'm sorry. That information is not available here. You'll have to speak with your doctor."

"Well, maybe we'll just have to take him to an emergency room."

"Ms. Barrett. I know you're worried, but your father is under very good care. Dr. Majani is an experienced surgeon. We've never had a problem before. If you go to the emergency room, I'm afraid you'll just incur a large expense, which won't be covered under your policy. Please try to work with the doctor."

"Could I ask just how good his outcome statistics are for this procedure?"

This hit Maxine Healy right between the eyes. No one had ever asked for such a thing. "I'm sorry. I don't think that information is available."

"Look, Maxine. I'm a case manager at Great Health Benefit. I know the drill. Both your company and mine keep profiles on every contract doctor. I want to know what Dr. Majani's outcome stats look like," insisted Jenny.

Maxine was troubled by the turn of this conversation. "Again, I don't have access to that information. That department is closed right now. Maybe you can call back tomorrow." Maxine wanted this conversation to end. Mercifully, it did.

"I'll call tomorrow, Ms. Healy," said Jenny, as she hung up. She turned to her parents, a look of stern resolution on her face, and her parents stared back in hope and gratitude that their daughter knew how to manage this behemoth system. "I'm going to see Dr. Shepard tomorrow, even if Majani calls back. I don't understand what's going on here, but I don't like it either. No one's taking any responsibility."

"Thanks, Jen," said her mother with damp eyes, reaching over to squeeze her daughter's hand. "It's so good to have you here. I'll sleep better tonight, and so will this crabby old bear."

They talked for a while, but the stresses of the day had tired everyone out. Jenny's father kept slipping into sleep, which seemed the best place for him in his discomfort. While her mother tidied up the dishes, Jenny stepped outside to breathe some sweet country air she missed in Los Angeles. As she walked into the night air, the wooden clack of the screen door striking its frame shot her back through time. The air was scented from the fragrant flowers in the yard. The little creek beside the house was flowing swiftly from spring runoff, babbling with the frogs and crickets to welcome her home.

The porch light illuminated the giant oak tree in front of the house, which bore many bruises from her and David's adventures as children. The tree was the most enduring chronicle of her and David's passage through childhood. A long, low branch was constricted and scarred by the chains that once held their swing set. Stab wounds from knives and arrows and spears dotted all sides of the 18-inch trunk. Rusted nails were all that remained of their once mighty tree fortress. At the eye level of a 14-year-old there remained the chiseled initials of their first few loves.

The night air was brisk, but comfortable. A crystal clear sky revealed the starlit vault of heaven that Jenny couldn't see through the haze and light of Southern California. Her feet glided through the soft crushed clay of the driveway, and the country night seemed to swallow her. She turned to see a view through the kitchen window of her mother's head bobbing as she worked, as she had done through countless summer evenings. Jenny heard the telephone ring and her mother disappeared. A few minutes later, the screen door creaked open and her mother called out. "Jenny, it's David."

She returned to the house to speak with her brother.

"Hey sis, got your message. Glad you're there. How are things going?" said David, always getting directly to the point.

"I'm okay. Dad's really uncomfortable, but he won't do anything. The doctor isn't being cooperative, the insurance company is dropping the ball, and I was just looking at your proclamation of love to Valerie Brunswick on the tree."

David laughed briefly, then asked soberly, "Are things serious? Do I need to come home?"

"No, we can handle it. Just got to slap some sense into these quacks. Dad's so disgusted that he won't go see anyone, but I've got a plan for tomorrow. Maybe pull out the heavy artillery."

"Uh oh. Is Jenny gonna nuke 'em with data? Flame their system until they cry uncle?"

"Something like that. Speaking of flaming, Dwick says hello."

"Dwick!" exclaimed David. "The old Demon Warlord. You hanging with the radicals again?"

"He's helping me on a project."

"God help you, Jenny. That man's brilliant, but he's completely nuts."

"He's mellowed since his kid was born. Anyway, message delivered."

"How's Mom doing? She sounds okay."

"She's holding up," Jenny assured him. "God, it's good to hear your voice, David. Do you think you can touch base over the next few days? I need some moral support."

"Sure. I'm hanging in Bangkok for the week. Pitching a new system to a few banks. Do the folks still have my computer up and running? When I get settled in the hotel, we can do a video conference."

"I'm sure they do, but I got this nice Axil Laser 9000 laptop we can use.

"Jesus, sis. Are you in the big bucks now?" said David.

"It's a loaner from my company."

"I'll start working for them tomorrow, okay? We'll try to put that together. How long do you think you'll be in town?"

"Well, I am away from my new job in only my second week. Still, I want to make sure Dad's out of the woods. We'll see."

"Great. You know how to reach me. Can I talk to Dad?"

"He's asleep. I really don't want to wake him."

"Sure. Talk to you tomorrow. Hugs and kisses. I'm off for a sandwich."

"Would that be a Bangkok sandwich?"

"Why sis, you embarrass me with your knowledge of Eastern habits. Bye."

Jenny's last act of the night was to leave a message on Mark's answering machine, a brief status report as she had promised, then the Barrett household retired into fitful sleep.

Chapter 24

On a hot spring day Ezra padded down the street approaching his house. Robins and sparrows darted through the bushy trees. He felt his skin draw tight in response to the sun, yet he absorbed the radiant energy like the trees, feeling fuller, stronger. His shoes scuffed along the walkway to the porch, stepping over weeds pushing through the cracks in the concrete. Life is hardy stuff, he thought.

He stopped at the mailbox, which was stuffed with advertisements for nursing homes. He wondered why, since he hadn't spoken with anyone except GHB about such plans. Ezra didn't realize how quickly an innocent query could become a marketing request. Many companies paid GHB great sums of money to learn of the members' needs. Everything was for sale.

He opened the thick front door and crossed over to the living room. A peace had settled on the house. Even the refrigerator was quiet. Nora was not on the couch, so she must be asleep in the bedroom. Wanting to savor the residual warmth from his walk, he plopped down on the couch, dumping the nursing home flyers on the coffee table. From force of habit his eyes scanned for the remote control, but he really didn't want the crass sound of television game shows disturbing his reverie. His eyes caught a folded sheet of paper from a writing tablet on the coffee table. Poorly formed letters peeked from under the top fold. It was not a handwriting he immediately recognized. With a grunt he snatched the letter up, opening it to discover an almost childlike cipher. He could just make out that the signature was "Nora," and he realized he hadn't seen anything written by her in a few years. His eyes strained at the closing above her name. "Goodbye my love." His breathing stopped. His eyes went wide.

Springing to his feet, he almost pitched over the coffee table. Stumbling through the hallway, he pushed open the door to the bedroom.

Nora lay bundled in the comforter, dressed in the robe he had given her at Christmas. Her eyes were closed and she lay more still than he had ever seen her before. Her skin was ashen white, offset by the jarring red of her fingernails. The corners of her mouth seemed curved up in a mysterious smile. She looked so peaceful and lovely, and he knew she was gone. He quickly grabbed her arm and felt for a pulse. It was cold and offered no resistance. He slipped his arm under her back and pressed his ear against her chest. Her heart was silent. Ezra began to sob. She had done this, he knew without reading the letter. She had taken her life to spare him any more pain. Rocking her back and forth in his arms as if trying to revive her. He felt that he had failed her. Then he thought of her pain and how sleep had become her only real escape from it. Was he calling her back for his own selfish needs? She was in God's hands, where she needed to be.

He stayed with her for half an hour. He gently embraced the finality of her act. "Till death do us part" kept leaping through his mind, the vows taken four and half decades ago that had seemed so theoretical, so distant. Now it was over. The woman he loved was gone. Nothing he could do or say could change it. In one instant their marriage had gone from an "is" to a "was."

Ezra realized there were many things to do, but he could not let her go right now. His eyes surveyed the bedroom and he saw a syringe on the table. Somehow, despite her palsy, she had used it, and it looked evil. As he shifted his weight and laid her down on the pillow, the note crackled in his hand. He smoothed it out and again examined the writing. The last message from his beloved. He read it slowly.

Dear Ezra,

I'm sorry I can't write more clearly, but I will try to say what I need to. In many ways this will be a sad day for both of us. However, in other ways, it will be joyous. By the time you read this I will have left this world. I'm sure of that, for I have spent the last week planning it. I want this to be a good death. If I hold on too much longer, it won't be. Too many other people will take over. I want this to be my decision alone. I wish the clinic had found the illness earlier, had given me the right tests, but we can't let that mistake ruin our spirit. Don't let my death blind you with rage. Look at what we had, not at what we've missed.

Leaving you behind is the hardest thing I will ever

do. Please do not feel that you have failed me. You have made this life as wonderful as I could have ever hoped it would be. I have had the pleasure of knowing you for almost fifty years. You have been my closest friend, companion, lover, and champion. You have painted so many smiles on my face with your wit and humor. You have been like a stone column of strength when I needed it. You have been tender and giving when I hurt. We have been on a very long road together. But now, I must leave.

The cancer is winning too quickly. Every day I feel it steal more of my life. I'm so thankful I've had this medicine to keep the pain at least tolerable, but even your miracle drug is failing. I have tried to be as good a companion as you have been. I don't want my image tarnished by months of disability, pain, and suffering for both of us. I see on your face the toll this ordeal has taken. I have lived as your wife and I will die as your wife, not as an invalid in a strange place. I know the anguish you feel as you try to make the best decisions for me. Let me ease your burden, Ezra. Let me exit knowing your last image of me is as I want to be, not what I'm afraid I'll become.

I saved a couple of bottles of medicine for this moment. Please don't be mad. Please understand that it is my love for you and all that we have had that I chose to leave now. I will arrive in Heaven with an image of your smile fixed in my mind. We will have eternity, Ezra. Nothing could give me greater peace.

Goodbye my love,
Nora

***

Jenny left the house early the next morning, using her father's pickup to stop in at the Shepard Clinic. Alex Shepard had been her family's doctor since they moved to Grants Pass, when she was four years old. He had always seemed old to her, even though he must have been active and athletic in earlier years, for he won many tennis tournaments at the country club. Dr. Shepard had followed Jenny through most of her childhood illnesses, her acne and weight problems of adolescence, and he was there to comfort her when she thought she was pregnant at 17. She wasn't. He gave her an intense, impassioned lecture and the incident was never mentioned again. Jenny imagined that her brother must have received the same lecture somewhere along the line.

Most kids wouldn't have the benefit of an enduring medical continuity today. There was little permanence in modern medical care. Most families changed doctors as often as they changed insurance policies. Different rules, different provider panels, homogenized care by a carousel of primary care doctors. Today's kids probably didn't feel much privacy either. Even if they had the courage to enter a clinic with a personal concern, seeing their name typed into computers would scare them away. They'd likely end up seeking street solutions, or "alternative health" options.

Jenny remembered with rage overhearing a conversation on the Venice boardwalk in Southern California. A dealer in crystals and metaphysical trinkets was approached by a frail 15-year-old. She asked him for a crystal that would serve as birth control. He offered her a ten dollar pink quartz necklace. Jenny exploded at the vendor, trying to protect the young girl from inevitable disaster, but the waif took the crystal anyway. It was all the medical care the helpless girl could afford.

The Shepard Clinic was located in a remodeled Victorian house, yellow with white trim, surrounded by well kept gardens. The age of the building became apparent on closer examination. Standing on the porch, one could see the blemishes of nicked and faded paint. Molding was missing here and there, floor boards were stained and warped, mold grew thick in the shade of the porch railing. Jenny could see the interior through the picture window, which looked brighter and more sanitary. She eyed the crystal door knob on the leaded glass entrance. As a little girl she had wondered if it was a precious stone that the doctor had received for saving the life of a king in some foreign land.

She entered the vacant waiting room and sat on a winged back chair. The room was rich in wood and ornate metal work. Antique medical and pharmaceutical equipment occupied some display cases. A local FM station provided the musical ambiance. Although Dr. Shepard must have redecorated since Jenny visited him as a child, the office seemed familiar and comforting. She never recalled dreading a visit to the doctor. His easy manner and playfulness had won her over. When required to give an injection to the child, he often pointed to some ever-present, and proudly won, bump or scrape on her skinny legs and suggest that hurt much more than a little "shot."

It was Wednesday, a day of light traffic in the office as she expected. Midweek golf was still a strong tradition among the physicians of Grants Pass. It had been at least eight years since Jenny had seen this country doctor, although she often heard about his life from her parents.

Jenny saw shadowy movement behind the frosted glass of the receptionist window. The dark wooden door opened and Dr. Shepard appeared, as robust as ever.

"Jenny, it's wonderful to see you."

"Dr. Shepard, thanks for seeing me." Jenny moved toward him to give him a hug as she used to do, but he extended his hand and averted his eyes. His smile seemed plastic and didn't radiate to his eyes. This puzzled Jenny, for she had never known him to be aloof. He ushered her into the hallway, then down to his business office.

"So what are you doing with yourself?" he asked.

"Still working in Los Angeles. Shuffling papers and talking to patients on the phone."

"Oh, yes, you work at a psychiatric managed care company. PsychHelp?"

"Progressive. However, they were just bought out by Great Health Benefit, so I'm now working for them."

"Great Health Benefit!" he said with some astonishment. "I guess they're taking over the world."

"Do they have a big presence up here?"

"Very big. Just about every physician and provider in town. I'm one of your guys," he said with a hopeful look of acceptance.

"Not one of mine, Dr. Shepard. I'm not even sure I'm going to stay there. It's a strange company."

Shepard looked at her quizzically, as if trying to decide if he could risk speaking openly, but seemed to think better of it. "Is this a vacation, or business?"

"The business of Dad, mostly. Mom got me worried, so I came up to see if I could help. I got in last night. Dr. Shepard, he doesn't look well at all. I'd like you to look at him."

The corners of Dr. Shepard's mouth drooped a little, betraying his discomfort with the request. "I thought he was seeing Dr. Majani over at Hubb Health?" he said.

"He's only seen him a couple of times and doesn't like him. Aren't you still his primary care physician, according to Axis Health?"

"No, actually, they've switched a number of my patients over to Majani."

"Don't we have anything to say about it? My family has been with you since I was a kid. You're the one my father trusts the most. You're on the panel for Axis Health, right?"

Dr. Shepard squirmed, but continued in a cordial fashion. "Jenny, I'd love to see Bill, but I can't control his insurance company. They're calling the shots."

"Well, just see him and we'll pay cash. They won't even know."

"Jenny, you know that's illegal. Physicians are required by law to bill and report every contact with a Medicare patient. It's a federal law, from back in the late 1980s. No physician in town can see Bill without Axis finding out about it. I can't risk breaking the law."

This is not going well, thought Jenny. Yes, she knew the law, but this wasn't the doctor she remembered. He seemed to totally acquiesce to Axis. There was no fight left in him, none of that strong patient advocacy she remembered. She felt he was just abandoning her father. "Why did they make my father change doctors in the first place?"

"More equitable distribution. My caseload was higher than they allowed. Said it was a violation of my contract with them. Everything's a violation. Damn contract is two inches thick." Shepard gauged Jenny's reaction to this protest. He had a similar contract with GHB.

"Well, we don't think Majani is the right doctor for this case. Dad's really sick, more than he should be, especially from a simple lap chole. I can't get Majani to see him or the insurance company to authorize another visit. Dad's afraid to go out of plan because he heard some people have been punished by even more doctor changes. You're at least on the plan."

"Jenny, probably every physician in Grants Pass is on the plan. They must report every Medicare patient contact. We can't see another doctor's patient without permission, but that's not the only issue. Hell, you work for GHB. You know how much power they wield. They were the first big company in town. Put a lot of docs out of business with their capitated contracts. Paying twenty cents on the dollar. Hell, I almost went under. They're too big. Don't ask me to take on Goliath."

"What are you talking about? Are you saying they aren't paying you? I watch them authorize care all day long."

"Authorizations are cheap. Payments are hard to come by, particularly in a company town like this. Over 85 percent of Grants Pass is enrolled in one of three programs. GHB and Axis Health have the lion's share. They have a thousand ways to whittle down their payments. I'd rather not piss them off."

Jenny felt bewildered and angry. Dr. Shepard had always been a role model of a good doctor to her. Now it was all about money and contracts. Maybe he was just old and crabby, wanting to retire. She looked at the weary man, seeing both pain and shame in his eyes. He looked back, almost pleading for understanding.

"Jenny, you really don't understand, do you?"

"Understand what?"

"How it is now. Out in the trenches. Delivering care. Being controlled by case managers located far away. How long have you been at Great Health Benefit?"

"About a week. Really haven't gotten my feet wet yet. I'm supposed to work on their new diagnostic computer program," said Jenny.

"You've never had any dealings with them before this week?"

"No. I heard they have a tough reputation, but they are very impressive technologically. They certainly have enough stuff to do good things. In answer to your real question, no, I'm not one of them. Like I said, I'm not even sure I'm going to stay there."

Jenny saw the old Dr. Shepard return. His eyes warmed up, his jaw relaxed. He leaned toward her and said, "Run, Jenny. Get out of there fast. They'll eat you for lunch."

"You seem to feel pretty strongly about this. What have they done to you, Dr. Shepard?"

"Jenny, I need to talk to the little girl who poked her finger in Mr. Mallen's harvester and almost lost it. The same girl who got a popcorn kernel stuck deep in her ear at a high school party. The one who pleaded to go on birth control pills because she couldn't restrain herself around Angus McConnell."

Jenny smiled at the recollections of her "medical" history. Dr. Shepard had always been there. "I never thanked you for the lecture. I heard Angus is doing time for robbery. You were right. Okay, what do you want to tell me? Is Dad really sick?"

"I don't know about Bill and honestly haven't seen him for months. But the system is sick, and the company you work for is, how can I describe it, . . . evil. Sinister. Ruthless."

During the next hour Dr. Shepard explained the history of GHB as he knew it in Grants Pass. The tricks, the manipulations, the bankruptcies. Bills unpaid, gag rules and threats of censure. Careers gone with the click of a mouse. The subservience of his profession to the bottom line MBAs. The corralling of patients. The demands for extensive proof of clinical need. The Big Brother of healthcare.

Jenny found it hard to believe that the company was as brutal and callous as Shepard described. "Maybe it's a bad regional manager?"

"It's no different with Axis Health. They all work the same way. They want total compliance," said Shepard.

"But you said there are gag rules. Those were outlawed a few years ago."

"How many companies have you read about being charged with gag rule violation? Jenny, you know they have extensive profiles and case histories on every physician and healthcare provider. There are 8,000 rules of practice and procedure. All they have to do is threaten to notify the licensing board of any questionable activity and a practitioner is dead in the water. Doesn't have to be true. Just 'a concern.' It's an electronic blacklist, transmitted through the community at light speed. Everyone will instantly know and be barred from referring clients. No appeal. That's one hell of a gag rule."

"Has that happened?" asked Jenny.

"More than you want to know. Remember Dr. Newland? Took out your tonsils. Blew his brains out last year. GHB didn't like him telling some mother that GHB waited too long to treat her daughter's meningitis with an expensive medication. Girl ended up with a cerebral infarction and a residual palsy. The parents went to the employer and the insurance commission. GHB retaliated by accusing Newland of some bogus improprieties in other cases. That was it. No more practice. The licensing board cleared him of any wrongdoing last month. Posthumously. GHB said they were just doing their duty."

"Jesus. Dr. Newland? I can't believe it." They sat in silence for a minute, Shepard trying to decide if he had just committed a grievous sin, while Jenny desperately tried to find a flaw in his assessment of GHB, but she knew it was true. She had already seen enough herself. Jenny slowly looked around his office at the dusty old books and journals. The signs of the old medicine, from an old doctor. Her gaze returned to Shepard's deeply lined face. "How have they treated you?"

"Like everyone else. They let you think you're on the edge, just about to be struck from the provider list. They'd much rather deal with large group practices anyway," said Shepard.

"And Axis operates the same way?"

"Pretty much, though they're not as sophisticated with technology. I can still bend the ear off a case manager and get my way. It just takes so much time."

"So you really can't help my dad?"

"Jenny, I'll do anything I can, but we can't do anything without the authority and the blessing of Axis. They won't listen to me, and they'd drop me like a rock if I disobeyed them. It's either Majani or one of their case managers."

A sense of defeat swept through her. Although she worked in the field of medicine, she had been insulated from these harsh realities.

Progressive had never been like this. She was beginning to understand the full measure of avarice in GHB. She wanted to help Dr. Shepard.

"Tell you what," she began. "I'm not sure how much longer I'm going to be with GHB, but I'll be happy to check on your profile and make sure it's in good shape."

"Thanks. It has become a strange world, Jenny Barrett. Hey, I think I hear my computer calling," Shepard said in response to some squawking noises from the other room.

The sound of the modem seemed to wake Jenny up as well. "You know, I might be able to check on some things right from here. Maybe you can help. Most of the provider profiling I've done is in mental health. If you want to look over my shoulder, I can probably pull up your profile right now."

"Are you serious? I thought that was tightly guarded."

"We'll see. I've got a special GHB computer out in the truck. You got some time?"

"To see my standing with the biggest insurance company in town? You bet."

Jenny retrieved the laptop computer from the truck, tucked away in her valise. Dr. Shepard showed her where to plug into the computer—fax line and also the power supply. The screen came to life with the GHB logo. A few keystrokes launched the dial-up program and her customized log-on script. It was 9:30 A.M. Pacific time, so the Net had heavy traffic. Although the little computer had a 56K modem, the best speed it could attain at this time was 36K.

The GHB logo appeared again, followed by a few seconds of computer handshakes, password checks, and security confirmations. Finally MOM displayed, "Welcome, Jenny Barrett. Your access level is four."

"This is the master computer that I have to argue with?" asked Shepard.

"Yes, it's MOM."

"How maternal and protective. She just wants to take care of everyone, is that it?"

"I guess it's pretty transparent, but you'd be surprised how well the employees accept her, I mean, it." Jenny's face reddened at the slip.

"They even have you hoodwinked. Jenny."

"Okay, I'm logged on so I can access the provider profiles. Let me punch in your name and tax ID number." Dr. Shepard gave her the data and his name popped up on the screen. What followed were pages of credentials, verified insurance coverage, hospital privileges, specialties, and administrative coding. Next came pages of patient names sorted in descending order by date of last treatment. Because of the heavy Internet traffic, the names scrolled slowly, taking four minutes to reach the end. The transaction totals were next to names, with a summary at the bottom. It revealed billings for the year of $58,000 and payouts of $21,000. The other $37,000 was listed as pending or denied.

"You need to get a better billing program, doctor. Look at all those denials. Your name has a ding against it for poor documentation."

"Nothing wrong at my end. It's your company that keeps losing stuff. Doris spends two hours a day arguing with insurance companies."

"But all these cases are missing something." She highlighted a name on the list, Rachel Blatt, and retrieved her chart from MOM. The denial said that the procedure code was missing from the insurance form. "See?" said Jenny.

Dr. Shepard excused himself to get the original chart, and returned with it opened to the page containing the insurance form. The procedure codes were there. "This is a copy of the original I sent."

Jenny was perplexed. Maybe it was just an oversight. She asked MOM to retrieve the original billing form and was presented with an electronic copy of the one in the chart. The codes were there. "I don't know how they were missed. I'm looking right at them. Maybe this was the corrected one you sent in."

"Jenny, I haven't even responded yet. If Doris had sent in another, she'd have noted it."

"You said this happens often?"

"Jenny, they don't want to give up the money. They play these stupid games that drive everyone crazy so they get to keep the money. All the time. Who are we going to complain to?"

"Dr. Shepard, why don't we call the Provider Relations Department and check into this? Maybe I can remove some of these dings on your record."

A few minutes later she was talking with Jamal DeWitt about the problem. Jenny played Dr. Shepard's secretary.

". . .so, could you please check your records?"

"I'm sorry, Ms. Barrett, there are some missing procedure codes and we can't take them over the phone. You'll have to resubmit the form," said Jamal.

"However, I'm looking at the form right now," said Jenny in frustration. "I'm looking at the codes."

"Well, they may be on your form in the office, but they are not on the form here."

"But I'm looking at the form there."

"I beg your pardon," said a confused Jamal.

"Mr. Dewitt, are you looking at the form itself?"

"No, the computer reports the error."

"Can you retrieve the original form?"

"Not without a supervisor's authorization."

"Could you please get it, and the form?" Jenny persisted.

"One moment please."

Dr. Shepard leaned back in his chair. "Welcome to healthcare in the nineties. This is what we deal with every day."

"Ms. Barrett," said a new voice on the line. "This is Joanne Bell, a supervisor. I understand there is a problem with your billing."

"Could you please call up the original bill submitted by Dr. Shepard?"

"I'm not sure we can. This is highly irregular. We have to be careful with this sensitive information. It would be simpler if you just resubmit the form."

These people were not going to cooperate. Jenny had a sudden inspiration. Using her mouse, she split the laptop screen in two and logged onto her workstation at GHB. She ignored the prompts for e-mail and opened up her own provider management folder. "What workstation are you at right now, Ms. Bell?"

"I'm sorry?"

"What is the number of your workstation? It's right on the monitor," said Jenny.

"It's 3-210. Why?"

Jenny didn't answer. She routed the insurance form from her own GHB workstation through the e-mail system to 3-210. She even heard DeWitt's computer play the e-mail announcement tone over the phone. "Would you please check that e-mail, Ms. Bell?"

"What? E-mail? Jamal, could you check your e-mail?"

Mr. DeWitt and Ms. Bell stood in amazement as Dr. Shepard's completed form was displayed on the screen. "I think you'll find everything in order," said Jenny. "Please process this claim as quickly as possible, and I'd like you to check on the accuracy of all the other denied claims as well. Apparently there's a computer glitch, and it's wasting a lot of valuable physician time that could be spent helping people."

"Who is this?" shouted Bell.

"I'll check with you next week to be sure this is all straightened out and we're all acting in good faith," said Jenny as she hung up the phone. The modem connection to GHB was still on-line.

Chapter 25

"Jenny, want a full-time job close to your family?" asked Shepard.

"No thanks, but you can bet I'll check into this glitch when I get back."

"It's no glitch, Jenny. It's how things work."

"Let's look at some other dings against you. The bad ones are highlighted in red." She scrolled down to Ryan Parson and pulled up the "report of untoward outcome." It noted Mr. Parson had a severe reaction to an antibiotic, requiring three days hospitalization.

Dr. Shepard's face grimaced with rage. "What the hell is that all about? It was their fault on the Parson case. They admitted it. I warned them that he couldn't tolerate the medication and needed this more expensive stuff, but they only authorized a generic version and he reacted to it. They took full responsibility over the phone."

"Well, it's in your record. Brings your rating down a whole point."

"How am I supposed to know this is in my record?"

"I'm beginning to think you're not supposed to know. Do they give you any reports or access to your profile? It's almost like a secret credit report. It's part of the 'proprietary' information that gives them a competitive advantage."

"What?"

"Sorry, just citing their advertising material. So, when the monthly outcome statistics are generated, this one will be calculated as your fault."

"Wait a second. Who gets these outcome reports?"

"Employers, the state, other managed care companies. It's just aggregate data. Your name isn't in them. It just listed as provider error," said Jenny.

"But when a case goes wrong, who decides whether it's company error or provider error."

"Ah, the company. Yeah, I guess that pinning the blame on the providers might be pretty easy."

"Then they tell the employers they're getting rid of all those bad doctors. Who designed this system, Jenny? Where's the accountability?"

"You're right, doctor. This is a screwy system. I e-mailed myself a reminder to fix up your file when I get back. And I know the head programmer. I'll ask him about these glitches."

"Thanks."

"Want to see the good side of MOM? Her real diagnostic skills?"

"The computer diagnoses? You mean it checks to see if all the digits add up?"

"No, it actually looks at the data and comes up with a decision. Got any tricky cases?"

"Not that I'll trust to that thing. But, yeah, show me what it can do," Shepard said with skepticism.

Jenny logged onto the diagnostic module, and the Caduceus logo was displayed on the screen.

"Caduceus? Do they really plan to take over medicine?" asked Shepard with thick sarcasm.

For the next half hour Jenny took Shepard through the same series of tests and trials she had done earlier in the week. They manipulated symptoms, changed lab results, added obscure readings, and detailed contradictory syndromes. Even by Dr. Shepard's standards, MOM performed impressively, rank ordering diagnostic possibilities, methodically recommending further lab tests or exploratory procedures, and even recognizing patient comfort as an essential element in the treatment plan. When they plugged in an obviously terminal cancer syndrome, MOM recommended pain management, at home care, social service support, and bereavement services.

"Well that's very impressive, Jenny, but I just had a similar case and GHB wouldn't authorize those services."

"The system isn't fully implemented yet, but I hope you can see the good that could come of this. It's a very smart system."

"I don't trust it, Jenny. I'm sure it has all the state-of-the-art bells and whistles, but who's driving the bus? An insurance company. They aren't doctors. They're businessmen. You're showing me the decisions made on clinical criterion, but GHB has been sued by a bunch of states for fraudulent sales practices with life insurance and investment counseling. Why would this be any different? I bet MOM has a lot more nickel-and-dime criterion she filters clients through before she gets to the medicine part. I don't trust it."

Jenny realized that she didn't either. Sitting beside Dr. Shepard, she viewed the whole clinical process from the front lines, which was something she hadn't done in years. The system was clearly out of balance. Big industry was driving medicine. The Dr. Shepards of the world were being run over by tailored suits and technology.

"Case in point," challenged Dr. Shepard. "Check out Dr. Majani. GHB doesn't have your father's medical records, but they probably have a profile of Majani."

Jenny navigated to the provider profiles and pulled her father's doctor's profile. It was very short. Majani was part of the Hubb Health Group, a large medical practice of 26 physicians. He was licensed in the US just last year, educated in Mexico, originally from Pakistan. There was surprising little listed about his surgical experience. His outcome stats were not impressive. Jenny asked MOM to do a quick study on his success rate with gall bladder surgery. After a two minute wait MOM reported, "Insufficient data; only three known surgeries, two with risk complications. Rating, Global Provider Rating–Average. Surgical Rating–Poor."

"I guess he's learning on your father," said Shepard gravely.

"But Axis said he was highly qualified."

"Welcome to managed care, Jenny."

"That's terrible. My dad may be seriously ill." Jenny saved the data on Majani to the laptop's hard disk. "Who's the head of the Hubb Group?"

"Albert Hubb, a semi-retired cardiologist," said Shepard. "But he's just a figurehead. You'll need to speak with the practice administrator, Leon Jewett. He runs the show and oversees the managed care contracts."

"I'm afraid to ask," said Jenny. "Do they have a capitated contract with Axis Health?"

"Completely. They severely underbid every other suitor for the regional contract. I hear they're in some financial difficulty. Got hit pretty hard with inpatient admissions last year due to a minor flu epidemic. Lots of elderly got pneumonia. They don't recover quickly, so expenses went through the roof. They've been tightening care ever since. Even laid off a few staff. Now they have to get authorization for a Band-aid."

"Maybe I should check their profile with MOM?"

Jenny, still logged onto MOM, pulled up the data on Majani's employer. She paged through the demographics and location pages to the outcomes profile. There was a red alert attached to the file. The Hubb Health Group was listed as emergency only, close case monitoring, no capitation. GHB severed their contract in November and now considered them providers of last resort.

"They must owe GHB a lot of money if they've dropped them," said Shepard.

"Well, it's more likely due to their lousy outcome stats."

Dr. Shepard gave her a doubtful glance.

"I've got to get Dad to another doctor. These guys are terrible."

"Look, I'm still on the Axis Health provider list. If you can somehow convince them to allow a second opinion, I'd be happy to see Bill. Jenny, you supervise case managers. You know the tricks. Hit them where they live. "

Jenny logged off and closed the laptop with a snap. "You're right. Are you going to be available this afternoon?"

"I can be. For you, Jenny."

"Great. Talk with you soon."

"And Jenny, thanks for helping me out with GHB."

"Thank you for slapping some sense into me. This is only the beginning. I will not put up with this crap. A friend of mine, Mark, a reporter, tried to tell me how screwed up GHB was, but I was too wowed by the glitz. I may be dense, but I'm not stupid."

***

Crandall Bream marveled at the efficiency of Elliot Mears. Since the letter mailing mechanism was already in place, Elliot could obtain, process, merge, and mail 1.8 million additional letters to likely abortion victims within the week. Cash was flowing into their coffers at an astounding rate. The money was split equally between the foreign bank accounts, the three men, and the purchase of more mailing lists. The four top managed care companies were pleased to comply with their request for list, particularly when Elliot mentioned the plan to take the project east of the Mississippi within the month, buying up to four million more names.

Elliot did press Crandall on an issue that caused the spiritual leader some anguish. "You know, we now have our own valuable list in the database. Many groups would pay handsomely to obtain it. We're approaching a million names of women who will spend forty dollarsfor medical privacy. Soon, someone, maybe another Christian group, will make an offer to get this list. It's so specialized, it might garner $1.50 to $2.00 per name. What do you want to do?"

Crandall wrestled with his conscience for an hour. Finally, he said, "Elliot, I don't like it. I feel a commitment to these women who paid us. I want to honor their pledge since they've sought redemption. But can we sell the list of the women who didn't contribute?"

"No, that's illegal. We bought one-time-use lists. They could sue us," said Elliot.

"How would they know?"

"These lists are 'salted,' sprinkled with a few bogus names and addresses that serve to track where their lists are used. That way, if a letter to I.C. Poorly arrives back at a GHB drop box with a credit card promotion, they know we misused or resold the list."

"Does that mean GHB has received the solicitation letter?"

"Most likely."

"Well, for now, lock the contributors' names away. Don't purge them. Just keep them secure," said Crandall.

***

Four of the bogus "salted" names were collected by a GHB runner from the scattered mail drop boxes. They crossed the desk of Madeline Szorba, Manager of Media Products, who was responsible for monitoring mailing list usage. She also did volunteer work at a teen pregnancy home, trying to help the girls reconstruct their lives and make some tough decisions.

Madeline was almost blinded with rage at the letter. She summoned her staff into her office and shared the letter with them, to be sure she wasn't just over-personalizing the issue. The two women and two men were unanimously outraged. Madeline took the matter directly to her boss, Noreen Cane, Director of Communication Services. She, too, was appalled at the letter, but was equally concerned about any liability or bad publicity GHB might share.

Madeline pulled up the original list requests from Crandall's group. At first look, it hardly made sense, for neither list seemed related to abortion, but then Noreen put it together. She was familiar with computer market research programs. "A sniffer program put this together. See, they matched up pregnancy tests with uterine surgery dates."

"Is that legal?" a staff member asked.

"As far as I know. They paid for the lists and used them for the contracted purpose. We can't prevent them from massaging the data, but this has the smell of a pretty big media event. We don't need a lot of bad press about private medical records," said Madeline.

Noreen sent copies of the letters to Carter Newton, with a brief explanation of her findings. An hour later, Carter was smiling at the boldness of Crandall's plan. He admired the daring scheme, even as he considered his options for damage control of GHB's reputation. He also e-mailed Noreen to delay any further data requests from Crandall's group until he could gauge any negative consequences. "God, I hope Senator Gray doesn't get wind of this," he reflected. As a precaution, he sent a memo to the legal department to render an opinion on any possible actions against Crandall.

The story of Crandall's letter broke in the media on Monday. Crandall was inundated with requests for interviews and comments. He was ambushed by reporters at Jerry's house, but slipped away with the promise of a press conference the next day. The Seattle Examiner ran the headline, "Crandall Bream Behind Abortion Scheme." Sound bites of Crandall appeared on the local news breaks throughout the day. He stuck with comments about "exposing the murderers of children" and "helping the women find forgiveness," on the advice of Jerry.

At the press conference the next day, he "opened his heart to all the victims of profiteering abortionists" and claimed, "what little we have received in donations will be used to further God's law." He was mercilessly grilled on the amount of money he had gathered, which he refused to divulge. He was also asked when the list of "sinners" would be made public. He stared directly into the cameras, trying hard to produce a sympathetic, compassionate expression, and said, "When God tells me that no one else will seek redemption, then I will close the window of forgiveness and publish the list of the damned." He wanted the "window" to be open long enough so they could benefit from this media exposure. He imagined all the women who received letters were running scared, hopefully straight to their checkbooks.

Finally, a reporter asked the question Crandall feared. "Where did you get these lists?" Crandall played it shrewdly, not wanting to reveal his hand before their current orders for new lists had been filled. "The servants of God have used only legal and legitimate means to find these sinners. It does not matter how we know, for God knows all. It only matters that we do know."

Interviews with prosecutors and attorneys general in the three west coast states produced ambiguous answers. Until it was discovered that laws were broken, they could do little. The letter never openly accused the recipient of having an abortion, so there was no libel. Organizations are free to distribute their messages and solicit donations through the mail. The medical information was obtained legitimately. However, given Mr. Crandall's previous arrest for unlawfully obtaining medical records, the source of these women's names was a major concern of the police. Mr. Crandall refused to answer this question. The law was stymied.

***

Greg Hepman broke up his staff meeting and returned to his office. He had fifteen minutes until the next team rolled in. While swigging coffee, he instructed MOM to pull up Jenny's personnel records. GHB needed to be sure not only of her level of integrity, but of the nature of that integrity. Was she a team player? A loyal company employee? If she was to have access to sensitive parts of MOM's program, they had to be sure she could be trusted. He paged through her resumé, academic records, employment history, annual reviews, and awards. An impressive gal, he concluded. She had managed a few information technology projects herself at Progressive. He found that odd because she hadn't displayed a remarkably high level of technical knowledge around him. Still, MOM had given her high technical ratings in her initial profile.

Paging through other documents MOM had collected, Hepman reviewed financial and credit reports, Jenny's health history, and even federal and state police reports, which contained only a few traffic tickets, no arrests, and no civil suits. Jenny came up clean. She paid her bills, did well in school, worked hard. Nothing appeared out of order, yet something kept nagging at Hepman.

The conclusion of the report noted Jenny's strong sense of morality, which seemed more dedicated to people than to institutions. This led to an unusual combination of technical proficiency and strong human interest. "Not unusual for a psychologist, except for the technical side," he thought. "Elaina was like that." Then it struck him. Of course, if his job was to see if Jenny could fit in Elaina's job, he might as well have MOM compare them. He pulled up the dead woman's profile for a side by side comparison with Jenny's. Similar ages, middle class background, both raised in rural settings.

He instructed MOM to plot the similarities of the women. In about five seconds MOM displayed a list of matched qualities. Highlighted in shaded blue was a juncture point of the two lives.

Hepman froze, eyes wide, mouth agape. They both attended the UCLA School of Psychology from 1991-1995. They were classmates! Did Jenny know Elaina? She must have, yet she had never mentioned it in any conversation with himself or with Carter. Could she not know Elaina worked at GHB? Was Elaina's full name never mentioned? Hepman couldn't remember.

The highlighted link on the screen seemed to glow brighter as Hepman grew more concerned. A glance at the other intersects on their respective transcripts revealed eight classes they had taken together. Hepman was flooded with feelings of anxiety, doubt, betrayal, and confusion. He wasn't good at managing intense visceral reactions. "Shit!" he said out loud. How could fate do this to him? He pulled up an image of Elaina. For a moment he was swept with sadness as he looked at her face, so full of life. Although she had betrayed him, he was shattered by her death. What a tragedy. Some outrageous mistake. And now it was repeating.

Shaking himself out of this trance of fear, he picked up the phone and called Carter.

"Mr. Newton's office," said his secretary.

"Amanda, this is Greg Hepman. I must talk to Carter immediately."

"He's on a conference call, Mr. Hepman."

"What's his schedule look like?"

"He's meeting with Rich Mehlman from claims and recovery in fifteen minutes."

"Cancel it. I'll take the meeting."

"Greg, I'm not sure I can do that."

"I'll take the heat. This can't wait and Carter will agree. I'll take responsibility."

"Okay, I'll let him know."

Twenty minutes later, Carter was up to speed on Hepman's discovery. "Christ, how did this happen?" Carter asked. "Okay, okay. She's only been here for a week. Maybe we've never really mentioned Elaina's name, so she didn't know. They've both been out of school for three years. How do we know if they even stayed in touch? Let's not overreact."

Sitting at Carter's console, Hepman pulled the profiles of the two women onto the screen. MOM discovered another juncture, a conference on Mental Health and Information Technology both women had attended just last year. Carter settled into his chair and asked, "So what can she really get? I doubt anything important, she's hardly been on the system. She doesn't yet know her way around."

"They have MOM at Progressive. She was a project leader," said Hepman.

"Well, she's in Oregon now. Did you check that there really is a sick father?"

Hepman searched Jenny's personnel file for her father's name, under "living relatives". He then pulled up the Barrett's address in Grants Pass. He logged onto the Langston Hospital computer in Medford, a GHB contracting facility. To pull the records on William Barrett, he used the permission code of an emergency admission. In 90 seconds, sitting at a terminal in Woodland Hills, California, Hepman confirmed that a man he didn't know, and with whom GHB had no relationship, had surgery two days ago in a hospital almost a thousand miles away.

"Looks legit," he assured Carter.

"Okay, we really don't need to panic. We have no reason to believe she's anything other than she appears. Harrington gave her high marks. We'll wait until she returns, then check her out closely. Greg, did you install the rat on her computer?"

"Yes."

"Great. We'll use it to get some answers. Until then, I don't think there's anything to worry about."

"Ah, there is one thing. We gave her a laptop to keep in touch and continue her work. It has a very high level security access code. She can get past the protective firewall and into MOM on a phone line."

"Pull the plug. Delete her access. Tell her we're having technical troubles. Even on the remote chance she's a spy for another company, I don't want anyone getting access to the Caduceus code. Got it?" Hepman had touched a sensitive button in Carter. A multibillion-dollar button. A future-of-the-company button.

The keyboard clattered with Hepman's machine gun keystrokes. "Done, sir."

***

Jenny hastily left the Shepard Clinic, walked to the pickup truck out front and left for home. She planned her strategy on the way. Maybe Dad would be feeling better when she got there. "Stop it!" she scolded herself. "Don't wimp out. This is bullshit medicine."

Dust flew up in the dry, warm air as the pickup roared to a stop in front of her house. She grabbed the laptop and started out of the vehicle, but saw it was surrounded by a whirlwind of dust. The powdery dirt particles could spell death to the computer, so she protectively hugged the machine and stayed in the cab until the air cleared. She used the time to compose herself. Panic was dangerous.

She spied her mother at the screen door, toweling her hands dry. Francis opened the door and asked, "Did you get to see Dr. Shepard?"

"Yeah, Mom. We had a good talk, a real eye opener. He'd be happy to see Dad, but we've got to get the insurance company to okay it. I think I know how. Is Dad any better?"

"He's asleep, hon, or knocked out on those pain meds. He hasn't been this sick since, well, I don't think ever. Jen, it's scaring me," said Francis Barrett. She turned to hide her tears. "You just hear about people our age getting sick and suddenly, boom, they're gone. I don't want to lose him."

Jenny came up from behind and held her mother tightly. Jenny's rebelliousness in her teenage years had estranged them, and when she went off to college the distance grew cavernous. Her character was more like that of her father, and she always seemed more willing to accept his counsel than mom's, but as Jenny settled into adult womanhood, she began to realize the gifts her mother had to offer. Their conversations had grown longer and deeper. Her mother could share more easily in Jenny's career challenges and began to treat her like an adult. The surest sign of that was right now, when Jenny comforted her mother in the face of this unthinkable loss. Two women, supporting each other. They had found a new friendship.

In the family room Jenny found her father asleep on the couch. His breathing was labored and his arms were drawn protectively across his distended midriff. Sweat beaded on his forehead and matted his hair. Jenny touched his skin and felt a fever. The man, always a light sleeper, didn't stir from her contact, probably because of the sedative pain medicine. His robe hung open, revealing a sweat-soaked tee shirt and boxers, and an alarming discoloration to his abdomen. Jenny recalled the frustrating conversation with Axis Health the previous night. This time she'd be armed.

"Mom, where's the thermometer?"

"I left it on the bathroom sink."

Jenny retrieved it and gently woke up her father. His skin was clammy and consciousness brought him immediate pain.

"Jenny! What's going on," he said in a moment of disorientation. He tried to raise himself, but his stomach provided a mammoth spasm of pain that sent a shudder through his entire body. "Christ," he screamed, trying to restrain his outburst.

"Dad, I don't like this at all. I think you have the wrong doctor. I'm going to get authorization for Dr. Shepard to see you."

"That's the only one I'll see. But how are you going to do it?" asked Bill.

"Do you still have David's computer set up in his room?"

"Yeah. We use it for e-mail," Francis answered.

"Good." Jenny read the thermometer. 102°F. "Dad, your fever is not going down. We need to get you to a hospital."

"Jenny, I won't let them treat me like a side of beef. They're going to cut and stick me just so they can make their payment. I'm better off without them." He painfully rolled over in protest, his back to Jenny.

Jenny touched his shoulder and said, "Dad, I'm gonna get you back to Shepard. Is that okay?"

Bill Barrett growled, "If you can do it, he's the only one I'll see."

Chapter 26

Jenny grabbed the laptop and marched into David's bedroom, plopping the laptop next to his computer. She pulled out the AC power supply, unplugged the phone line from the back of his computer and plugged it into the laptop. She fired the machine up and within a few minutes had again logged onto MOM at GHB.

"Invalid log-on. User name not valid. Please try again," was the message on the screen.

She clicked the log-on script again, thinking it must have just encountered a glitch over the long telephone connection to Los Angeles.

"Invalid log-on. User name not valid. Terminating connection."

"Damn," she said out loud. "What's wrong?" Maybe the script was corrupted. She decided to log on manually. Jenny opened up the script file to obtain the log-on information and then re-dialed MOM. The machine wouldn't accept her name, even though it had done so not an hour earlier. Jenny needed to get into the system to use MOM. Her plan was to use the advanced diagnostic skills of the expert computer system to document her father's need for more aggressive treatment. If Axis and Majani wouldn't listen to her, they would damn well listen to the preeminent diagnostic computer.

Jenny picked up the phone and dialed GHB. She requested Greg Hepman's number from the operator, but was told he was unavailable. She then asked to speak with Mable Jackson.

"Yes Jenny," said the familiar voice.

"Mable, I can't seem to log on from up here. Is there something wrong with the computer?"

"Not that I know of, honey. What do you need?"

"My father's really ill. He was treated by a quack surgeon who was dropped by GHB. I need to get some data so I can wake these people up," explained Jenny.

"Have you called Hitman?"

"He's busy. I've got a message into him."

"How about support services. Maybe they can get you on?"

"Good idea. Mable, I hate to ask this, but if you find Hepman could you have him call me at this number?"

"Sure, honey. I know what it's like when it's about family. If they can't help you, get back to me. I don't have your high level access to MOM, but maybe I can help. Let me transfer you to support services."

She heard a few clicks, then a male voice answered, "Support Services."

"Hi. This is Jenny Barrett, a new employee. I'm up here in Oregon with one of your laptops. I can't seem to log on to MOM, even though I did just an hour ago. Could you help me?"

"Sure. Jenny Barrett. Let me check your access." The man muted the microphone while he queried the computer. Jenny sat on the silent phone for about two minutes, then he returned, with a more cautious tone of voice.

"Ah, miss. I'm going to transfer you to Mr. Hepman. He'll help you."

"Thanks. Hello, Greg. This is Jenny."

"Jenny, how's your father?" asked Hepman.

"Not well. We're worried. I was trying to log on to MOM and the system shut me out. What going on?"

"Well, I'm not sure. Shouldn't have done that. Let me check." She heard keyboard clicks, then some discussion in the hallway. "Jenny, the network guys say everything is okay here. Must be a mess up in your computer."

"Can we fix it, Greg?"

"Not over the phone. Not at your level of access. We'll have to wait till you get back in town." There was something stilted and affected about the way Hepman was speaking to her.

"Greg, isn't there any way to fix this while I'm up here? I hate to be out of touch."

"Sorry. However, we'll be meeting with Carter when you get back and everything will be straightened out."

What did Carter have to do with this, Jenny wondered. It seemed Hepman had let something slip. Carter had something to do with her access. This wasn't a technical glitch. She'd been locked out. Why? Had they discovered her association with Elaina? Not now. She desperately needed that computer access, but Hepman wasn't going to help.

"Okay, Greg. Sorry I can't do any work while I'm up here. I'll try to get back there as soon as possible."

"Yeah, I'm sorry too. Look, I'll be meeting with Carter today at one. Want me to bring anything up?"

"What meeting is this?"

"Just a planning meeting with the Caduceus team."

"No. I don't have anything to say right now, but ask Carter if there's anything I should be working on. Can I give you a call later to check in?"

"Sure. I'll be done around 2:00," said Hepman.

"Thanks," she said absently as she hung up.

An idea had intruded into her thoughts. Hepman would be in a team meeting from one until two. That means he wouldn't be logged onto MOM. She had his script saved on the laptop, so maybe she could still access MOM. It would be a risk, but it sounded like things might not be too good for her anyway down there. Yeah, she could try to get on briefly while that meeting was going on. Get what she needed and be off before anyone knew. It was just noon.

The house was quiet. Her father remained asleep on the couch. Her mother had taken some desperately needed time away from home to run errands. It was a good time to check for messages. Daisy would have automatically scanned for midday e-mails by now, so she decided to check in. This would also verify that the laptop was really functioning correctly. The link to Daisy was quick and flawless. Hepman was bullshitting her.

The fast modem made communication a pleasure. Daisy played a funny voice mail from Mark, with exotic plans for her return. A few friends had called in sympathetic concerns for her father. Dwick had left two e-mails and a voice message.

"Jenny, contact me ASAP. I have your information, and you're a prize winner."

An odd message. She checked the e-mail, which was essentially the same, except it further requested that she log on from a secure workstation over a direct Internet link, not through GHB. It was becoming easier to sympathize with his paranoia. Jenny launched the terminal program on the laptop, but thought better of it. Who knew if this machine was keeping a log of all of her activities? It could easily capture her conversations, her log-on IDs and passwords, even record a conversation. For security, she unplugged the phone cord and inserted it back into David's old machine, then fired it up. Within a minute she was at Dwick's web site. She e-mailed him to announce her presence, and soon he was on-line. David's computer had a more primitive voice modem, but it was functional enough for their purposes.

"Jenny, have I got some news for you. Are you sure you're on a secure line?"

"Yes, Dwick. I'm at my parents in Oregon, using my brother's old computer. What's up?"

"Two things. First, about Carter Newton. Bad guy. Really bad. Got busted in Massachusetts in a big life insurance scam. Before that he was an administrator for a small doctor owned clinic. Got caught with his hand in the Medicare till. Cut a deal with the prosecutors and sent away the doctors. Not a pretty scene."

"Why would GHB want him?"

"Cause he gets the job done. Upper management keeps bailing him out. He's got major balls to go after big deals."

"And the other thing, Dwick?"

"Ah, I've got a slight confession to make. I took the liberty of copying Elaina's computer disk the other night while we talked."

"You what? How could you do that? We were working together the whole time. The system was tied up looking for clues. How could you download over a billion bytes without me knowing?"

"Thank your T1 line, Jenny. It's like the Alaskan pipeline of data. Anyway, you wanted me to check it out, so I did. And guess what? I found Waldo, and his pockets were full of this giant program called Caduceus. It's a killer. Literally. It has all these formulas for computing healthcare, except it mostly finds ways to avoid paying anyone anything."

"Yes, I saw some of the code. Looks like it's written in C++ language or something."

"Right you are girl. I ran it through a nifty little program that graphically charts the whole thing. What the program does, how it does it, what it considers. I produced this flow chart that is awesome and scary as hell. Jenny, this is the evil empire."

"So what do you want to do?"

"Well, the bad news is this is just the beta test copy, version 0.97 or something. I think this is what they showed the government. It's mostly the medical computation part, but I can see references to the subroutine that comes before this. Some big sections of it are missing. Like how you have to stand on your head, wiggle your ears, and whistle 'Dixie' before the computer will even consider authorizing treatment. Also, there's references to all sorts of bad stuff. It's just not here, but we know where it is, Jenny. These are real bad guys, I just know it. They're hurting people. Badly. I know no one else has seen this code. We need to blow the whistle on these guys."

"How? Can't you just show someone that code?"

"This is too old and incomplete. We need to get the updated source code."

"How do we do that?"Jenny asked, starting to tremble with both fear and anticipation.

"Send Waldo back in. I know where this stuff is now. There are all sorts of addresses listed. There's some guy named Hepman who seems to have the bulk of the code. I want Waldo to pay his computer a little visit."

"Are you going to copy the code from MOM?"

"No, that wouldn't work. That object code is already compiled into machine language. Just about impossible to reverse it. We need the source code, before it's compiled, what the programmers actually write. It's sitting on this Hepman's computer. In fact I have one of his passwords, which I found on our disk. I'm sure it's no good now. People at that level change passwords at least monthly."

"They change weekly," corrected Jenny.

"Well, I have a program that may be able to predict what some future passwords would be. It's tough with only one password. If we can get another, it makes it a thousand times easier to project the pattern someone uses for their passwords. What we got is still better than nothing."

Jenny hesitated in telling Dwick about what was sitting on her laptop Hepman's current password. She was being pushed into overt sabotage and subterfuge, which was not in her nature, but she could also feel her rising hatred of this company and the "new medicine."

"I don't know, Dwick. This is some serious stuff. It's not what I do."

"Jenny, there's one other thing you need to know. The stuff on Elaina's computer. A guy like this Carter Newton would consider it a life-and-death issue for his company. What the hell was a threatening voice mail doing on Elaina's computer? I didn't hardly know the woman, but if she was your friend I gotta think she was a straight shooter. Jenny, these kinds of trade secrets are worth millions of dollars on the open market. Maybe more. What I'm saying is, Elaina could have been killed for this."

Dwick had finally pierced through Jenny's denial. It all painfully made sense to her. Like a lightning bolt emerging from dark thunderheads, the landscape suddenly seemed clear. All of this was frighteningly possible. A dark evil sat within the core of this company: the way clients were treated, the usurping of power over doctors, the commitment to technology over humanity. She knew Elaina would have been shocked by these actions. Maybe she tried to do something and was stopped.

"Dwick, Are you sure?"

"Jenny, we need to get back in there. I know you think I'm a wacko. Hey, I wear the mantle proudly, but we've got to stop this shit.

"Look, I think I can get you in again one more time. They gave me a computer to keep in touch. It had a high-level access, but they just pulled the plug on me this morning for some reason. Maybe they found out I knew Elaina. Anyway, when the guy, Hepman, was setting this thing up, I kind of copied his log-on script."

"You copied his script? Jenny, I'm proud of you. I'll recommend you to the hacker hall of fame. You've got a second password from Hepman?"

"And access through the firewall, I think, but my guess is I can only use it once. All hell will break loose if they catch me."

"Just say when, Jenny,"

"Today, just after one, Pacific time."

"What? Why so soon?"

"When they pulled the plug on me I called Hepman to see if he'd fix it. He gave me some bullshit answer, but did mention that he'd be in a meeting from 1:00 until 2:00 today, which means he won't be on-line. If I tried to log on while he was on-line MOM would, of course, blow the whistle immediately. However, if he's tied up in a meeting, we can probably sneak in. I need to get access to MOM's medical database to help my father. I'm going to take my shot just after 1:00. Do you think you can piggy back on my login like you did the other day?"

"You got it, babe. Hey, we can even route the call through one of my bogus web addresses. They won't have a clue who it was. I'll have to hustle up with Waldo, figure out the routing to Hepman's machine and back out. Can you give me his log-on information now? That would help."

Jenny pulled up the script from the laptop and read the information to Dwick.

"Okay. You log on to my web site after 1:00. Click on the 'support' button and then head for the 'GHB button,' which I just added. I'll piggyback there and we can invade the palace together. I'll drop the Waldo agent off and he'll make his way to Hepman's computer. It may take awhile before he resurfaces."

"Tell me again what Waldo actually does?" asked Jenny.

"Okay. Waldo is like a computer virus, except he doesn't destroy data or wreck machines. Instead, he slips inside a big machine and collects information. He jumps from one computer to another, cruising the network, looking for information. When he finds it, he copies it, compresses the data, and sticks it in his pockets. He sneaks all around the system, blending in with the other computer code so he can't be seen by the main program. Eventually, he completes his assignment and finds a way out to the Internet. Then he comes home. Got it?"

"Yeah. Pretty amazing little guy. See you at 1:00," said Jenny as she signed off. It took two attempts to correctly type the log-off, her hands were trembling so much. This scheme was far beyond anything she had ever done before. It ran against her ethical nature, and she knew it was illegal. But then, GHB was hurting millions of people. The greater good for the greater numbers. Didn't Lincoln say something about that?

The pounding in her ears was deafening as her blood pressure spiked from anxiety. She felt she was on the brink of disaster, as if compelled to jump out of an airplane with an unreliable parachute. Even as the resolve to push ahead solidified in her gut, her mind raced with doubt, ambivalence, and confusion. Jenny needed to regain control, for it would require the greatest stealth to invade MOM without leaving an obvious trail. A picture of Indiana Jones picking his way through the booby traps of a sacred cave came to mind.

Jenny focused her thinking on her tasks. The laptop would have to be used, but it might log the whole invasion in a file which Hepman could retrieve. She could destroy the hard drive after the invasion. Hepman had already documented the failure of the machine. She could drop it off the roof. No, too obvious and not even a sure way to destroy data.

She could do a wipe out and restore. Yes. She'd back-up the system now, before the invasion, then do the deal. After the invasion, she'd copy the important data to David's machine, completely erase and reformat the laptop hard disk, then restore it from the backup as it had been before the invasion. All evidence would be erased. Yes, it would work. She linked the laptop to David's computer, plugged in a tape, and launched the backup program.

William Barrett stirred loudly in the living room. Jenny went to check on his progress and found him essentially unchanged. His stomach was still impossibly swollen, his breathing labored, and sweat drenched his clothing. Dr. Majani had not called back to check on his patient. Jenny went to the bathroom to retrieve a towel soaked in cold water. She gently swabbed the sweat from her father's face and neck. His eyes fluttered open, and he looked dazed and lost for a second.

"Oh, hi Jenny," he said with a weak slur. "Where's Mom?"

"She ran to town on some errands. Should be back in awhile. How are you feeling?"

"Terrible. Sweaty, hot, nauseous. My back is killing me. I need to go to the bathroom." He tried to get up, but winced in great pain. "Guess I'll need some help," he said sheepishly.

Jenny braced her leg against the couch, wrapped her arms around his shoulder, and rolled him to his feet. He wobbled for a moment, then took an uncertain step. Together they maneuvered the hallway to the bathroom and onto the commode.

"I'll step outside, Dad, but don't get yourself in trouble. If you feel faint or you can't do something, let me know. This is no time for modesty."

"I'll be okay."

Fortunately, the family had always been comfortable with nudity, giving acceptance to bodies of any size or type. This not only gave the children a comfort with their own bodies, it diminished the embarrassment with other bodies as well. David and Jenny were using the Internet long before it was widely popular, and they had the inevitable adventures of downloading pornographic images. Fortunately, the Barrett family values helped the children view the airbrushed flesh and raunchy activities as minimally entertaining aberrations, unrelated to their own lives. They knew what good sex and good love was, and that it wasn't depicted in these pictures from the wild and wooly web.

At his signal, Jenny entered the bathroom and helped her father back to the couch. He seemed drained of energy by the little excursion, and he asked for help being propped up to watch a movie. He uncapped a medicine bottle and took two pain pills. Jenny plugged in his requested videotape, and offered to make him a cheese sandwich. By the time she returned with the meal, he was fast asleep. She noticed a discoloration on his abdomen, a light maroon stain under the skin, about six inches around. She was tempted to call the doctor again, but knew they would likely give her the runaround again. In a little while she'd have what she needed to beat these fools into action.

It was a quarter to one, fifteen minutes until she launched the most desperate and foolhardy plan of her life. Was she just being suckered by Dwick to let him attack the establishment? Was it even remotely possible that Elaina was somehow killed by this corporate giant? Was her career about to go up in smoke?

No, she decided. She had seen enough to know in her heart that this was true. It was not the place for her to work. It was evil. Not just greedy. Not just ruthless. It was evil. The sinister voice message from Carter found on Elaina's computer was unmistakable as a threat, and Elaina then disappears into a hospital and dies the next day. What if they do the same to her? Dwick was right. They were gambling on millions of dollars. What did Mark say the average cost of a hitman was in Los Angeles? Fifteen hundred dollars. Pretty cheap solution.

At 1:05 P.M. the backup was complete and Jenny reconnected the laptop to the telephone line. A calm had come over her. Helping her father had strengthened her resolve. She looked at a picture of her and David on the wall, peering into an open computer box when she was 16. David had taught her well. She wished he was here now, but she felt confident in her task.

Jenny clicked her way to the web site destination, and there on her screen stood a cartoon character, a long, thin man wearing a orange striped shirt, a green and white sock hat, blue pants, and oversized glasses. Waldo was waving to her. Dwick greeted Jenny as she arrived at his web site. "Waldo is all set to go."

"I can see that," she laughed. "Is this really a state-of-the-art program waving at me?"

"This is the most advanced intelligent agent software around. Your Hepman will have to be pretty good to find him."

"Let me assure you, he's pretty damn good. But not as cute as Waldo."

"I'm better. And cuter. I've got some surprises coded in this little guy.

"Once we get past the protective firewall, how long will it take you to plant Waldo?"

"About two nanoseconds. That's if I stop for lunch. You won't even notice me, Jen."

"Will you be recording the whole process?" asked Jenny.

"Of course. Can't lie to you, but I doubt I'll find anything valuable. Are you okay with me seeing what your doing?"

"Sure. You'll be impressed with the part of MOM I'll be using. It's really kind of sad. The machine could be used for so much good. Too bad the bean counters are driving."

"Let's go, Ms. Jenny."

"Yeah, let's do it. If Hepman is still on-line, he'll get an alert from MOM. Maybe he'll think it was just an errant log-on. But if it happens a second time, we're dead."

Chapter 27

Inside the McCracken Pharmacy in Boise, Idaho, Henry Abrams, a slow-witted box boy pushed his broom over to Betsy Waller. He had a long, thin face that was ridiculously accented with a small goatee, framed by slick-back black hair, and arms that seemed to hang to his knees.

Betsy, in stark contrast, was quite round, fully 220 pounds at 5' 4", with a face like a frying pan and a girth that gave her difficulty fitting into movie theater seats. She peeked at the world through brown eyes buried in puffy slits of swollen pink flesh framed by mousy brown hair. She was dressed in her typical long-sleeve, checkered frock, with white frills on the sleeves and hem. Stubby, edematous fingers, stained brown from her chain smoking, resembled the German sausages she voraciously consumed.

"I thought you was pregnant, Betsy. You shouldn't be smoking," said Henry.

"It don't matter," she said dismissively. "This here is a special baby. Nothing can hurt it, 'cept the fires of Hell. Fires of Hell. Fire in the hole. Fire in the hole. Fiery whore, I'm a fiery whore," she mumbled on.

"Oh yeah," interrupted Henry. With a devilish grin he said, "I forgot. How long you been pregnant now?"

"Going on 48 months," Betsy answered, rocking back and forth. "48 months. Four to eight mumps."

Betsy was quite mad. Or more precisely, schizophrenic. She lived at a mental health board and care facility two blocks from the pharmacy. At 26 years old, her fate had seemingly been sealed by an almost indelible diagnosis. She survived on social security disability, for her parents had abandoned her when she was nine years old.

Her illness had not been noticeable back then, and in fact may not have even existed then. Years of neglect and abuse from the two cruel and embattled parents took its toll on her ego, which slowly dissolved in repeated cycles of physical, mental, and sexual abuse. Thankfully, Betsy's birth had severely compromised her mother's fertility, so she had no siblings. The mother felt cheated and took out her resentment on the youngster daily. Child protective services workers were frequent visitors to the home, but nothing was done until the parents disappeared one day when Betsy was nine. She finished her childhood living with four different foster families.

Henry swept his way to Betsy's side and brushed his hand against her fleshy buttock, which gained her attention. "Want me to get you some more cigarettes? I can if you let me do it to you." Betsy had bartered for many things in her meager life this way.

As an adolescent, she had been thin and wiry, naturally shy, and her face was usually healing from self-inflicted gouges and sores. No one befriended her, and she only received attention as the butt of jokes or as a sexual outlet for cruel boys. She eventually joined a teenage underground group that fancied itself a satanic cult, although mostly they worshiped marijuana, beer, and strange ritual dancing that often led to sex. Yet even this exotic crowd became uncomfortable with Betsy's increasingly bizarre ramblings.

Betsy truly believed in the satanic rituals. She embraced them with all of her chaotic might, believing that only the wicked could love her. Most of the original group members outgrew this rebellious stage, but Betsy sank deeper into its mystery. New, younger teens would join as the older ones left.

Eventually, a runaway psychopathic boy named Vinny joined the group and dominated the confused souls. As distorted as Betsy's values were, she still cared about others. Vinny cared about nothing. During one evening's ritual he disemboweled a cat and set it aflame. It was more than anyone in the group could take. At 19 years old, Betsy went over the edge and was hospitalized for an acute schizophrenic breakdown. She never fully recovered and lived in eternal fear of the boy's return. She thought he was Satan's child.

After a year of hospitalization with massive dosages of anti-psychotic medication, Betsy stabilized sufficiently to be released into the community. Spring Manor Board & Care provided a supervised living center with eight other disturbed patients. Her psychiatric care consisted mainly of pumping anti-psychotic medicine into her twice a day. She had done well for four years on a new but expensive medication, risperidone.

Great Health Benefit acquired Betsy as part of a Medicaid contract two years ago. MOM immediately re-computed the cost benefit of the expensive medication, but even for a computer, it was a "no brainer." A month's supply of risperidone cost $150. An older anti-psychotic drug, chlorpromazine, was available as a generic for thirty dollars per month, even though it was less effective with Betsy and had more side effects. MOM had never had a hallucination or been tormented by demons. Her programming couldn't weigh the importance of these symptoms, so twenty-four months ago, GHB switched Betsy and 6,000 other patients to the older and cheaper medication. Betsy's voices and inner turmoil returned. Her demons were slowly winning.

The residents of Boise suddenly saw a dramatic increase in the number of psychotic people on their streets, while the local news covered ever more bizarre events. Civic leaders speculated about where all these crazy people had suddenly come from, not realizing they had merely crawled out of the urban woodwork because of mental health cost cutting. MOM had little sense of Boise's community. The machine was programmed by people in Los Angeles, where "community" had little meaning.

Henry eyed Betsy's chest, but without a bra, her breasts were indistinguishable from the rest of her body. The side effects of the current medication and her inactive lifestyle had caused her to balloon to enormous size. An odd consequence of this was the rounding of her face, which made her appear almost angelic, with reddened cheeks and dimples. She was significantly better than Henry was used to getting in the last year.

"I'll give you five packs of cigarettes if you let me do ya," he whispered to her. "That's what Randy said he paid."

"Randy didn't ever do nothing with me. He's a lying lingwey," said Betsy, not even looking at Henry. "Don't nobody get inside my cuddly coo. I've got the special one in me."

"Oh please," he pleaded. "How about a little blowing? That won't hurt nothing."

Betsy was getting upset at Henry's persistence. This caused her to erupt in audible squeals and grunts, a sign that the demons were escaping. The curious noises frightened Henry, and he backed away. She lit another cigarette, even while still holding a burning one in her hand. She tossed the shorter one at Henry's broom. "You get going now," she shouted. "Zachariah come down in your canly come," she said as a nonsense alliteration that had great meaning to her. Henry was bright enough to know Betsy was headed for an explosion, so he quickly exited to the storeroom to take care of his disappointed desire in the rest room.

Betsy left the pharmacy and waddled down the street, with the glow of a soon-to-be proud mama. Four years ago she'd had an abortion, but she truly believed it hadn't worked and she remained pregnant for 48 months. Why else would she be so fat now? She was really a thin person. She used to put a filled hot water bottle under her dress just to look more pregnant, so people would stop teasing her, but then she got fat and didn't need it.

Ever since that "rambling preacher man" had come passing through the board and care, she knew she was pregnant. And not with just any old baby. No, this one was special. This was Satan's baby.

A battle had been waging in Betsy's aching head ever since she came to realize the significance of the package she carried. "Kill the Beast," the voices in her soul would say. It was in her hands to save the planet from Satan's return, but she knew that was pointless. The doctors kept telling her she wasn't pregnant, but she realized that was because Satan was so good at hiding things, even making her bleed sometimes, just like a period. She wanted to kill the child herself, but figured Satan would just get someone else pregnant. "Canly Come," she said in frustration.

Betsy creaked up the porch stairs of the Spring Manor Board & Care, maneuvered through the front screen door, and finally plopped herself on a worn, velvet couch in the community room. It was a sizable living room for the 90-year-old Victorian home, but now it served as a social-recreational center for the residents. A conversation occurred around her about whether Angela Moss, a 22-year-old schizophrenic, should get a pet. Adam Branskowski, a 38-year-old neurologically impaired PCP burnout was trying to help. Max Barenstein, a 66-year-old mid-stage Alzheimer victim, was coming in and out of the conversation.

"I always had pets," said Angela. "Maybe I can get a bird or a fish."

"A bird would be too noisy. Get a fish," growled Max, and immediately his mind left the room.

"A fish would be good," said Adam. "A bright angel fish."

"What do I need to keep fish?" asked Angela.

"A tank. If you get a few fish, you must get a filter for the fish."

"Gefilte fish?" asked Max, whose mind had just returned. "You can't have a gefilte fish for a pet. You eat gefilte fish." The conversation degenerated from there.

Betsy spied an envelope in her mailbox slot, which was a surprise since she hadn't received mail in ten months. The staff was happy for her too, for only government agencies ever wrote to Betsy. The religious logo on the letter brought them hope. Betsy took the letter to her room and shut the door. It was a short letter, but her mind was so unfocused and crowded with voices it was hard to remember the beginning of a paragraph by the time she reached its end. She studied the letter for almost an hour. Dates and places meant little to her. She saw that it was about money, forty dollars. It was also about abortions or birthing. The letter talked of redemption and lists of the damned.

Then she got it. It was as if the heavens had opened and the light of God illuminated the answer. Betsy Waller believed that Crandall Bream's letter was from the father of her child. He wanted her to come to Seattle so he could be there for the birth of his son. This was proof that she was the chosen one, and she could save the world after all. She'd go to Crandall-Satan-Bream and deliver his child. Back to the fires of Hell.

***

Jenny directed the powerful little computer to contact GHB using Hepman's log-on script, yet the system seemed to stall, flashing a spinning hourglass icon on the screen. The grains of digital sand ticked off the seconds of blocked access as the icon spun in rhythm to her rising fear. Her eyes were transfixed on the rotating symbol, as if it was drilling into her mind. What's wrong? Hepman must be on-line, she thought. Panic grew to nausea in her stomach. MOM must be freaking out by the log-on. She's getting ready to shut us down. Jenny's breathing stopped, while black fears shot deep roots into her soul. She felt she was losing control.

"Network congestion encountered," reported the terminal program. Dwick's laughter erupted over the computer speakers. "Whew, that had me going for a minute," he said. "I forgot about the lunch crowd."

Of course, she thought. People everywhere in the Pacific time zone were checking their e-mail messages after lunch. The sagging infrastructure of the Internet was clogged from the massive access. Suddenly she saw the GHB logo, and the machine launched the log-on script. Within seconds she and Dwick were past the firewall and inside MOM.

"Done," said Dwick an instant later.

"Great." Jenny then steered a direct path to the sample cases under Caduceus, MOM's expert system. She pulled up a 66-year-old male case example, configured his physical description to match her father, and gave him a lap chole gall bladder surgery. MOM displayed the profile of normal recovery. It was nothing like her father's current condition.

"Your dad had gall bladder surgery?" asked Dwick.

"Yeah, Monday. He's not doing well. I pulled up a normal case. Now I'm going to enter Dad's current symptoms and see what MOM says is going on."

After displaying the symptom form, Jenny filled in her observations and the few measures she knew: persistent 102°F fever, a distended abdomen, nausea, weakness. MOM, now knowing the area of concern, displayed a more precise symptom checklist. It asked about back pain, which Jenny had assumed was simply his age-old problem; then it asked about skin condition, lab values she didn't have, and any noticeable subcutaneous discoloration, which she confirmed. MOM then asked for the surgeon's name to check outcome statistics, displaying an alphabetical list of all credentialed surgeons at Langston Hospital. She scrolled to Majani and highlighted his name.

Finally, Jenny ran out of data. She clicked on the "diagnose" button and MOM displayed a "Please Wait" message, then a report appeared on the screen:

Alert
Immediate Intervention Required
Patient John Doe 455

This is a Patient Alert. Patient profile is not consistent with normal post-op recovery. Symptoms suggest serious compromise of patient's health, most consistent with organ trauma during surgery. Probable iatrogenic scalpel laceration of pancreas or bowel during surgical procedure. Suspect internal bleeding, increasing infection, risk of peritonitis without antibiotic treatment. Authorize immediate emergency admission, collect listed lab values, physical exam of patient, and possible surgery to repair organ damage. Attending physician, Dr. Majani, is not authorized for this surgery. Attached is a list of recommended surgeons for Langston Hospital. This patient's data will be transmitted to crisis case management team. Recommend status reports every eight hours. This is a priority one case. Significant risks of death, costly outcome, and serious financial liability. Please confirm that action is being taken now.

cc: Crisis Management's team
        Hospital
Attachments:
        Authorized physicians list.
(Note: Action terminated: Sample case. No action. [Code 23-12])
MultiAxil Outcome Management System. Caduceus ver. 3.9
End Report

"Oh my God, sounds pretty serious," said Dwick. "Is your dad really that sick?"

"Sure is, and now I can get these clowns moving." Jenny saved the report to her disk, which still contained the earlier saved profile of Dr. Majani. "I'm gonna whack these guys."

"Jenny, we've been on this system for almost fifteen minutes. If Hepman finds he can't log-on I'm sure he'll come crashing through a back door and try to trace this link. We'd better get out of here."

"I've got everything I need." Jenny logged off from MOM, but kept the connection to Dwick. "I've got to call 911. Tell me quickly, what do you think will happen next?" she asked.

"Waldo will get to Hepman's computer the next time it comes on-line. He'll hide on the hard disk in an invisible file and search the disk for data. He'll compress it, wait for the next log-on, and work his way through the network to the firewall program, then make the jump to the Internet. He should be home in a few days."

"You sound like a proud papa, Dwick."

"I guess I am. I've spent a lot of time on this little critter. I hope to scare the wits out of corporate America with him and make a bundle protecting them from guys like Waldo."

"I'm glad I'm on your side, Dwick. Give me a call when Waldo gets home."

"Will do. Take care of yourself, Jenny. Get your dad some help. And get the hell out of that company," he said as the connection terminated.

Francis Barrett arrived as Jenny finished dialing 911, explaining her father's severe condition and her fear of moving him. They immediately dispatched the emergency medical team.

"You got the okay?" asked Francis.

"Give me five minutes. Do you have Dr. Majani's business card?"

Francis plowed through her pocketbook and produced a card with the Hubb Health Group logo. Jenny took the card back to the computer and launched the fax program. "Mom, get Dad ready to go. I'm going to get authorization for Dr. Shepard." She pulled up MOM's reports on Majani's questionable skills and the probable diagnosis of her father, then she drafted a cover sheet.

To: Mr. Jowett, Clinic Administrator.
From: Jenny Barrett.
Re: Emergency care of my father, William Barrett.
Urgent Message.

My father is in immediate need of treatment which your clinic is responsible for providing under our contract with The Axis Health System. I am demanding immediate release of my father for treatment by another physician, Dr. Shepard, within the hour.

Your clinic has not acted in good faith and has actively deceived my family about the qualifications and credentials of Dr. Majani. Attached is a record of his training and experience that shows he was neither experienced nor successful in the surgery he provided.

Additionally, I have attached the diagnostic opinion of the leading expert medical decision support computer in America today. It documents the severe risks my father is subject to and the necessary steps needed to assure his recovery. Should you fail to act on this data, you will be sued for gross negligence and malpractice.

A copy of these documents is being transmitted to Axis Health in an effort to promote your compliance with their contractual agreements.

Attachments: Two (2).
Majani Provider Profile
MultiAxil Management System Diagnostic Summary.

Jenny then called Axis Health's 800 line and quickly wove her way through the voice mail system.

"Thank you for calling Axis Health System. This is Alicia, how can I help you?"

"This is Jenny Barrett. I'd like to speak with a supervising case manager regarding the care of my father, William Barrett."

"Is there a problem?"

"Yes, but I need to speak with a supervisor. Oh, and do you have a fax machine on the floor near you."

"Why yes."

"Could I have the fax number? I have an important document to send. Please hurry."

Jenny jotted down the fax number while the attendant searched for the supervisor. She redrafted the letter for Axis and transmitted it from the laptop on the data line. A few seconds later a soothing yet professional voice was heard on the line.

"This is Carol Bowen, nurse supervisor. Can I help you?"

"Thank you, Ms. Bowen. I just faxed some documents to you regarding my father. I'm a case manager like yourself, over at Great Health Benefit. I'm very concerned with the post-op care he's receiving from Dr. Majani of the Hubb Health Group. I'm sure his record must be on your screen. I spoke with one of your case managers yesterday and was told that Dr. Majani was experienced in the lap chole procedure, but when I ran his provider profile through our system I found that we were deceived. His stats are terrible. Additionally, the Hubb Group is in deep financial difficulty due to cost overruns on their capitated contracts. You basically dumped my father with a poorly rated provider and now he's desperately ill."

"I don't . . . Who is this?" asked Bowen.

"Please, just walk over to the fax machine and pick up the document on Barrett. I'll wait."

The call switched to hold music for about two minutes, then Bowen returned to the line.

"This is your profile?" she stammered in disbelief.

"Yeah. Look, let's talk straight. We both know the drill. This is a bad doctor in a questionable group. I want my father switched back to Dr. Shepard within the hour. I'm taking him to Riverview Hospital here in Grants Pass. I expect you will authorize his admission, even if it's not a contract hospital."

"I don't know if I can do that."

"Sure you can," Jenny assured her, trying to take command of the situation."Look at the damn symptom list. It was produced by our expert computer system, MOM 3.0, if you know anything about it."

"Your computer did this?"

"Yes. Using the Harvard Medical School database. Do you want to challenge it with your system?"

"No. I'll accept this, at least until a physician examines your father. However, we do have an exclusive contract with Hubb Health. We can't just pull their patients away."

"Ms Bowen, you do it every day. I've appraised Hubb of my intentions and their risk of malpractice and fraud charges for their actions to date. I expect the administrator will not give us any protest. Let's just do this right, okay?"

"Okay, we'll authorize admission for emergency evaluation," said Bowen.

"Could you repeat that, I want it on voice mail? And could you state your name?"

Bowen hesitated, but as she glanced over the documents she realized the most expedient way to manage this. "This is Carol Bowen, case supervisor at Axis Health. I will authorize an emergency evaluation of William Barrett at Riverview Hospital. Dr. Shepard is authorized to evaluate. Is that sufficient?"

"Thanks, Carol. I owe you for this. Please transmit the authorizations and I'll get my father in there."

"I'm sorry if there has been any inconvenience, Ms. Barrett."

"You did well," said Jenny as she hung up.

"Mom," shouted Jenny. "Dad's going to Riverview. Shepard is authorized to see him. Let's get going." The EMT vehicle pulled into the dusty driveway and the two uniformed attendants were greeted at the door. While Francis helped Bill prepare for the ride, Jenny called Dr. Shepard. She had his service page him, and within a minute he was on the phone.

"Jenny?" he said.

"It's a go, Dr. Shepard. We got you back on the case. Authorization is headed for your office. We're taking Dad to Riverview. MOM, the computer I showed you, says he probably has a cut pancreas or intestine. Can you see him, doctor?"

"Within the hour. Great work, Jenny. How'd you do it?"

"You don't want to know."

The administrator of Hubb Health saw the wisdom of transferring care and offered no resistance. Within the week their Axis contract had been terminated.

An hour after Bill Barrett arrived at the hospital, he was transferred to an operating room for emergency surgery. The discoloration under the skin was caused by bleeding from a cut to his pancreas made during his prior, lap chole surgery. An infection was roaring through his abdomen. Tubes drained the fluid from his oversized belly. Dr. Shepard stood beside the bed shaking his head. "Much too close," he kept saying.

Thursday evening found Bill Barrett out of immediate danger and feeling much better, having been thoroughly "nuked" with intravenous antibiotics. Jenny and her mother sat in his semi-private room munching cheeseburgers, which was not as cruel as it might sound since Bill had no appetite. His spirits, on the other hand, were quite high.

"God, I can see my feet again," he said. "I feel like I gave birth to a Volkswagen."

"Well, you almost went the way of the Yugo," chirped Francis.

"Jenny, I owe you big time for making this happen. Dr. Shepard said another day at home and I might have been beyond help." He extended his hand to her, stretching the plastic tubes from his IV. Jenny took his hand and squeezed it tight while looking at the fire that had returned to his eyes.

"Hey, you're the only Dad I get, and you're still under warranty. We gotta keep you running right."

"You must have showed them some spunk to get me back to Shepard. What did you do?" asked Bill.

"She kicked their cyber-butts!" said the proud mother. "I came home and there was Jenny, pulling down this report from some super-computer and getting the goods on Dr. Majani. Then she blasts the reports all over the country about how rottenly the clinic has treated you and what this expert computer says you need. Shut those guys up real quick."

Francis leaned on Jenny's shoulder and mussed up her daughter's hair like she was a ten-year-old. Jenny leaned back to echo the support, greeting her mother's eyes with warm appreciation. The praise from her parents was beginning to embarrass her. William Barrett's eyes lingered on Jenny's lovely face, his heart filled with pride at the accomplished young woman who sat by his bed.

"If you're going to thank anyone," countered Jenny, "thank David for all those hours he let me play with his computers. I am glad I could help. You gave me so much when I was growing up. I'm glad I could give a little back."

Friday morning found Grants Pass enjoying a pastoral spring day. Since there was no telling when she'd get back up here, Jenny decided to stay until Sunday, clearing it with Carter Newton's office at GHB. By Friday afternoon Bill Barrett was walking comfortably around the hospital floor, nosing into the nurse's business and trying hard to make himself a pest. He was clearly out of the woods.

The weekend would be filled with visits and talks with her mother. Jenny withheld all but her general concern about GHB's corporate "culture," not sharing any of her more sinister suspicions. On Saturday David called and they managed to set up the video phone on his old computer. The two women brought David up to speed on his father's condition, which gave him some guilt for having been so out of touch. Her mother overheard a brief version of the invasion of MOM and how her daughter got the provider profiles and diagnosis on Bill. David was impressed, but understood that this violation of corporate security likely meant Jenny was on the way out. He was immensely proud of his sister.

"Did I hear right, that Dwick rode in with you?" asked David.

"Yeah, he had to drop off a package," said Jenny.

"Uh-Oh. I'd better check out my insurance coverage. I don't think GHB is going to fare well in the next few weeks."

Chapter 28

The massive form of Betsy Waller eased into a gun shop on Elm Street. She had seen guns as a teen, and briefly lived in a car with a guy who kept a 9-millimeter automatic in his waistband, but she didn't know much about their operation. She approached the man at the counter, who was polishing a knife blade.

"Can I help you, Miss?" he asked.

Betsy tried her best to sound cool and rational, but her anxiety and excitement were unrestrained. "I'm seeing the Armageddon of Satan round the corner. Will a gun bridle that wormster?" She complimented herself on how clearly she had stated the issue.

"Beg your pardon, ma'am?"

"I gots to help my child," she said, rubbing her immense belly. "He's a coming, He's a coming. I need to be ready, ready like rain. Rainy day ready for the coming."

"Ma'am, I don't think I can help you with that."

"Oh, you got to. Please, mister, you got to. Get to. Get a gun to. I've got thirty-six dollars. Please let me get a gun for that wheezy weasel wormster."

"Well, there isn't any gun in the store for under a hundred dollars. Besides, you have to have a permit."

"A permit. Give me a permit. I permit you."

"Can't do that. You go down to the police department and tell them you need a gun permit. They'll help you out." The man sat back down on his stool, disengaging from the conversation. No way he was selling a gun to this loon.

"Can I see a gun? Look and touch. I've never held a bullet gun."

"Then will you go to the police?"

"Yes," Betsy said eagerly.

The man pulled out a 38-caliber Police Special, checked to see that it was unloaded, and handed it to her. Betsy instantly hated the cold steel. She touched the hard barrel and suddenly recalled, through the thick clouds of her memory, another gun pressed against her face. Some boys in a field, messing with her. She couldn't retrieve the entire memory, but she quickly handed back the gun. "I don't like guns."

"Good for you. They can hurt people," said the clerk.

Betsy was about to leave when her eyes caught sight of a basket filled with handcuffs. She picked up a set and asked, "How much for this?"

"Fifteen dollars."

"Okay." An idea began to form in her twisted mind. She gave the man a twenty dollar bill and put the device in her purse, took her change and left. The man felt relieved that she didn't buy anything dangerous.

Betsy's next stop was the bus station, where she purchased a ticket to Seattle, Washington. She hadn't been out of Idaho in ten years, so there was some exhilaration to her thoughts. Fortunately, she only had to say one short sentence clearly, "Seattle, one way." Such a trip meant she would be missed at her facility, but it wasn't unusual for residents to take off for a day or two. They generally returned from their little "vacations"in good shape, and the police did not have time to search the neighborhood and try to distinguish between the homeless mentally ill and those who had an address.

Betsy returned to her room and chased thoughts around her chaotic mind for the remainder of the day. She asked for another dose of chlorpromazine to help her thinking. GHB had cut back on her allotment, which contributed to her constant low level symptoms. However, occasionally she could get an extra pill for "agitation." She tried to figure out what an enormously pregnant girl could do to hurt the devil, but her internal voices kept distracting her. Then, for an instant, she saw a solution. It was perfectly clear, but it was fading fast. She rubbed her stomach and tried to associate the image with her soft belly. She concentrated with all of her might. Yes, it would work, but she needed some help.

Henry Abrams was loading shelves at the pharmacy when Betsy approached him.

"Henry, I'm needing to know something for truth-in-all. How big can you blow a hot water bottle?"

The box boy turned to her with a screwed up expression on his skinny face and said, "Huh?"

"Blowing up hot water bottles? How big they turn into, balloonish," said Betsy.

"Well, I can't do it very big myself. But I once saw Leonard Nelson blow up one with a bicycle pump. Sucker was bigger than a basketball. Then he poked it with a rake and it exploded, just about blew my eardrums out."

"I need some. Four or five."

"Why?"

"Don't ask the rumcackle question. I just do. But I don't have money."

Seeing an opportunity to negotiate, Henry said, "Well, they're pretty expensive, you know. We only carry the good stuff. If you want me to be giving you some, I'll have to get something back."

Betsy expected this and was resigned to it. "Okay, I'll blow you."

"No honey, I want the real thing."

"No! No one goes in my cuddly coo. That's my baby's place."

"No deal then."

After 15 minutes of negotiation, Betsy relented and agreed to meet Henry in the men's room at 5:30. She wasn't sure what would happen. Maybe that Satan baby would reach down and grab his pecker and yank it off. She figured that baby must be smarter than Henry. At 5:30 sharp Henry and Betsy walked unseen into the bathroom at the back of the storeroom. At 5:33 Betsy came out with four hot water bottles, two cartons of cigarettes, and a lighter. She also scooped up a razor sharp box cutting knife on her way out. Henry still had his penis.

***

Mark Lipton sped down the Santa Ana Freeway, his car twisting and rolling through the coiled ribbons of asphalt and concrete that turned Los Angeles into a macramé of roadways. Occasionally, he passed under an elevated pedestrian freeway crossing, all of which were caged in hurricane fencing to block adolescents and miscreants from the urban sport of brick tossing at the speeding autos below. As a reporter, he'd covered a few senseless deaths and injuries because of this macabre recreation, for which he prayed there was no official scorekeeper. The drivers of Southern California were the most attentive in the world, for they needed to watch in six directions at once as they traveled from any point "A" to point "B." Commuting, like intimacy, was not for the faint of heart.

Mark hated working on Saturdays, especially when the 98-degree

Santa Ana Winds dropped the humidity to three percent and the waves of the Pacific beckoned from the nearby shoreline. Instead of enjoying the sailing gulls and warm sand, Mark mentally replayed his conversation with Jim Witcomb from last night.

"Look, I'm pulling in a favor to get you in with Senator Gray tomorrow," said Mark's editor. "He's conducting hearings on managed care and may have already had one of the Great Health Benefit executives on the hot seat. You'll recall, Gray now heads the Joint Subcommittee on Health Insurance Reform. He's been focusing on all this health information floating around in cyberspace: who's guarding it, who's selling it, and who's actually matking the decisions on care."

"Lucky us. Our own Senator in a plum position. Can't I just do a telephone interview? I'm sure there's little that can be gained by either of us disturbing our weekends."

"Mark, he's one of the few guys in Washington I trust. Gray has always been a strong consumer advocate, though it hasn't been easy for him. He's still considered an outsider, despite two tours in the House, which means he still has some palpable ethics. I think he can help you, and you may even help him."

"Help him? Aren't we supposed to be impartial? I mean, theoretically."

"Get out of here," said Witcomb, shooing Mark away. "Speak with Eddie in Gray's office. You'll get about a half hour tomorrow with the Senator. If he likes you, or you add something to his arsenal, maybe an hour. Take all your notes on Great Health Benefit with you."

The notes sat beside Mark as he saw the exit sign for Knott's Berry Farm, a local theme park. The tip of Disneyland's Matterhorn slipped past on the right as he entered the city of Anaheim. He'd played basketball inside the attraction many years ago, on a staff court tucked deep inside the ersatz mountain. Soon he exited the freeway and headed for the foothills. He missed Jenny and wished he could be with her in Oregon right now. She had left a message saying her father was in the hospital and much improved. That was a relief. She also mentioned something about that guy Dwick discovering a big story in a computer. He'd try again to speak with her tonight and planned to be at her door tomorrow night when she returned.

Mark had been impressed with the profile materials Witcomb had given him in preparation for this interview. Gray and his wife seemed like regular people. As a consumer advocate, Gray had caused some major upheavals in industries as diverse as car rentals, medical equipment, and Internet service providers. He was particularly hard on scams against the elderly. His wife was no slouch either, now recognized as an artist of some note. One of her works had decorated the cover of <u>Los Angeles Magazine</u>.

The winding hillside roads took Mark high above the flat lands, past houses of increasing worth, size, and elegance. He finally entered a gated community and was questioned briefly by a guard. He then made his way to the gated front of the Senator's home. As the iron barrier opened to admit the car, Mark was struck with the incongruity of the easygoing man described in the bios and the fortress he lived behind. Then he remembered that the Senator had kids.

The house sat on a hillside and was approached via a driveway that snaked down to a flat front yard. The house was not especially large or palatial, although it was smart and nicely appointed, with a white tile porch, walls of stucco and Spanish tiles, and tropical flora securing privacy all around. He parked in front of the home on the side of the double-wide driveway. He wasn't quite to the front door when it swung open and Donald Gray emerged, greeting Mark with a broad smile and pumping handshake.

"Welcome to the homestead, Mr. Lipton."

"Thank you, Senator, and please call me Mark.

"If you'll call me Don."

Mark was escorted into an airy living room, plush white with a matching Steinway piano dominating the center. The room looked far too elegant to sit in, and Mark was guided through to the patio overlooking the pool. The two sat at the glass patio table and a maid asked about drinks.

"Can the reporter have a nice German beer while on assignment?" asked Gray.

"Only if we talk about international issues. Be sure to mention Europe at some point."

The Senator gave Mark a standing tour of the backyard, pointing out plants, sculptures, and landscaping features from the table as the maid popped open the beers. "If you look into that far corner of the yard, you'll see the view Emily painted that was featured on the cover of <u>LA Magazine</u>."

"A beautiful place."

"So, Mark, " said Gray lifting his beer. "Here's to the European Alliance." They sipped the luxurious ale. "Jim Witcomb says you're one of his best reporters. I read your story on clinics ripping off the elderly. Great work. I've been looking forward to speaking with you."

"Thank you. Say, am I keeping you from your family?" Mark said as he looked around.

"Emily and the kids are doing some shopping chores, then we're all off to Knott's Berry Farm for some log fluming. They'll be back in an hour, at which time you'll officially lose me."

"Fine. I'm sorry to disturb your weekend as it is, but there are some questions I need to ask. Mind if I record?" said Mark as he withdrew a small tape recorder.

"Can we just keep it simple?" said Gray, touching the back of Mark's hand in a gentle but firm decline. Mark put the machine away. "I'll give you some background material to relieve your note taking. Let me tell you about the Joint-Congressional Health Insurance Reform Committee." For the next twenty minutes, Gray told Mark the scope, breadth, and history of the committee. A folder containing much of this material was placed beside Mark by the maid. He leafed through the documents, confirming what the Senator was saying.

"Then I ended up as full chair after the unfortunate stroke of Senator Small. Since then the committee has been trying to understand the mechanisms of care measurement and monitoring used by the big managed care companies. They've taken over so much of the Medicare and Medicaid burden that medicine has become disturbingly centralized. Some doctors, mostly in small practices, are complaining that they can no longer stand up for their clients. From my days as a consumer advocate, I remember how lonely an advocacy position can feel."

"So, as I understand it, you're currently looking into the rules and regs that control how medical care is dispensed to patients."

"Pretty much," agreed the Senator, "but existing law has hampered the investigation. As you know, much of the control is being handled by information systems, which do most of the routine eligibility determination. I can understand that. However, I also understand that computers are increasingly dispensing medical advice and decisions. I'm concerned about how that works, yet the managed care companies are under no obligation to show us their computer code."

"How can this be?" asked Mark. "Something as essential as medical care and you can't look at the charts?"

"Oh, we can review charts. We just can't see the exact formulas for care. This has all happened so quickly, there is little formal law on the matter. We're trying to bend existing law to fit the circumstances, like the regulation of credit histories or drivers' licenses, but we're largely at the mercy of the large companies."

"You can't just look at the formulas for care? After all, Senator, with Medicare and Medicaid, they really are the government's patients."

"Yes, they are our patients and no, they don't and won't let us see the programs. Can't say that I blame them, really. A large firm like Great Health Benefit can't afford to let the competition see its inner workings. It's a tight, competitive market. Axis would pay dearly for their formulas. I wouldn't trust the government to keep them secret. I also wouldn't want them in my pocket, they're too valuable. It's a bit like those stories you hear of a poor kid getting killed over a designer jacket, except this might be worth tens of millions of dollars."

"Senator," began Mark, to add seriousness to the question, "you're saying that no one is watching these guys. How do you know they're not just keeping the millions of dollars the government pays them while denying legitimate care to the people?"

"Unfortunately, I'm sure that is going on, particularly among the more predatory insurance companies. Yet to be honest, they have us over a barrel. We've been getting reports and complaints from some constituents, but overall the reports have been pretty favorable. Surprising, since the population might be getting sicker. It's like the tobacco industry. Happy faces, mounting body count. The GDRs, sorry, the global death rates are up for a few of these companies."

"Global death rate?" asked Mark with a grim look.

"Sorry. That's an industry term. It refers to the total death rates for a particular company. In fact, they're trying to come up with a better name. Like 'LSR,' longitudinal survival rate. Anyway, the GDR for a few plans is quite alarming . . . Axis Health, GHB, Vanguard."

"Isn't that your proof that they're hurting people? What do the companies say about that?"

"Well, as British Prime Minister Disraeli used to say, 'There are lies, damn lies, and statistics.' The managed care companies say this is a good thing. It is testimony to their greater caring and efficiency."

"And how does a higher death rate transfer into better medicine?"

"Easy. The two biggest rebuttals from the managed care companies are that, one, they take sicker patients, and two, they don't milk them for money like private, fee-for-service doctors do. You know that about 80 percent of medical care funds are consumed in the last few months of a patient's life. They say death rates are increasing because they are not artificially prolonging the painful death process just to squeeze out more money. Patients die earlier, but with more dignity, and since they are taking our "sicker" patients, of course that skews the statistics."

"Do you believe this?"

"I believe it's total bullshit. Unfortunately, we don't have much data to counter it."

"What do you mean?"

The Senator looked around as if under surveillance, then said, "I think the increased death rates are due to tight fists, not warm hearts. Bottom lines, not natural causes are killing people. Still, it's going to take years to get the statistics straight on this, many years. And these guys will get filthy rich and thousands of people may die. However, I just can't get much attention on this issue."

"Why is that?" asked Mark, as his pen flew across the yellow pad.

"The industry mounted a brilliant campaign against all the 'greedy' providers, doctors, and healthcare providers who were ripping off Medicare. It was largely the work of a very few bad apples, but the industry kept the spotlight on greedy doctors to keep the attention off themselves. In fact, they offered to help Medicare track down these evil doctors and confiscate their Mercedes. The current Presidential Administration bought it. Gave the managed care industry almost total control. It's like we were worried that the eggs in the chicken house were being snatched by some weasels, so we threw a couple of wolves in the chicken coop to stand guard. Now those wolves are looking pretty fat."

"I don't understand, Senator. The Feds check on banking programs and credit programs. Why can't they do medical programs?"

"Whole different beast. Banking is pretty much adding up the numbers. We don't care how they compute it, just that the interest rate matches what they publish. So we look at a customer's account with $1,000 at 7 percent interest and figure out how much he should have been paid. We don't need to see their formula, we just need to know it produces the right figure. But healthcare isn't like that. It does matter how the care is computed, or what the program considers.

"So you can't get them with statistics and you can't see the formula for care."

"I'd give anything to see one, but it's off limits for now. Private, secret formulas. Just as long as the companies obey the law, there's nothing we can do." Gray leaned over slightly to Mark as a gesture of a confidential statement and said, "I thought we had a lead on some computer code, from a disgruntled employee, but she never came through. Disappeared."

The reference made Mark hesitate. Could it have been? "You had an inside track to a computer?"

"Thought we did. It would have been grand. Just to see the actual clinical decision trees of these companies. Talk about a smoking gun. We might have gotten a court order to open up the whole machine."

"What company was that?"

"I'd rather not say, Mark. Officially, I'm not sure I really know how it would have been viewed. The code might have been stolen. I can't be an accessory to grand theft. Only if there was extremely incriminating evidence in the program could it be used for further investigation. I'm just saying it would have been interesting."

"Senator, was it a Hispanic woman who approached you?"

"Why, yes."

"From GHB?"

"Ah, possibly."

"Elaina Ruiz?" Mark dared to ask.

"Yes, I think that was her name. Are you using her as a source? If so, I'd love to speak with her about that big computer, what do they call it, MOM, I think. I thought the company must have bought her off, or she got cold feet."

"She's dead, sir."

"She died?"

"In January. In a psychiatric hospital, a mysterious death due to a medication reaction."

"I'm sorry. Was she a source for you?" asked the Senator.

"No, she was an acquaintance and a friend of my girlfriend, Jenny, who now works for GHB."

"I'm sorry to hear that. Let me get this straight. Your girlfriend was a friend of this Elaina woman, who died, and your Jenny now works for GHB?"

"Yes, sir. I believe she is in much the same job position. They're both psychologists with computer expertise."

"Then I'm not sure we should be having this conversation."

"I'm sure that we should, Senator. I'm worried about Jenny. I've been researching this company for a couple of weeks. I can hardly find anything good that's been said about it. As you must know, they're being sued or investigated by several state attorneys general. Their life insurance and investment divisions have been involved in multiple billion-dollar consumer fraud settlements, and now they've taken over the medical care for millions of Americans. Jenny has seen inside MOM, their computer system."

"She's seen the coding of MOM?" exclaimed Senator Gray.

"I don't know about that, but she's been telling me about the inner workings of the program. Apparently, it's making most of the decisions about healthcare. Jenny has been trying to tell me how crazy and evil it seems, but I didn't understand the meaning or the scale of it until now. I think she can get you the code."

The Senator's eyes lit up like a child's on Christmas morning. "She'd work with us?"

"I'm pretty sure. She's fed up with their system."

Gray's face suddenly grew serious. He looked at Mark with a measure of doubt. "There are big stakes in this game. I don't want to be left out on a limb. I can't afford to jeopardize the investigation, limited as it is. I'll need to be sure who you are."

"I understand. Check with Jim Witcomb. Look at my record. I'll introduce you to Jenny. I promise, we'll keep you clean," Mark assured.

"You know, asking someone to become a whistle blower is an invitation to hell. I wouldn't want her taking any unnecessary risks."

"She's a strong woman, sir, and she really hates what she's seen so far. I've heard her voice the same concerns about formulas for care that you have. She says MOM is being used to hurt people."

"Was there some connection between this Elaina woman's death and GHB?"

"I'm beginning to think so, but there's no hard proof," said Mark.

"Did the police investigate?"

"No need to. It seemed to be an accident, but too much is adding up and I'm worried about Jenny. Apparently there are very few computer-savvy psychologists around. Jenny thinks she is in Elaina's job. GHB doesn't know of their past friendship."

"Son, I don't think you realize the scope of what we're dealing with. If GHB and the others get their way, the federal government will turn over billions of dollars to them to manage the healthcare of much of the country. I feel like that Chinese dissident who was trying to stop the tank in Tiananmen Square, except these guys are rougher. They would squash anyone who got in their way."

"Jenny will be back Monday. She's in Oregon helping her sick father. I'll be speaking with her tomorrow."

"I'll be leaving for Washington Monday evening. We'll have to talk Tuesday. The committee meetings go on for another two weeks. I can reschedule the GHB people if it looks like we can get something."

"What do you need, Senator?"

"Anything that will dramatically illustrate the need to look at these computer systems, how they decide things, how we can remove the veil of privacy. I'm alone in this right now. The President, the Congress, and even the courts may be siding with the insurance industry to solve our healthcare problems. The numbers look good, but if we can show them that the numbers come at the cost of people's lives, it won't look so good to anyone."

The sound of the front door opening was followed by merry

shouts of family greetings. Donald Gray stood up to introduce Mark to the members of the family, but didn't sit, signifying that the meeting was over. Mark stood up to be walked to the door. The Senator stopped at a desk, rustled some papers, and withdrew some kind of flyer.

"Mark, have you seen this?"

Mark took the flyer and read it over quickly. The name and address were blacked out, but the content of Crandall Bream's letter was astounding to the reporter. "Where'd this come from? You have a crazy group in Washington?"

"No, it was sent to me by a local constituent. Apparently there are thousands of them flying around. I don't know if it's legit as to its data, but what interests me is where the group got the mailing list. This is just the kind of corrupt use of medical records that could sway Congress about the need for more government controls. If you come across any information, please let me know."

"I think I may have heard something about this. I'll check it out."

"Thanks. I've put a couple of staff on it myself. I want to know if any laws have been broken. Here's my private phone number, Mark. Joyce can always track me down. Let's see if we can get together on the phone Tuesday."

"Are you under much pressure to wrap it up?"

"A little. Since I have such minimal support from anyone in Washington on this issue, I think they see it mostly as an exercise in futility. There's also a PR element to it. The committee in part gives the appearance of serious investigation even if it's a sham. Appearances are everything in Washington. However, if we get some hard evidence, we can use our visibility to command some attention. It might open up a real investigation." The said their goodbyes and Mark left the house.

Chapter 29

During the flight back home on Sunday night, Jenny took time to think deeply about her circumstances. The visit with her parents and the battle for her father's health had given her a more enlightened perspective on her job, her work, and her life direction. The invasion of MOM had produced a jarring look into the black heart of GHB.

Over the weekend Dwick had e-mailed copies of MOM's decision flow charts from Elaina's portion of MOM's . Although incomplete, the diagrams revealed that the Caduceus Project was a sham. Rarely would a patient's symptoms be considered by the master computer. Instead, at every decision point, MOM would branch out to a subroutine designed to find ways to avoid payment for treatment. Little comments in the programming code referenced efforts to lie, cheat, deceive, miscommunicate, or sue to avoid cash outflow. What Jenny had experienced on her father's behalf occurred daily, in millions of cycles per second.

Jenny remembered a client session during an internship training at the Veteran's Administration Hospital. A disabled vet she worked with was the only survivor of a helicopter crash during an exercise. He was burned and broken, in flesh and spirit, trussed up in a bed unable to move. Traumatic stress and survivor guilt had thrown him into a suicidal depression. It wasn't that he could really do anything to kill himself, but without his will to live the medication might not have been sufficient to heal him. Jenny saw him every day. She coached him, cried with him, scolded him, and came to love him in a protective way. The young man's spirit returned, and he was able to focus on recovery. Today, her services would be replaced by a pill, at twenty cents a dose.

The lights were on in her townhouse as she approached. Mark was there, using his old key to let himself in. A warmth spread over her at the thought of him on her couch. She needed his company, his firm embrace. He was so much more mature, talking of settling down. Her caution flags were still up, and she knew she was too hungry for comfort to trust her impressions right now, but she could hope it was true. She had spoken with him over the weekend, outlining her adventures and hearing of his enthusiasm after his meeting with Senator Gray.

Mark sprang to the door as she entered, wrestling with her luggage and a shopping sack. Surprisingly he said nothing, no jocular kidding or wisecracks. He held her firmly as they stood in the doorway, feeling her body, smelling her hair, pressing his face into her neck. It wasn't lustful. He was trying to squeeze her soul.

Finally he broke his hold. "Welcome back, pretty lady. How's the family?"

"Everyone's well now. They all send hugs and kisses to you." She parked her luggage by the couch and plopped down into its cushions. "Dad's a whole lot better. Mom and I had some good talks. I feel recharged, but tired."

"I've got some exciting things to tell you, but they can wait till later. Can I make you a snack or ply you with wine?"

"Wine will put me under, Mark, completely."

"Is that what you need?"

"Absolutely."

Mark brought out a Pinot Noir and filled a large glass. Jenny took a few sips and then curled up under his arm. "I need someone to take care of me tonight."

"You've got it, babe. The cyber-warrior returns to the home fires, victorious. Time for some R & R."

It was just 9:00 P.M., but Jenny was spent. Mark collected her discarded shoes, pants, and coat while she stretched out on the couch in her tee shirt. She was asleep in seconds. Mark moved her to the bedroom and set the alarm for 5:00 A.M. so they'd have time to talk in the morning.

The sounds of a traffic report on the radio pulled Jenny from a disturbing dream. She had been running along a beach at the foot of some huge bluffs. A fifty-foot tidal wave was approaching and she was running to escape being crushed on the rocks, but her feet sank in the sand up to her ankles, tortuously slowing her progress. She felt like an insignificant speck caught between colossal forces. It didn't take Freud to analyze the meaning of the dream.

Mark's arm laid across her stomach, his bushy head buried in the pillow. She stroked his arm and reveled in its difference from hers. It was hard, rough, lumpy with musculature. She clasped his hands and felt his strength. She was still haunted by dream residue and wanted some protection from the giant wave.

His arm began to move slowly from her hand, as if he was turning over in his sleep, but it stopped at her thigh, and gently plunged between her legs. "Good morning sunshine," he said with a grin. "What's for breakfast?" They laughed and grabbed each other.

"Maybe your favorite, if you're good."

He was good. And it was good. In the warmth of the morning bed they made slow, casual love. It was more an affirmation of their reunion than a passionate release. Their bodies set a rhythmic cadence, occasionally interrupted by hugs and laughter. Their serial climaxes were in close step, and they kissed and stroked until the traffic reporter returned on the radio to drive them from bed. They showered and dressed with calculated efficiency, to gain some time together at breakfast.

"So what did you learn on your trip, Jenny Barrett?"

"That I don't want to have anything to do with GHB. Dwick, the guy you met on my computer, showed me the program code that Elaina had acquired. It's evil, Mark. The company exists to cause people harm. There is profit in pain and suffering, and GHB wants it all."

"I'm glad to hear that. My research says pretty much the same thing. I'm running a story this week on the Progressive merger, complete with all the GHB corruption. Since you're leaving, can I use your inside information for part two?"

"Yeah. I want these guys to hurt, like all the people they've hurt."

"I spoke with Senator Donald Gray. Jenny, he was contacted by Elaina just before she died. He had no idea why she suddenly disappeared. When I told him the circumstances of her death, he became very concerned."

"Dwick knows a lot about this computer program. He says its worth millions and GHB would kill to keep it hidden."

"Can Dwick give me and the Senator copies of the program? Poor Gray is flailing around in DC trying to get Congress to open up the vaults of these 'expert' computers. Under present law, there's no way to look inside. The Feds have to take GHB's word for what its programs do."

"He could have a copy, but it's incomplete. An early beta test version. We infected MOM with a virus-agent while I was visiting up in Oregon . . .”

"Infected MOM? Hah. I always knew you were a hacker in sheep's clothing," Mark laughed.

"Yes, I'm afraid I'm guilty. I had to do it. I think I told you GHB suddenly locked me out. I had to help my dad, and that was the easiest way. They may have discovered my link to Elaina. Anyway, I have a feeling things will be different at work today. However, as I was saying, Dwick invaded with me and dropped a virus-like program into MOM. It's supposed to gather up MOM's program source code and deliver it to him. It's got a cute name. Waldo, like 'Where's Waldo'."

"You hacks are nuts," he said in intimidated awe. "So when is this Waldo supposed to deliver the goods?"

"Soon. Dwick's not sure, but probably in a couple of days. He'll e-mail me immediately, but first he'll have to process the data. There are millions of lines of code. We couldn't hope to understand it all, but he's got a program that reads the code and produces a flow chart about what the program does, what variables it considers, the decision processes, the advice it gives. It would be enough to let you and the Senator know how MOM really works."

"So, you'll work with Gray?"

Jenny pondered the magnitude of the commitment she was about to make. It went completely against all her principles of career building. Yet after the visit home, she knew what values were more important."Yes. I owe it to Elaina, and to myself. I never thought I'd be a whistle blower, but this is really evil stuff."

"Would you talk with him if I get him on the line?"

"Right now, Mark?"

"Yeah. It's the middle of the morning in Washington, DC."

"I really don't have much to tell him."

"I know, but I want the two of you to connect. I'm worried about you. If he speaks with you, knows you're a real person who knew Elaina, I'd feel a little more comfortable. If anyone hassles you, you'll have some backup."

"Okay. I'm diving into my Cheerios. If you can get him on the line, we'll talk."

Mark dialed the number and got hold of Gray's receptionist, who patched him through. "Senator Gray? This is Mark Lipton. Yeah. I'm with Jenny. I'd like you two to touch base. Tell her what you need." He handed the phone to Jenny.

"Hello?" she said, unsure how to address a Senator.

"Jenny. It's good to have you aboard. Mark says you may have some valuable information for our efforts here."

"I hope to have some soon. But what exactly are you looking for?"

"Anything that will get me inside that computer, MOM. We need to know what these companies are doing with these information systems. Can I count on you?" asked Gray.

"I'll give it my best effort."

"I'm sorry about Elaina, Jenny. Mark told me she was your friend."

"She was a great person. I miss her."

"Maybe we can make this right," Gray said. "Complete her work."

"As I said, I'll try my best." The tinge of manipulation in his speech annoyed her, but then, he was under a time pressure and was desperate. "I'll talk with you soon, Senator."

She looked at Mark like a frightened puppy.

"We'll be careful. I don't want to lose you now. Just play stupid at work. I'm going to be sleeping here for a while, if it's okay with you," asked Mark.

"Thanks. I need you."

"I need you, Jenny." She saw his eyes dampen before he looked away. In their closest moments she had never seen him cry. Maybe he had finally become a man? "Hey, I've got to get going to work," he continued. "Let's pick this up tonight, after work. We'll go to dinner and plan the rest of our lives. Okay?"

She kissed him on the cheek so he didn't have to face her. "You got it."

***

Carter Newton had just sat at his desk when Amanda, his secretary, rang through the first call of the day, from Norm Kepper, an attorney in GHB legal services.

"Norm, whatcha got?" he asked, sipping his first cup of coffee.

"Mr. Newton, I think we have to take this mailing list matter very seriously. The entire office here feels there is a potential for disastrous liability exposure and media slam if we're identified as the source for those lists of women. Doesn't matter that it was a legitimate request. Abortion is too hot an issue."

"What do you propose?"

"I'll contact this Bream organization and rattle a saber about fraudulent purposes and the hazards of implication. I'll imply that if the press and the government come down hard on them, we'll jump on them too unless they keep our names out of it. At least till this all blows over," said Norm.

"Sounds good. Keep me informed."

Greg Hepman was ushered into the office by Amanda as she dropped some papers on Carter's desk.

"Amanda, I'm not to be disturbed until further notice. Okay," said Carter.

"Got it," was the crisp reply.

***

Jenny logged onto her computer at GHB at 8:35 A.M. Her e-mail box was stuffed, but many of the memos were routine general announcements, which she dragged on screen to her virtual trash can. A note from Hepman apologized for the failure of the laptop communication program, and advised her that he'd pick up the machine at her workstation around 10:30 A.M. Jenny had already reformatted and restored the laptop's hard disk to what it contained just before the invasion of MOM. No "footprints" were left for Detective Hepman.

A note from Carter Newton requested a meeting with her tomorrow at 9 A.M. regarding the rollout of the final Caduceus project. He asked that she run some specific sample cases to gauge how staff would receive MOM's consultation on complex cases. Besides a section meeting at 2 P.M., Jenny's day was open. She noted that her security level had not been changed. Maybe the laptop failure was a true glitch, she wondered.

Three floors above her, Carter Newton and Greg Hepman watched Jenny log on from a four-inch video window on Carter's monitor. "She can't tell that the camera is on?" he asked Hepman.

"No, the signal light is off. It still operates, and if anyone else calls her it will flash on, but for now, she has no idea she's under scrutiny."

"What are these graphs along the bottom of my screen?"

"They're the bio-stress readings from the 'rat' we installed. When she touches her mouse, the electrical conductivity is measured here, her pulse here, and hand temperature here. As you can see, she looks pretty relaxed, so we're recording her baseline. When we flash our test material on the screen, we can easily measure her reaction."

"What's this graph here?" asked Carter.

"That's a voice stress meter. The psychiatric case workers use it to assess suicide and homicide risk in our clients, and Workers' Comp staff use it to detect deception from claimants. If you speak with her directly it will give you a clear picture of her credibility. When she starts working on those sample cases, we'll find out what we need to know."

"Great work, Greg. So did you follow up on her log on activities from Oregon?"

"Yeah. My staff tracked her calls. Seems she checked the billings for a Dr. Shepard, who used to be their family physician. She slapped the staff around and got them to agree to pay his claims. Pretty clever girl."

"That was it? Seems innocent enough," said Carter.

"I'm not so concerned about what she did, it's how well she did it. This girl is extremely knowledgeable about the system. I'd almost say she could be a hacker. She's playing too innocent for her level of skill."

"Maybe she just doesn't want to seem like a propeller head dweeb, not with that lovely brown hair and delicious figure. Say, can't we get some X-ray cameras so we can check a little deeper?"

Hepman smiled. "Actually, we have them. Penetrating infrared scanners. They can see right through clothing, bouncing a signal directly off skin. Produces a very high resolution black and white image. I saw them demonstrated at a trade show. The booth was packed. They had models in business dresses wearing leather bathing suits underneath. The rays penetrated the fabric, but couldn't get through the leather. A very impressive demo."

"We'll have to look into those cameras."

"She's calling up the first sample case," alerted Hepman.

"Okay, what should we expect?"

"Look, she's paging through the case record. It's a tough call about a child who needs eye surgery, but has terrible insurance coverage. I wanted to put her nerves on edge a bit. When she gets to the utilization report, she'll see Elaina's name and signature. That should tell us something about her association with the woman."

The men watched the bio-stress meters fluctuate as Jenny moused her way through screens. As she explored the case material, her tension rose in sympathy for the imaginary child who was at risk of losing an eye. Hepman tapped some keys which produced another window on Carter's screen reflecting what was on Jenny's monitor. The image of Jenny was so clear that they could tell what portion of the monitor she was reading.

"It's on the next page," said Hepman.

Jenny clicked to pull up the utilization review report. Carter and Hepman watched her eyes drift down the screen. The "rat" pumped her biological readings through the system. Then her eyes fell upon Elaina's name, and in an instant, all bio-stress readings flew to the top of their graphs. Jenny's eyes were wide, riveted to the bottom of her screen. Redness appeared in her eyes, followed by moisture that brimmed on her lower eyelid. There was no mouse movement, she was frozen in time. MOM quickly added megabytes of data to Jenny's psychological profile. Her reaction left no doubt about the significance of the name on the screen.

"Shit! Look at those readings," screamed Carter. "God damn it. How could this happen? She must have been friends with Elaina, and she probably knows that she's dead. Shit, shit shit."

"Look, Carter, I don't think there's been any damage. We traced Jenny's activities in MOM. It's all been pretty benign stuff. We'll just downsize her out of here. She doesn't know anything that could hurt us. There's no evidence she has the Caduceus program. There's no problem."

"I hope you're right, Greg, but we have to see how deep this goes. What does she know? Who has she spoken to? Greg, pull up Elaina's personnel file and get me her parents' phone number."

"Why?" Greg asked, but Carter had slipped deep into thought and Greg knew to just please his boss. "Here it is."

Carter dialed the number.

"Allo?" answered Mrs. Ruiz.

"Mrs. Ruiz, this is Carter Newton at Great Health Benefit."

"Oh, Mr. Newton. It's so good to hear from you."

"How are you doing?"

"Okay, I guess."

"The reason I called was about the memorial fund for Elaina."

"Oh, yes. That is so wonderful. She would be so proud."

"Well, we're planning a little dedication for the memorial fund, and we wanted to contact some of Elaina's friends and colleagues."

"Si, that would be nice, Mr. Newton."

"We have a list of all the people who attended the memorial service. Still, I'm sure there are others who weren't able to attend. Old friends, students, and colleagues. Maybe you can help us find these people."

"I'd be happy to."

"Has anyone contacted you since the service?"

"Oh, yes, so many people have called. Just last week a college friend came over to visit."

"How nice. Who was that?"

"Let's see. Jenny. Jenny Barrett. A sweet girl."

"She was a college friend?"

"Yes. They understand computers so well. I gave her Elaina's old computer. Maybe she can find someone who can use it. Do you want to invite her to the dedication?"

"Yes, I would," said Carter almost crushing the phone in anger, "And any other friends. If you would be so kind, I'd appreciate it if you would send me a list of the friends we don't know about. I know Elaina had a lot of friends."

"I'll do it, Mr. Newton." Mrs. Ruiz jotted down Carter's address and promised a list by the end of the week.

"Shit," said Carter for the fifth time in as many minutes. "Is this some kind of set up? Now she has Elaina's old computer."

"Carter, it was thoroughly erased, degaussed with a 1,000 watts. No data could have survived that electronic zapper. It would be like throwing a floppy disk in a microwave oven. I'm sure it was just a generous gesture," replied Hepman.

"Greg, this is a ten million-dollar project. Someone stole some code. You know damn well it was Elaina. Can you tell me that Jenny doesn't have it? Or worse, someone like Senator Gray!"

"Let's not panic. I swear, there was nothing left on that computer."

Carter pulled himself together. "Thomas Baldwin is scheduled to appear before Gray's committee this week. I don't want any new evidence suddenly appearing at that meeting. I don't trust Jenny. You said yourself that she was withholding her computer knowledge. I know you're good, Greg, but this is too spooky. Let's get a plan together and move her out of here."

Jenny's image was still on the monitor, now set in a contained, emotionless expression. Mable Jackson was seen beside her, speaking in a jovial fashion. Carter could have had Hepman turn on Jenny's microphone to eavesdrop on the conversation, but he had heard enough already.

What he didn't know was that Mable had seen Jenny's reaction to the case material, and came over to comfort her. With subtlety and innuendo, Mable let Jenny know that GHB had the power to monitor its employees, despite what Hepman had said. It was enough to pull Jenny back to composure.

Hepman's beeper went off as he and Carter considered their options. Fred Travis, one of his staff, flashed Hepman a 911, an emergency code used only for the highest priority system issues. "Great," he thought. "I don't need a system crash right now."

"This is Hepman," he told Fred on the phone. "What's up?"

"We've had an infection."

"What!" His bark was so loud that it startled Newton.

"We've got a virus or agent in the system. MOM picked up the trail twenty minutes ago. We haven't isolated it yet, but we've shut down the firewall so if it came from outside it can't escape to the Internet."

"How'd it get in?" asked Hepman.

"Don't know yet. Could have been a remote link or an inside job."

"You think it could be an agent?"

"Could be, but we've detected no damage yet," said Fred.

"Well, shut down the firewall gateway so it can't escape. I'll be right down."

"One thing you should know, Greg. It passed through your workstation."

A cold sweat erupted from Hepman. His eyes turned away from the questioning glare of Carter. "Get it. Now! I don't care if you have to shut down most of the system. Get it. I'll be right down."

Reluctantly, Hepman faced Newton. "Bad news. MOM's detected an invasion, probably an intelligent agent. We haven't found it yet, but we shut down its only escape route."

"What the hell is that?" demanded Carter.

"It's like a virus, only it doesn't destroy data. It usually just steals it."

"Great. What the hell is this one doing?"

"We're not sure, but it apparently went through my computer. Oh my God . . . that means it had access to MOM's source code."

Carter winced in pain, then recovered in anger. "Kill it, Greg. I don't care how, just kill it. And try to find out where it came from. I want blood."

"Sir, it had to be an inside job. That's the only way it could have singled out my computer."

"Still think she's innocent, Greg?" said Carter with heavy sarcasm, eyeing Jenny's image on the monitor.

"What do we do?"

"Can you monitor her phone line?"

"Sure."

"Including her home phone?"

"That's much harder."

"Can you get a list of who she calls from home on the caller ID?"

"Yeah, we have access to phone records."

"Good. Then all we have to do is silence her," said Carter.

"How?" Hepman paused. He was on dangerous ground, but

barreled on. "That isn't what happened to Elaina, is it?" he blurted, fearful of the depth of Newton's determination.

"No, no. Greg, there are many ways to buy silence. We have an entire psychological profile on Ms. Barrett. I'm sure I can find some weakness. Don't worry, I'll handle it personally. You go kill that bug."

Chapter 30

Carter watched Jenny navigate through the next sample case on her screen. He needed to know if she would betray the company. If he could hypnotize her and put a self-destruct mechanism in her, he'd do it, but that was science fiction. What was needed was science fact. He pulled her updated psychological profile. It had grown to twenty-eight pages, including the results of the subtle tests on loyalty, trust, intimidation, values, and conscience. With a click he rank-ordered Jenny's most important influences. Family headed the list, followed by friends, community, professional integrity, scientific truth, and generosity. Fear of her own death ranked very low. Fear of other people's death ranked higher, particularly the death of family members.

The safest action for data security was to kill her, but that might raise too much suspicion, Carter thought. It might prompt an investigation. There were some people in this company who were so sentimental that they couldn't appreciate the risk of tens of millions of dollars, or that Carter's career hinged on this project. He considered other options. Maybe an accident far away? Or maybe the right kind of threat?

Carter called his underworld assistant and explained what he needed guaranteed silence. They discussed the best way to approach this, given the circumstances and the personality involved.

"Can you do this?"

"Mr. Newton, that *is* my business."

"I mean, you can't damage her, unless there is no other way."

"That remains to be seen. I can assure you she will not be damaged, at least not in any obvious way. Often a tiny wound can be much more persuasive than a large one. You should see gang members in the emergency room after a rumble. Just minutes ago they were bravely facing off against an attacker with a knife, yet when a nurse approaches with a syringe, the young toughs cringe and cower. It is not the power of the weapon, Mr. Newton, it's the meaning of the threat. She will be handled well and your message will be delivered. Still, if I deem it necessary, she will need to disappear. Agreed?" asked the man.

Carter was assured that this was manageable and reluctantly agreed to let the man make the call. The assistant needed as much data as possible, so Carter e-mailed the entire profile to a secure and private web site. The money would be in the man's account soon after lunch. "Oh, and one other thing. Get that God damn computer."

"Her computer?" asked the man.

"Apparently she has the other woman's computer," said Carter.

"I though it was sanitized when I used that de-gassing device?"

"I was assured the degausser would do the job, but I can't afford any slip-ups. Take the damn machine."

"I will check my e-mail and bank account after lunch. Goodbye Mr. Newton."

***

Greg Hepman tore through MOM like a Stealth fighter. He pulled up every virus detection device he owned and had his staff systematically check through MOM's thousands of nooks and crannies. The virus-agent could be anywhere, on any hard drive, or stuck in some virtual memory location. If the agent was just a virus designed to destroy code, they could easily recover it from the system's many backup tapes. If it was an agent sent to steal code, it was much more serious. The cyber-creature would grow to a sizable package, even if the data were compressed.

Time was pressing hard on them to find it, for all data communications outside GHB had been suspended, to prevent the agent from escaping. At most they could keep it down for about three hours. Upper management would never authorize longer down time. It was costing close to $3000 per hour in lost productivity and job backlog.

Hepman launched four of his own intelligent agents, which flew through MOM like honey bees, stopping at specially chosen data "flowers" to check out their integrity. At 11:18 A.M. one of those bees disappeared. Something had killed it. It was last detected on a new and hardly used computer network server on the third floor, Server 12-23.

It was just one jump away from the firewall server. Hepman duplicated his bees and sent them en masse to Server 12-23, searching for anything out of compliance or bearing his workstation ID.

Waldo was found on hard drive E with his "pants" bulging from stored data. Somehow, the agent had commandeered three gigabytes of disk data space without being detected. Hepman was anxious to learn how it had done it, but first he had to secure the critter. He was fearful of a self-destruct feature should the agent be detected by the master program, so he first copied the hard disk to a writeable CD-ROM. This essentially created a "frozen" duplicate specimen to insure a replicable copy for autopsy, then he switched to a hard drive utility program and carefully lifted the agent and data off the machine, storing it on an auxiliary hard drive in his office. He then scrubbed all the data off the network server, and told his staff to restore it from backups and get it back on-line. Hepman also alerted Newton that the crisis was probably over.

In Hepman's opinion, Waldo was a work of art. It was beyond anything he had seen before. The little virus-agent was a tightly packed program, ingeniously invisible, and incredibly adaptable. It was a credit to MOM that she had detected it. A self-destruct mechanism was built in, and Waldo's code had begun to decompose just when Hepman captured it. Its signature name was there, and some of the protective devices, but, alas, some parts of the agent code had been lost.

When Hepman pulled up the executable code in his graphics program, the icon of Waldo stood on his screen, casually smiling in his funny clothes and knit hat. "What kind of ego would have dedicated code just for this silly icon?" he thought. Hepman carefully dissected the layers of programming code, looking for addresses and destinations. He wanted to find out who sent this creature, and he looked forward to sending its creator a message. Hepman hacked on the agent code until 8:30 that evening. He could piece together a few important parts. He wondered what the word "DWICK" meant.

"What does this memo mean, Mable?" asked Jenny, curious about the firewall alert. "What's going on?"

"I'm not sure, honey. Last time they shut down the firewall it was due to a security breach. A virus or something, but all I got was the same memo saying it would be down for a short time."

Jenny went cold. Waldo must have been found, or at least suspected. The plan was falling apart. If they discovered Waldo, they might trace it back to her. That was a criminal offense. People went to jail for hacking and planting viruses. What the hell was she doing in this nightmare?

With her brain half-fried with worry, Jenny nodded through the afternoon section meeting. Every time the conference room doors swung open, she expected Carter Newton to walk in with a police escort to cart her away. After the meeting, back at her desk, she received a notice that the firewall was functioning and outside communications had been restored. She didn't know whether that was good or bad. Another glitch? She didn't care. She just wanted to go home.

The workday ended uneventfully. No calls. No confrontations. Nothing. By the time she got home her tensions had reduced markedly. Mark would meet her for dinner at around 8 P.M. A cheese sandwich quelled her appetite. "Daisy, play messages," she commanded her computer. Her mother's voice emerged from the speakers, reporting all was still well. "Daisy, delete message. Daisy, check e-mail." The computer logged onto her Internet provider, but reported only junk mail. Nothing from Dwick. "Daisy, take note. Update resumé, contact a head hunter, and stick my head in a bucket of water. End note." Daisy unquestioningly recorded her Master's instructions.

Carter Newton was still at his desk at 7 P.M. He felt like there were too many irons in the fire, any of which could burn him in the ass. His phone rang, but Amanda had left for the day. The caller ID said it was Norm from legal.

"Yes, Norm."

"I just had an amazing conversation with a Mr. Jerry Stack of Mr. Bream's organization, the one who did the abortion mailing. Apparently they had requested more mailing lists from us and were informed that GHB will not honor their requests. He said he wanted to cut a deal with us. Part of it is his silence for more names."

"Okay. What's the other part?"

"This is a little over my head, but he said someone above me needs to hear this. It's about Senator Gray."

"Senator Gray?" said Carter with obvious excitement. "What is it?"

"He wouldn't tell me. He would only speak with a senior executive who was, ah . . . troubled by a Joint-Congressional Committee. I'm not sure what he was talking about, but I promised to pass it on."

"Thank you, Norm. I need to talk with this man."

"He said you would, and left this number. He'll be there until 10

P.M. running a television show, and tomorrow all day."

"I'll give Mr. Stack a call to see what he has. Can we trust him to keep silent if we give him more names? Or are we digging a bigger hole?"

"No way to know," said Norm."He seemed to grasp the issues. Said he wouldn't name his sources so they could trust him later. Seemed like a realistic position. Good luck, Mr. Newton."

Carter was desperate to get anything on Senator Gray. Thomas Baldwin was hounding him. MOM had come up empty on medical history. The man seemed clean.

Carter dialed the number.

"The Bream Children's Life Project," answered the cheerful female receptionist.

"This is Mr. Newton of Great Health Benefit. I'd like to speak with Mr. Stack."

"One moment please." He was on hold for about 90 seconds.

"Hello, Mr. Newton. I'm Jerry Stack. Thanks for getting back to me so promptly."

"One of my attorneys said he had an interesting conversation with you. I think he said you wanted more mailing lists."

"Yes, we do, and we have no interest in implicating you in our project. We've used lists from many sources, but GHB is one of the largest databases. There's no way any single source could be compromised."

"So you want an authorization to process your order?" Carter asked.

"Please. And as a show of good faith, and to get a certain Senator off our backs, I'd like to give you a piece of information that I'm sure you can use. I imagine GHB has some very influential lobbyists in DC who would know how to, let's say, make the Senator see reason?"

"I'd love to have such a piece of information. It sounds like it might serve both our interests."

"Believe me, it will. God works in many strange ways. I can only believe he sent this information to us to help our cause."

"Yes, God loves a winner." Unfortunately, that was the most holy statement Carter could conceive. "May I have the information?"

"Can I be assured that we will get our lists?" asked Jerry.

"Absolutely. I'll call it in tomorrow morning."

"Could you e-mail me right now with an authenticating signature, confirming your support for our request?"

These guys play hard, thought Carter. He quickly drafted a brief memo, inserted his authenticating virtual signature, and sent it to the e-mail address that Jerry specified. Ten seconds later he heard a "ding" over the phone from a computer, and Jerry confirmed receipt of the memo.

"Thank you. Now, if I can have a secure e-mail address, I'll send you the material you need. It is self explanatory, and you can verify it with your own data. In fact, it came from your machine."

"Please, tell me."

"Emily Schuster-Gray, the Senator's wife, had a late stage abortion three years ago."

"What! Are you sure?" exclaimed Carter.

"Absolutely. We have a confirmed pregnancy test in June and the record states she was ten weeks pregnant. Eleven weeks later she had a D & C for uterine fibroids. No baby appears. No miscarriage reported. Where did the baby go? I think the public has a right to know that the Senator who champions for their healthcare rights, and his wife, kill babies."

Carter was speechless for a moment. What a find. "How the hell did you dig this up when the press couldn't find it?" Nor us, he reflected.

"They don't have God on their side. Or a very special computer programmer."

"You say you're positive about this?"

"Mr. Newton, feel free to use your own resources to check it out. I hope the Senator will be informed of your findings quickly, so we can all get on with our tasks."

"Yes. I agree. I will act on this immediately. Thank you, Mr. Stack. May God be for you."

"Yes, may God be *with* you, Mr. Newton," offering a soft correction to the unsaved soul.

Jerry's package arrived in Carter's e-mail within ten minutes. He closely inspected the materials and called up what he could to confirm it with MOM. It was all there, with no mistakes or omissions. It must have taken a special mind to even think to put these two facts together, Carter thought. He should hire Bream's programmer tomorrow.

With the pride of a knight delivering the head of an enemy to the king, Carter Newton composed and transmitted a memo that would make Thomas Baldwin's day. It would make his month. Sometime tomorrow, Senator Donald Gray would receive the most devastating package of his life. He would, of course, protect his wife from the attacks of the press. This would effectively neutralize him so that no significant legislation would be coming out of his committee.

***

Mark met Jenny at TGI Fridays around 8 P.M. The place was crowded and noisy, with a mixture of dinner patrons and sports watchers. The couple was shown to a window seat that lay just on the border of the rowdy crowd. They ordered mostly from the sides menu. Mark had a draft Killian's Red, Jenny the house Chardonnay.

"Any word of that Waldo character?" asked Mark. "I want to slam GHB with the next installment."

"Not yet. Should be soon now, unless MOM found him. I feel like I'm quietly watching a battle between Dwick and Hepman, kind of a cyber-tennis match."

"I hinted to Witcomb about the material. He's excited."

"Let's take it a step at a time."

Mark ordered another round of drinks and made his pitch. "Speaking of taking steps. Jenny, being with you has made for one of my happiest times in years. I've been thinking a lot about what I want to do and who I want to do it with. I want to make it work again."

"Mark, I do too, but did it ever really work?" Jenny was not going down easy. She'd be a complete fool to take him back so quickly and repeat the pattern again. "How do I know you're willing to share your life now?"

"You don't, I admit it. I've just had some . . . experiences that seem to have sobered me up from the free and easy life. I think I can give a lot more now, but you may have to take a little less than you want. Jenny, you can get a bit controlling you know."

"So what happens if I get, in your opinion, controlling again. Is that your ticket out of here?"

"No, I want to break through that barrier. I realize it's something every couple has to do, wrestle around to see what we each have. I've looked in your eyes, Jenny Barrett. I've seen your soul. It has the things that I want. I've looked in the eyes of a lot of women. They don't have it."

"That sweet talk will definitely get you laid, but I'm not sure it will get you a commitment."

"A chance. That's all I want. I don't want to just get laid, although you are definitely in a world-class league. No, I want you to trust me with your life."

"You're getting too dramatic, Mark."

"Sorry, I'm not really good at this, but you know exactly what I'm saying.

The crowd at the bar had expanded and people were bumping against their table, trying to get a view of the overhead TV. Suddenly, a burly Asian man seemed to stumble and fall across the table, spilling their drinks. He appeared to be fairly drunk.

"Sorry, folks," he slurred. "Somebody pushed me." He rose from the table and teetered a bit. "Oh, shit, I spilled your drinks. Sorry 'bout that. Let me get you some more."

"That's okay," said Mark. "Go have a good time."

"No, I insist," he said to Jenny, looking her over with close scrutiny. His gaze lingered too long, making her uncomfortable. "Let's see, you're having a red beer. Killian's?"

"Yes," replied Mark.

"And the lady, white wine?"

"Chardonnay," she said with a polite smile.

"Coming right up," and he stumbled off toward the bar.

Jenny grabbed some napkins and began to dab up wine from her pants and blouse.

Mark noticed her drenched pants. "I didn't realize he got you so good. Want to leave?"

To their surprise, before she could answer him the man appeared with the drinks.

"Anything else you want, just let me know," he slurred.

They thanked him and sent him on his way.

"I'm okay, let's just finish these drinks and our conversation on neutral ground."

Mark took a long gulp of beer, then said, "What do I need to do to earn another chance?"

"I don't know. Just be there for me. It may take me awhile to get back on track. So much is happening. I can feel myself spinning out of control, and you know how I get when that happens. My dad almost died. I work for the evil empire. Elaina's death. Maybe we're both just grabbing on for dear life. I love you, in all the right and wrong ways. It's the wrong ways that keep messing us up. Now may not be the best time to make this call."

"You're too damn wise, woman." Mark said as he leaned back in his chair and almost fell over. "Wow, these beers are packing a wallop tonight. Okay, let's call a truce, with dating privileges. I will take it as an opportunity to prove myself to the fair cyber-princess. I will hang out, cook, clean, and talk to your computer." Mark leaned forward and nearly knocked over his beer.

"You look like you've had quite enough. Do you think you can drive?"

"Sure, I think so." He rose from his chair and seemed to use it as a brace to stand up.

"Look, I'd better do the driving. I'll scoot you back tomorrow to get your car."

"I'm sorry Jen. I didn't think I had that much to drink. Maybe I'm coming down with something?"

"Could be, with your wild and wooly lifestyle."

Chapter 31

Jenny poured Mark into her Camry and drove the few miles to her home. By the time she switched off the ignition, he was asleep. She was barely able to rouse him enough to get him into the condo. He fell on the sofa and was soon snoring in deep slumber.

"Mr. Party Animal," said Jenny with a grin. "You try to worm your way into my bed, then you fall asleep on the couch."

She smelled of beer and cigarettes. Removing her clothes didn't help, so she jumped into the shower. She was a little buzzed herself, and the warm water flowing over her body helped put bad thoughts out of her mind. "For tonight," she thought, "I'll just enjoy the romantic efforts of a very nice guy, who, unfortunately, is dead drunk on the couch."

The light in the bathroom flickered for a second, then again. Another power outage, she wondered. A second later she was plunged into darkness.

"Mark, are you messing around?" she called out loud.

Jenny could see through the frosted shower door that the place was dark. That meant stumbling to the kitchen to get a flashlight, maybe candlelight if Romeo would wake up.

She stepped out of the shower, grabbed the towel on the door and reached for the light switch just to check it. There was a swift movement in the darkness. Suddenly a hand covered her mouth with a vice-like grip while an arm encircled her chest.

"Don't make a sound or you're dead, Jenny," hissed a deep male voice.

Terror shot through her like an electric shock. A scream tried to emerge from her throat, but the passage was sealed shut. She clutched at the hand on her mouth and tried to break away, but the arm tightened on her chest like a python, crushing the breath from her body. Her mind went white with blinding terror. She pulled and pushed against the attacker, trying to bang against the wall or shower to wake up Mark, but the assailant easily anticipated her moves and the effort was futile. He was too powerful for her.

"Jenny," said the harsh voice in a low whisper, "we need to have a serious talk. Right now."

The man used her name again. The phrase somehow focused her mind for a second, helping her to get a grip on her panic. Why would he know her name? From the mailbox? Was he stalking her?

She stopped struggling and tried to regain her balance. Her heart was pounding in her ears, the copper taste of fear permeated her mouth. She was naked while in the grip of an attacker. She was blind in the darkness. What did he want? Was he armed? If he meant to kill her, wouldn't she already be dead? Unless he wanted to rape her. God, where was Mark? Shit, he's passed out on the couch. A scream began to emerge from her soul, but the firm hand clamped her mouth shut. Her ribs began to ache from his choking grasp. The restricted breathing was making her feel light-headed.

"I have a knife," said the man. Jenny felt a cold hard object slide across her stomach, then it was pressed against her face. It seemed to sear her flesh. She froze. Her eyes tried to make out a form in the mirror, but he was merely a dark shadow clamped onto a white, thin body. She shuddered to realize that she might be staring at her own death. Terror swept through her again like a cold wind, but she somehow held some composure.

"I don't want to hurt you, but I will if it is necessary. Your friend Mark can't help you now. I carried his very unconscious body to your bed so that we can talk in the living room. I need you to cooperate. I'm going to release you now and turn on the light. Can I trust that you will not scream?"

The hand cautiously slipped down to her chin. "Yes," she said in a tearful squeak.

"If you scream, this knife will be plunged into your throat."

He released her, stepped across the bathroom, and flicked on the light. He immediately looked familiar. He was Asian, Filipino. A very bland face of little distinction.

"You're the man at Friday's!" she exclaimed.

"Yes. Sorry for the simple con, but I needed Mark incapacitated for the evening. When I replaced your drinks, I added a special kicker to Mark's. Roofies are wonderful things. The date-rape drug. It seems to have knocked him out cold. We're here alone now."

Jenny pulled the towel around her for cover.

The man raised the knife in a threatening gesture. "No, Jenny. I want to see that beautiful body. Drop the towel."

Jenny stood there, paralyzed for a few seconds. The man drew his finger along the knife blade to reinforce his message. Jenny let the towel slip away. The man stepped up to her. Her shoulders were slumped, as if she were trying to curl up in a ball to hide. He grabbed her shoulders firmly and made her stand straight up, pressing her back against the cold wall. His hand slipped down and roughly grabbed her right breast. She began to cry and tremble. Jenny closed her eyes to help mute her reaction. She knew if she ran she would die, yet for an instant, that seemed a quicker, more desirable end.

"Look at me," he commanded.

Jenny opened her eyes and stared straight into his menacing black orbs. A thick, muscular arm was placed across her throat, pressing her against the wall. The man's other hand drifted down to her loins. He gently stroked her pubic hair, then she felt the cold steel of the knife blade against her labia. Her trembling became spasms of fear. "Please don't hurt me," she cried.

The knife came up to her left breast. The blade rotated so that the cutting edge rested on her protruding nipple. He drew the knife ever so slightly to the right, which sliced like a paper cut into the erect tissue. Jenny cried out in shock and jumped in pain, but the weight of the man trapped her in the corner. She watched as a single drop of blood wept from the small wound.

"Don't move," he commanded. With his forearm pressed firmly against her throat, he captured the drop of blood with the knife tip, then licked the red drop of life off the cold steel. Jenny was too numb to feel it. His dark eyes returned to hers, and a sinister smile spread across his face.

The man took a step back, leaving her standing alone. "Don't worry, Jenny, I won't hurt you too much." *I certainly can't leave any tissue damage,* he thought to himself. "I'm of an unusual sexual persuasion, one you'd probably rather not know about. However, part of my job here tonight is to make an impression on you. I find that's easy to do when you're standing naked and bleeding in front of a man with a knife. Go ahead, put on your robe now. Quietly. I need you to be quiet. I'll kill you if necessary. I think you believe me."

Jenny retrieved her robe from the hook on the door and put it on.

He motioned for her to leave the bathroom. Her mind was racing. If only she could run out the door. No, he was too quick. Her legs were like jelly. She had no weapon in the condo, which was probably just as well. The man guided her into the living room, then toward the sofa. Suddenly, she felt a sharp sting in her right buttock, and she let out a slight yelp, more of surprise than pain.

"Ouch," she whimpered. "What was that? What are you doing?" She turned to see him replacing the cap on a small syringe with a short needle, like those used by diabetics. He sat on the sofa near her work desk. She sat on the chair at the desk, facing him.

"What was that?" she screamed, rubbing the stinging spot on her buttock.

"Part of my persuasive plan," he replied. "You have violated a sacred trust, Jenny. A company trusted you and you betrayed them. Now you must pay the price." The man reached into his pocket and withdrew a small vial of yellow liquid. He handed it to her saying, "I've just given you a triple dose of this marvelous concoction."

Jenny turned the bottle upright in her fingers. It was labeled in red, "Live Virus—Highly Dangerous. Use Extreme Caution." Under that warning were words she could hardly believe: HIV—AIDS. Active Virus type C.

The coldness in his face highlighted his dark, empty eyes. They told her that this was true. In an instant her future had been taken away. Not an hour ago she was considering a life with the man she loved. Now she was hearing her death sentence.

The man saw it coming. Tears sprang from Jenny's eyes. She twisted and turned in the chair. The scream emerged from deep in her soul. He calmly rose and slipped behind her. Jenny was hardly aware of his movement, so lost in her own agony. His hand covered her mouth just as the terrible scream emerged. "Noooooo . . . "

Though muffled, the scream was long and agonizing. It was a mixture of sadness and rage that her life should be taken away so easily. These were large and evil forces that cared nothing for her. She screamed for the love she would miss, for the children she would never have, for the pain to her family. Evil surrounded her. It was even inside her now. She felt hopelessly lost.

The man held her in restraint for a few seconds even after the scream subsided. A quiet resignation came over her, a veil of denial at the reality. She dried her eyes on the sleeve of the robe, then stared vacantly at the man. He sat her down and returned to his seat across from her.

Before she could speak, the man held up a finger to quiet her. "I'm sorry, Jenny. It must be this way. You are now HIV–positive, although it won't show up on any test for another two months or so. In about six to twelve months you will develop AIDS symptoms, repeated infections, skin sores, possible lung problems. The size of this dose will cause it to act quickly. Doctors will try you on AZT and other drugs, but by that time you will be massively infected. Your immune system will be completely compromised and you will wither away. You've handled AIDS cases before. It's a horrible way to die. As you know, there is no antidote."

"Why?" she whispered, staring at the floor.

"Because you may hurt my client," the man answered.

"What client? What are you talking about?"

"In due time. You'll probably make an educated guess. But we need your cooperation."

"I haven't hurt anyone. I'm a nobody. What the hell is going on?" Talking seemed to give her strength, even though this seemed too unreal, like a wild nightmare.

"We need your cooperation."

"You come in here, infect me with AIDS, and want my cooperation?"

"Yes, it will all be explained, and I think you'll see the wisdom of the plan."

"Can I have some water or something?" she said, gaining some control through denial and emotional distancing, trying to understand what was going on.

"Certainly," said the man. "I'll get it, but please don't do anything stupid. Your friend Mark is in no condition to move. So if you run, I will be left with only him."

The man lumbered across the room toward the kitchen, keeping an eye on his hostage. He had a clear view from the kitchen sink. It took every ounce of what little willpower she had left to get a handle on her thoughts. What the hell was happening? Why would someone want to kill her? And so slowly? Who does this guy work for? Could this be about GHB and MOM? She wasn't thinking clearly. Where was help?

Jenny's panic rose to a level that triggered her instinctual coping reflexes, the ones she had learned as a river guide. She scanned the room for resources, but saw only Daisy. Could Daisy call the police? Yes, but he would hear the modem dialing, in fact, he'd hear her giving the instructions. The room was so quiet. What could Daisy do? Then she had an idea. At the very least she should record this conversation.

She glanced at the computer and saw that the monitor power was turned off. Good. If Daisy starts recording there would be no sign, except for the flashing disk access light under the desk. The man was heading back into the room.

Her mind raced. Commands. How to get Daisy to record. "I can't whisper it. Maybe I can shout it quickly." He held the glass with a paper towel and handed it to her. She drank it down. The flush of coolness helped to further clear her thoughts. "Think, girl!" she commanded herself. A sentence. The words. Work them together. Her mind worked with an idea for a second, then it just burst out of her. She was angry and scared, but had nothing to lose. Jenny compressed the fragments of her courage into an emotional wad and threw it out with all she had.

"Hey, I'm not just some dipsey DAISY. TAKE NOTE, mister, I don't have a clue what's going on," Jenny shouted.

The man was more taken aback by the force of her comment than its awkward sentence structure. Out of the corner of her eye Jenny saw Daisy's hard drive light up. The computer only heard the commands "DAISY" and "TAKE NOTE," which launched the memo program. Daisy could probably record a half-hour of conversation before she ran out of disk space. Now for some answers.

"I see you've regained some composure, Jenny. Good. I need you to be thinking clearly."

"Can I know what the hell this is about?"

"Yes, you must know. I will try to keep it simple. My employer needs your cooperation in the matter of their new computer program. It seems you have some sensitive material that could fall into the wrong hands. It would cost the company tens of millions, maybe hundreds of millions of dollars. That's a steep price to pay. You might be the only one with this sensitive information, so we need to insure your silence."

"Can't you just buy me out? Isn't that the traditional way of the business world?"

"Yes, with certain personalities. However, a computer, MOM I think it's called, did a thorough profile of you and found that you're plagued by a strong social conscience. Money just doesn't do much for you. At least, it doesn't buy the security we need."

"So you're going to kill me slowly? What would keep me from talking to the police if I'm going to die anyway? What sense does that make?"

"None at all. You're absolutely right, Jenny. All of this is for show. I haven't given you AIDS, Jenny. That was another ruse. It was only saline. You should live a long and happy life, as long as you cooperate."

Disbelief spread across her face.

"Yes, it's true, but this is not a pointless gesture. I needed you to feel the real threat of death, particularly delivered in such a simple way. A casual stick out of nowhere. The reason we are here, the reason I have impressed you with terror, is to demonstrate our power. You needed to feel the very real fear, to be pushed around by forces you couldn't understand. You needed to know that we can strike at will."

"I believe you," she assured him.

"Good. Because if you ever collaborate with the enemies of GHB, including Senator Gray, a syringe containing real AIDS virus will be inserted . . . into your brother, David."

"What! What does he have to do with this?"

"Absolutely nothing, except to guarantee your silence. We needed to show you that we mean business. We can and will infect your brother as easily as we almost did you. Maybe even easier. He would feel the same sharp sting while walking down the street. A man with an umbrella or cane would apologize for his carelessness and disappear into the crowd. Within two years your brother would be dead from a painful and merciless disease. All the fear and rage you just experienced would be his. For real."

"I get the picture."

"Good."

"May I ask, why didn't you just kill me?" Jenny asked.

"Too messy. Too many questions. Apparently there was a similar problem in January. That poor girl died. I believe you're in a related job position. Wouldn't do to have two psychologists die in the same job within the year. Why, OSHA would be all over them, plus the FBI. This is much better. Everyone gets to go on living, as long as you cooperate."

He killed Elaina! They murdered her in the hospital. The revelation produced a torrent of conflicted feelings. This man was a killer, a hit man for GHB! Yet she was still alive. He was talking to her. He could have killed her and Mark instantly if that was his plan.

As she continued to scrutinize the menacing figure, Jenny felt oddly comforted by his words. Though she was still under threat, it was something she could control. After staring death in the face, it was a great relief to feel in control of something. There was no way to know if he was lying, but she needed to believe that he wasn't. Another peek towards the desk confirmed that Daisy's hard disk light continued to blink.

"I must collect some items for my employer. Apparently you have a copy of sensitive data on a computer. I must have that as well as any backup tapes." The man looked at Jenny's computer and her heart sank. All would be lost now, she thought.

The man rose and turned to her desk. He looked at the monitor on top of the desk and then scrutinized the machine standing on the floor. Elaina's machine. It still had cables attached to it. He began detaching them and hoisted the metal box and placed it on the desk. He was taking the wrong computer.

"Can I keep my monitor?" she asked, in part to test his knowledge.

"Monitor? Oh that. Yeah, we only need the CPO," said the hit man, misstating the letters for "CPU." "Where do you store your backup tapes?"

"I'll get them for you." Jenny walked to the fireproof safe and retrieved the tapes. The man followed her and firmly pushed her aside after she opened it. He rummaged around, examining other tapes and disks with innocuous labels. He removed the tape with the name "Elaina" scrawled on the label. He seemed satisfied that all was secure and returned to the desk. He didn't notice anything wrong, so he scooped up the computer box under his arm.

"What happens now?" asked Jenny.

"I believe you will have a meeting with your superiors, who will have my report regarding your probable cooperation. You should expect a small severance package and a good recommendation for your next job. Still, don't let my casual demeanor fool you. Your brother will die a most horrible death if you break your word, the man warned."

"I understand. What if it gets out anyway. What if someone else blows the whistle. How will you know it's not me?"

"We'll make our best guess. We could be wrong, but hopefully, all of this will be behind us. If you know of anyone else who might blow the whistle, you would be wise to let your superiors know. It would be a tragedy to lose your brother to a mistake."

Jenny politely opened the door for the man, who lumbered through with the machine under his arm. She restrained herself from saying "thank you" in appreciation for her life. "I hope I never have to see you again," she said.

"Trust me. You never will. Even if I'm paid to visit you again, you will not see me. There will be no point to further talk."

Jenny closed the door as the man was swallowed up in the darkness. She threw the deadbolt and turned her back to the door. Her hands were trembling. A cold feeling penetrated to her very soul. She collapsed on the floor and cried. The crisis was over, her defenses were lowered, and the fear rushed in. She quietly wept and trembled, agonizing over what to do.

A faint beep brought her back to the present. Daisy was announcing that the hard disk was full. Jenny had forgotten the recording of the conversation. She sat at the keyboard and called up the memo file. It took up 834 megabytes of space. God knows when the computer stopped recording, and she couldn't bear to listen to it now. "Discipline, girl," she told herself. "Don't do anything stupid." However, knowing what was stupid in this nightmare was difficult.

Jenny highlighted the enormous voice file and sent it to the Jaz drive, which still contained the copy of Elaina's computer files. For four minutes she watched an animated icon of papers flying into a folder across the screen, representing the digital copying process, and then it was done.

Another impulse from Jenny's rational side pushed through, the safety of redundancy. Jenny pulled open a drawer and withdrew two more Jaz disks. Ten minutes later she had three more copies of the threatening conversation. Then she withdrew a blank backup tape and inserted it into her machine. She launched the program to back up the voice file and Elaina's computer data. The tape whirled as she walked out of the room.

"Daisy, Internet," she commanded. The machine responded in half-time because of the many tasks it was doing simultaneously. Jenny e-mailed her brother to call her as soon as possible. She also left a voice mail at his company.

Jenny wanted to take another shower, to wash off the filth and grime of the last hour, but as she looked at the bathroom door, the fears of sudden darkness came rushing in. For all the terror and pain, there were no physical marks on her body. Her nipple had only a faint reddened line from the shallow cut, while the bump on her hip could easily be a mosquito bite. No evidence of the terrorism, yet she felt completely violated.

She cleaned up the condo, put on her night shirt, and lay next to Mark in bed. His breathing was slow and regular. She nudged him a few times to see if he would awaken, but he was still out cold. Jenny tossed and turned for a while, then stripped a blanket from the bed and went into the living room, curling up on the couch. Sometime around 4:00 A.M. exhaustion set in and she mercifully fell asleep.

***

The tour bus made the trip from Boise to Seattle in twenty-four hours. Betsy Waller had not focused on anything but her plan. She had no idea where she was going to stay, but she figured Crandall Bream would take care of her. Stepping off the bus at the station, she picked up her simple suitcase and waddled to a phone booth. She dialed the phone number on Crandall Bream's letterhead.

"The Bream Children's Life Project," answered a female voice.

"Hi. I got the Breaming letter, I want to come talk with him and thank him for my baby."

"I'm not sure I understand," said the voice. "Did you have an abortion?"

"Yeah, a time ago. I'm gots a baby in me now. Mr. Bream been to the cuddly coo."

"Just a moment, please." Betsy was placed on hold while the receptionist paged Jerry and filled him in on the call, then he took over.

"Madam, my name is Jerry Stack, Mr. Bream's associate. How are you?"

"Very happy as hamming horner. I'm as big as a house. I want to give my money and show thanks to the Crandall Bream."

"You say you're pregnant," asked Jerry.

"Surely am, almost 48 months now."

"For eight months," said Jerry, who was also trying to communicate with the receptionist about the show schedule. "Well, you're welcome to come to our ministry any evening. Mr. Bream has an evangelical television show every day at 7:00 P.M. at the Metro Studios. You're welcome to come down and give him your pledge. I think it would be a grand gesture for a mother-to-be to take such an honorable action. Mr. Bream would be very pleased. Where are you staying?"

Betsy looked around the phone booth. "By the bus station."

"That's quite close by. Would you like me to send someone to pick you up?"

"That would be nicely godly."

"It's 3:30 now. Would you like to come tonight?"

"I'd love to. Canly Come, I'd love to."

Jerry didn't quite catch the phrase, but he was so excited about the public relations coup he was about to secure that he let it pass. A pregnant woman making a contribution for her past sins. How perfect. "Where shall we meet you?"

"Bus station. I'm the big pregnant flower dress with pockery pinehepples."

Jerry laughed, then said, "Fine. We'll see you at about 6:30?"

Betsy exited the phone booth, found a quiet place under a tree, and sat on her suitcase. A distinct biting odor emanating from the suitcase, which she would have to mask with something or they would discover her plan. Lots of perfume, maybe. And wash really good.

Chapter 32

Mark awoke at 7:15 A.M. with a huge hangover. Blurry-eyed, he stumbled into the bathroom to relieve himself and splash water on his scruffy face. He found Jenny curled up on the sofa. It did not appear that she had a peaceful sleep. He sat next to her and gently shook her awake. Jenny's eyes flew open with a start and she bolted upright, startling Mark. Was last night a dream? Did a strange man really deliver that terrible message? Her eyes fell on her desk. Elaina's computer was gone. It had been real.

"You okay, babe?" asked Mark.

"I don't know. I feel like something terrible is happening. Mark . . ." She had to tell Mark to cancel his story in the <u>Chronicle</u>.

"Jesus, I really got smashed last night. I'm sorry. Guess I blew the evening."

"Mark, ah . . .a man was in here last night."

"What?"

"Hear me out. You've got to believe me. You were drugged last night. At Friday's. That Filipino man who spilled our drinks. He slipped you some drugs. Roofies, I think. You passed out and he came after me. He didn't touch me, but he said I can't speak with anyone about GHB. Not Senator Gray, not anyone. If I do, they'll kill my brother David."

Mark sat in utter astonishment. "Are you sure this happened? It's not a dream?"

She began trembling as she nodded toward her desk. "He took Elaina's computer."

Mark saw that the machine was gone. He exploded in worry and frustration. "This all happened and I was out for the count. Shit. Are you okay? God damn it, I let you down completely. What an asshole I am! Did he touch you? Hurt you? Oh, Jenny." Mark grabbed her and held her close. Jenny cried in his arms. His protection, even after the fact, made her feel more secure.

"Mark, we had no idea. You were targeted, just as I was. There was no real harm done. He said they have targeted my brother because it's the best way to insure my silence. As far as I'm concerned, they have it."

"Can you trust a man like that?"

"Do I have a choice? He pretty much admitted that they murdered Elaina."

"Holy shit! Jenny, let's get you out of here."

"Mark, we can't just run. They said I'm okay as long as I don't talk. I'm done talking."

"Jenny, lots of people are investigating GHB. My first story is out this week. What if someone else spills the beans? They might kill you and your brother."

"I know. Mark, what can I do?"

"Maybe Senator Gray can help," Mark suggested.

"They said talking to Gray will kill my brother."

"Maybe I can make some arrangements. Like a witness protection thing."

"Mark, I don't have very much evidence of anything. I've got nothing to sell. The bad guys won. All I want to do is walk away. I'm not here to save the world."

The phone rang. It was 7:45 A.M. Jenny picked it up, "Hello?"

"Hi, Jenny. This is Amanda, Carter's secretary. He's scheduled a vital appointment at 9:30 A.M. today in his office. Just you. I need to confirm that you can make it."

Jenny reeled in dizziness and sat on the chair. The final showdown, she thought. I'm to be quietly removed. Clear out your desk. Then to Amanda she said, "Yes, I'll be there." She hung up without a goodbye.

"Jenny, I feel like shit. I talk all this love and commitment stuff, then I let you down."

"Mark, shush," she said, putting a finger to his lips. "No one can take away the last few days with you. I want to be with you. I need you more than ever. You can't leave me now."

"Never."

"You talk with Senator Gray, Mark. See what he can do. Explain what happened, but I'm not risking my brother."

Time was slipping by, so they showered, dressed, and left, both lost in their own thoughts and fears.

Jenny stopped at the door. "Dwick!" she thought. "Waldo is still in MOM. I gotta stop this." Jenny dashed across the room, yelling at her computer. "Daisy, Internet, Dwick."

Daisy ran the log-on routines and routed the browser to Dwick's web site.

"Error. DNS server not found. URL site doesn't exist," was reported on the screen.

"What?" Jenny sat at the keyboard and manually entered the web site address. Same error message. She tried sending an e-mail to Dwick's address. "Address not found." She tried some old backup addresses. None worked. Dwick had dropped off the Net. Had GHB found him? Did he close shop and run? Was he dead? Had Waldo returned? Was the little agent dead or alive? Panic stirred in her gut, hovering just below the surface. She was losing control.

Jenny ran to the bathroom and took a tranquilizer, aprazolam. Then she took a second. She returned through the living room headed for the front door, but spied the Jaz drive. She popped out the disk with the copy of Elaina's computer and the hitman conversation, labeled it "Elaina," followed by a dividing horizontal line, then "Hitman." She then tucked it in her personal calendar.

Her home no longer felt secure. Opening her desk drawer, she put the other Jaz drive disks into special mailers, addressing one to her parents' home and one to Mark's. Pulling out the new backup tape of Elaina's computer, she stuffed it in an envelope.

Jenny looked at Daisy and saw a sitting duck. The bad guys may realize their mistake and come back. She couldn't lug Daisy around with her. She needed to dump Daisy's data in a safe place. Oregon. Yeah. Jenny called her mother.

"Mom?"

"Hi honey. I was going to call you today."

"I can't talk. Gotta get to work. Mom, could you do me a favor and turn on David's computer and modem?"

"Sure, honey. Right now?"

"Yes, I'll wait."

A three minute pause, then her mother was back.

"Up and running."

"Thanks. Look, I'm going to upload a giant program to his computer. It may take all day, so don't disturb it, okay."

"No problem. By the way, the medical staff wants to kick your grouchy father out of the hospital. He may be home tomorrow."

"Mom, that's great. I'll talk with you tonight, and could you try and find out where David is? Tell him I need to speak with him tonight."

"Will do. Talk with you soon."

Jenny instructed her computer, "Daisy, dial David." Daisy obeyed, detected the squawking of David's computer modem and established a link. Jenny then took control of his machine. She cleared all the files off his "D" drive and then told Daisy to compress and copy every file on her system to David's system. Data bits started flying. It would probably take up to four hours to complete the task. But there would be a copy of her computer in Oregon. Somehow, Grants Pass still felt safe.

On the way to her car she dropped the mailers in the condo mailbox and put the backup disk in her own mailbox, just to have it out of the apartment. Redundancy gave her comfort and a sense of control.

***

Joyce received a hand-delivered flat manila mailer envelope from a delivery man that morning. Although it was stamped "Eyes Only" for Senator Gray, she had no idea where it came from or what it contained, yet somehow it reeked of evil. She summoned an office courier and had the package run down to the mail office for a quick X-ray scan, just to be safe. Upon its return she broke the seal and skimmed the contents, which contained only a letter and two copied newspaper clippings. Her mouth dropped open as she read. She hadn't made it halfway through the first page when she quickly resealed the package. She knew life in Washington could be vicious, but this was obscene.

She buzzed Donald Gray. "Senator, I have an urgent package that you must see immediately. Could you send Ella out here to watch the desk?"

"Yes, Joyce," replied Gray. He knew his secretary was not prone to petty interruptions. Turning to the aide he said, "Ella, be a dear and watch the front desk for a few minutes."

Joyce appeared pale and sickly as she entered with the package. "Donald, I'm so sorry to give this to you."

The use of his first name during business hours suggested this was a personal matter. He accepted the package, withdrew the contents, and watched his life disintegrate in the heinous and threatening language of the cover letter. Someone had found out about Emily's abortion! He was swept with nausea and fear.

The language of the letter described enough details to convey that the author had solid evidence of his wife's tragic pregnancy and its termination. In included a condescending reference to "protecting" his wife from public scandal and embarrassment, but only in exchange for important concessions from the Joint Committee. He was to dance to their tune or face the grisly music, and he was forbidden from quitting. If Senator Gray tried to withdraw from the committee, the author said they would immediately release the materials to the public. Donald was to stay and comply with their demands, or they would destroy his life. The letter ended with a prayer for the couple's salvation.

The two clippings were newspaper articles describing the "cover stories" of Emily's absence from the social scene due to some unknown illness. There was enough material here to capture the national media attention for a week. If the scandal broke, the Conservatives would undoubtedly try to boot him from the chair, if not the committee. He would lose reelection. Worst of all, Emily could be scarred even more deeply from this past tragedy. His children would be dragged into this as well. Senator Gray started to tremble with fear and rage.

Donald sensed a comforting hand on his back and looked up to see Joyce weeping as she read over his shoulder. He was about to become a puppet, inextricably attached to strings that would make him dance to a fiendish piper. There seemed to be no escape.

Emily Schuster-Gray felt a deep shame blow through her like a cyclone. She sat in an upholstered winged chair in their Washington apartment, across from Donald, who sat on the bed. The letter bobbed up and down in her hand as her breathing became short, almost panting. Of all the feelings that had coursed through her since the abortion of their poor fetus, shame had never been one of them. Nevertheless, now she looked at this letter from the perspective of her enemies, from the callous press, and from the public's reaction to her husband.

Donald rose from the bed, sat on the arm of her chair, and held her tight. "I'm sorry I've brought this to you," he said. How odd, she thought, that he should be apologizing to her. Was this her fault? Was it anybody's fault? Had there ever been another choice in this sad chapter of their lives?

She took his hand and kissed it gently. "What do you want to do? You've worked so hard and for so long. It can't all be just gone now. There has got to be options." Her eyes pleaded with him to find an answer.

"Emily, this is a savage business. We knew that coming in. I won't let it destroy us, or our family."

"I won't let you sell yourself out. That isn't the man I married, and it's not the father of my children."

"Emily, they hold all the cards, and they're threatening to show them to everyone. If I fight or if I leave, they'll crucify us, but we can acquiesce. Big deal. So they won this round. There are plenty more battles to fight. Hey, this won't be the first do-nothing committee in Washington."

A fire was lit in her eyes. "I won't let you talk like that. This is not what we're about. You've never been bullied before. Now you let them, just to protect me. I won't stand for it."

"Honey, it's just a stupid committee. We can't destroy our lives over it. Hell, nobody wants this committee to produce anything anyway. There will be other committees, better opportunities."

"Don't lie to me, Donald. Is that how infected you are with this Washington disease? You can't even talk truth to me. There are no more committees. You're dead if you run again. This secret is sitting in the hands of the enemy. You know what that means. Donald, I've stood by you through all of your career. I've never caught you in a lie. Please don't start now. We can do this together."

"I don't know how, without hurting you."

Emily's eyes cleared of her pain. Her brow furrowed in a look of determination. She sat up straight and cradled her husband's face. "Then let them try to hurt me."

"What do you mean?"

"They only have power if we give it to them. They're counting on you protecting me above all else. They're confident you won't even mention it to me. They probably expect you'll just roll over and fade away, giving them the farm as you leave. But we can control this. We can take the initiative."

"Emily, don't," begged Donald.

"I'm not going to be bullied by these assholes. I'm not ashamed of what we did, and no two-bit God Squad extortionist is going to banish me to the dark corners of the world."

"Emily, you don't know what they'll do to you. The press can be merciless. You'll be painted as a murderess, a child killer, a woman with no soul."

"So what else is new? Look at the crap I've read about you. You're still here. The kids and I still love you. You got reelected."

"This is different."

"For the last time, stop bullshitting me, Donald. It is not different.

We can take control of this. I will not go down the drain like the rest of the greasy slime of Washington."

"What are you going to do?"

"I'm going to disarm them. Take away their big stick. I'm going to go public."

Donald had seen that look in her eyes before. It was not negotiable. His wife had set her course. Direct confrontation was futile. At best he could buy some time. At worst, she would roll over him like a train. He had little with which to negotiate. It seemed everyone had cards but him. His arms fell around her shoulders and he sighed in resignation. His wife would take a bullet, just so that he would be free.

***

Jenny arrived at work at 8:45 A.M. The building looked sinister in its cold steel and glass. While exiting the car she remembered the Jaz disk in her calendar. For security, she removed it and placed it in the glove compartment. She didn't want to enter the building. She thought of the Jews entering a concentration camp, not certain if a doorway held life or death. Yet the atmosphere inside the glass cube was normal and no one seemed to pay her much attention. Mable Jackson was not at her station. Jenny had hoped to see a friendly face.

The computer lay still on her desk, asleep. She fired it up to open a window into the soul of MOM, watching the boot-up routine with dispassionate interest. MOM told her that she had e-mail. One message was from Carter about the meeting this morning. The next was from Greg Hepman. Under subject, it just said, "Sorry for your loss." She opened the mail message and her breathing stopped. Death was on her screen. Comical, absurd, egomaniacal death, a fatal slash at any last ray of hope for redemption.

In the center of her screen lay Waldo, face down, drained of color, a large dagger protruding from his back. An "X" covered each eye, the cartoon symbol of death. Dwick's intelligent agent had been found and destroyed. That Waldo appeared on her screen indicated that Hepman and Newton knew of her involvement. She could not suffer any more blows today. GHB had won, completely. She only hoped that Dwick was safe and not in jail under charges of data theft.

From his office, Carter Newton and Greg Hepman scrutinized Jenny's reactions on the video screen. The bio-graphs told the tale, Jenny knew about Waldo. She was a party to the breach. They would get to the bottom of this very soon. "Look at her sweat," said Hepman.

"I knew she was smart. Too smart, but not smart enough for MOM."

"You have to admit, Greg. She had you going, just like Elaina. You bought it hook, line, and sinker. You're a sucker."

Hepman took offense at the comment, but didn't challenge his boss. Besides, there she was, squirming like a hooked worm. "Don't screw with the big boys, honey," he thought to himself. Then to Carter he said, "I guess I'm surprised she came in today. She must not have known we were on to her."

"She knows, but she has nowhere to go," said Carter with a smirk.

The bio-graphs of Jenny slowly settled down, turning from elongated red bars of anxiety to short blue stumps of resignation. To contain her dread and despondency, Jenny had been forced to mentally shut down her emotions, becoming cold, detached, and momentarily indifferent. She was exhausted. There was no fight left in her. She could only think of putting one foot in front of another and walking away.

For half an hour she watched the logo of GHB bounce around her screen as MOM waited for instructions. There were none to give. Jenny reviewed the events that had brought her to this juncture. It all seemed so impossible. Just a few weeks ago she knew who she was and where she was going. Now, she was about to walk into the office of a powerful and angry man, to hear what her future would be. Would the police be there? Would she ever work in the field again? She had seen GHB destroy professional careers with the click of a mouse. What would they do to her?

At 9:25 A.M. Jenny reluctantly rose from her chair and mechanically walked to the elevator. She pressed the call button for the elevator. She crossed the threshold and pressed the key for the fifth floor, just under the key for the seventh floor penthouse. For a brief instant, a vision of her sailing off the roof of GHB trampled through her mind. The elevator doors closed, and she ascended up to hell.

Amanda greeted Jenny in an overly friendly way. The secretary sprang up and hustled her into Carter's office, where Jenny found him finishing a telephone call. It was just the two of them. He beckoned her to sit in a chair beside his desk, next to his computer monitor. She saw that her personnel file was on the screen. The cursor was flashing in the box next to one labeled "hire date." It was ready to receive the "termination date."

". . . and what was that final number?" Carter said to the caller. It was Hepman, reporting on Jenny's phone activity. He had cross referenced the dialed numbers with a national reverse phone directory, where you can type in a number and find out who it belongs to. Senator Gray's name had popped up. Carter hung up the phone.

"Jenny, how are you doing?" asked Carter, stretching back in his executive chair and openly admiring her figure. "I hope you slept well last night," he teased with a cruel grin.

"I'm fine. What do you want to do?" she asked with a stone face.

"What do I want to do? Sorry, there are rules against what I want to do. But then, rules don't seem to mean much to you. I was wondering if you had recently had any visions or premonitions about how you can best serve this company. As I understand it, MOM had a funny little visitor, who was filling his pockets full of proprietary things. I think you know something about that, don't you?"

"A little. Not very much," she replied, staring at his shoes.

"I think you know a lot about it. Fortunately, we stopped it. Your little elf is dead, as you saw. The integrity of MOM is assured. We're back on-line and in full operation. I think you owe us an apology."

"Is that what you want?" asked Jenny.

"Oh yes. That, and a whole lot more. I was just about to fire you, when I realized how valuable you could be. I think you have many things you can contribute to this company, Jenny."

"I'm not sure what you mean."

"You're a beautiful, smart woman who has possibly violated some very important laws. People have lost their professional licenses over less. You don't seem to get it, Jenny. Healthcare is now a business, an industry. The terrible irony is that you professionals carry all the liability and business carries all the profit. Time to grow up, Ms. Barrett. You need a mentor, a protector, someone to show you the right way to climb the career ladder."

Carter was toying with her. "Was he seriously planning on keeping her around?" she wondered. Her skin crawled at the way he was trying to manipulate her.

"I don't see why you were so quick to betray us, Jenny. We're just like any other company, trying to make a buck. You could do a lot worse."

She couldn't contain herself. "Mr. Newton, this company is the incarnation of evil. It is rotten to the core. You have incredible resources to do good, yet you choose to do nothing but hurt and kill people, and shovel profits. This is not what I plan to do with my life. I want out."

Carter burst into a rolling, menacing laugh. "Jenny, you are a hoot. You come in here, try to sell us down the river, steal our company secrets, and then you get all high and mighty."

Carter suddenly pushed his face within an inch of hers. "You'll do exactly what I say you'll do. You're in big trouble, girl. You've already received the message. Don't fuck with us," he hissed. "Your actions have threatened tens of millions of dollars for this company. You thought you were smart enough to get in and out. You even spoke with the honorable Senator Gray, as I understand it. Well I'm sorry to report, he won't be able to help you now. He won't be able to help himself. You are on your own."

At the mention of Senator Gray's name, Jenny blanched white in fear. In the back of her mind she had placed a small beacon of light at the end of this long tunnel. It had been Senator Gray, and now they snuffed it out. She began to weep.

Carter's face was still inches from hers. He smelled her perfume, looked longingly at her silky, brown hair tossed around an exquisitely chiseled ear. A red rash of fear blotted her neck and shoulders. This was going to be grand, he thought. Carter stood up, grabbed a box of tissues and held it out to her. Jenny pulled out three and blotted her eyes. She couldn't look at him, for she felt so weak, and that would only satisfy this monster. Her eyes fixed on the credenza behind his desk.

Her eye caught a curious, fleeting movement in the corner of his computer monitor. She quickly glanced over at the screen, but saw nothing except her personnel folder, the cursor still flashing on "termination date." Just as she was about to look away, an orange cursor, no it was a ball, bounced along the top of the document. Jenny squinted to see what this curious thing was, but it disappeared. "Must be a screen saver," she thought. A little hand appeared from behind the document, then a leg. Another ball appeared in the upper right screen. It commanded her complete attention, and Carter turned to look at what was stealing his thunder.

Finally, Waldo walked full form through the screen. The comical character then seemed to jump to another window. Two Waldos entered from the right, and four more crawled over the top. Within seconds eight Waldos were running around the screen. Some had skinny pants, while others had bulging pockets. Jenny could hear Amanda laughing in the waiting room. Carter picked up his intercom.

"Amanda, what's going on?"

'I don't know, Mr. Newton. They're everywhere. Those funny little characters are crawling over everyone's computers. We can't get any work done, they're too funny."

"They're everywhere?" He didn't wait for a reply, hanging up and dialing Hepman. Busy. He tried again. Busy. He dialed the operator and had her break into Hepman's line.

"Greg, what the hell's going on?" Carter demanded.

"We're infected. Waldo has metastasized. He's multiplying exponentially, running all over the computer. We're trying to stop the flow without crashing the system."

As if struck by a sword, Carter Newton suddenly saw the grand purpose in this. "Greg, did you shut down the firewall? Is there still access to the Internet?"

"Shit, I forgot all about that. You're right, these guys could be headed right out of here. Let me check."

Torturous seconds ticked by as Carter's screen became a blurred madhouse of orange, white, and blue characters running around.

"Jesus Christ! There's a flood of data flowing out the firewall gateway onto the Internet. It's a mob scene. This virus is carrying away our programs!" shouted Hepman.

While hanging on the phone, Carter heard Hepman yelling at his staff, "Pull the fucking plug. I don't give a shit. Pull the plug. Shut the entire service down. Fuck the protocol. Hit the switches. Yes, all of them. I don't care, pull the fucking plug out of the wall. Why is this server still on-line. . ."

Carter hung up on the madness. He could no longer see the document on his screen, only a churning cauldron of three primary colors. The agent-virus completely overran MOM. Nothing would function.

The legions of Waldos spilled onto the Internet and spread like a bloodstain on a sheet. Thousands of them were destined for prearranged sites, pockets full of data, for collection by Dwick and his cronies, and thousands more were randomly spewed around the Internet, carrying packets of MOM code all over the globe.

Tracing their routes was impossible, for at each stop they would duplicate again. The infrastructure of the Internet sagged under the load, slowing communications for nearly two hours. The proprietary wall of GHB had crumbled. Their secrets were soon to become common knowledge, traded like jokes or Doom strategies in on-line chat groups.

Carter turned ashen white. This had happened under his watch. He was viewing the end of his career. This woman had caused his ruin. Hate filled his heart. He wanted to hurt her, badly. Maybe he should make the call now, right in front of her.

Jenny rose from her chair. She was grinning. Her cheeks were flushed with the color of life. She looked at the visual melee on the screen, and then turned to face Carter.

"You're history Jenny," he said with a menacing scowl.

"Fuck you, Carter. I'm out of here." At the office door she stopped to face him. "Oh, and the threat your errand boy delivered last night. I have it all on tape. I think you need a little mentoring in this type of business. You should definitely hire a less talkative hitman. See you in Hell," she said, slipping through the door, leaving the man to a glorious agony.

Carter Newton saw his career being chewed up by a cartoon ebola virus. It almost turned his own entrails to liquid. There would be no recovery from this nightmare. His future was in ruins. He had lost the company's crown jewels. That self-righteous bitch had done this. He picked up the phone and dialed. Into the receiver he said one simple line.

"Do her now!"

Chapter 33

At 6:30 P.M. Betsy was prepared for the arrival of the van taking her to Crandall Bream. She had dressed in her prettiest outfit, which looked like all of her other outfits. The billowy skirt and high lacy neckline allowed her to conceal the surprise perfectly. Her stomach was so immense from the extra baggage that she looked as if she was going to deliver at any moment. Her new "breasts" hung heavy in an oversized brassiere, but swayed naturally. She doused herself with cheap perfume stolen from a local K-Mart. Jerry was stunned at her size when she lumbered up to the car.

"Ms. Waller?"

"Hi. I'm the purgley one. Surprised how big I am?" asked Betsy.

"Looks like you're carrying twins."

"More like four, five, or six," she said with a smile.

Jerry popped out to hold the door open and help Betsy up the steps of the van. There was something peculiar about her, but he couldn't place what it was. Her stride? Her immense body? A slightly smeared smile? He wasn't sure. The fumes from the bus terminal were overwhelming. Jerry slapped on her seatbelt and climbed into the driver's seat.

"I've got to make a quick stop, but the station is only five minutes away. You comfortable, Miss?"

"Yes, I am, thank ya."

"Where's your husband?"

"He'll be along soon, I'm certain he's moving for me now."

"Well, he's a mighty lucky fellow to have a woman like you."

Jerry pulled into a service station and topped off the gas tank. As he re-entered the cab, the acrid smell of gasoline seemed to permeate the interior. He smelled his hands, which stank of fuel.

"Hope this gas doesn't make you ill. The smell should be gone in a second."

"Canly come, Lord. Canly come," she chanted. A dribble of sweat rolled down her cheek as she gritted her teeth and tried to hold onto her demons. Her medication was wearing off. Betsy tried to concentrate on the road ahead, but in the shadows of her peripheral vision the side streets were turning into moving rivers of tar. The rustling tree leaves were like wiggling hands, but she interpreted this as applause for her brave mission. She massaged her belly rhythmically with her hands, which afforded some comfort. Jerry didn't quite know what to make of this odd woman.

"Don't think I've ever heard that phrase, ma'am. Is it 'canly come,' Like Kingdom Come?"

His comment startled Betsy. She hadn't realized she uttered the words out loud. It was as if Jerry had reached into her mind and extracted her most intimate thoughts. She replied, "It means happy homily. I heard it long ago."

The van bounced into the parking structure of the TV station and Jerry pulled to the curb. He let Betsy in through a side door, then wove through a system of tunnels to an elevator. Soon they entered the third floor studio, as indicated by a plastic sign.

"Okay. The audience is already seated. You'll be up front. The show starts in ten minutes. Crandall will speak for about five minutes, then ask for people seeking redemption. That's your cue. Just stand up, walk around to the side steps, and walk onto the stage. You'll have to walk to the center, because all the cameras are focused there. Crandall will ask you your name and then give him this envelope,"he said as he slipped one into her hand. "We'll get the donation later. Then say whatever you want. Crandall will help you if you get tongue-tied. When it's time to go, Crandall will walk you about halfway to the stairs. Just keep walking down and return to your seat. Is that easy enough?" Jerry asked.

"Yes, yes, yes, canly come. Yes. We can do it. Zachariah will see it," Betsy said. Jerry hoped she wouldn't say too much.

The crowd roared as Crandall made his way to the far corner of the stage. He waved at everyone, but Betsy knew it was only to her. She saw the horns sprouting from his head, eyes blazing yellow, and fingers like little daggers. A forked tongue dampened his lips. She saw his skin as pebbled, like a reptile. It was Satan for sure. She stroked her belly, which whooshed like a water bed. Her hand slipped into a pocket hidden in a pleat, touching her tools. Soon it would be time. Betsy closed her eyes and rocked gently. "Canly come, canly come," she chanted with barely moving lips.

The stage manager gave the final countdown and Crandall burst onto the stage amid a roar of applause, yells, and hallelujahs. Crandall welcomed the saved and praised their commitment to the fight for the lives of unborn children. As he preached about the list of the damned and its imminent publication, his eyes scanned the form of Betsy Waller. "Holy Mother of God," he thought to himself. "She's gigantic. I'd better get this over with before she drops the kid right here."

Crandall quieted the crowd and announced that they had a very special person seeking redemption. His eyes fell upon the rocking Betsy, who almost involuntarily rose from her seat. Her heart was pounding in her ears. She couldn't hear Crandall, but she saw him gesture for her to come on stage. She tried to run, but the demons wouldn't let her. The snake-eyed man kept calling her. "He wants his baby," she realized. "I must give him back to Hell."

Betsy stumbled onto the stage at the top of the stairs, her body seeming to flow in four directions at once. Crandall didn't move, but he began clapping as she approached. Betsy's right hand was away from the audience as she fished in her skirt and withdrew the handcuffs. Cupped in her hands, out of view of the audience, she clipped one half of the handcuffs to her left wrist. Crandall faced the audience as he extended his hand to welcome the portly woman.

Her hand clasped his, and casually locked the remaining cuff around his wrist as she kissed his hand. Crandall suddenly felt that familiar sensation of cold steel around his wrist. "Gotcha, Satan," she said in triumph. Crandall turned in perplexity to see what was going on. Again her hand slipped into the pocket, emerging with the box knife and the lighter. Crandall recognized the knife instantly and pulled away, but he was inextricably attached to this mad woman.

Betsy raised her hand as if to strike, so Crandall covered his face with his arm. She then plunged the knife blade deep into her abdomen, drawing it up in a slitting motion across her belly. The dress spread open as the hot water bottle exploded its stored gasoline all over Crandall and Betsy. The cameramen and audience couldn't see the knife. It looked as if she had grabbed her stomach in response to a pain, then broke her water. Betsy then sliced across her chest, exploding two more hot water bottles in a spray of acrid, stinging, volatile fluid.

Crandall pulled desperately away, but her bulk was too much for him. He stumbled forward and fell on the floor, in the spreading pool of gasoline. A stage hand ran to his aid, but slid on the slippery fuel and flew off the stage. Betsy looked at the fallen Beast, grabbed his reptilian hand, starred into his lifeless yellow eyes and said, "Take your son to canly come." Crandall saw the lighter in Betsy's hand, and the horror of his predicament hit him full force. Jerry sprinted down the center aisle, while the audience tried to make sense of the frantic activities.

Crandall and Betsy exploded in a crackling ball of fire. Smoke and flames roiled toward the ceiling, popping floodlights and melting insulation. The overhead microphones captured the screams of Crandall Bream and the stage audience, blasting them into the homes of his 20,000 television viewers. The cameras rolled as flames consumed the twitching figures. Bream thrashed against the charred hulk of Betsy, unable to escape as the fire consumed him. No one could get within twenty feet of the fireball, which melted a handheld camera dropped by the operator as he dove for cover. Some stage hands tried to spray the fire with CO_2 extinguishers, but it was futile. Before his greatest audience ever, Crandall Bream was burned alive.

***

Three days after Nora's death, Ezra sauntered up the porch steps as usual, though dressed in an ill-fitting black tuxedo that seemed to suck every ray of light from the fading sun. He was returning from Nora's funeral. It was a small affair, mostly friends, her sisters, and some cousins. Even Bob had attended. After the ceremony the group had assembled at cousin Gene's home for refreshments and condolences. His longtime neighbors eventually dropped Ezra at home.

The mailbox was still being stuffed with nursing home promotions. Ezra had no doubt who provided Nora's name to them.

GHB was giving him fits. They had run some tests on Nora's body without his permission. They claimed it was part of their total healthcare program. Studying the causes of death could lead to longer life, they said. "So could a competent diagnosis," thought Ezra. With no apology, GHB said they routinely reviewed the deaths of their members to help gauge the success of their programs and the accuracy of their treatment protocols. The implication was that by providing all the care for a client they essentially "owned" the body. Ezra was too weary to fight them.

GHB was also concerned to know the exact cause of death, since she had recently been diagnosed as a substance abuser. Did this shorten her life expectancy? Did she consume more than the recommended amount of pain medicine? Did she take any illicit drugs that could have impaired her treatment? Did the drugs prevent her from donating organs? Did he know that many GHB members were waiting for organ donations? What right did he have to deprive those people of useful organs?

The tone of the "outcomes manager" from GHB was severe and threatening. She referred to criminal prosecutions and civil penalties. If they discovered criminal activity, it might affect the company's liability in Nora's medical claims. Ezra might be held responsible for a greater share of the costs. Ezra smiled at the implications. "With these guys it's always about money," he reflected. He wanted to send them a gift-wrapped package of plastic explosive.

Ezra noticed that there were six phone messages on the answering machine. Everyone he knew had been at the funeral. He pressed the button and heard the "urgent" request from GHB to contact their offices. He skipped to the next message. GHB again. And again. Before he could listen to the next message, the phone rang.

"Hello?"

"Mr. Whitney. Ezra Whitney?"

"Yes, who is this?"

"Mr. Whitney, I'm with the claims division of Great Benefit Health. I'm an attorney here in Los Angeles. I need to talk with you about your wife."

"My wife is dead," he shouted, tears welling up in his eyes.

"Yes, I'm sorry for that. Unfortunately our toxicology lab has come up with some disturbing results. It seems your wife had been taking large quantities of both prescription and illegal drugs. Were you aware of that?"

"My wife was in great pain. Your company wouldn't help."

"Mr. Whitney, I'm afraid this could lead to some serious charges against you. As you are aware, illegal drug use is often punished not only by jail time, but by confiscation of personal property, like your house or your car."

"What? I try to help my wife and they are going to throw me in jail?" questioned Ezra.

"I'm afraid they could, Mr. Whitney, but I'm prepared to help you through this problem. We feel a commitment to look after our customers," said the lawyer from Los Angeles.

"How can you help?" said Ezra with mild amusement.

"We can agree not to pursue these charges if you agree to take out an annuity policy on your home."

"I don't understand. What does this annuity policy do?"

"Let me assure you that it allows you to keep living in your home as long as you want. All of your medical expenses are covered as they have been in the past, but upon your death, GHB takes possession of the house."

"And then what?" snickered Ezra.

"Well, they'll do with it as they see fit. However, the point is, you'll get to live out your days in your own home, no jail, no confiscation. We guarantee it."

"Is this through my insurance company?"

"Well, we're a partner to your health insurance, Great Health Benefit. We're Great Home Annuity and Life."

"And if I don't go for this deal?"

"I'm fearful the long arm of the law may destroy your golden years."

"You've already destroyed them, but let me think about it a couple of days. Okay?" he said, while dropping the receiver down on the phone cradle. "It's always about the money," he said out loud.

Their threats did not affect him. The pain in Ezra was constant now, a deep emotional pain. It wouldn't go away, so he decided he needed to go away. Life without Nora was an odd affair. She had been a companion to him even when she wasn't there. Now no eyes were looking after him. He was alone. He fit in nowhere. There was little reason to hang on.

That evening Ezra took out the stash of bottles Bob had sold him and filled three syringes. He had read about techniques of suicide from accounts of Dr. Kevorkian and the Hemlock Society. It was important that the lethal substance be injected gradually. To be sure someone called on him tomorrow, he had made a lunch date with Nora's sister. He wanted to be discovered early, but dead.

Ezra picked up a syringe and grabbed an alcohol swab. "What am I worrying about germs for?" he laughed to himself. Around him on the bed were family albums and mementos of his and Nora's life together. His despair ran deep, particularly as he hated leaving this world while the bad guys were winning, but there seemed little he could do. GHB would soon be denying care for him, just as they had with Nora. Maybe this is what they really wanted.

Ezra held the needle to the light and gently pressed the plunger until an amber drop appeared at the tip. He looked past the needle to his wedding picture. The house was again quiet. It creaked like his bones as the sun went down. He couldn't help feeling a bit like a quitter, but he held onto his resolve. It was time, and he was ready. His eyes scanned the room one last time. He inhaled the sweet, warm air from his open window.

The phone rang. This was not a time to speak to anyone. He wanted to die. It rang again and again. The dial on the answer machine was dark. He had turned it off. Maybe they'll go away. The phone rang for the eleventh time. Ezra shifted in frustration and put down the syringe. "Shit, I can't find any peace," he said with gruff impatience as he grabbed the phone.

"Mr. Whitney," said the female voice.

"Yes."

"My name is Jenny Barrett. I'm sorry to disturb you at this sad time, but I'd like to talk with you about your wife."

"I just talked with you animals today. She's dead. There is nothing more you can do to me. I will not give you my house."

"Mr. Whitney, I know you won't believe this at first, but I'm trying to help you. I know all about the antics of GHB and what they've done to you. We're trying to stop them. I'm working with Senator Gray to expose their evil practices. We need your story to help us."

"My story?" said Ezra in a soft whisper.

"I'm looking at all they've done to you and Nora. I know Nora died last week. I see all you've done to try and save her, but I need you to come with us and tell the story to America."

"My story?" was all he could say. He looked toward the heavens and said, "Nora, they want my story."

***

Jenny awoke when a sliver of sunlight snuck through the vertical blinds of Mark's apartment and marched across her eyelids. Reluctantly, she was pulled from her sleep, but resolutely refused to rise from the warm bed covers. Mark's rhythmic breathing was again reassuring; it was all over. She had spent the last three days in his Pasadena gated community, in part to be far away from GHB and also to be close to him. Tomorrow she would fly to Washington, DC to testify before Senator Gray's committee.

She snuggled her cold bottom against Mark's warm hip and reviewed the events of the last couple of days.

When Jenny left GHB that last day, she instinctively knew it was over for Carter. The cloud of fear instantly evaporated, for the great, proprietary secrets were finally revealed. She had been only a small part of the scheme. Carter had much bigger fish to fry now. She let her brother David know of the threat, but felt confident he was too far away, and there was little benefit in silencing her. Waldo had seen to that.

The Tide of Waldo, as the GHB invasion came to be known, washed up on the cybernetic shores of every major Internet site in the world, including many in Washington, DC It carried the flotsam and jetsam of MOM's coding, not in complete packages, but with choice words and notations. The list included the cynically labeled "Death Before Disbursement" subroutine for computing AIDS care, or the "Lost Claim Form" branch of the "Standard Barriers to Payment" program. Jay Leno even used references to the "Pull the Plug: Coma Cost Containment" module. The next morning the nation was chanting a new version of an old joke. What's the best way to spread your intimate secrets nationwide? Telephone, tell Geraldo, and tell managed care.

At first, there was no way to see what the funny little characters carried in their pockets, but as chat room participants began to compare notes, it was discovered that there was a method to this madness. Each recipient had a little bit of the secret, something like a burger company contest where matching tokens or pieces of a puzzle must be assembled to win the big prize. Cyber-surfers kept finding little tokens tucked into mail boxes or a web site. The secrets of MOM rained down on the web like confetti.

The blizzard of Waldos helped cover the tracks of the primary invasion team. This collection of linked Waldos picked up the coding of MOM as an organized network, filing through the web and then reassembling the code piece by piece on one of Dwick's secure Internet sites. The Waldo forces were able to rebuild MOM's programs line by line. The soul of MOM was laid bare.

Dwick quickly massaged the pieces into an organized whole, then had his utility programs munch through the material, the branches, decision points, and subroutines, to graphically represent what this massive program did.

The death of Crandall Bream garnered most of media attention for a week. It received better ratings than the Branch Davidian shoot-out. News stations initially tried to veil the grisly footage to avoid shocking viewers, but the shark-fest of ratings wars and cable channels quickly brought slow-motion closeups to the screen. The Seattle Weekly Reader, an extreme left tabloid publication, proclaimed in a banner headline, "CRANDALL BREAM BECOMES TOAST OF THE TOWN." Many silent victims of Crandall's extortion plot took private joy in watching the monster consumed in the fires of Hell that he had so quickly spewed on others.

Jerry Stack was not a natural, or even capable, leader, so with no captain at the helm the steamship Bream quickly crashed on the rocks. Crandall Bream's organization collapsed amidst investigations by federal and state agencies, insurance companies, and class action suits from victims. All the "The Bream Children's Life Project" assets were frozen, so Jerry packed his family off to the Cayman Islands. He was wise enough to leave behind a large enough pile of money to keep his adversaries occupied in a financial wrestling match.

To aid in the restoration of women's privacy, and to try to restore some community credibility "without admitting guilt," GHB sent a team of programmers to evaluate Elliot Mears' "sniffer" program. After two days of examination, the team proclaimed that the program was seriously flawed and had mistakenly identified thousands of women as abortion victims. That, at least, was the pubic comment, which helped women to come forward without necessarily admitting to an abortion. This media coverage freed women from the threat of the List of the Damned, yet programmers who knew Elliot Mears also knew this was merely a public relations gambit. Elliot's program actually worked quite well. In fact, Elliot and his program were secretly hired by another religious group for $80,000.

Emily Schuster-Gray could have tried to duck behind the PR statement about the flawed program, but she knew the data was out there somewhere. She agreed to work with her husband's media advisors and eventually held a press conference that placed her as a symbol of women's lost privacy.

With Emily's consent, her physician provided an overview of the sad events that lead to her decision to terminate the pregnancy. Her pastor, a moderate pro-lifer, yet old and tired of the grim squabbles between Christian denominations, stood beside Emily's humanitarian decision. "This child suffered from an innocent and unfortunate act of man, not an act of God. I could not fathom the pain such a child would have endured for its brief and futile existence. I will not condemn this heartfelt act of mercy. I have touched the remorse and felt the loss of this couple. I have the greatest admiration for their courage in the face of such grim choices. Let no man judge, lest he be judged."

Quietly, the media focus shifted from the sources of donations to the sources of the women's names. Jerry threw them the GHB lists to get the reporters' attention elsewhere. The public suddenly became concerned with cyber-access to personal medical data. Senator Gray's committee quickly became center stage in the battle for privacy. Thomas Baldwin was scheduled for the Joint Committee meetings the next week. Jenny and Dwick had provided a thermonuclear data bomb to drop on his head.

When Jenny finally got a hold of Dwick she scolded him like a fishwife.

"Where the hell did you go? You scared me to death. I thought they had carted you off to jail," said Jenny.

"Sorry, Jen. I had to prepare for Waldo's return. It squeezed every resource I could muster. I had to close the web page so the Waldo troops had a way to come home. Sorry if I frightened you. But, shit, ain't it the greatest thing you ever saw?"

"Dwick, you'll never know. I was sitting with my boss, who was just about to flush me down the professional toilet, when your little guy went bouncing across the screen. I thought I'd die of laughter when the big honcho went into manic overload."

"Oh, I guess I forgot to tell you that Waldo had some replicating DNA code stored in him."

"Thanks a lot. They put a picture of poor, dead Waldo on my computer screen. I thought the game was over."

"Sorry I didn't clue you in, but I figured ignorance was bliss. It's the old one-two punch. I led your fellow, Hepman, around by the nose, or rather, Waldo's nose. He probably thought I was nuts for wasting code on that silly icon, but the spawning code sat right in Waldo's head."

"You're a sick man, Dwick."

"I can't believe I made the national news. Well, not me, but Waldo. Did you hear Leno?"

"Yes,' said Jenny, "And all the media talking about the little bits of GHB code."

"I'll tell you, when I saw the margin notations and subroutine names on the samples from Elaina's computer, I knew this was big. I've never seen such arrogance and contempt for people embodied in a computer program."

"Wait till they see your package. The Joint Committee is going to slaughter GHB."

"You take the credit, girl. I'm on the lam."

"Are you in any danger? I mean, for invading their computer?"

"Sure. All they have to do is find me," he chuckled. "All the really cool programmers know my signature. This has got to be the best calling card ever, but the police will never find me.

"Are you sure?"

"Well, could you? Think about it, Jenny. Who am I?" Dwick challenged.

Jenny scurried through her memories of every contact she'd had with Dwick over the last four years. He had always been Dwick, an acronym. The Demon Warlord Invader and Code Killer. That's all she knew. "Dwick, what is your name?"

"Interesting question, isn't it? Maybe I'll answer it someday. Of course, the real question may be 'What am I?'"

"You're a certified wacko, sweetie, who saved my butt. Thanks," said Jenny.

"Thanks yourself. But you forgot 'space alien.' You don't think a mere human could be this brilliant do you? Hey, did you check out all the graphic analysis of MOM's programs on your e-mail?"

"Just scanned them, but they're frightening. They reek of greed. How could programmers write those callous notes about people's care? Like that big MOM module called KTM. It means Keep-The-Money. What pomposity must have written that."

"They thought no one would ever see it. Next time they'll be more crafty. Still, that's what keeps me in the sport. Use the data well, Jenny."

"I'll take it all to Washington. The Senator believes he can get this admitted into evidence. What a grim program it is. All that computer coding designed to lie, cheat, and kill. For all that effort, it would have made more sense to do it the right way."

"Hey, it's the grand corporate conspiracy. I finally got one, fresh on my hook. Paranoia can pay off after all," said Dwick.

That conversation was yesterday, then Dwick vanished. Two days later, Senator Gray's office received a DVD disk containing six gigabytes of GHB data, programs, analysis, and flowcharting. It mapped the road to digital Hell.

Chapter 34

Mark stirred in his sleep and rolled over, flopping an arm across Jenny's chest while inserting his pinky in her eye.

"Thanks, I love you too," she said, flinging his arm away.

He opened his eyes for a second of disorientation, then nuzzled into her neck and said good morning. Other portions of his anatomy awoke as well. Checking the clock, he realized they could squeeze in some wake-up eroticism before he had to dash off to work.

Fifteen minutes later, they were both in the shower. Mark bolted early and flew out the door.

"You're leaving tomorrow for Washington?" he asked.

"Yeah. Can the Chronicle spare their top reporter? There will be some great material at the hearings."

"I'm trying. I'll let you know later. Bye," and he was gone.

After a light breakfast, Jenny dressed casually and prepared for a trip to her home. She was running out of clean clothes and wanted to check her mail. The danger had passed. Carter and GHB were in turmoil.

She skipped down the steps and walked to Mark's parking space, which contained her Toyota. She pressed the remote alarm switch on her key chain and the car let out a chirp as it deactivated the alarm and unlocked the doors. Jenny threw a bag of dirty clothes into the back seat and sat down.

The engine roared to life as she auto-locked the doors. A news station on the radio advised her of traffic patterns. As she reached for the seatbelt, she heard the unmistakable chirp of the alarm system again. Her door locks popped up. The passenger side door flew open and a blur of an Asian man sat down in the passenger seat. A gun emerged from his waistband while his broad smile sent chills through her.

"Hello, Jenny. Good to see you again. Drive away. Immediately!" he said, pushing the gun against her ribs.

Her breathing stopped and her eyes constricted in tunnel vision; all she could see was the sinister black bore of the gun. It was the hitman.

"Move it," he commanded. He cocked the gun.

Jenny slid the car into reverse and crept backward, almost hitting an approaching van.

"Watch it, Jenny. We don't need a wreck, It might be fatal to you."

Her knuckles were white as she clenched the steering wheel. What the hell was he doing here?

As if reading her mind, the man said, "In answer to the obvious question, I'm here on business. If you cooperate, you live. If you don't, you die. Fairly simple choice." He pressed the gun firmly into her cheek to remind her of the terror of the other night.

"What do you want?" she asked, almost running a red light in her distraction.

"We're going to your home. You still have something that belongs to my employer. I also understand you made a recording of our little talk. I want that too. When I am convinced you are powerless, I will leave you to your life. If you don't cooperate, I'll be forced to switch to plan 'B', and you don't want to know what that is, I assure you."

Jenny stole a look at his face and was instantly convinced he was lying through his cavity pitted teeth. She was about to die, with or without her cooperation. Carter's last stand. She imagined the executive taking pleasure in ordering her death. She had been too cocky, baiting him. Now she faced a killer.

"Jenny, don't get any heroic ideas," he continued. "This is Los Angeles. At any time I can shoot you, coast to a stop, and walk away. You could stay slumped at the wheel for hours." In his left hand he held a device that looked like a calculator, which he placed in his pocket as she watched.

"It's some kind of high frequency scanner recorder. When you press your little remote alarm device, it transmits a high frequency sound code to disarm the card. I used this to record the code, then all I had to do was play it back, like a tape recorder, and your car door locks sprung open. I love these high-tech gadgets, but I think people put too much faith in technology. Don't you?"

They were near the Foothill Freeway, and he signaled her to take the on ramp. Jenny mentally scrambled to make some sense of this, to find a solution. If she's on the freeway, he probably wouldn't shoot her at 55 miles an hour. That gave her about thirty-five minutes to think up a plan. As she mentally clawed for shreds of sanity, her car almost side-swiped a truck in the next lane. The killer jabbed her painfully with the gun, commanding her to straighten up.

"Talk with him," she commanded herself. "Find a weakness." His thick hands and muscular arms did not reveal any obvious weakness. He could crush her skull like a melon. "Talk," she commanded herself again.

"I thought I wasn't going to see you again."

"Hey, I lied. What do you expect? I'm a criminal."

"Will you really let me live?" she pleaded.

"I have no reason to kill you if I know you can't hurt anyone." He said this looking sincerely into her eyes, yet the corner of his mouth betrayed just the hint of a smile. The sadistic hit man was a recreational killer, and she caught him planning his fun for the night.

The Toyota merged onto the Golden State Freeway, where traffic was slower due to congestion. They cruised at forty miles per hour past an optimistic sign that set the speed limit at 65. Jenny knew that when she exited the freeway all hope would be lost. She racked her brain trying to think what to do. Jump from the car? Not with her seat belt attached. Honk the horn? He'd beat her, or shoot her. Spin out of control? He'd shoot her when the car stopped.

Something nagged at her, a memento of wisdom her father had imparted to her in the past. Something about a weapon. Weapon in the car. No. The car is a weapon. That's it. A car is the biggest weapon you'll ever control. If you hit someone with two tons of steel, they usually don't walk away. He said this when she was a teen, dating some odd characters. What was that again? Riding or driving, a car is the biggest weapon.

How can I hit him with the car? No, hit something else with the car. She checked to see that he wasn't wearing a seat belt. She had air bags, but at sufficient speed they wouldn't work alone. "What if I kill myself in the process? Well, if you get home, you're definitely dead," she mentally yelled.

The man casually perused the contents of her car, opening the glove compartment and rummaging through it. He withdrew the Jaz drive disk and read the label. His quizzical expression transformed into a big smile. He looked gloatingly at Jenny, saying, "This is my lucky day," while flashing the disk label "Elaina and hitman".

They sped along in the right lane, the hit man's eyes looking her up and down. A half mile ahead she saw an orange CalTrans road maintenance truck stopped by the side of the freeway, yellow light flashing. It had a high rear stake bed, full of emergency blockades. She couldn't see anyone in the cab through its rear window. Did she have the guts to do this? Her mouth was so dry her tongue seemed glued to her teeth.

Using a standard psychotherapy technique, Jenny took a deep breath and relaxed her hands on the steering wheel. She tensed her stomach, then made it relax. For a few seconds she imagined lying on a Hawaiian beach with Mark, feeling the warm sand, hearing the gulls, smelling the sweet air. She calmed herself down, then turned to the hit man while edging the car's speed to 45 miles per hour. The CalTrans truck was coming up quickly and she would steer directly into it, but he mustn't know, or he'd grab the wheel. Taking full command of her will, she relaxed her jaw and face muscles, trying to find some inner peace to hold on to. She let the car drift to the right, but realized she had to engage the hit man or he'd notice her plan.

"You know," she said, turning a friendly face to him. "There's one thing I think you should realize. Elaina was my friend, you fucking scum."

The broad face smiled. "Why I'm touched that you . . ."

In an explosion of metal, glass, and steam, the Toyota crashed full force into the rear of the truck. The car spun back onto the freeway as the truck was knocked ten feet forward. Air bags deployed instantly, securing Jenny in a pneumatic womb while the unbelted hit man flew off to the side and collided with the hard, unforgiving edge of the truck bed. Jenny's last memory was of her crumpled hood coming toward the front seat and a flash of white blocking her view, then blackness.

Jenny awoke beside the Golden State Freeway, lying on a stretcher. The fumes of traffic stung her nose. A hand stroked her forehead. It was attached to a mustachioed young man dressed in an EMT uniform. Her eyes had difficulty focusing.

"You okay, Miss?"

Jenny tried to rise, but a stabbing pain shot through her neck.

"Hey, take it easy. You've had an accident. You don't seem to have any broken bones or even deep cuts, mostly just little glass nicks. Still, I bet your neck hurts from that impact."

"I'm Jenny Barrett," was all she could think of to say.

"Yeah, we saw your driver's license. We're just about to take you to the hospital for X-rays. It's 9:10 A.M. The accident happened about twenty minutes ago." Turning to another EMT, he said, "Jeff, she's ready."

They hoisted her into the emergency vehicle. No other patients were inside. Images were starting to come back to her. The man. In the car. She turned with a questioning look on her face to the technician. He knew what the answer was to her unasked question.

"I'm sorry. Your friend wasn't so lucky. He flew out of the car and landed on the pavement. We had to chopper him to USC Medical Center. I'm not sure how he's doing. He's in surgery now. He couldn't be at a better hospital," he said for encouragement.

"I. . . see," Jenny squeaked out, then fell back on the gurney.

"Say, we couldn't find any ID on the man. Who is he?" asked the EMT.

"I don't know. I think they sent him to kill me. I have him recorded on disk. Please don't let him go."

The technician couldn't make any sense out of what Jenny was saying. Since she appeared to be physically intact, though suffering a reactive trauma to the accident, he suggested that she close her eyes and rest. She was out in a second.

Jenny heard Mark's voice in the hospital room, speaking on the phone. Soon she realized he was speaking to her parents. Her eyes flew open and she instantly felt much stronger. "Tell Dad he raised a tough daughter," she said. Mark spun around with the phone, draped himself across her to awkwardly manage a hug, and hooted for her parents.

"Tell him yourself," he said, handing her the phone.

"Hi Mom and Dad. I'm okay."

"Jenny, we were so worried," said her mother.

"What happened in that car? Mark says some strange guy was with you," asked Bill.

"Yes, I was trying to run away with a Filipino hit man, but he got too possessive."

"What? Don't joke around, honey," said her mother.

"Dad?"

"Yeah."

"I want to thank you for those driving lessons."

"What do you mean? You just got into an accident."

"I'll tell you later, but I just want you to know that you saved my life. We're even."

A perplexed Bill Barrett babbled on with questions, but Jenny let Mark take over. She swung around on the corner of the bed and slowly sat up. The clock said it was 1:30 P.M.

"God, I guess I was out for a while," Jenny said.

"The hospital staff says it's normal. Sorry to tell you this, but they can't find anything wrong with you. Doctors say you'll hurt all over for a few days, but nothing is broken," said Mark.

"I feel like I need three days in a hot tub."

Mark got serious. "Was that guy in the car the hit man you talked about?"

"Yes. What happened to him?"

"I think he just retired," said Mark. "He's got serious brain damage, probably will end up a hemiplegic. Broken bones all over, crushed spine, damaged organs, tubes running in and out of him. I told the police he was probably the guy, so they're keeping an eye on him. Why did he come back?"

"Carter Newton. I'm sure he sent him. The guy said he wanted to get that recording I made of him threatening me the first time, but I could see in his eyes he was lying and that he planned to kill me. I hope they string Carter up by his balls."

"I've got to tell you, for Carter it's much worse. They have him strung up by his balance sheet. The stupid prick."

They postponed the trip to Washington a week to ensure Jenny's full recovery. Detectives from the Los Angeles County Police Department took a strong interest in the Filipino hit man when his gun was found in the wreck of Jenny's car. His mental state had deteriorated, owing to the trauma of the crash and the serious pain medicine he was given. The police read him his rights, but he only wanted more morphine. His lips became extremely loose, his well-honed skill at lying had disintegrated in a brain hemorrhage. He required only minimal security, for there was little concern about him running off anywhere. The hit man was severely and permanently crippled, and most willing to cut any deal. He gladly threw them Carter Newton.

Further digging into Elaina's archived computer files found some notes she had made just before her final admission to the hospital. Carter's last voice message to Elaina was viewed in a new light, given the recent events with Jenny. After two days of increasingly precise police questioning, Carter realized that the hit man had become a fountain of information. An attorney suddenly appeared to take on the

Filipino man's plight. All questions from that point on were filtered through the lawyer, but it was too late. They had spilled Carter's beans.

Jenny and Mark smiled as they watched the evening news, featuring Carter Newton, flanked by officers, as they escorted him to jail for booking on suspicion of a contract murder.

Daisy took a surprising voice message from Larry Harrington, the ex-CEO of Progressive, inviting Jenny to call on his private telephone number.

"Mr. Harrington?" she asked, as a familiar voiced answered.

"Jenny. Thanks for calling. I've been following all the incredible events at GHB."

"I know. I'm sorry they pushed you out of Progressive. You're one of the best leaders in the business."

"I don't know if you'll say that after I apologize?"

"Apologize?" asked Jenny. "For what?"

"For putting you in danger. I had no idea GHB was so ruthless. When they took over Progressive I knew they were bad, but not that they were evil. I recommended you for that position just to put some soul into GHB's cold heart. I never told you that, and I feel I owe you an apology."

"Mr. Harrington, I've never been so scared in my life, but I wouldn't hold it against you. No one could have guessed. It all turned out for the best. I'm glad I could finish Elaina's work. You made that happen. Thank you."

"Jenny, if you need anything, just let me know."

"How's your wife doing?"

"Very well. She's responded beyond expectations to radiation and chemotherapy. Now we're both bald. She's doing fine, and I know you will be too. Maybe I'll see you in Washington. I've offered to testify at the Joint Committee hearings about privacy and electronic medical records."

"About GHB?"

"That, and the sad state-of-the-art in medical privacy. How competition is driving out the responsible providers and encouraging corruption. I won't bore you with the details until I testify," promised Harrington.

"I couldn't think of a finer person to expose the system. "I'll be there too. Thank you, Mr. Harrington."

The scandalous program coding of MOM and the Caduceus team caught the attention of regulators and brought them sniffing at every

GHB doorway. The company's stock dropped 15 percent on anticipated suits by clients. When Mark's newspaper article revealed that many of GHB's recent hires were employees recycled from the parent company's other corrupt financial and life insurance branches, the conglomerate teetered on the brink of bankruptcy.

Thomas Baldwin was headed for Senator Gray's committee with his pockets turned inside out. He felt naked and exposed; the man he had trusted had destroyed the company's reputation. GHB needed a villain, a renegade, a sitting sap to hang all this corruption on. Carter Newton was elected, for he had blood on his hands. Baldwin covered his own ass by giving the media a perfect scoundrel.

Baldwin produced a report that showed the company began having doubts about Carter in November. He disclosed that Carter had openly voiced concerns about Elaina, who was quite troubled by the clinical decisions MOM was making. Carter suspected she was involved in an incident of computer invasion and code theft, but he couldn't find any hard evidence. He reportedly bullied an admission out of Elaina and threatened to smear her name, charge her with a felony, and petition that her psychology license be rescinded. Unfortunately, Baldwin was not told of these insidious acts of Carter Newton.

Elaina wouldn't budge, so Carter came up with another plan. He suggested that she agree to spend a few days in a psychiatric hospital, which would sufficiently damage her credibility so that no investigative agency would take her seriously. However, when a search of her home still produced nothing, Carter decided the safest course was death. Baldwin said he only heard from Carter that Elaina had confessed and was terminated.

Baldwin was only speculating, of course, and would never have supported such outrageous behavior. He was, unfortunately, out of touch with the California operations in his office on the East Coast and didn't hear of the poor girl's death until much later. He had even suggested a memorial fund in honor of the fallen employee.

As project leader, Greg Hepman was also summoned to Washington to answer questions about MOM's coding. Hepman had become a shattered man, unprepared for the sudden and overwhelming events that embroiled him in a nasty business. His secret fear, that Carter had ordered Elaina's death, had been all but confirmed by the police. In some small way Hepman felt responsible for the world losing a smart and beautiful woman, even if she did manipulate him for information. He knew the human values Elaina held and was impressed by her commitment to patients. He hated Carter Newton now.

The magnitude of Dwick's invasion had shamed Hepman in the computer community. Even with the assistance of Jenny, an insider, his defenses had proven inadequate to protect the company jewels. Had this been medieval times, he would have been ordered to fall on his sword. Instead, Hepman, on the advice of the company attorney, fell in step with the "hang Carter" mob and answered the committee's questions honestly.

The project leader provided some chilling sound bites at the hearings.

"Mr. Hepman," asked Congressman Wade from Illinois, "What are we to make of the programmer remarks in MOM's code? Do these represent the company's antipathy and callousness towards their own clients?"

"Mr. Wade, MOM has the potential for helping more people more quickly than any other single machine on earth. She is as perfect a physician as anyone could dream of. Yet without a soul she is at the mercy of her many masters. Carter Newton encouraged the team to use the most profit-minded terms to keep the group on the track of money. Basically, clients could only reach the wisdom of the Caduceus program after MOM had confirmed they could make a profit," revealed Hepman to a stunned audience. Yet this was just the beginning.

Jenny took the witness chair after Hepman, staring intently at Senator Gray to draw her attention away from the tortured knot in her stomach. The media spotlight fell upon the Oregon country girl who soon electrified the viewing public with a detailed and documented account of her immersion into the corrupt heart of GHB. Jenny's odd blend of clinical empathy and computer proficiency gave the country an intimate description of the collision between humanity and technology. Weaving compassionate feelings with cold logic, her descriptions proved unsettling for either side of the brain.

In preparation for her testimony, Dwick and Jenny had packaged over 80 gigabytes of documentation, including material from Elaina's computer, producing GHB's worst nightmare: the complete disclosure of their formulas for healthcare. It was soon clear that MOM was programmed to violate most medical ethics and a number of state and federal laws. The company's claim of proprietary rights fell on deaf ears, for once the public had a glimpse of GHB's dark soul, they wanted nothing short of an electronic exorcism, or a lobotomy, or even a torching of the monster "expert system."

Jenny had visions of peasants storming the Frankenstein castle. As the public's hunger for vengeance rose, Jenny felt compelled to defend the technology. At her request, Lawrence Harrington helped with the preparation of her testimony.

On the witness stand she asked that the committee not to lose sight of the real villains, who were made of flesh and blood, not wires and silicon.

"Senator and honored committee members, " Jenny said, "As I describe the horrendous and despicable events that occurred at GHB, I'd like to make it clear that I am not here to condemn the technology that was used to hurt millions of people. In reality, MOM can do no more or less than she is instructed to do. It would be criminal to discard this wondrous technology just because an evil empire chose to use it for selfish purposes."

"I, and hundreds of my colleagues, have used the same technology to bring urgently needed help to people all over this country. We've diagnosed a child with a rare blood disease in the backwaters of Mississippi. We've drilled through a myriad of contradictory symptoms to discover a masked ailment. We've called upon a community to help save the life of a suicidal teen. I believe that, in the hands of responsible practitioners, these tools rival the magnificence of antibiotics, MRIs, and laser surgery."

"I know the committee has reviewed the sample cases MOM used to develop and display her clinical expertise. Systems like these, though still in their infancy, are vital to the future of medicine. If we are to provide the greatest care for the greatest number in a cost-effective way, we cannot do it with horse-and-buggy technology. The precision of diagnosis, the management of health resources, and the outstanding research that can be compiled in seconds are all blessings we cannot discard. The question is not whether medical records will travel on the information highway, but rather, who will be driving the bus."

After this brief assertion of the importance of information technology, Jenny spent the next two days detailing the corruption that permeated the great corporation. America gasped at the sorry state of privacy and dignity in the "new healthcare." It was clear private industry did not have the need or the interest in protecting patients' rights. Medical information was too valuable, too profitable, and too powerful. Employers, insurers, physicians, marketers, and even police agencies all felt entitled to ladle vital data from the big vats of computerized medical records. In fact, about the only group with no access to the data was the patients themselves. However, the rules were about to change.

The evening Jenny rapped up her testimony before the Joint Commission hearings, Mark arrived in Washington. He had already written two feature stories on GHB and another was in the can for tomorrow's edition of the <u>Chronicle</u>. Mark showered and shaved, then lay in his briefs on the sofa watching TV, just catching Jenny's image on CNN.

At 6:15 P.M., Jenny arrived and fell into Mark's lap as he watched the news.

"So how is it the <u>Chronicle</u> can afford to let their soon to be Pulitzer Prize winning reporter come to Washington?"

"Because that's where the story is. Besides, I'm not letting any of these high-powered DC boys get a line on my woman."

"Your woman?" questioned Jenny."I don't recall seeing your brand stamped on my butt."

"That's not where I'm going to put it."

"Let me guess. You plan to use that big, throbbing branding iron you carry around."

He brought out a small package, a ring box. "No, I was thinking more along these lines."

"I don't know if I'm ready for that, cowboy. What if I just want to run with the herd for a little while longer?"

"Jenny, I know what I want," said Mark in a more serious tone. "I want you to make me crazy with your techno-dweeb talk. I want to watch you grow old and toothless. I want to feel you next to me every morning. I know exactly what kind of relationship I want."

"And what's that?"

"For the full answer, you'll have to speak with a guy named Ezra Whitney."

The next morning, Jenny Barrett helped Ezra Whitney down the long aisle to the table in front of the committee. Senator Gray sat in the center, his wife in the audience. Ezra had physically deteriorated since the death of Nora, and he shuffled with an uncertainty that stopped the din of conversation in the large room. All the observers tensed as he neared the chair in front of the microphone. They extended their collective will to help him make it without falling.

Ezra's case was one of many that the Waldo agent brought to Dwick. The case had been flagged by GHB for collections, and Waldo thought the coding meant it was an important subroutine. About 230 names were accidentally collected this way.

Ezra Whitney touched Jenny's arm for support as he sat down. The audience expected a frail sound to emerge from the fragile figure, but a surprisingly firm, authoritative voice filled the meeting room. His eyes stared directly at Donald Gray, as the Senator had suggested, and Ezra unfolded his story of terror, harassment, and pain from GHB, the principal Medicare providers for Ohio. It was a story familiar to many who had suffered their own personal trials.

Ezra pleaded for help and guidance in finding ways to provide assistance for the people eaten up by the new systems. His fists clenched as he cried for his lost love, even thought he knew her spirit was still alive. He glanced out at the sky through a high window, focusing on a puffy cloud.

"Nora. They're listening to our story."

The End